"Reloaded Version 2013"

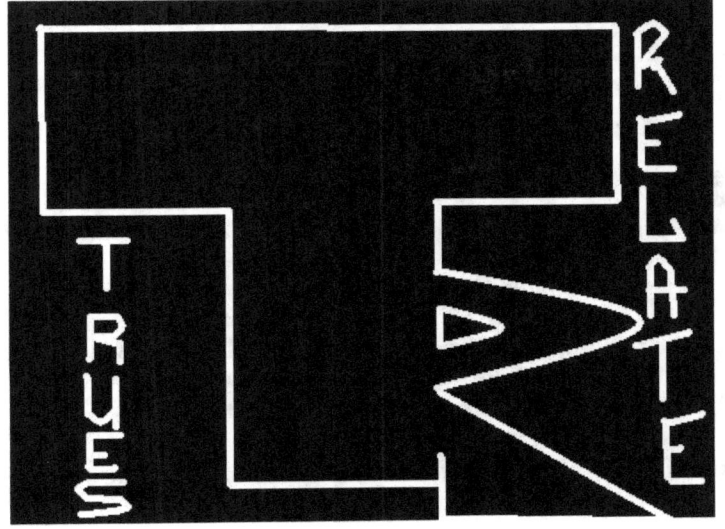

The Making of AJAY
"Every Man"-RELOADED,
A Time Will Reveal Novel

The Making of AJAY- Every Man, RELOADED, A Time Will Reveal novel

Published by True's Relate Publishing
The Making of AJAY
"Every Man"-RELOADED,
A Time Will Reveal Novel
Library of Congress Control Number:
Copyright ©2011, 2014 True's Relate publishing/LTBROWN
REGISTERED TRADEMARK-MARCA REGISTRADA
ISBN: 978-0-9844701-8-1 & 978-0-9892092-6-7
Printed in the United States of America
Set by: True's Relate publishing
Cover design by : Gregory Spencer of Misvision Graphics
info@misvisiongraphics.com
Logo design: JayRocOne [@ age 9] JayRocOne Designs]

Requests for information on ordering, scheduling the author
for signings and
appearances should be addressed to:
"Contact us" tab on
Black Coffee's websites:
www.truesrelatepublishing.com
www.blackdollone.com

Fan page: Author Black Coffee & True's Relate publishing, LLC
Facebook Group: The Time Will Reveal-RELOADED series Crew
Nation #Crew4Life
On Twitter: http://Twitter.com/AuthorBlkCoffee

Manuscript Preparation: Black Coffee
True's Relate publishing company
P.O. Box 2911
Gulfport, Ms. 39505
blackdollone@att.net

PUBLISHER'S NOTES

Dedicated to the diehards and book junkies who love the Time Will Reveal series!

=====================

THE TIME WILL REVEAL SHORT STORIES

#1 MORE THAN 4 ADMIRERS-RELOADED
"The Threat to a Legacy."
#2 MR. WRONG AND THE RATS-RELOADED
"Sweet Ray, Sonya, Shuntay & Tina"
#3 THE CREW'S PRIORITY-RELOADED[TBA]
"The Females of the Crew"

ORDER THE FULL SERIES AT:
www.truesrelatepublishing.com
www.blackdollone.com

The Time Will Reveal-Novel series
TIME TO LEARN-RELOADED part 1
TIME TO GROW-RELOADED part 2
TIME TO LOVE-RELOADED part 3
TIME TO KNOW-RELOADED part 4
TIME TO FEEL-RELOADED part 5
The Making of AJAY- Every Man-RELOADED
TIME TO SHOW-RELOADED part 6
AJAY AND EBONY 1- Time To Give part 7[TBA]
AJAY AND EBONY 2- Time To Live part 8[TBA]

<u>The Making of AJAY- "Every Man"</u>
The Intro

This novel is a detailed book on Anthony "Ajay" Jackson, Sr and his coming of age. The *"Time Will Reveal"* series starts on June 3, 1989 with "TIME TO LEARN-RELOADED part 1." It references things in Ajay's life, *prior* to that day. My readers requested more about *this* character. This novel is my attempt at giving them more insight into Ajay.

By the end of "TIME TO FEEL-RELOADED part 5", Ajay is a husband, father of 6 and a full time superstar in the NBA. But he still has only 1 son out of his 6 kids. I decided that the set up of this novel would be based around Ajay having father to son talks with his only son Ajay Jr known as Lil Ajay, starting from when Lil Ajay was age 6. Which means the *"real time"* of this novel starts in September 2005 when Lil Ajay had just started 1st grade. The coverage you'll get of Ajay's growing years will come to you with him telling his son about his life and how he came to view things in the world based on what he went through and learned as he was growing up. He started these discussions to help Lil Ajay understand how to deal with older girls who are after him. Plus what legacy he was born into. If you've read "MORE THAN 4 ADMIRERS" then you already know about the enemy situation Ajay and the males learned of because the men in the crew are the protectors of their families. The males are reared very different than the females. So what Ajay is doing in these talks is making sure his only son knows what to look for. While at the same time, making sure he knows who he expects him to be.

Although the conversations take place starting in 2005, I have titled the sections with dates and in some cases seasons or holidays, to help you navigate the period of time in which you're reading about.

With that said, it's time to get to know *Anthony Devante' Jackson Sr* better known to all of you as *Ajay*. From his parents, he's called Ant but his government name is Anthony. That is for Ebony, *ONLY*.

I hope you enjoy this novel and please don't forget to add your review for all other Black Coffee novels & short stories online using the author page link is on my website. www.truesrelatepublishing.com

Send a your name, photo and hometown in Facebook group: The Time Will Reveal-RELOADED series Crew Nation #Crew4Life. I'll add your review here: http://www.blackdollone.com/Reveiws-and-Covers.html

As always, thank you for your continued support and be sure to pick up the rest of the series which is listed at the end of each installment.
- Author Black Coffee #ABC

V

The Making of AJAY- "Every Man"
Chapter 1-Making The Man

"Every woman wants to be made love too, thoroughly. That's the only way she'll know she has you. But a real man won't kiss nor give that kind of treatment to every woman. That's only for his one and only and the one he wants to have and hold forever. Thorough love making is an art, son. That's something Jackson men are known for and you'll have to hold up for that name too. The art of loving a woman takes a lot of preparation. You have to study her, learn what she likes and what she doesn't like. Not every man can do that because he's never been schooled on what it takes to satisfy his woman. But my daddy told me and I'm gonna make sure you know it too. Pussy will be coming at you from every angle and direction. That's because of how you'll carry yourself. All men fuck. But only real men make love. I learned how to please my woman. Your mama is well taken care of, in ways you can see and ways you'll never see. My number one thought when I lay eyes on her, is what new ways can I please her and leave her smiling. I'm thinking like that even when she's not around. Don't ever leave the woman you love, wanting more. Because she'll find it somewhere other than with you, if she has too. For a Jackson man, that's a no-no. We don't share our woman sexually, with anyone. She has to have morals. She has to be a woman who keeps you on your toes too. With positive shit. Good shit that's for the betterment of you. She can only chastise you when it's for your own good. You have to be man enough to know that she has the right to do that. The good ones just seem to know when to do it. To keep her faithful, you've gotta have the upper hand long before the sex starts. A real man has it and maintains it, even after she submits to him. I have it and that's a fact. Good loving keeps your home peaceful. Keeps your woman smiling, in her place and happy. Good loving keeps the order in your relationship and in your life too. But your best loving is only for that one woman. The one that you love. You give her your all and your best. She's the only one who can see the intimate side of you, son. You don't show that to every woman you fuck around with. Only the one you wanna keep and you can only keep one. So choose wisely."

Lil Ajay has come home with a head full of questions and wants his pops to help him understand, why there are girls from 5th grade writing their names with his on their notebooks, clothes and lockers, at school. And he's only in 1st grade.

"Son you're a Jackson man," Ajay says, "You're a female magnet. They're gonna want you. So understand this. You can get all the pussy you want. But you must use protection and pick the right girls."

"How do I know who are the right ones?" Lil Ajay asks, "All the girls at my school say they wanna go wit me. They want me to be they boyfriend and I don't even like them."

"You're only gonna *really* like one girl, son," Ajay says, "But you can fuck all of them if you choose too. As long as you make it clear to them that they will not run you or be around you later. Nor will they decide when and if they get to be around you or if you fuck with them or not. There's only gonna be *one* girl in your life that you're gonna allow to do that. And you'll wanna give her anything you can because she'll be *just* that special to you. I went through the same things when I was young, like you are now. It can be frustrating, son. Because you know things that most six year olds don't know. I don't want you to let it upset you and that's gonna be the most work because it'll get on your nerves, most of the time."

"It's getting on my nerves *now*," Lil Ajay says, "But I do wanna feel on some of them because they're cute. But I don't wanna make them think they can keep coming to me like I'm suppose to do it, just cause they want me too."

"Ant this is the very reason I started talking to you in a regular way, as soon as you could understand words," Ajay says, "You're not packed with a lot of patience and some people are gonna misread that and say you're mean. You're not mean. You're just selective and you're smart enough to know what you want and what you don't want."

"I don't want them saying we go together," Lil Ajay stresses.

"My pops and grandpa use to tell me these same things," Ajay says and smiles, "And I've looked forward to the day when I could pass this on to my own son. Ant, you're my only son and I need for you to get this right. I'm gonna tell you how it was for me, so pay attention. Here it goes."

Anthony Devante' Jackson Sr nicknamed *Ajay* by his paternal grandfather Allen Devante' Jackson Sr, is the type of man most women refer to as a myth. He's a good man and an able bodied man. He's head

7

strong, book smart, gangster street wise and dominant. Plus he has an over-average talent in basketball and the very efficient art of pleasing the woman his heart desires. Her name is Ebony Eloise Brown-Jackson. Ajay often refers to her as *"baby girl."* From as far back as he can remember, he has wanted her undivided attention. In his pre-teen days, he wasn't able to get it which only made him want her more. He wanted to love her bad enough to learn how to do it properly. He was determined he was going to make her love him too. He had too. She was the kind of girl his mother always told him she wanted him to be with. His father had always talked about how precious Ebony was and he was as protective of her as he was of his own daughters. Ajay wanted the honor of being her protector. He didn't want anyone else to approach her without his permission. Rather they were in his crew or not. She was perfect. To him, she was the most precious person he knew and he was going to take care of her and make sure she maintained that special part. They grew up next door to each other and he'd picked her out to be his wife by the time his mother Jo was registering him for 1st grade. He wanted John Brown's baby girl and he was going to find out what he had to do to have her. Then he was going to do it. She was going to be his and *only* his. She wasn't even school age yet. But he knew if he was ever going to have a girlfriend. It would have to be her. From a very young age, he never believed he had any other options to choose from. She was the girl he wanted and he was going to have her.

By 2nd grade, he had made such a name for himself that he could've had his choice of any girl within his reach. Many girls who were twice his age, would go through outrageous acts and carry themselves in loose fashion just trying to have him for their boy toy. But he wasn't raised to settle for anything less than the absolute best of the bunch. He wanted a virtuous girl. A girl with morals and the type of mentality that wouldn't allow a boy to treat her in any other way except special, like a princess. A girl who took pride in the fact that she wasn't just *any* other girl. The kind who was choosy about those who could be in her company and who could talk to her. While in her company, that boy would have to speak to her in the correct manner or he wouldn't ever get any positive feedback from her. Ajay wanted a girl like that. One who demanded he be all he could be. While at the same time, be all about her because she knew she deserved it. He wanted a girl who had been raised by strong parents. A girl who had been taught to value herself more than material things or anything that money could buy. Ajay was always selective about the types of people he spent his time with. To be in his company, you had to be about moving

8

things and having something worth having. The girl who would have his attention was going to be the type of girl that every man would want. Basically he wanted a girl who deserved him too. A girl who was an open and easy target, could never hold his interest. No matter what age she was. He wanted the best. A girl just like his mother. A female version of himself. Ebony "baby girl" Brown was just such a girl. She was raised by people whom he both admired and respected.

Ajay was raised by strong people. His legacy says and shows as much. His mother was the oldest daughter of a segregation era pioneer. Allen Saul Williams lost his life fighting for the civil rights of all people. He wanted a better life for his children. Ajay's mother, Joanna Williams-Jackson had been raised to be a virtuous woman. She married Allen Devante' Jackson Jr, who was a freedom rider and so was his father Allen Sr. Jo and Allen Jr gave birth to Ajay on July 11, 1974. He was their only male child and they raised him to be a leader. A *man's* man. He wasn't allowed to have missteps while he was growing up. Which naturally made him hard around the edges. He would grow up to be a hard nose type with very little patience for any path except his own. His parents demanded he get it right the first time. They knew that for a young black male in America, he would seldom be afforded the benefit of the doubt. He had to carry himself upright and be strong in his convictions. Coming from such a demanding upbringing, he had very little patience for anything regular or minimal. He was raised to strive for the best life had to offer and never sell himself short or take a loss. Being a young kid and having such high expectations placed on his shoulders, also made him wise beyond his years. He carried himself like a man, early in his life. Which caught the eyes of many females. Most of those females were much older but she would have something to hold his interest, short term, if she wasn't a girl like his mother. Because he didn't believe in wasting his time. He wasn't raised too. Once the older girls were able to get some attention from him and saw that he was able to carry on a conversation equal to theirs and sometimes even more adult than theirs. They were hooked and wanted to know him better. They wanted him as their boyfriend but he was mentally mature and head strong too. He wouldn't go with a girl who didn't meet the standards his parents had raised him to look for. He wasn't only mature mentality though. His physical being was big in stature as well. He was nearly 4 feet tall at age 6 with a body to match. He descended from big and tall men with bold bodies that stood out in a crowd. By the time he'd passed to 3rd grade, he was the height of the 6th graders at Abe Lincoln Middle school. But he was still at Beachwood Elementary. Many were already labeling him as a lady killer. They thought surely he was getting a lot of girls because he was already sexually active. He wasn't penetrating any girls before 3rd grade. But he'd already experienced the oral side of sex, from the receiving end. He'd gotten head several times before actually doing the whole act. But it would be the summer of 1982, before he started 3rd grade, that he would experience his 1st sex with penetration. It was just after he'd turned 8 years old. He had a dress rehearsal for real sex, during the spring prior to his 8th birthday. It was with the same girl who would eventually give him his 1st experience with pussy. *Let's venture into the life of Ajay, from a boy to the ideal man from the Time Will Reveal series.*

}June 1981{

Ajay's parents had given birth to another girl in February, whom they named Erica. Ajay had 3 sisters now. Lynn was a year older than him. Nina, who was a 1 ½ years younger and Erica, who had turned 4 months old in June. With his upbringing, Ajay automatically felt like he had to be responsible for all of them and he was ready for the job. He was 6 years old and about to turn 7 the next month. But his manhood urges had already kicked in. He started to notice girls a lot more in 1979 when he'd started Kindergarten at public school. He liked certain things about certain girls. But none of the girls at his school made him feel as though he had to look for them. Even though he had sisters, there wasn't many girls who hung around them other than the girls from their crew and a select few, outside of the crew. That was by design. Their parents were very particular about whom they linked up with and whom they brought home to visit. Ajay knew from his father's teachings that he wasn't to get fresh with a crew female unless he wanted her as his girlfriend for life. There was only 1 girl whom he saw in that way. She was his sister Nina's age. But she still wasn't old enough to play outside without her parents yet. She stayed indoors and played with her baby dolls and her pet Scottish Terrier, which she'd gotten from her daddy for her 3rd birthday, 2½ years ago. Her brothers were Ajay's best friends and he had already let them know, he wanted her to be his girlfriend in the future. That way, he knew they would look out for him. Ebony's 2 older brothers was 2 of the males in Ajay's crew. 1 was older than him and they called him Jb. Her other brother Tank was 7 months younger than Ajay. He was Ajay's best friend from his age group. There were older guys too. Big Chill, Stoney, Rob and Ajay's cousin Brad Jr were all older then Ajay by 3 to 5 years. Big Chill was their leader and the oldest of all the boys. He was already popular with many of the females too. That was an advantage for Ajay because having crew brothers who were double digit in age, brought the older girls around him. And there was a lot of girls who hung around his crew. Ajay was becoming good in basketball during that time as well. When the girls were around and he played and beat the older boys, that brought him positive attention from the older girls. He liked that a lot because he didn't have to put forth any effort to get their attention, which he didn't want to do anyway. He knew they wasn't the type he could be with in sight of his parents. So he would tell them they could find him at his after-school job.

His family owned a detail shop in University Heights. That was Ajay's first job. He worked there every afternoon and every Saturday. There was only 1 thing that could pull Ajay away from his crew and that was basketball. Because he was going to play basketball daily, no matter what or where the game was being played. He had to go and find where the best competition was. Him and his crew brothers were tight and they went everywhere together. So if Ajay got invited to go play a game. They all went. This left the fathers to do all of the cars including drying them, which was the job of big Chill's crew. So to solve that problem. The fathers erected a basketball court in the spare parking lot, next to the shop. That way they could keep Ajay and the guys there and working. That was ideal for Ajay because he loved to make his own money. Just as much as he loved to play basketball. At age 6, the ideal job for him would've been to play basketball for money. He would even hustle up money on the side as he played basketball games by placing bets. He won a lot of money that way. He would offer it to his mother first. But she never took any of it. She told him to save it for a rainy day and that's exactly what he did. He was saving his money by the time he was in 1st grade. He was already *very* particular about how he spent it and whom he spent it on.

A lot of girls would come around the detail shop looking for the older guys in his crew and some of their fathers too. Ajay always got their attention. That was pretty much because he never seemed to want it. Nor did he put in work to get it. He gave them a take it or leave it type of attitude. This made females who wanted time with him, work even harder to get that time. And even after getting his attention. They still had to work hard to keep it. That was a job in itself. He loved females a lot. But he didn't want to love them in a way that made them hang around him for longer than that day. Or long enough for him to get a good feel off them or whatever he saw as their worth to him. The females often thought he was

11

a teenager because of his size and his mentality. So they would naturally offer him the same things they were providing to the older boys in his crew. *Sex.* They would talk to him about having sex or doing sexual things. That's what made him curious. It wouldn't be long before his appetite for sex and sex acts would peak. He had many offers and dress rehearsals with different girls before he actually indulged. He experienced oral sex long before he got to the penetration side of it. He wasn't even 7 years old when he first got his dick sucked.

It was on Father's day weekend in 1981. The girl was nearly 15 years old which was more than twice his age. She was the friend of a girl who was hanging around to have sex with his crew leader, big Chill.

Chill, who had just past to the 7th grade, had already turned 12. The girls who came around him were always his age or older and never the virtuous type, just like the girl who gave Ajay his 1st head job. Like the others, she thought Ajay was older because he was of size and his conversation was on point too. He hadn't turned 7 yet but his penis had outgrown his age. It was 6 inches long, which was man size to any 15 year old girl. After getting his attention for a few hours, that girl thought she was special. She wanted to be his girlfriend but he wasn't about that. Not with her and he didn't pretend to be. Ajay didn't mix words. He spoke his opinion bluntly and that seemed to have started at birth.

"You sucked my dick already," nearly 7 year old Ajay told her that Friday night. He added, "What makes you think I'm gonna be yo man?"

"Cause I like you a lot," she had said.

"But you done gave me head without even being my girlfriend," he said, "I ain't wit that, Lil mama. You're too loose for me. You done already gave another nigga head too. I'm already knowing that. So hell nah. If you wanna suck me off, we can do that. But I can't be yo man because I'll never be able to trust you. See the girl who's gonna be mine, ain't gonna fuck wit nobody but me. You're already out there and the streets know it. Let's do this if you want too. If you don't wanna give me no more head. That's cool too. I'm out."

That worked on that girl. He got head from her that day and another 6 times that year. Even though she knew he didn't want anything else as far as him having to claim her as his own, was concerned. Nor did he have to bother to keep in touch with her. She made herself available to him whether he got with her or not. She would always hang around. She had promised him she would give him her pussy too. And all he had to do was to let her know when he was ready for it. He never got around to it because she got

12

pregnant before that summer ended. And for Ajay, she was all the way over and out of his life. He wanted nothing else to do with her, her body or her mouth from that point on. He suggested she stick with the guy who had gotten her pregnant because he didn't want that kind of drama in his life. Not over a girl he didn't want. But she wasn't even sure who had fathered her child.

"Then that's zero for you," he'd said, "I don't even want no head from you no more. Bye."

That was the last conversation he had with that girl. He moved on to several other girls during the summer and fall of 1981. He turned 7 and was headed to 2nd grade. He would get head many more times over the next year. He took it in stride. 1 of the most notable head jobs he'd gotten was from a girl named Monica Keyes. Monica was 15 years old and came to Cleveland from Seattle to stay with relatives after the eruption of Mount St. Helens which happened on the 18th of May, just 4 months prior to meeting Ajay. Her family's Seattle home had been destroyed and they had come to Cleveland to stay with her uncle and his family until her parents could rebuild. Ajay met Monica at his cousin Brad Jr's 10th birthday party on August 14th. As soon as she saw him, she approached him.

"I can't believe you ain't wit nobody," Monica had said, "*Damn* you're so cute. Where yo girlfriend at?"

"I don't have one," Ajay had said bluntly.
From his experience, that had always worked and it worked on Monica too.

"Well damn," she said, "I need to be your girlfriend. I tell you one thing. I bet I wouldn't be leaving you by yo self at no damn party. Not as fine as yo ass is, baby."

"Well I'm by myself," Ajay said, "So what's up?"

"You got somewhere we can talk in private?" she'd asked him.
The party was at Chill and his father Paul's house, which was always a packed scene. Ajay and the crew guys could always use the spare room to get busy because Chill was always using his own room and so was big Paul.

"What you trying to do?" Ajay had asked, "Cause I don't wanna talk. I need to get some lips. I know you can suck a good dick, right?"

"Let's go," Monica had said, "Let me show you what I'm working wit."
They went upstairs to the spare room. No sooner than they were inside and the door was closed, Monica was on her knees in front of Ajay. She was undoing his pants for him. He backed up and sat on the edge of the guest bed and brought her with him. She got to work on him and he thoroughly

13

enjoyed it. He knew she'd had a lot of practice because her head game was superb.

"You got a big sweet ass dick, Ajay," she had said as she sucked him off.

She made him shiver a lot which was a first for him. She sucked his balls and that was new for him too. She asked him to let her take the condom off so she could swallow him. He was feeling so good, he almost allowed it. But he remembered what his father and grandfather had told him about diseases. He didn't want to risk that.

"No. Just keep doing what you doing," he said and she did.

She sucked him until he came. That was the best nut he'd gotten so far. It made him weak. So weak that he had to lay back for several minutes to catch his breath and to get his strength back. She laid next to him and tried to kiss him but he declined.

"I don't kiss on the mouth," he said.

"If my period wasn't on. I would fuck you Ajay," she said suddenly, "I wanna feel this big ass dick you got."

He said nothing. He hadn't penetrated a pussy yet and that part made him nervous. He wished her period wasn't on because he would've loved to have gotten that 1st time out of the way. It wasn't going to happen that night. Once he caught his breath, he got up and discarded the condom. Then told her he had some crew business he had to get to and they had to go. He'd learned *that* getaway line from big Chill. It always worked. Him and Monica went back downstairs to the party. She hung around but Ajay didn't say another word to her for the rest of the night. In fact, he actually got head from another girl in that same room before he headed home. Later he heard Monica gave head to Chill that night too. Chill told Ajay that she had talked about him while they were getting to the act. Ajay smiled briefly. He knew his rep would build with the right girls talking him up. And with a talker like Monica putting the word out about him. He knew his head totals would increase. He was just fine with that too.

The word had gotten out that he had a big dick. Some teen girls were afraid to try sexing him all the way. He didn't sweat it. He knew his 1st penetration would come before long and it did. It was spring break week of 1982 when he had come close to getting his 1st pussy. But the real thing wouldn't come until later that year, in the summer of 1982 after he turned 8 years old. It would happen the very same day his crew leader big Chill was taken into custody by family court and sent to Juvenile detention for the 2nd degree manslaughter of Neal Palmer. *Let's explore.*

14

}January 25, 1982{

Tank turned 7 and had his daytime party at his parents big John and Pearl's house. Ajay went to this party because he knew he would see Ebony. After the cake was served, all the kids were left to play in the basement. All the children were playing together except Ebony. She sat alone on the basement steps holding her Scottish Terrier which she had named Lady. She watched them play. Ajay noticed her sitting alone, so he went and sat on the steps next to her.

"Hey cutie pie," he said.

She didn't say anything nor did she look at him. She just brushed her dog's hair.

"You can't say hey to me?" he asked.

She still didn't say anything. Suddenly she got up, took her dog and went up the stairs. Ajay thought about following her but he didn't. He knew she was going to her mother's side. He knew his mother was up there with Pearl too. He figured if Ebony saw him up there. She would probably tell them that he was bothering her. Then his mother would fuss at him. So he stayed in the basement but he wasn't in the best of moods. 8 year-old Jb noticed that he wasn't mixing with the rest of his crew. He was moping around and looking uncomfortable. Jb approached him right away.

"What's up, Ajay?" he asked.

"Your sister act like she can't *stand* me. I don't know why."

"She's just shy, Ajay," Jb had said, "She do that to everybody. It's cool. Man she's still a baby. All she do is draw, play wit her dog and play with her baby dolls. She play with Nina, T-baby and Ree Ree. But they have to come over here. Daddy got her spoiled like that and she ain't *finna* talk to no boy yet, bro."

"I know that man. But I wanna make sure she knows that I like her, that's all," Ajay told him and he sounded desperate.

"Give it time, bro," Jb said, "Me and Tank got yo back. When she do talk to a boy. He gotta be crew anyway. You the only one that's gonna do for me, Tank and most likely my daddy too. Just chill out. You good."

With that, Ajay calmed his nerves a bit. He still couldn't figure out why every other girl came at him and wanted to be his girlfriend. But the 1 girl he wanted for his girlfriend wouldn't even speak to him. He took that in stride too. He wasn't going to give up. He was going to ask her big mama for advice. Because she knows everybody's business in their crew.

15

The next day, big Al called Houston so Ajay could talk to Ebony's big mama.

"Hello," big mama said.

"Hey big mama Eloise, it's Al," big Al said.

"Well hello," big mama said in an excited voice. "How's everybody and where's Ajay? Did he ask you to call me again?"

"Yes ma'am. He's right here," Al said as he chuckled. "Maybe Joanna and I will get to talk to you and poppa Percy, once he's done."

"Okay baby. Put him on."

Al gave Ajay the phone and some privacy. Ajay spoke to big mama and got right to his reason for calling her.

"I still can't get Ebony to speak to me, big mama," he said, "What am I doing wrong?"

"Nothing, sweetheart," she says, "Ebony's still very shy and unlike you, her mentality is still very young. But she isn't quiet because she hates you. She doesn't hate you. My namesake doesn't have a hateful bone in her body. She's most likely quiet because either she doesn't know what to say. Or she's afraid to say it. You know everybody thinks you're mean but I know you're not."

"I wouldn't be mean to her," he said, "I *like* her. I ain't never liked a girl before. Not like I like her. But she won't say nothing."

"She's my namesake and a little bit of her mother too," big mama said, "And my Pearl takes awhile to warm up to people too. Just give it a little more time. But whatever you do. Do not give up. Okay?"

"I'm not gonna give up," he said, "Thank you, big mama."

That's all he wanted to hear her say. He wanted to know he still had her blessings and support of him pursuing Ebony. He gave the phone back to his father. He was good to go and he definitely was going to keep speaking to Ebony until she said something back.

}March 1982{

The precursor to Ajay's 1st real sex was with Marsha, the 12 year old niece of his neighbor Miss Lou Robinson. Marsha was from Milwaukee. She was in Cleveland spending spring break with her aunt. She set her eyes on Ajay 1 afternoon while he was playing basketball with Jb, Stoney and Rob, outside of his house where Al had put up a basketball goal for him. The boys had been playing for nearly an hour on the dual driveways shared by Ajay's home and Ebony's home. Al and big John had the goal set up so

16

Ajay had a regulation sized half court to work on his game. Marsha made her way through her aunt's backyard. She stood by the back fence and watched him play. She thought he was already a teenager because that's how he carried himself. Plus he was hanging with the older boys too. She couldn't take her eyes off of him. She thought he was the prettiest boy in the world. He had very dark skin, entrancing eyes and shiny braids. He wasn't wearing a shirt while he played basketball and his chest was built. His abdomen was ripped too. He looked to be about 14 years old and he hadn't even turned 8 yet. That was still 4 months away. He wore a shiny gold rope chain and he had a sparkling diamond earring in each ear. They were earrings he had bought with some of his own money too. He had on a pair of long red *Nike* shorts with the *Julius Erving skywalk* emblem on them with the shoes to match. She watched him. He didn't even smile, not unless 1 of the guys had tried to take him to the hoop and he stole the ball and scored on him. He had nice game for sure. He had to be at least 14. She was sure of it. She had to talk to *this* boy. So she hung around watching them play for another hour until he finally took a break. That was the only way he was leaving the court because him and Stoney never lost to any of the other 2-man teams they played. Ajay was drinking *Gatorade* when she approached him.

"Hey I'm Marsha," she'd said, "My aunt lives in the house behind yours, back there."
She was pointing to the house so he would know where to find her. He wasn't impressed. He thought she was cute but basically average. He knew she was older than him too and that was typical.

"How do you know where I live?" he'd asked.

"I watched you play basketball from my window yesterday," she said, "Then when you got done playing. You went into that house right there."
She pointed to Ebony's house. Her aunt's house was located behind big John and Pearl's house. Ajay didn't correct her. He was always over at Jb and Tank's house. That was the only way he got the chance to see Ebony because she didn't come outside unless they were leaving. Or during the warmer months, when everybody was enjoying 1 of their many cookouts. This spring, she had visited his sister Nina a few times and she'd started to go across the street to big Chill's house. But she rarely played outside unless they were having a family get together. It was fine with Ajay if Marsha didn't know where he lived because she wasn't going to be visiting him.
"So what are you about to do?" Marsha had asked.

17

"Get cleaned up and go kick it wit my crew," he said, "Why?"

"I was just wondering if you would wanna come over to my aunts house and hang out wit me?" she asked as she blushed. "I'm at home all by myself. My aunt Lou is gone to work and it ain't nobody gonna be there but me."

He figured this was about to be another 1 of his older girl experiences. He was use to those by now.

"What time do you want me to come back there?" he'd asked.

"After you finish getting dressed," she said.

Then she wrote the phone number in his hand and said,

"Call me when you're on the way. So I can come downstairs and open the door for you."

"Cool," he said.

She looked happy and accomplished as she skipped back home. Ajay waited until she went through the back privacy fence. Then he darted into his own house to go take a shower and change clothes. He was going to get his 1st piece of pussy in a matter of hours or so he thought. He was *way* ready.

Ebony came over to visit Nina while Ajay was in the shower. When he got out and was going into his room, Ebony and Nina was coming back up the stairs. He was wrapped in a terrycloth half robe and he wanted Ebony to see him in it. But she still wouldn't even look at him. Not for longer than the few seconds it took for her to go from the top of their stairs and into Nina and Lynn's bedroom door. She was so shy or afraid. He wasn't sure which 1 it was. Ebony had turned 6 years old on Christmas day. She had always been the loner type and everyone knew it. But Ajay wanted to change that. He wasn't a real people's person and Ebony talked to even fewer people than he did. But she was best friends with his sister Nina, his play cousin Rebbie and T-baby, who was Ebony's 1st cousin. She would play with them when they were all together. But only her big mama, her brother Tank, her parents and big Chill could get her to hold a conversation. Ajay wanted to be in that number and he wasn't going to rest until he found a way to make that happen.

She's right there. I gotta say something to her again.

"Hey cutie pie," he'd said to Ebony as he stuck his head inside of Nina's bedroom door.

"Why you calling me that?" she'd asked him.

She said something!

18

"Because you're pretty to me," he said, "I just want you to know that, okay?"

"Well alright," she said and turned her back to him without another word or even a glance.

He was devastated but he took it in stride.

That's my girl, right there. She ain't easy.

That's what he thought to himself as he went back into his own room. He was about to get dressed so he could talk to his father before he went to Miss Lou's house. He took the phone with him and called Marsha while he got dressed.

"Hello," she said, answering on the 1st ring.

"What's up? Is this Marsha?" he asked.

"Yea this is me, Ajay," she said as she giggled. "And what's up is that I'm waiting on you to come and keep me company."

"I'll be there when my sister and her company leave," he told her.

She thought maybe he was babysitting his younger sister. But what he'd actually meant was he wasn't going to leave as long as Ebony was there and he could see her.

"So what time yo aunt getting home?" he asked.

"Late," she said, "She get off real late at night, like eleven. And she don't make it home until midnight."

"Good," he said, "Then I got time to knock that thang off, then ha?"

She laughed flirtatiously and she giggled a lot too. Then she asked,

"Do you wanna get busy wit me? Is that what you're talking about Ajay?"

"What else am I coming over there for?" he asked, "To watch TV? I got a TV in my room. I can watch TV at home."

"What you wanna do?" she asked while she still laughed.

"I want some pussy if I come over there," he said boldly, "What you think? You wit that?"

He wanted to see how far she was willing to go because whether it be her or 1 of his other 20 options. He wasn't going to go through spring break without getting to the good part. His new 7 inches had started to get hard and throb for no reason and he'd had enough of masturbating. He'd also had enough talks with his father, grandfather, big Chill and the crew men too. Plus he'd had a lot of practice with putting on condoms. He knew that was rule #1 with the men in his crew. If he wasn't with the girl he was going to be in a real situation with. Then he had to wrap it up. His father only

19

wanted him to be with a girl from their crew. And namely Ebony. She was the daughter of his parents best friends. Ajay was definitely alright with that rule. But for now, he was ready to know what it felt like to lose his deposits while actually in the act. He was ready to get his 1st piece and he wanted it before he went back to Beachwood Elementary and finished his 2nd grade school year. He knew his father had experienced sex by age 10. His father had told him early sex was apart of his genetics. Ajay wouldn't be 8 years old until this July. But he was ready to find out what it felt like to bust a nut while doing the real thing. Marsha was willing or so he thought. He knew he was.

"I knew you was like that," Marsha said as she started to laugh really loud. "I could tell you was already getting up on the girls. You got that look. Yea you're like that. You're just after these panties."

"Yea I am," he said, keeping with the ornery demeanor because that always worked on those types.

He knew he would never approach Ebony like that. But it was working on Marsha, just like it had worked on Monica Keyes and every other girl, thus far.

He asked, "So you wit it or what? Cause I got money to get. I ain't gonna waste my time if you ain't comin off no ass."

"Okay," she'd said, "Come on now."

"Are you a virgin or what?" he asked.

"No," she said, "I know what I'm doing."

"Cool," he said, "I'll be over soon as I can leave."

"Okay."

"Bye," he said and hung up the phone.

His father had warned him not to have a virgin that he wasn't willing to keep because they would be naturally emotional. He'd spent his entire life being aggressive with his talking points and he was raised to be honest about what he was feeling. His experiences with females, up until that point, was the reason he was like that. Being honest was a mentality he would never have to unlearn to have Ebony. She would see through him if he wasn't telling the truth because she was being raised similar to him. Thus far, the girls he had messed around with were always talking to him like they were going to run him or be in charge of him. He wasn't okay with that. His father raised him to be the man, always! And to never concede to anything unless it was what he was willing to do. He wasn't going to be led anywhere. The more he acted uninterested in them. The more the girls wanted him. That philosophy would never work on the 1 girl that he liked.

20

He would talk to Ebony and get no response at all. He knew if he tried to talk to her aggressively, she most likely wouldn't even reciprocate. Even when he complimented her, she didn't give him a positive response. He was baffled by her actions and according to his father, the girls who aren't ready to go for whatever he said. Were the ones to look into more carefully. And those who was ready to drop their drawers at his whim. Was a girl for the moment and not 1 to keep around. He didn't care about the other girls and how they took his demeanor because they didn't count toward his future. Only Ebony's reactions bothered him and he still hadn't figured out why or how to handle it. But he was going to learn what it took for her to talk to him and smile when she did.

I can't wait to talk to big mama again. She'll know what I need to do next.

Ebony was still in Nina's room after Ajay had gotten dressed. He wanted to see if he could get her to talk to him. Or at least smile for him. He had to see if she liked him, even just a little bit. So he went into Nina's room to see what the 4 girls were up too.

Ebony had brought her baby dolls over to play with Nina. T-baby and Rebbie had come over so they could all play together while their mothers was at Ebony's house doing the final preparations for the crew's April celebration. Ajay's oldest sister Lynn was going to turn 9 years old next month. His cousin Terrell would be coming from Boston to celebrate his 11th birthday, along with her. Ebony's grandparents was coming from Houston to visit and celebrate 28 years of marriage too. Ajay loved Ebony's big mama and he couldn't wait for her to come. He loved talking to her about how much he liked her granddaughter. Big mama liked that he liked Ebony and she would always encourage him to make sure Ebony knew it too. He planned to do just that. Ebony was still at his house and he was going to talk to her again.

"This all y'all got to do all day?" Ajay asked the girls.

Rebbie giggled while T-baby gave him a mean face. They hadn't turned 6 years old yet. But 6 year-old Ebony just stared at him while Nina got to the business of getting rid of her annoying only brother, who would always disrupt their play time.

"Get out of my room ole big headed boy!" 6 year-old Nina screamed. "I'm gonna tell mama! You're always messing wit us. Get outta here and close my door back! You don't want me to go in your room!"

"I can come in here," he fired back. "Shut up, wit yo lemon head."

All the girls laughed. All except Ebony. She just stared at him but didn't say

21

1 word. Seeing her was his reason for the interruption. Something in her eyes said she liked him. Only she seemed to be afraid of him. He just wanted her to say something nice to him and he would leave them be. So he went for broke.

"Cutie pie is this all you like to do?" he asked Ebony as he reached out and was attempting to touch her face.

She slapped his hand away and said, "You better not put your hand on me, boy. I'm gonna tell my daddy."

The girls giggled but Ebony still didn't. She just kept staring at him. Feeling dejected, he said, "Y'all some babies anyway. I gotta get to my crew. Where some big people at who don't play with baby dolls and toys all day. It's time to go get some money with the big folks. I need to get on my grind anyway. I can't be wasting my time wit no babies."

"Well why don't you go on ahead then!" Nina fired right back at him and he left as he slammed her door behind him.

He left Nina's room feeling angry. But even more than that, he was disappointed. He liked Ebony a lot. But she hated him or that's how it seemed to him. He went down the stairs and headed to Chill's house. All of the males were over there hanging out while the mothers gathered at Ebony's house. He had to talk to his father, grandfather and big Chill before he could go knock off Marsha at Miss Lou Robinson's house.

But after he was out of the room, Ebony asked Nina, "Where is he going?"

"Over big Paul's house," Nina said, "They got to play cards and domino's. That's what boys do, I guess."

"Oh," Ebony said.

"Ajay is *so* mean," T-baby said.

"Sho is," Rebbie said, "He can fight too."

"He's big," Ebony said, "He's not mean to me. He always smile at me. But he is mean to people sometimes. Just not to me. Maybe because he's too big. He's bigger than big Chill."

They all laughed. Ebony still didn't.

Then Rebbie said,

"Ebony you're mean too. That's probably why he ain't mean to you."

"Cause she'll punch him," T-baby said and they all cracked up laughing.

Ebony didn't laugh still. She didn't like what her cousin said. She didn't even know why she didn't like it. But she knew she didn't like it at all. Still she didn't say anything else to defend it. They continued playing with their

22

toys but Ebony was quiet throughout the remainder of their play time, while her 3 friends chattered on about who was mean and who wasn't.

Meanwhile Ajay had made it to big Paul's house and settled in with the men and boys. His father and grandfather was there. Chill and his father big Paul was there too. Along with Ebony's older brothers Jb and Tank. All of the crew men were there or on their way. Ebony's father John was on the road. He drove 18-Wheelers for a living which kept him away from home, his family and crew for 2 week intervals. He would be home in time for the April celebration though.

"What it do, Ajay?" Chill asked him as he glided in and took the seat between his father and grandfather.

"Nothing," Ajay said still feeling dejected. "I'm just *chillin*, bro. What you got for it?"

Chill grinned. He knew Ajay wanted to get a hit of some weed. He also knew he must've had some head lined up because he generally liked to be buzzed when he did that.

"Come holla at me," Chill said and they went out on the back porch to talk. Immediately Chill asked, "What's up?"

"Miss Lou's niece wanna do me," he said with a straight face.

"Oh shit!" Chill said in a excited tone, "You're about to get that virgin bug off you?"

"Fo sho," was Ajay's reply. "But I want my buzz first so I can be in busy mode when I get over there. I don't wanna waste time talking. I don't wanna be her boyfriend. I just wanna get to the nut."

Chill cracked up laughing and said, "See why I call you my brother? You ain't got time for these ho's. See me. I have to be careful now that I got a girlfriend. Renee don't take shit. She be beating these ho's asses if she think they on me."

"She's crew ready though, damn near," Ajay had said, "Big Paul and my pops said that."

"Most definitely," Chill agreed, "She's gonna be crew. See that's gonna be my wife one of these days, bro. She's over there at mama Pearl's house with Lynn, Jan and all the rest of the ladies."

They laughed as Chill pulled out a sack of weed and rolled 1 up. Then he asked, "I know you got some rubbers, right?"

"Yep," Ajay said, "I'm bringing two wit me."

"Ah shit," Chill said as he lit the weed. "You need to really hit this muafucka then. You finna bust *two* nuts."

They laughed as they smoked weed together. Jb and Tank soon joined

23

them. Jb would be turning 9 on the 4th of July and a week before Ajay would turn 8. Tank had turned 7 in January. These 4 spent a lot of time together because they lived closest to each other.

After Ajay was done smoking, he talked to his father and grandfather about his mission. They gave him some pointers and soon he was on his way to visit Marsha. Tank and Jb were going to be his lookouts. They had to make sure no one caught him going in there or coming out. And definitely they wasn't going to allow him to get caught inside of that house. He let them know Marsha thought he lived in their house. Jb recommended that he call her from their phone to let her know he was on his way.

"She's gonna look outside when you say you're coming," Jb said, "And she'll see you coming out of *our* house."
Ajay took his advice and called from Pearl's phone. Now Jb and Tank had the re-dial option if they had to get at Ajay right away. He hung up with Marsha and headed out on his mission.

After Ajay went through the privacy fence, Jb turned to Tank and said, "I knew Ajay was gonna fuck before me. He about to be in the league with Chill, junior, Stoney, Arthur and Rob. Hell I'm gonna be the next one to bust though and I want Lynn. Ajay know about it already and he's cool wit it."

"He like twin," Tank said, "He told me he like her a lot."

"I know he do," Jb said, "But Ebony ain't ready to do what Ajay is doing. I told him to just get her to smile and like him first. Then later on they can go together."

"Yea he told me that too," Tank said, "He said he don't want her to do nothing with him but just say she's his girl. And don't never like no other boy."

"Yep and we're gonna handle that part for him," Jb said, "Our little sister gots to have a man from the crew. *Period*. That's what daddy said too."

"Big Al said the same thing about Ajay and all of his sisters," Tank said, "They gonna have to be wit crew too."

"You like Nina, don't you?" Jb asked as he smiled.

"Yep," Tank said, "And she likes me too."

"Cool," Jb said, "But y'all gotta wait awhile. Big Al and daddy will have to tell us when we can date the crew girls. I don't know if I can wait though."

"I don't either," Tank said, "But big Al and daddy said we all need
24

to stay wit our crew when we pick our *real* girl. The girl that we wanna bring to meet them."

"It's a good thing he said that," Jb said, "Cause we already like the girls in our crew. So they can help keep the mama's from fussing at us when we start going out. I want Ebony to be wit Ajay when she grow up. I know he ain't gonna let shit go wrong for her. Daddy put me in charge of making sure the house stays safe and he told me don't let no boys come around here trying to talk to Ebony. He said he'll make sure she gets with who she's suppose to be with. Big Al said the same thing to Ajay. He said he ain't gonna be bringing no outsiders up in his house. He said he wanted Ajay to date inside the crew. So who the fuck else that leave for him if it ain't gonna be Ebony?"

"He already like twin," Tank said again. "And he told big Al that too. And he said big Al told him she was a good girl."

"I know and that's good," Jb said, "Cause Ajay don't like nobody that his daddy and his granddaddy don't cosign."

"Big Al treats twin like she's one of his own daughters already," Tank said and him and Jb laughed.

Marsha was standing in the back door when Ajay got there. She said, "Hey Ajay," as she opened the screen door and walked him in.
"I was starting to think you lied to me," she said once he was inside.

"I don't lie," Ajay said quickly, "That's one thing I don't do. My pops taught me that. If I didn't wanna come. I would've just told you I didn't wanna come. But I'm here now. So what's up?"

"Can I have a kiss?" she asked as she blushed.

"Yea," he said.
They kissed on the mouth but Ajay didn't allow her to use her tongue.
He wasn't familiar with her mouth and he didn't know where it had been or who it had been on. His father and grandfather had always preached that to him too. Never get that intimate with a girl that you don't know everything about because she could be passing something on to you that you don't want any parts of.
"Where's your room at?" Ajay asked her.
He was ready to get to it, get it done and get it over with. He didn't want to hang out with her for long. And not at all, if she wasn't going to keep her word to him.

"It's upstairs," she said but she didn't head that way.

"We going up there?" he asked.

25

"Okay," she said.

She started toward the stairs and paused. Then she turned around and asked, "Can we sit on the couch and talk first? I wanna know if you got a girlfriend. If you do then what is her name and where's she at right now?"

"Why?" he asked, already becoming impatient.

"Because I don't have a boyfriend," she said, "And I want you to be my boyfriend."

"You don't even live here," he said, "How is that gonna work?"

"I come here on every school break," she said, "I can asked my auntie to let me come for all breaks and holidays. How about that?"

"I thought you said we was gonna get busy if I came over here," he said and he was out of patience at that point.

"We can but I want you to be my boyfriend too," she tried.

"I don't want a girlfriend who don't live here," he said, "And you don't live here. Plus you already had a boyfriend. That mean I can't be number one. That ain't gonna work for me. I'm number one or nothing."

"Why you gotta be like that?" she asked.

"That's how it is," was his reply, "Are you ready or not?"

"No," she said, "I don't wanna have sex with no boy who ain't gonna be wit me."

"See ya," he said and headed for the door.

"Wait Ajay," she said, "Don't leave. Please come sit down and talk to me first."

"I didn't come over here to talk," he said, "That's not what you said when you invited me over here either. I'm out. In a minute."

Just like that, he was gone. He left out the door royally pissed off. He hated to have his time wasted on an expectation that didn't happen.

Tank and Jb could see him as he headed back and they met him at the gate.

"Damn Ajay," Jb said, "What happened?"

"Yea what happened, Ajay?" Tank asked.

"Not shit," he said, "She wanted me to watch TV. I told her when I first called that I didn't wanna hang out. So fuck it. Let's go see what big Chill bout to do. Since we off today."

The 3 of them headed to Chill's house so they could get up with him, Arthur, Jr, Stoney and Lil Rob. Then get out on their blocks and collect their money.

Ebony had spent the rest of their play time trying to figure out why

Ajay was nice to her but no one else. Neither of her friends came up with answers that satisfied her. Before long, she went to her house and played in her room alone. But it didn't take her 3 friends long to make their way to her room to play. They could never seem to play right unless it was the 4 of them. It was just a whole lot more fun with all 4 of them together.

}*June 14, 1982*{

The leader of the 3rd generation of the crew was made official on this date. Kenneth *"Big Chill"* Ramon Payne turned 13 and had a huge all day party. His father big Paul pulled out all the stops. He had a daytime concert where *Roger Trautman* and *Zapp* performed in the middle of the strip mall parking lot in front of their Detail shop. The place was packed.

"Chill your party is off the damn chain, man," Stoney said as Rob and the other guys agreed.

"Big Paul got some juice," Rob added.

"He got papa Brown and poppa Percy to hook it up," Chill told them. "They know mister *Eddie Levert*. He's with that group *The O'Jays*. Pops said they know *everybody*."

Every few seconds a partygoer would run up to Chill and tell him his party was the spot or the place to be.

He smiled and said, "Yea and this is gonna always be the spot and the place to be. Remember that."

Renee was standing with him as the compliments came in and she smiled big too. She was always telling Chill that he had major power and that folks loved to attend whatever his crew's name was on.

Renee asked, "You said you wanna have your own club one day, right?"

"I am *gonna* have a club one day," Chill said, "It's gonna be for my whole crew though."

"You should call it *The Spot*," she said, "The *Chill* spot. Everybody would know where to come because after today. Anytime you have a party. People are gonna show up."

"True that," Chill said as he gave her a kiss and smiled at her.

"I'm gonna be there. I know that much," Renee said, in a matter of fact tone.

"*Fasho* you gonna be here," Chill said, "I'm keeping you girl. I told you that. Stop sweating these ho's. They don't mean shit to me. You gonna be crew queen soon as you make thirteen in November. So get your mind

27

ready, get it right and get it set on that, Miss Renee Stewart. Because you're gonna be in charge of making sure all the girls from *my* crew have their heads on straight. And y'all are gonna be down for each other. No matter what. Do you feel me?"

"I feel you and I'm wit that," she said and smiled.

They continued to enjoy the party. All of the parents were there with even the smallest children. Ebony was there with Pearl and big John. They were in 1 of the side store's which was where the party food was being made and served. That store was the 2nd largest at their strip mall and it would 1 day become a restaurant for the crew. Ebony was inside cooling in the air conditioning. She had brought Lady and her favorite baby doll with her. It didn't take long for Ajay to find her. He walked in and walked right up to her and smiled. This time she smiled back. His heart fluttered. He felt butterflies which was definitely unusual for him.

"Hey cutie pie," he tried.

"That's not my name," she said as she rubbed Lady's coat down with her hands.

"You like your dog a lot, don't you?" Ajay asked.

"Yes," Ebony said with excitement, "She's so pretty. Don't you think she's pretty?"

"Yea," he said, "Can I pet her?"

"Okay."

Chill came in to get a cool drink. He saw them seated together and went right over to where they were sitting.

"Hey baby girl!" Chill said with excitement, "You came to my party? Now I know it's the place to be!"

Ebony cracked up laughing as did Chill and Ajay. This was new for Ajay. He hadn't seen this side of Ebony but it was 1 thing he could see right then and there. And that was that she had a beautiful smile. Even with 1 of her front teeth pulled out as every child usually goes through around 6 years old. She was still *so* pretty to him. It was something about seeing her happy that made him feel good and made him want to be in a good mood.

What is wrong with me?

Ajay decided to let Chill do the talking for awhile because he seemed to have the magic touch. The object of his affection was laughing, smiling and even talking too.

"Chill do you see Ajay petting my baby?" she asked.

"I see that," Chill said, "You ain't never let nobody outside of big

28

John's house pet Lady. Unless they was cool like me. And it's okay to let Ajay pet her because he's cool too. Did you know he's like a little brother to me since I don't have one?"

"He *is*?" she asked as she looked at Ajay and finally gave him the once over.

"Yea," Chill said as Ajay just smiled and remained quiet.
He didn't want to mess up or break anything about that moment.

"Okay then," Ebony said. Then she looked at Ajay and said, "Chill says you're cool. Chill is cool too, ha?"

"He's cool, *Fasho*," Ajay answered quickly and he couldn't stop smiling for anything.

"Chill is my big *bigger* brother," she says, "He don't let me get hurt or nothing. He always make sure I stay safe when I'm outside."

"I like hearing that," is all Ajay said but he wanted that spot.
He couldn't stop watching her smile. She was busy making sure Lady liked being petted by him. And from all accounts and reactions from Lady. She did. She had fallen asleep laying on Ebony's lap.

"Lady likes you to rub her," Ebony whispers, "She went to sleep."
Then Chill says, "Ajay got a gentle stroke. That's from shooting all of them bottom of the net shots when he plays basketball."

"I see him playing on our driveway everyday," she says, "Every time I hear the ball bouncing and I look outside. I see him. He be making all his shots too."

"He's gonna go pro one day," Chill said.
Ebony looked at Ajay and asked, "What's pro?"

"It's the N-B-A," he said, "Have you ever heard of doctor Jay?"

"The basketball man?" she asked.

"Yep," Ajay said, "The basketball *king*. He's my favorite player. He's a professional basketball player already. And that's what pro means. Professional."

"Oh," she said and looked at him seriously. "You're gonna do that one day? Be a pro..fess..shun..all?"
Ajay smiled and said, "I want too, yea. That's why I practice so hard."

"That's so cool," she said and giggled. "They gonna put you on TV if you be like doctor Jay."
Ajay just smiled and Chill said, "Oh yea. He's gonna be on TV, Fasho! And I get to be at the games too. I'm gonna be yelling *That's my Lil brother that's killing y'all!*" he said and laughed. Then he said, "Then I'm gonna tell Ajay to dunk on em!"

"I can't dunk yet, Chill. But I will in a few years," Ajay said. Then to keep the conversation going, he said, "I gotta keep pumping the leg weights. I can get the rim already though."

"I saw you hanging on the goal one day," Ebony said and laughed.

"You did?" Ajay asked, "Where was you at?"

"In my room window," she said and smiled.

"Oh okay," Ajay said, "Did you like that?"

"Yes," she said, "It looked like it was a lot of fun."

"Well now that I know you like watching me do that," Ajay said, "I'm gonna be doing that every time I'm out there now."

Chill laughed. He liked seeing the 2 of them having such a pleasant conversation. He'd never seen Ajay so attentive to anyone. It was a good look and he wanted to make sure they kept talking pleasantly.

"Oh baby girl. He knows how to fix your handle bars on your bike too," Chill said suddenly.

"He can?" she asked as she looked at Ajay.

"Yep," Chill said, "He can put a whole bike together."

"Can you fix mine?" she asked Ajay.

"Yes," Ajay said, "I'll do it tomorrow if you want me too."

"I do because then, I can keep up with Tank when he rides fast," she said and smiled. "My handle bars always twist around and I feel like I'm gonna fall off. Then he speeds up and leaves me. So then I have to just go back to my yard and wait til he comes back. I wanna ride down the street too but he won't wait for me."

"If I fix them for you. Will you go riding wit me and Tank?" he asked, "I'll tell Nina to go wit us too."

"Okay I guess so. If my mama say I can," she said, "My daddy has to go back to work before I get up tomorrow. I'll have to ask mama if I can ride down the street."

"Well I'll fix em for you. No problem," Ajay said and smiled.

She smiled back and said, "Well I have to go and let Lady lay down. My daddy told me not to hold her while she sleeps because she'll get lazy. My daddy have to leave in the morning so I'm gonna go and let Lady lay down and sleep. Then I can sit on my daddy's lap before it's time for me to go home."

"Oh alright," Ajay said somberly, "I'll come over and fix it when I get up. Before we have to come to work tomorrow. Okay?"

"Okay," she said as she eased up and stood to her feet.

She carried Lady to her doggy bed and put her down while Ajay watched

30

her, the whole way. He had a look on his face like he was in a trance until Chill got his attention.

"Hey bro," Chill said and laughed. "Let's go handle some business, right quick."

"Okay," he said as he stood up and followed Chill to the door.
He looked back at Ebony before leaving out. But she never looked back at him. That made him feel sad. But he was happy they'd talked and for that long too.

Him and Chill hit the strip mall scene and got up with the rest of the guys. They had street stuff to do. Ajay felt light on his feet, all of sudden. Like he could float to the rim if he had a basketball in his hand at that moment. He just smiled and kept up with his crew.

The next morning Ajay got up and tightened Ebony's handle bars. While he was at it, he set her gears to the fastest mode which would make her pedals easier to rotate. That would allow her to pick up speed quicker on her 3-speed bike. That would also make it easier for her to ride with Tank. He was going to make sure and be there to ride the next time Tank pulled his bike out.

It was 2 days later when Tank decided to ride his bike. Ajay was ready to ride too. But he wanted to bring Ebony along and he knew he had told her he would bring Nina too. He went and got Nina and helped her bring her bike out. He knew that would work for Tank as well and it did.

"I told daddy you fixed Ebony's bike," Tank said, "He called when he made it to Memphis last night. He said to tell you thanks."

"No problem," Ajay said, "I told her I was gonna fix it so she could ride wit us and keep up."

"It's *souped* up now, man," Tank said, "I rode it to Monica's house while you was at Chill's with that ho yesterday. It's fast. You worked them pedals a loose."

"Monica gave you head didn't she?" Ajay asked and laughed.

"Yep," Tank said and laughed, as his attention went to mama Jo's side door.
Nina was coming out. Her bike was already outside waiting next to Ebony's. Ajay had a suggestion for his younger sister.

"Nina go get Ebony, so we can all ride together," Ajay said.

"She's not gonna go nowhere," Nina said in a bossy tone.

"Just go tell her and see what she say," Ajay insisted.

31

"Okay," Nina said and ran into Pearl's house.

Within minutes, Ebony appeared at the door. She was dressed so cute in her pink and white short set. Ajay smiled. Ebony didn't. She looked afraid. He had to change that.

"You ready to ride wit us?" Ajay asked Ebony.

"Tank gonna leave me," Ebony tried.

"I'm not gonna leave you," Ajay said, "Come on."

First she stood next to her bike and grabbed the handle bars with both hands. She pushed forward on them to see if they would move. They didn't. She looked at Ajay. He smiled. She didn't. Next she straddled it while still testing the handle bars as she guided it down the driveway and to the street. She readied herself to ride it by placing her foot on the pedal. Then she pushed off with the other foot and started to roll down the street. Ajay, Tank and Nina rode behind her. Everything was going fine until she started to pedal and realized the pedals were a lot looser than before.

"My pedals messed up!" she yelled.

"No twin. Ajay souped it up for ya!" Tank yelled but Ebony started to scream.

"My bike is broken! It's broken! No!" she yelled as she stopped in the middle of the street.

Ajay tried to explain to her what he'd done but she wasn't hearing it. She wasn't hearing either of them. She was angry as she jumped off of her bike and let it fall onto the pavement and ran back home crying.

"I'm telling my daddy you broke my bike!" she cried as she ran to their front door and disappeared into the house.

Ajay felt horrible. He didn't know what do or say at that point. He just looked at Tank with a helpless expression.

"She'll be cool, Ajay," Tank said, "I'll make sure she knows it's not broken. She just spoiled like that. She don't know that her bike is ready for the road. I think she just scared to go down there anyway. Let her stay home."

He picked up her bike and ran it back to their yard and parked it in front of their shed. Then he hustled back to where Ajay and Nina was still waiting and looking puzzled. Ajay didn't want to ride if Ebony wasn't going. But he knew Tank still wanted him to accompany him.

So to make it even, he said, "Nina take your bike and go back home."

"Ah Ajay," Tank protested.

"She ain't going if Ebony not going. Period."

Ajay helped Nina guide her bike back to their shed. She didn't seem angry about not riding her bike, as she headed back inside of Jo's side door. Ajay looked at Ebony's bike, then at his basketball goal. He thought about what she'd said at Chill's party. He looked up at her bedroom window and there she was, looking down at him. It startled him at first. But then he smiled and waved. She didn't do either back. She just stared at him with a blank expression. He had no words for this one as he backed away toward the street, still looking up at her. He hated the feeling he had at that moment. After all the strides he'd made and finally got to the point where she not only looked at him and smiled. But she talked to him too. She had even let him pet her dog. Then her face glowed when she found out he could fix her bike for her. He did and tried to fix her woe with Tank, at the same time. By making it speed up faster but she didn't like it and she got upset.

"What the fuck do I do now?" he whispered to himself.

He dropped his head and went back to his bike and Tank, who was still waiting in the street. They rode off on Tank's mission. Tank was talking a lot but Ajay didn't say more than 1 word for each answer. He wasn't happy. He felt like he had to start all over and that annoyed him a lot.

Chapter 2-A Day To Forget To Remember

Ajay and Lil Ajay are having another conversation. Lil Ajay thinks it's funny how his mother had acted toward his pops when they were little and he wants his little sisters to be the same way.

"Lannie and Lea gotta be just like mama," Lil Ajay says, "They better not let no boys trick them into being no stool either. Papa Al told me to make sure of that too. But I didn't know mama had a dog when she was a little girl. That was a girl dog though. I want a pit."

Ajay laughs and says, "I figured you would want a tough dog but we still have to see what your mama says about it. Your nana Jo wasn't having it. She was not about to let pops get me what she called a killer dog."

They both laugh and Ajay adds, "Son we're gonna have these talks every time I'm home. At least once a week or four times a month. I have to make sure you're *more* ready than I was. Because the world has changed a lot. Internet and cell phones wasn't even around when I was your age and definitely not where everybody had them. But nowadays everybody has a cell phone and the internet. You can reach millions of people in a second and they can reach you too. As a father, that's cause for alarm. I had 4 sisters to look out for and if we would've had the internet I would've known all of their passwords, so I could see what they was talking about and who they was talking too. Because as a boy, I knew and you'll know just what a boy's game is by the way he talks. And I'm looking for you to help me make sure that nobody gets into your sisters heads with crazy shit. Nor bother them or disrespect them. Not even online. Are you wit that?"

"I'm wit it pops and I got you," Lil Ajay says, "I like hearing about your life. You are the man, just like I always say."

"Yea son but Ebony is that woman who helped me to become the man that I am today," he says, "I wasn't always like this. I fucked a lot of females and fucked around with even more than that. But she was always the one who helped to keep things in order and on point."

"So you was getting head at six and seven but when did you get to the real thing?" Lil Ajay asks.

"Oh yea I got to the penetration right after I turned eight years old," Ajay says as he chuckles. "You might beat my record though, son. Because I beat my dad and he beat his. Grandpa Al was twelve when he started and pops was ten. But I started at eight. You know miss Lou that live behind nana Pearl, right?"

"Yes sir," Lil Ajay says, "So your first piece was with the same girl who wanted you to watch TV wit her when she came for spring break?"

"Yea she came back for the summer," Ajay says, "Marsha from Milwaukee. Here's how that went."

}July 17, 1982{

Back in May of 1982, Ajay's parents had given birth to another daughter whom they gave the name Pamela. Ajay just saw her as more responsibility for himself. That's just how he always viewed his sisters because of the teachings from the males in his whole crew. He also watched how his mother and father carried on their loving relationship. He really liked how his father treated his mother and how he loved all of his kids. Ajay knew he would be a man just like big Al. He wanted to have his own kids one day, so he could carry that on and he wanted Ebony to be the mother of those kids and his wife too.

It was July 17, 1982. He had turned 8 years-old 6 days prior and had a big party on the double driveways. Marsha had gone back to Milwaukee after spring break and finished her 8th grade school year, then returned to spend the summer with her aunt Lou. Mama Jo had invited her to Ajay's party last week and she came. But Ajay didn't even acknowledge her. He saw her as a liar and a tease. He wanted no parts of her because what she had told him she wanted to do with him. She didn't do. He had wanted to get his 1st piece and that didn't happen. So to him, she was just like the other girls who wanted to latch onto him for their own gain and he wouldn't get anything out of it for him. But what he didn't know about this 2nd coming of Marsha, was she had come back to Cleveland for 1 reason and 1 reason only. That was to show him that she really did want to get busy with him and she didn't want him to be angry with her. All she needed to do now was to figure out how to get his attention again. That was going to take a whole lot of work because since her last visit in the spring. The 1 girl that Ajay liked had become interested in learning to play basketball because she wanted to swing from the rim just like she'd seen him do.

Ebony had seen Ajay playing basketball every day and that was when he seemed to be at his most relaxed state. She wanted to learn it too. She also figured since her girls seemed to think that she was mean as well. Then maybe she could find out if basketball could be something that could change that for her too. She was going to learn it and get good enough at it, so she could play a game with Ajay. Her plan was to see if they could play basketball together and while playing, she'd tell him that she took up for

35

him when her girls had called him mean. Maybe then, he would forgive her for getting mad about her bicycle. She knew he had worried a lot about her actions that day in the street. Because he had gone through the trouble of calling her father on the road and asking him to please let her know that he was sorry for changing her bike speed. She was over the whole bike situation by now and she wanted to find a way to let him know that she was. The only thing she could think of, was telling him during a game of basketball. Which was when he seemed to be in the best mood. He wasn't mean, in her eyes. He had took the time to pet her dog to sleep. A mean person wouldn't do that. Tank never even did that and he was her closest friend in the world besides Nina, T-baby and Rebbie. Ebony planned to get Ajay to prove to her girls and others that he wasn't mean and he liked them all. So after the bike incident, she had started to go outside on the double driveways more and she asked the big boys to show her how to shoot. After school had let out for the summer, Ajay wasn't always there on a day-to-day basis. In the early summer, he was already on basketball teams with other 6-8 year olds whom the adult men thought would really be good enough to compete in the game on higher levels. Al and the other men had him competing all over Cleveland before July. Ebony figured she'd better get good at it before she could even asked Ajay to play with her. She knew who she was going to get to teach her. That would be big Chill.

Big Chill was the big brother type to her and all of the crew, who was his age and under. Everybody looked up to Chill. Even Ajay did and she could tell that already. So Chill was the first one she sought out to teach her this game and he was more then willing to help. Big Chill had turned 13 in June and was on his way to 8th grade. So to Ebony, he knew everything. He had a lot of power and a lot of folks who looked up to him, at his young age too. Nobody seemed to want to be on his bad side, so Ebony clung to him. She told him she wanted to know how to shoot basketball, so her girls wouldn't think that she was mean. She also told him that she didn't see Ajay as mean either, though a lot of others seemed to think he was.

"He put lady to sleep at your party," she said, "A mean person wouldn't play with a girl dog."
That brought a laugh out of big Chill. She had always been able to talk to him and he never reminded her that she was just a baby. He took the time to talk to her about whatever it was she wanted to talk about and he never tried to make her act any older than what she was. He was an only child being raised by his dad because his mother was killed, years before. Ebony

36

was 3 years old when she died and she could vaguely remember her. But there are lots of pictures of her, all over big Paul and Chill's house. Her mother has a picture of Chill's mother in their living room, as do all of the crew homes that Ebony visits. She knew Chill's mother had to have been an important person in all of their lives. Including her parents and their friends, because they all had lots of pictures of her and pictures of them with her.

Chill started teaching Ebony how to shoot basketball before the spring ended. But the date in the lives of Chill's generation of the crew, that would forever change their history and for some of them, their ability to ever trust others outside of their crew circle, was *July 17, 1982*.

Big Chill was the leader and a certified member of what Ajay and his inner circle called *The Crew*. Ebony, the apple of Ajay's eye had passed to 1st grade along with Nina, T-baby and Rebbie. Ajay's best friend Tank had passed to 2nd grade, Jb and Lynn had passed to the 4th grade and the popular Ajay would be going on to 3rd grade, for the next school year, along with T-baby's 1st cousin Jan.

Big Paul's house had become the host house for the men of the crew, after his wife Willamena was killed. Ebony went over there every day that summer to work on her jump shot with big Chill. It was late morning when she went over on July 17th. Big Paul was preparing to host another domino's game that afternoon. That was something him and the men did often, on their days off and weekends. An outsider named Neal Palmer was a regular at their all-male parties. But on this particular day, he had shown up extra early. Only Paul was home and Ajay's father big Al was there with him, getting the house ready for the other men to arrive. Paul, Neal and Al played a few practice games and shot the shit while Chill got out of bed and went to shower and get dressed. He knew Ebony would be coming over there early, looking for him so he could help her work on her shots. Big Chill had another engagement to get too. But he had to put in the work with Ebony before he could leave. Paul, Al and Neal had an argument during the practice games. Neal had gotten heated but it didn't advance further than words. Paul had to get more liquor before the other men arrived and he had asked Al to drive him to the store. It was during the hour while they were gone and Chill was upstairs in the shower, that Ebony had shown up.

Meanwhile across the street, Marsha had gone to Pearl's side door looking for Ajay. Pearl had answered and invited her to come in, then headed up the stairs to get the boys up. Ajay had spent the night with Tank

37

and Jb, as he'd often done. The boys got up and got dressed, then came downstairs. Ajay went outside with Marsha. Tank and Jb already knew they had to lookout for him, if he decided to go to Miss Lou's house. So they prepared themselves for that, while Ajay talked to Marsha on the double driveways.

"What you want wit me?" he asked Marsha in a very impatient manner.

He didn't like it 1 bit that she had come to Ebony's door looking for him. But he also remembered that he had allowed her to think that he lived there. He didn't want her to know where he really lived, so he let it go at that.

"I wanna do what I didn't do last time," she said to him, "I promise I won't flake out. That's why I came as soon as aunt Lou left for work. I came back to Cleveland for you."

"Are you living here now?" he asked.

He wasn't really interested in where she lived. He was wondering if he was going to have to come up with a tactic to avoid her for longer than just an occasional visit.

"Not yet," she said, "My mama said I still have to come back to Milwaukee to go to school."

"So what's up?" he said, "More lies?"

"No," she said, "I want too."

"Then let's go," he said and they headed to Miss Lou's house.

He wanted to get out of sight before Ebony came back outside. He knew she had gone over to Chill's house and they would be outside soon on Chill's driveway shooting ball. He didn't want her to see him leave with Marsha nor did he want her to know that he did. But he had no idea of what was about to happen across that street. While he would be giving up his last bit of innocence. A pedophile who had nestled in with their fathers and crew, was attempting to steal the innocence of the 1 girl who stayed on his young mind. What was about to happen to Ebony, would send her into a shell of distrust when it came to intimacy and mare her ability to see the vaginal touch from a male as something to be desired.

Ajay and Marsha went into Miss Lou's house and straight up to her bedroom. She wasn't going to waste time, this time around. Because she could tell by his demeanor that she wasn't going to be given a 3rd chance.

"So this is your room?" he had asked.

"Yes," she said, "I use to watch you play basketball from this window."

He went and stood next to the window with her. He could see his father's car pulling into big Paul's driveway across the street from Ebony's house. He wanted to get this first time done, so he could join the men at Chill's for what would no doubt be a discussion on how the first time was for him. When he turned his attention back to Marsha, she was already naked. She had taken off her own clothes and was standing next to the bed, smiling at him. She had breast and they were nice and firm. He had never seen a girl completely nude before, so he took in the sight for a few seconds. Then he shed his own clothes and got on the bed. She followed him.

"So you wit it this time ha?" he asked while rubbing her breast.

"Yes," she had said.

He rubbed on her breast before he took 1 of her nipples into his mouth. He was doing what had been explained to him by his father. After she seemed ready. He reached over to his shorts pocket and pulled out 1 of the 2 condoms, he kept with him and put it on. She was laying on her back. He climbed on top of her and used his fingers to find his target. It took him all of 5 seconds and he was inside of it. Just like that, his vaginal virginity was over. He was now on his way to being a complete man. Marsha was moving her body against him which gave him a sensation that he didn't have any words for. The only word that came to his mouth was, "Oooo," and he said it many times. The sensation was good and he was enjoying the feeling he was getting. It didn't take him long to lose those deposits that until today, usually wound up in his hands or on his spread. But not this time. Today they were sitting at the tip of the condom he was wearing and he was breathless. He pulled out and looked down at his member. He knew he would never forget this day. He couldn't find any words for Marsha and suddenly, he felt like he needed to find an escape.

"Where's the bathroom?" he had asked.

"The door next to mine," she said as she sat on the side of the bed using her hands to brush her hair down.

He got up and pulled his boxers and shorts back on and went to find the bathroom. He could hear Miss Lou's phone ringing as he looked in the bathroom mirror and smiled. He was no longer a virgin and he felt damn good about that. He pulled his shorts and boxers down, pulled the condom off and flushed it in the toilet. Then he got a clean towel from the linen shelf there in the bathroom, washed and cleaned his member and pulled his boxers and shorts back on. He didn't need a 2nd time, not right now. He had to give himself time to take in this moment that had only lasted about 5 minutes. But it seemed like it had taken him a lifetime to finally get to it. He knew from then on, that was an act the other girls would have to be ready to do. Whether they gave him head or not. He already knew he wanted to feel the inside of a pussy again. He could hear Marsha rushing back up the stairs and she was calling his name. He thought surely her aunt had come home and he was about to be caught in that house. He looked out of the bathroom window searching for an escape. That bathroom window faced in the same direction as Marsha's bedroom window. He could see his house, Ebony's house and across their street to Chill's house too. And at Chill's house, there was police there! He could see Tank and Jb rushing through the path and privacy gate heading to Miss Lou's back door. They had to be coming to get him and he knew instantly something was wrong with his family. At that point, he didn't even care what Marsha was calling him for. All he wanted to do was to get to his shirts and shoes, get them on and get the hell out of there. He needed to know what was going on at his brother Chill's house and he had to know immediately. His father's car was parked in Chill's driveway. From the bathroom window, he could see that lots of people had started to gather outside of Chill's house.

Suddenly he heard Marsha yell, "Ajay! Ajay! Jb just called for you and said you need to come home! Something's happened at mister Paul's house!"

Ajay rushed out of the bathroom and back into Marsha's room. He could hear Tank and Jb banging on the door.

"Go let them in," he said to Marsha.

She jetted back down the stairs to open the door while Ajay got his shirts and shoes on. By the time he got to the top of the stairs, Tank and Jb was already at the bottom looking up at him.

"What's going on?" Marsha asked Jb and Tank but they didn't respond.

Ajay darted down the stairs and said, "Let's go crew."

"We gotta get to Chill's, man," Tank said as they headed to the door and exited while Marsha continued to ask what had happened.

They never answered Marsha because they were raised to know that crew never put their business out to outsiders. And besides, Ajay didn't know what had happened and he damn sure didn't want to find out at the same time an outsider did. Him, Tank and Jb hit the door running. Ajay never even said another word to Marsha.

"Call me later!" Marsha shouted as the guys raced back toward and then through the privacy fence.

"What's going on?" Ajay asked as him, Tank and Jb ran right

40

passed Pearl's side door, on toward the street and toward Chill's house.

They made it to the street just in time to see the police and a juvenile counselor escorting big Chill to an unmarked police car. His hands were behind his back and he was wearing handcuffs. Stoney, Rob and Ajay's cousin Jr had made their way over to where Ajay, Tank and Jb had stopped to observe. No one was allowed in the yard. Jr and the guys already had the story.

"What the fuck is going on?" Ajay asked, "Why are they taking Chill away?"

"He shot that fool Neal," Stoney said, "He jumped on Chill while big Paul and big Al was gone to the store getting liquor for game day."

"What the fuck did he jump on big Chill for?" Tank asked.

"Cause big Paul and uncle Al had said they was gonna whoop his ass when they got back, if he was still talking shit," Jr said.

"Yea so that bitch ass nigga must've decided he would go in on Chill since he knew he couldn't beat his pops," Rob added, "I knew he was a bitch. I never liked that nigga."

Ajay's cousin Richie Rich and Tank's cousin June had made it there with their parents, by that time. They all stood together watching as Chill sat in the back of the unmarked car. Stoney, Rob and Jr gave them the story as they had heard it. The 8 males in Chill's crew now knew why their brother and leader was being taken away. Ajay looked up and saw his father coming out of the house. He was holding Ebony in his arms. He could tell that she'd been crying. He knew she was upset to see Chill taken away because he was her basketball coach and her bigger big brother too. Seeing her upset only made Ajay angrier.

"Neal dead?" he asked softly.

"Dead as a door nail," Rob said, "Chill popped that fool for putting his hands on him."

"He better be dead or I was gonna kill him, if he wasn't," Ajay said as he walked away from them and went toward his father.

A police officer tried to impede Ajay's progress but he yanked his arm away and before the officer could say anything more, Al spoke up.

"Officer let him on through," Al said, "That's my son and he's just trying to check on his father, is all."

The officer moved out of Ajay's path so he could get to Al. He had to know what happened and also what was wrong with Ebony too.

"Pops is she okay? Or you okay?" Ajay asked Al and then Ebony.

"Yea son," Al said, "She's a little scared with all of this drama

41

going on around here. But she's fine and you know I'm okay because I'm still walking."

Al tried to smile but Ajay could see that he was royally pissed off. He figured he had wanted to do away with Neal Palmer himself. But Chill had beat him to it. Ebony stared at him with tears in her eyes but she said nothing. Al was already in meeting mode, at that point.

"Go get the guys together, son," Al said to Ajay, "We're gonna have a crew meeting at our house, after we get this mess cleared up. I'm taking Ebony over here to Pearl and I'll be right there."

"Okay," Ajay said then he looked at Ebony and asked, "Are you alright?"

She shook her head yes but she started to cry again. He didn't believe she was okay. She wasn't looking like she was okay. She looked scared out of her mind and that only made him even more angry. As Al went to meet Pearl on the sidewalk and deliver Ebony to her arms, Ajay let the other 7 guys know about the meeting. He never took his eyes off of Ebony until she was out of his sight and safe inside of her own house.

After the streets were clear and all of the crew men and the boys were inside big Al and Jo's house, that's when Al and big Paul let the guys know Chill's circumstances.

"He's going to training school for nine months," big Paul said of his son. "He's taking one for the crew, only because he got to that bitch ass muthafucka before I could dead his ass. That Neal was the lowest part of the scum of this earth. He might as well have been with big Jake's old snot nose ass. I can't stand a nigga that don't know how to be a real man. And neither one of them bitches know what being a true man is. We've got mister Wheeler working on keeping my son locally. In the meantime, I want all of you young crew fellows to move as one. Stoney and Rob will step in and lead until March. That's when my son can come back home. Is that understood?"

They all said, "Yes sir!"

Then Al stood and said, "Chill will still get to go to school while he's there and he'll learn a trade that he can use once he's back home. During the time that he's gone, we're gonna get each one of you to where you need to be in order for you guys to be able to hold him down. Both while he's in there and certainly after he's back home. We have to protect our families, our women, the girls in our families and our elders. My father is gonna take the floor and make sure that each one of you know the legacy that you will be expected to protect."

With that, Al Sr took the floor. He told them about the beef with Jake Johnson and that it wasn't over and would never be over until Jake Johnson and anybody who sided with him was killed. Ajay knew about the beef already. His father and grandfather had been telling him about it since he was old enough to understand and process information. But he had no idea that his grandpa was going to tell them about a health problem that he had too. A serious medical problem which was just as common in males as breast cancer was in females.

"I also found out this morning that I have a severe case of Prostate cancer," Al Sr said.

He didn't sugar coat things at all because he knew his prostate cancer was beyond repair and that it would eventually take his life. He told them that on that day too. Ajay couldn't even measure his anger at that point. He didn't know what to be mad about first or the most. His brother going away, his dad getting into a fight, his grandfather telling him that he had cancer and would not live much longer or seeing the apple of his eye distraught and him not knowing what the hell he could do to fix any of it.

"Anybody got anything they wanna add?" Al Sr asked.

"I just wanna hurt somebody," is all Ajay could say, "I got my first piece of pussy today and I thought this was gonna be a good day. But right now, all I wanna do is hurt somebody."

The older men chuckled briefly before Al Sr said,

"Fucking is something that every man loves and wants to do. But after that nut comes, it's just like a person who gets drunk because he's feeling down or depressed. The problems you had before, will still be very much there afterwards. And in some cases, there may be even more problems than before you got that nut."

Everybody laughed at that comment except Ajay. He didn't feel like laughing at all. All he could think about doing was some damage and he still wanted to know if Ebony was okay. He knew now that Neal Palmer was dead and since he wasn't able to kill him, He wanted to do some type of damage to somebody else. *Anybody* else. And he didn't give a damn who that somebody else turned out to be.

The day after Chill left seemed like the saddest day of his whole life to Ajay. He had sat in his room most of the morning. He knew he had to go to another basketball camp, the following Monday and he knew Chill was proud of him for doing so well in basketball. Ajay was hand picked to be on the communities team with boys who were much older than him. But that

43

didn't feel so good, right then. He worried about big Chill and if he was going to be alright while he was locked away somewhere. He worried about his grandfather. He was worried about Ebony too. She had witnessed it all and he knew she was probably never going to come outside again.

"This is so fucked up!" he yelled as he sat in his room alone.

Suddenly he grabbed his basketball and started spinning it on his fingertips like he had seen Dr J do, so many times. He started thinking of some new things he could try outside on his half court. He had stress to get off of his mind and he knew the only way he could do that was to take it the court and relieve it. But he had to see Ebony's eyes again. He felt like he would be able to see if she was okay, if only he could look into her brown eyes. He headed down their stairs and out the side door.

He knocked on Pearl's door. Tank answered, invited him in and they headed upstairs to Tank's room. Jb was already out with Stoney, Rob and Jr handling the business that they were going to do with Chill before that bullshit ever happened yesterday.

"Where's Ebony at?" Ajay asked as soon as he got inside Tank's room and closed the door behind him.

"Twin in her room," Tank said, "She ain't talking to nobody either. That shit fucked her head up bad. She got Lady in there wit her. She ain't fucking wit nobody but her dog, right now."

"Let's go check on her," Ajay recommended.

"She not gonna say nothing, man," Tank tried.

"That's alright," he said, "I just want her to know that she ain't gotta be scared. Ain't nobody gonna fuck wit her."

Tank could see the desperation in Ajay's face and although he didn't fully understand it. He said okay and they headed back out of his room and down the hall to Ebony's door. He could tell Ajay wasn't going to let it go. Ajay wanted to see Ebony's face and the look in her eyes. It was something about the way she looked at him when she was in his father's arms that told him she wanted somebody to protect her. He wanted to be that somebody. Especially now because Chill wasn't there and neither was big John.

Ajay and Tank went to her door and knocked. She didn't say anything and they thought she was asleep. But suddenly she opened the door without saying a word. She opened it and went back and sat down at her desk. Lady had followed her every move.

"What you doing in here, twin?" Tank asked and she pointed to a picture she was coloring.

"You wanna come shoot basketball wit us?" Ajay asked.

She shook her head to say no but the way she looked at Ajay made him feel like she had something else to say but she just wouldn't say it.

"Well anytime you wanna shoot basketball," Ajay said, "Let me know. You can shoot with me until Chill comes back, okay?"

She shook her head affirmative and her eyes seemed to smile at him. He figured it was because she was happy to know that Chill would be coming back. He knew she didn't know where he went or if he was alright. So Ajay assumed that him saying Chill would be back, had brightened her day because it showed in her eyes. But that wasn't all of it.

"We're going outside to shoot basketball twin," Tank said, "If you want too you can come out there with us. Come on Ajay. Let's go."

Tank got up to leave the room. Ajay followed him reluctantly. He wasn't ready to leave Ebony, just yet. He watched her watch him, as he followed Tank to the door. She watched him until he disappeared down their stairs, then she went back to coloring her picture.

Jb, Jr and the guys had just returned from their mission. Jr was going to be 11 that year but he was nearly the same height as Ajay. His father Brad Sr had started to let him drive the car as long as he was in the car with him. The guys had gone out to The Point where papa and granny live. They had to pick up some food from them and deliver it to 1 of the neighborhood homes out there for a family who had fallen on hard times. That was something the older generation of their crew did weekly. Jr and the guys played basketball with Tank and Ajay but Ebony never came outside. She didn't even watch them from her window either. Ajay knows she didn't because he was watching her window and hoping she'd look outside. But she never did.

The following week was T-baby's 6th birthday party and Ajay had left for his first basketball camp away from Cleveland. He would be gone for 2 weeks. Big Al had gone with him and so had Al Sr. That was the loneliest time for Ebony. No Chill, no Al, no Ajay and her daddy wouldn't be home for 5 more days. Her cousin T-baby had a birthday party at her house and they all went. Renee's younger brother Wesley had come to visit Renee at Chill's house, where she stayed more often then she stayed at their mother's. Wesley was 7 years old and he was cute just like Renee. He got along with all of the kids at the party except for Richie Rich. Wesley stuck close to Tank and Jb while he was there and he had told Tank that he thought T-baby was very pretty.

"That's my first cousin," Tank said, "She in our crew too."

"She's pretty," Wesley said, "That boy that's over there by her. Do he like her too?"

"That's Richie," Tank said, "He wanna like her but our girls can't have no boyfriends until their daddy say they can. Richie wanna be her boyfriend one day but he gotta wait."

"He keeps trying to fight me," Wesley said.

"Probably because he saw my cousin smiling at you when y'all was talking," Tank said, "Richie Rich don't like no boys that ain't in our crew. He probably think she likes you and he want her to like him."

"Well I *do* like her," he said, "And if I find out she likes me. I'm gonna tell my big sister to let her to call me when I get home. And if Richie try to fight me today. I'm gonna bust his nose."

"Nah man don't get in no fight with my crew because we all have to help him," Tank said, "My big mama is here from Houston. Go talk to her. Tell her what he's doing and she'll make sure it get fixed, okay?"

"Okay that's cool," Wesley said and him and Tank got back to the party.

Big mama had come up to visit the day before Ajay left for his camp. He got a chance to talk to her before he left and he was happy about that. He told her how he felt about the bicycle situation and how scared Ebony looked that day on Chill's porch. He asked her to make sure that Ebony was okay until he comes back. Big mama smiled and assured him that she would talk to Ebony while she was in town.

Ebony spent that entire 2 weeks that Ajay was at camp, at her Granny's house with both sets of her grandparents. Only leaving to go to T-baby's party then back to The Point. She had asked to spend a lot of time with her elders. She had told her big mama that she wanted to go with them because big Chill was gone. But on the day that Ajay returned home. She wanted to go back to her mother's house. She was very adamant about getting back to Shaker Heights.

Ajay was only going to be back home for 1 week before he had to leave for a weekend camp that was opening in Toledo. Jb was going to that camp with him.

Tank and Jb was waiting on the driveways when Al Sr, Al Jr and Ajay pulled up. Ajay got out and gave them some dap. The first thing he wanted to know was had they heard from Chill and how had Ebony been doing while he was away.

"Chill answered all of our letters and he said he was okay," Jb told him, "He said he done already made him a crew in there."

"Twin doing fine," Tank said, "She on her way back from the point. She been out to papa's house since you been gone."

About that time, papa Brown pulled into Pearl and John's side of the driveway. In his car, he had granny, poppa, big mama and Ebony. The grandparents got out and hugged Ajay and the boys, then headed into Pearl's house. Ebony stared at Ajay from the car to the side door of her mother's house. Still without a word from her, Ajay felt like she was glad to see him. It was in her eyes. She watched him from the doorway too until her papa closed the door. Ajay knew he was going to go to their house as soon as he put his bags down in his room. And that's exactly what he did.

When he got over to Ebony's house, she still didn't talk to him even after he accompanied Tank into her room. But it was something he saw in her stare that kept him feeling positive about his mission to win her over. For Ebony, she saw something in him that she liked. Not in a sexual way but it was in a protective way. It was something about his persistence. It was something about that boy that everyone said was distant and didn't care to be nice to others. It was just something about that big boy that made her feel safe. Something that she felt like she needed then, especially with Chill being gone. She was going to find a way to make sure he was her friend because she wanted to feel safe. To her, he was a person that didn't fear anything or anybody. Chill was that same way. She also found out that it wasn't hard for her to get his attention. Her girls always said he didn't like nobody nor did he like to hang around them because they were girls. But that was never the way she saw him. He came to her room or to wherever she was, whenever they were at the same place or in the same space. He played with Lady too and Lady liked him so much that she had started to go to him as soon as he came into her space.

He is a good protector and he's big too. Nobody's gonna mess with him.

}Fall 1982{

Ebony would watch Ajay even more after they started back to school and she was at Beachwood Elementary with him. Ebony and her girls were in 1st grade and Ajay was a 3rd grader. Everybody knew him and yet he never seemed enthused by all the popularity. He still smiled at her when he saw her at school, which caused others to stare at her too. They were probably wondering why he was so nice to her but never showed that

47

side to any of them. As far as she could tell, he didn't seem to have a problem with her watching him even if she still wouldn't talk to him. He would just talk to her and smile at her while she stared at him with a straight face.

That's gonna have to work for now. I'm just glad she's looking at me and not at nobody else.

The fall semester was filled with basketball, football games and family celebrations for the Cleveland crew. Stoney, who was the 2nd in line to lead the crew, turned 13 on the 20th day of October. Big Paul had a party for him too and it was slamming. Him and the rest of the crew was missing Chill tremendously. He called and talked to his entire crew during the party. Of course, he talk to Renee longer than anyone.

"I miss you so much, baby," Renee said, "That one visit a week just ain't enough for me. I can't wait until you get home."

"It won't be that much longer," Chill said, "You'll be crew in less than a month."

"I don't wanna have a party until you get here," she said, "Big Paul asked me about it and I told him I wanna wait until you get home before I celebrate anything. What kind of party is it gonna be without my man being here?"

"I knew you was gonna feel like that," Chill said.

"Of course I do," Renee said, "I told Wesley I would come by mama's house and see him for my birthday. I miss him and he misses me too. He can't wait to get out of that house, just like I was ready to go."

"I heard he likes T-baby," Chill said as he chuckled.

"He does," Renee said and laughed, "He wants me to tell her to call him but I wanted to talk to you about that before I did anything."

"Well I think Richie Rich got his eyes on her already baby," he said, "And that's crew from birth. The grandparents are pushing for them to get together but you never know. Richie Rich got some anger issues since his dad ain't around all the time, like all the other fathers."

"His little sister is so beautiful," she said, "She's almost a year old. But baby I can understand him being upset. His father beat his mother up and had to go to jail and rehab. He watched him beat her up for a long time, just like I use to see my step-dad beating on my mama. And he would beat on me too, for no reason. That's why I never go back over there, even though he's in and out of jail too."

"I'll kill that muthafucka if I ever see his ass anywhere around my

48

set, baby," Chill stated, "Ain't nobody gonna be hitting on my girl."

"I don't want you to do anything to him," she said, "I don't want you to be away from me anymore, after this is over with. Wes is gonna end up killing him when he gets bigger though. I told him I want him to go live with our aunt and play mama. She lives in Akron. He said he told mama he wanted to go and she told him to take his ass on."

"That's so fucked up," Chill said, "And on top of that, she takes his side when he fuck with y'all wrong. You ain't never going back there. I already talk to my pops about that and he's okay with you staying with us and your friend Tonya too. She's going through the same shit you did."

"She like's junior too," Renee told him as she giggled.

"He like her too," Chill said, "He told me that in six different letters. When I get home, I'm gonna get them straight. She gonna come stay with us so we can get her groomed to be his crew girl."

"I like that and she's gonna love that baby," Renee said and giggled, "Is it okay if I tell her?"

"Fasho," he said.

His phone time was up and he had to hang up and get ready for bed check. "I'll see you in two days when pops come to visit, okay?"

"You know it," she said, "Junior and Tonya already said they're coming wit us."

"That's all good," Chill said, "I'll see ya."

"In a minute," Renee said and they hung up.

The fall seemed to have whizzed by for them as they waited eagerly for Chill's time in the Juvenile system to end. Everybody was busy with school and Ajay had basketball too. Nina and Ebony turned 7 years old in December and Tank turned 8 the following January. They were into their 2nd semester in no time. Everybody was looking forward to Chill coming home in March and finishing his 8th grade year at school with them. Nobody was looking forward to seeing Chill more than Renee, Ajay and Ebony.

Renee's brother Wes moved to Akron with their aunt for the 2nd semester. Renee was happy knowing he was in a better environment but she was sad that she wouldn't be able to see her closest family member on a weekly basis anymore. The only thing that kept her on positive ground was the fact that Chill was coming home in 2 weeks. She was finding it hard to focus on her 7th grade classes. Her mind was on her man and she only had to wait 13 more days before she could see him and hold him again.

Chapter 3-Seeing Signs Of Trouble Early

}March 1983{

Chill returned home the 1st day of March. His crew was delighted to see him and no one was more excited than his girlfriend Renee. She had stayed faithful to him and really bonded with his crew while he was away at training school. The older crew girls had started to refer to her as their crew queen because they knew she was about to become officially crewed up. Her best friend LaTonya had met and befriended all of the girls too and she was already sweet on Ajay's 1st cousin Jr. LaTonya was from Detroit but she had moved to Cleveland to stay with a surrogate family who was distant relatives of her deceased father. Her and Renee had met at Abe Lincoln middle school and became fast friends. After Chill went away, Renee and LaTonya became like sisters. LaTonya or Tonya as they refer to her, spent many nights with Renee at big Paul's house. By the time Chill got back, she was like a member of the family and very necessary to Renee. Since the day Chill found out Tonya liked Jr, he started to play his role of matchmaker. He knew she was crew material already because she mirrored Renee in her resolve and mentality. Jr and Tonya were both in 6th grade at the time and 11 years old. He figured it would be a year or so before they would become an official couple but he was laying the ground work to make their transition smooth. Jr was already crew destined and Chill wanted him to have a girl who was fit to be crew as well. Jr had written Chill letters about his interest in Tonya, so Chill got out and went right to work making sure they had ample opportunities to spend time together.

On Chill's first evening home, big Paul had an initiation party for Renee. It was during the party when Chill insisted that Jr and Tonya had to be a couple while they attended his girl's party. They were both okay with that. They hit the dance floor for 3 straight songs and for the rest of the party they were inseparable. Once Tonya and Jr started to talk to each other and hit it off, Chill was excited. He was ready to spend some alone time with his girl and now that Tonya had someone to keep her company. He could do just that. But first he had to find out about Ajay's sex game and whatever else was on his mind.

"So what's good, little bro?"

"Man I'm glad you home, bro," Ajay says, "It's been some weird shit happening with Richie Rich."

"I know he's tripping because his pops is gone," Chill said.

"Yea but he's killing animals and shit like that."

"What the fuck?!!!"

"He showed me and Tank some kittens floating in that ditch behind they house," Ajay said, "He told us he was the one that drowned them too. He even showed us the stick wit a rope tied to it that he used to hold them down wit."

"Ah hell nah! Are you for real?"

"I'm serious as a heart attack, bro," Ajay said, "And Chill he hung a turtle from a tree and beat it with a bat until the shell busted open. Then he set it on fire. It was still burning when me and Tank got down there. Tank ask him what it was and he told us the whole story. Plus he said he had killed a puppy that belong to that old man on the corner of his street that always be *bitchin* about his grass. After that was when he showed us the kittens."

"I'm gonna get at his ass tomorrow," Chill said, "We can't have no dumb shit like that going on. He needs to get some counseling, just like his old man is getting right now."

"He needs something, bro," Ajay said, "When he showed us those dead kittens. I punched the fuck out of him dumb ass. I guess since he didn't wanna get caught up in what he was doing. He didn't tell nobody that I socked him. He knew if he had told on me for hitting him. I would've told them why I hit his ass. So he just went inside aunt Anna's house and cleaned his nose. Chill during that whole time he just kept laughing. I was about to rush him but Tank begged me not too. He wanted me to tell you about it and let you get him right."

"That's a bad sign right there," Chill said, "I'm definitely gonna get on that shit pronto. Don't even sweat it. I got him, alright?"

"Alright man," Ajay said, "Cause if I see some shit like that again. I'm fuckin him up right there on sight. That's some weird shit to be doing, bro."

"Understood bro and I would cosign you on it if you did beat his ass for that type of behavior," Chill said, "But let me try to get at him first though. You just focus on yo hoop game, okay?"

"Okay."

"Now tell me what else you been up too because I know you was on that first time action, on the day I left," Chill said and smiled.

Ajay told him about his 1st encounter which happened on the day he had gotten sent away. He also let Chill know that he'd had sex many more times while he was gone too.

"So you're a regular now?" Chill asked Ajay as he chuckled.

"Yea man," Ajay said, "I know what I'm doing now. But Chill these girls don't even really turn me on. I just hit it and keep it moving. I don't even wanna spend time with them, like that. Bro these girls is ho's, man. I could never even bring them home. I ain't gonna be tied to no ho, just know that. Because my pops and grandpa would disown me if I brought a ho home and mama would tell her to her face that she wasn't welcomed in our house."

Chill cracked up laughing and said, "I would too and I would disown your ass too bro. No ho's will be welcomed around me nor my crew. Not as ladies of my crew. I would never sign off on no shit like that for none of my crew brothers. You're gonna have a girl that's fit for you Ajay and she's gonna be crew. I already got an idea about who it's gonna be too. But we'll get into that later on. Right now bro, you know I just got home and I gots to get to my girl. You gone be alright?"

"Yea," Ajay said, "But I can still remember Ebony's face from that day. She was scared. I know she was. So I looked out for her while you was gone."

"I'm sure that wasn't work though, right?" Chill asked as he smiled.

"*No,*" Ajay answered and smiled, "But she won't talk to me no more though. Not like she did at yo party. She got mad because I changed the speed gears on her bike. She was screaming at me in the street too. Since then, she ain't said nothing to me. She just stares at me anytime I'm around her now. I guess she thinks I'm mean now too."

"Nah she don't think that bro," Chill told him, "She told me that last spring. She said everybody calls you mean but you're not mean to her."

"I wish she would talk to me then," Ajay said, "That's all I want her to do is say something to me."

"Give her time, Ajay," he said, "She just made seven. She's still got a long way to go to understand what you're looking at her about. But mark my word. Big Al, big John and my daddy already got y'all matched for each other. But it's gonna have to be done right with these girls in the crew. She won't be a fly by night either bro. She'll have your heart. She'll be your wife, one day."

"I know that," Ajay said and he couldn't help but smile, "I don't even wanna do nothing wit her but talk to her. I wanna let her know that whenever big John say she can have a boyfriend. Then I wanna be him."

"I'm gonna tell you like papa Brown and poppa Jones told me," Chill said, "Just steady your road son. Know who you are and what you were raised to look for and who you come from. You'll get there."

"Alright," Ajay said and he continued to smile.

He knew Chill was giving him his blessings to date Ebony one day and that was music to his ears. Then they said they would see each other later and deal with Richie Rich the following day.

"Alright I'll see ya," Ajay said.

"In a minute, crew."

With that, Chill went to his room with Renee. Ajay went home to shower and change his clothes. All that was on his mind at that moment was doing whatever he had to do to get and keep Ebony's attention on him. He was going to spend a lot more time at Pearl and John's house, that was for sure. And at school, he was going to make sure that Ebony saw him at every opportunity.

The next morning before school, Chill asked big Paul to give him, Ajay, Rich and Tank a ride. Chill talked to Rich on the way and by the time big Paul dropped Ajay, Tank and Rich at Beachwood Elementary. Rich knew what was expected of him. He knew that if Chill ever heard or could prove that he had done anything else as vile as what Ajay had told him about again. That all of his crew brothers was going to beat his ass daily. That was what they called, *"Going into the Circle."* It was punishment for a crew member who did or acted in anyway unbecoming to the crew code of honor. Rich said he hadn't done anything else since the day that Ajay hit him. Chill took his word for it but Ajay found it hard to trust what he had said. Ajay was sure Rich was still going to do more and he let him know that he wasn't gonna wait for no vote about whooping his ass.

"If I see proof that you did something else. I'm just going in on you right then and there," Ajay said.

"And I'm gonna help him," Tank added.

****

A week later, Ajay's grandfather Allen Devante' Jackson Sr became very ill and had to be hospitalized. He was admitted into East General hospital where Ebony's mother Pearl worked as an RN. From the day he went in, he was weak and in a lot of pain. Ajay found it difficult to look at his grandfather and not get angry. Al Sr was in such bad health that his doctors advised Al Jr to notify all of his family. Al's mother had passed on in 1980 and the only relative he had left besides his father, was his older sister Jessica. She was 10 years older than Al. She had lived in Cleveland

53

while she attended college. But she had met and married a caucasian medical graduate named Jonathan Layton and moved back to their childhood home of Boston Massachusetts. Al called Jessica in Boston and told her to come right away.

By the weekend, Jessica was there and she had brought her 11 year-old son Terrell with her. Ajay was happy to see Terrell but he found it hard to be in a good mood with his grandfather being so ill. He didn't even want to play basketball. All he wanted to do was hang out at the hospital, after school. From the time of her arrival, his aunt Jessica didn't seem to Ajay like she was as concerned for her father's health as she was about his wealth. Al Sr wasn't in any condition to discuss what his last will contained, so Jessica brought up the matter to Al Jr. Al Jr told her that wasn't the time nor the place to discuss what their father had. But Jessica was relentless. She persisted with the matter and got unruly when she couldn't force her brother to get the paperwork together so she could see what all her father owned. She even started to insinuate that Jo was the reason Al wouldn't tell her anything about the assets. She accused Jo of trying to get her hands on an inheritance that was rightfully hers. That was when Al and Jessica got into a very heated argument in the hallway of the hospital. Jo tried to intervene and let Jessica know that she had no knowledge of her father-in-law's assets. She suggested that her and Al stay focused on their father's well being and not his money.

"And I advise you to mind your own damn business," Jessica said to Jo, "This is a discussion between my brother and I, so butt out bitch!"

"That's not necessary Jessica and my name is Jo, not bitch," Jo said and remained calm.

But Jessica became very disrespectful to Jo which seemed to be her intentions, all along. She insulted Jo and her upbringing and that irritated both Al and Ajay. Ajay became angry to the point that he had to get involved. First he tried telling Terrell to calm his mother down but Terrell just stood there quiet and looking dumbfounded as he leaned against the wall. Al stood in front of Jo and dared his sister to say another disrespectful word to his wife. He demanded that she apologize or leave the area. But before she could do either, Ajay started to insist that she apologize and he wasn't willing to stop his future actions even if she had.

"Don't call my mama no names," he said as the sclera or the whites of his eyes turned a dull shade of pink, "Her name is Jo and that's what you better call her."

Jo put her arms around Ajay and tried to get him to calm down because she

54

could tell that his blood had rushed to his head, indicating that he was highly upset. She tried rubbing the top of his braids and wiping the sweat from his brows but that wasn't working. He had started to breath harder as he looked from Jessica to Terrell. Though he wasn't yelling, his eyes and hands showed that he was very close to becoming physical. Jessica wouldn't even acknowledge him which only angered him more.

With her son Terrell standing right there, Ajay said,

"Apologize to my mama or Terrell gonna have to hold up for you since I can't hit a female. But you not gonna talk to my mama like that. My pops told you to apologize and you need to do that right now."

His body was tensed and Jo knew he was going to fight soon, if they didn't get this matter resolved. Jo asked Al to take Ajay outside to get some air. Al turned to put his arm around Ajay but Ajay had wheeled away from his mother and punched Terrell in the face and yelled,

"Tell her to apologize or I'm gonna beat you to sleep!"

He continued punching Terrell who although he was older, was no match for Ajay's assault. Jessica came to her sons aide. She pulled him away from Ajay's punches but Ajay kept advancing on him and beating him handedly. Jessica swung at Ajay and that's when Jo hit her. Immediately hospital security converged on the scene and they were escorted away from the public floor to an empty clinical area to be questioned and the police were summoned too.

Jessica wanted Ajay and Jo arrested and she was yelling it to the top of her voice. Although security was telling her they understood her request and they would handle it with the police momentarily.

Once the police arrived, they told Jessica that not only could they not arrest a Juvenile unless they had committed an adult crime. But the matter would have to be taken up with family court because no charges had been filed. Jessica wanted something in writing. The police told her that she would have to file charges if she had been assaulted. She didn't press for Jo to be charged but told them her minor son had been assaulted. Only because she knew she had swung on Ajay, who was a minor before Jo advanced on her.

"Your son would have to agree to the charges and then you can file them on his behalf," the officer had said.

Terrell was against it. He just wanted to let the nurses finish attending to his cuts and scrapes and that be it. But Jessica wasn't going to be satisfied with him if he didn't make a record of how his injuries happened and she was going to make his peace non-existent, if he had left her with the losing end of this fiasco. So though Terrell didn't want to press charges on his 1st cousin. His mother insisted. Terrell pressed assault charges and 8 year-old Ajay was charged and detained for an assault on his 11 year-old cousin. That only angered Ajay even more. Because his mother had never gotten her apology. Al was allowed to take his family home and the staff at the hospital recommended that they didn't visit Al Sr together from then on.

After leaving the hospital, Jessica moved her and Terrell's things to a hotel suite which she had rented with help from the police departments community officer. She was playing this up huge. Her and Al didn't speak to each other after that day and it was largely because Jessica never answered when he tried to call her nor did she return any of his messages. She stayed in constant contact with her husband, back in Boston. He was definitely accepting of her pleas that her brothers family and way of life was beneath them and she should sever her ties with the whole mess, as soon as possible then get back to Boston.

****

On the 17th of March 1983, Chill and big Paul had a remembrance for Willamena. That was the 4th year anniversary of the car accident which had taken her life. Renee consoled Chill the entire day while he wept and remembered his mother. He was also upset to know that Al Sr wasn't going to be coming home from the hospital. They had only given him a week to live. As soon as Chill heard that, he sent Renee to get Ajay because he knew he wasn't taking it well and he was right. Ajay was beside himself with grief and anger too. But that was only the beginning.

It was 3 days later, on March 20th when Allen Devante' Jackson Sr died from the complications brought on by Prostate cancer. That's when things took a turn for the absolute worst for Ajay Jackson. It was going to take something major or someone very special to save him from himself. The death caused him to reflect on the lose of his 1st grandmother big Joanna, who had died when he was only 2 years old. He reflected on how sad the family was 4 years ago, when Chill's mother died. Plus the death of his 2nd grandmother Bertha, in 1980 took him through changes where he would fight rather than talk. Al Sr had always been the 1 to talk to him about compassion and taking the time to hear a person out if he cared for them and not see violence as his only option. Now that grandfather was gone and so was Ajay's patience.

56

Jessica and Terrell were still in town for the funeral. Her husband Dr Jonathan Layton flew in from Boston to make sure his face was seen. But didn't try to bridge any gaps between himself and Jessica's brother Al. Nor had he changed his mind about Jessica making up with Al. He viewed their middle class lifestyle as less than his and he had wanted Jessica to separate herself from them, almost as soon as they had gotten married. Al Sr had never warmed up to Jonathan either. He had truly missed his only daughter who was his oldest child. But she opted to listen to her husband to keep peace in her marriage, was how she told it. Though the crew tried to reach out and be comfort to her, Jessica wasn't receptive of it. Ajay wasn't one of those who reached out to her. He had written her and Terrell off since the fight. Jonathan was never on, as far as he was concerned. Terrell didn't want friction between him and Ajay. While in town, he had big John or Greg Sr to pick him up from the hotel each day and bring him to Al's house so he could be around Ajay. But Ajay never acknowledged him. Terrell wanted to play basketball with him, after the funeral service was done and Ajay wouldn't even speak to him. Let alone play with him. Jonathan had encouraged Jessica to remain in Cleveland for the reading of her father's last will and testament and she did just that. The tension she held toward Al wasn't gone and it wouldn't be leaving any time soon.

It was 12 days passed the funeral before Ajay even came outside again. Ebony had reconnected with Chill. She still liked shooting basketball but she wanted more than that. She had witnessed the sadness of her best friend Nina and her family next door, as they went through the process of saying goodbye to Al Sr. She couldn't remember ever seeing Nina or Lynn so sad. She figured death had to be a hurtful thing. Even more, she didn't get to see Ajay smile the whole time. He didn't even try to get her to talk to him nor did he watch her like he had done prior. She figured he must've been hurting too and she was afraid that he would turn mean to her, like he was said to be with others. She didn't want that to happen so she went to Chill for help.

"Chill I wanna play basketball today," she said.

"Okay baby girl," Chill said to her, "Grab the ball from the pantry and let's go for it."

"Okay," she said and she ran to the kitchen.

She got the ball and returned. Chill was waiting for her by the front door. He said, "Let's do this. I need to see if you got that form down that we was working on before I left."

"I do!" she yelled in excitement as they headed out to his driveway. But once they got outside, she revealed a concern of hers that he had to help her resolve. It was actually going to not only be his pleasure but his duty as their generation's leader to see that it happened.

"Big Chill, I think Ajay is sad," she told him.

"Yes he is sad," Chill said to her.

"That's because he don't play basketball no more. That's why he's sad. Can you tell him to come play wit us so he can laugh again?"

"You got it baby girl," Chill said, "As a matter of fact. We can walk over there right now and get him. What do you think? I need to get at him about a few things anyway. So I can do that while we're over there. How about that?"

"Okay!" she yelled as she took his hand and walked with him across the street to Jo and Al's side door.

They went in together to see if Ajay would come out and play basketball with them.

Ajay was upstairs in his room where he'd spent the majority of his time in the past 2 weeks, listening to his father's cassette tape of the Isley Brothers. That's all he had done since burying his grandfather.

Chill and Ebony came in and spoke to everyone in the front room. Nina, Lynn and Jo got hugs from Chill and Ebony.

Then Chill asked, "Where's Ajay?"

"Still up in his room, Chill," Jo said, "See if you can get him out of there for me, please. He's gonna turn in on himself if he don't go on and grieve for his grandfather."

"I got it mama Jo," Chill said and he left Ebony downstairs with Nina and went up to Ajay's room.

He knocked on the door but he got no answer so he knocked again. The 2nd time he called out his name and Ajay finally opened the door. Chill could see that he was tormented. He went on in the room, closed the door and sat down in the chair. Ajay plopped down on his bed and turned the volume down on his boom box.

"How you feeling Ajay?" Chill asked.

"Like I could hurt some muafuckin body," Ajay said, "That's why I'm trying to stay in my room. I don't know what I would do if I go outside and somebody piss me off. Terrell keep coming over here but I don't wanna fuck wit him. His mama disrespected my mama and he didn't say shit. He didn't do shit about it either."

"Do you want me to talk to him?" Chill asked.

"I don't care who talk to him," Ajay said, "I'm not."
Chill continued to talk to Ajay until he finally got him to look at him while they talked. Chill wanted to get Ajay to come outside and cheer up, so he went for broke.

"I came over here with Ebony," Chill said, "She wants to play basketball and she asked me to come and see if you would play with us. So what do you say?"
Ajay looked at him. He almost smiled but he didn't. He just stared at him. Then he finally said, "She's outside?"

"She's downstairs waiting on us," Chill said.
Ajay got up immediately and put on some suitable clothes to keep warm in the Cleveland March weather. He strapped up his new Dr Jay Converse leather sneakers and went downstairs with Chill.

He caught sight of Ebony as soon as he was halfway down the stairs because she was waiting at the bottom, looking up and waiting for him to come down. She watched him the whole time that it took for him to descend the stairs. Ajay could see it in her eyes. She was happy to see him. He could tell that she was happy he had decided to come downstairs because her eyes was smiling at him.
Though he still didn't expect to get an answer, he asked,
"Hey cutie pie. You came to get me to play basketball wit you?"
She said, "Yes. Will you play with Chill and me?"
She said something back! Oh it's on now!

His smile was huge as he said, "Yea I'll play basketball with you anytime. Chill don't even have to play. We can play all by ourselves. Cutie pie you can come get me to shoot ball with you *anytime*."
He even chuckled after he said that and that brought a huge smile to his mother's face as well. Ebony was delighted and she couldn't hide her excitement either.

"Okay," Ebony said and she giggled hard as they headed out of Jo's side door.
Chill stood back and smiled as he watched them go out the door together and both of them were almost skipping. Jo thought it was cute too.
She laughed and said, "Well I'm glad somebody could get him to go outside. Chill he's been really down since his pawpaw passed away. I need you to help me to get him back to normal."

"*Ajay?* Normal?" Chill asked as if she was asking for the impossible and they both chuckled.

59

"Yes," Jo said, "Just get him back to Ajay normal."

"I've *gotta* admit it was most likely Ebony that got him out there," Chill offered, "His face lit up when I told him she was down here and she was the one who asked me to come and get him. He got right up and got dressed. Shoot he left me in the room trying to get down them stairs."

"Well that's alright with me," Jo said, "I may need to call her over here to get in behind him more often then."

"It just might work," Chill told her and continued to laugh.
Chill and mama Jo talked for a little while. She wanted to know how he was holding up after the remembrance of his mother.

"It's still hard for me to accept that she's gone, mama Jo," he said, "I would love for her to have met Renee."

"Renee is a great young lady and she's perfect for you, Chill."

"I agree and I'm keeping her," Chill said, "You got my word. She reminds me of my mama the way she can see right through me, if I try to lie to her," he said and laughed.

"That's a crew woman for sure then," Jo said, "We know we're not suppose to be lied too and we'll sniff out a lie in a heartbeat."

"I'm on it," Chill said, "Well let me get on out here and see how Ajay's doing. But I have a feeling he's all good for right now."

"Okay son," Jo said, "I'll see you, Paul and Renee for dinner."
Chill said okay and headed out to the driveways.

Ebony and Ajay was already shooting basketball when Chill made it out there. Ajay was helping her with her form and showing her how to hold the ball correctly whenever she attempted to shoot.

"Make sure your pointer finger or your index finger, whatever you wanna call it," Ajay said, "Make sure when you shoot and flip your wrist. That index finger needs to grab for that hook on the rim that's in front of you. The hooks are those things that hold the net up, okay? Whichever hook is in front of you when you shoot. Try to make that pointer finger grab it or wrap over the top of it, alright?"

"Alright," Ebony said.
She tried it exactly as he had instructed and she made it.

"Ah yea!" Ajay said and his voice was full of excitement, "You hit nothing but nets!"

"It worked!" Ebony exclaimed joyfully, "Chill did you see me?! I made it! All nets!"

"I see you, baby girl!" Chill yelled back just as excited. Then he said, "I think I need to let Ajay take over as your coach. What do you think about that?"

"Will you, Ajay?" Ebony asked with baited breath.

"Yea I will," Ajay said, "I can do that."

He smiled at her. She liked that he was smiling again. He looked so happy when he smiled and he was cuter too. He didn't look mean at all. That was what she'd wanted to see.

She said, "I'm glad you're not sad anymore. I don't want you to look sad all the time. People think you're mean when you look sad Ajay. So I want you to smile, so they don't keep saying that, okay?"

"You got it," Ajay said as he continued to smile at her, "As long as you smile at me and talk to me too. I can do that. Shoot that'll *make* me smile."

"Okay!" Ebony said again with a lot of excitement in her voice and she was elated.

She had helped Ajay to get his smile back and now she could tell her cousin, his sister and Rebbie that he wasn't mean. He just get sad sometimes, just like everybody else.

Her and Ajay played basketball for another hour. Soon Tank, Jb and the guys showed up to play some real games. Terrell had come by and went to Tank's house. He knew Ajay was still angry with him so he had tried to get Tank to fix things. Tank told him he would try and he suggested they join Ajay and Ebony on the driveway and they did.

Ajay still didn't say anything to Terrell. He just picked teams quickly. He got Jb and Ebony on his team. They played Chill, Tank and Terrell. Terrell had to hold Ebony and that's when Ajay said something to him.

"I dare you to hurt her," Ajay said.

"No way," Terrell said, "She's too pretty for me to hurt her. I'll let her shoot."

"You gonna make me hurt you, cousin," Ajay said and he wasn't smiling, "I'm in a good mood so just stop talking about how pretty Ebony is and all that junk. Just play ball or you can leave."

He took the ball out and passed it to Ebony. She passed it right back. She had watched them play from her bedroom window enough to know that she had to keep moving around to get open for a pass and a shot. She did good. Ajay and Jb made sure she got a chance to score a basket too. She had a great time and so did Ajay. He was on the way back to Ajay normal. Ebony was happy to see Ajay smiling and back to playing his favorite game. She

61

was proud of herself for getting Ajay to come out of the house. She was very happy about that and so was his mother Jo, Chill and everybody else who'd been feeling the wrath of his grief.

The next week was spring break. Marsha had come back to Cleveland but she didn't get to see Ajay. Him and Jb had gone to camp in Indiana. When Ajay left, Ebony left too. She went to her granny and papa's in The Point. Big mama and poppa was still visiting and had been since Al Sr's funeral.

The grandmother's decided to make pies for the upcoming Sunday family Easter dinner at 1st Baptist Church of Cleveland. That had been their home church since the 1st generation migrated to the city. All of the crew was members there. Easter Sunday was known as family day and for the crew, it was always a huge event. Granny and big mama brought Ebony into the kitchen with them so they could teach her how to make and crinkle pie crust. They knew that would be a good time to talk with her about her feelings and see if there was anything she wanted to talk about.

"I wish I could bring Lady over here with me when I spend the night," Ebony had said, "I know she's missing me. Mama said she always stays right by the side door the whole time when I'm gone."

"Well she's waiting for you to come back," big mama said.

"We'll get Jackson to go get her and let her come out here where you are," granny offered, "Would you like that?"

"Yes!" Ebony said with excitement.

Granny sent papa to get Lady from Shaker Heights and bring her back to The Point. Her and big mama continued to talk to Ebony while they all made assorted pies. Ebony didn't add very much to the conversation but she did listen a lot. They talked about Ajay and the fact that he liked her already. Just listening to them talk, Ebony could tell that they knew Ajay liked her. She didn't understand just *how much* he liked her. She knew she had helped him to get his smile back and she felt good about that part. She felt like that was the reason he liked her and he had probably told the family about it. Ajay had a reputation for not being open to many people. He wasn't 1 to reach out to anyone unless there was something he felt was important to him about that person. Her grandmothers knew he was grooming himself to be the man that Ebony would date, once she was old enough and ready too. She listened to them as they talked. She pretended she didn't understand what they were talking about but she understood them well enough to know that there was something about her that made

62

the best things come out of Ajay. Also something that made him want to be a better person. That made Ebony feel very special.

****

When Ajay and Jb returned home the Saturday night after spring break, Ebony and Lady went right back to Shaker Heights.

The next day was Easter Sunday and everybody had on their finest clothes. When Ajay's family came out to load up in their car for church, Ebony's family was doing the same. Ajay got a glimpse of Ebony and she saw him too.

"You look nice, cutie pie," he said with a smile.

"So do you," she said and smiled back.

"You wanna play ball when we come from church?" Ajay asked.

"Yes," she answered.

"Cool," he said.

They both got into the cars with their family's and went off to Easter service.

After church, they all had dinner on the church grounds. It was a great time had by all. Once that was over, all of the families headed to Shaker Heights and gathered at Jo, Pearl and big Paul's homes. It was celebration time, like the crew did it. All the kids were outside playing on the lawns. Ajay and Ebony played basketball and were joined by Tank, Jb, Richie Rich, June and the other guys. Chill and Stoney even played and so did Jr and Rob. Ebony was the only girl playing with them. But soon Lynn joined them and wanted to play too.

"Oh God," Ajay said as he laughed, "Sis you can run good. But you ain't no ball player. If you gone play ball too. Then you're gonna have to be real good because you're my sister. You can't be half ass. That'll make me look bad."

"Shut up and throw me the ball," Lynn said, "When Terrell was here. I played him and beat him."

"That ain't saying nothing," Ajay said, "Ebony beat him and she didn't even let him score."

They all laughed and continued to play. Lynn scored on Richie Rich and he acted out negatively. Ajay warned him immediately.

"You better slam that ball to the ground, cousin," he said, "Act like you wanna throw it at my sister again and you gone feel me. I hope yo ass try me too."

Richie Rich didn't say anything. He just threw the ball in and kept silent. But Ajay could tell he was working something out in his mind. Richie Rich knew Ajay was very protective of all of his sisters and to harm 1 of them would be suicide. But he noticed how nice Ajay had started to be to Ebony. He figured Ajay had to have liked Ebony because of how cordial he acted around her. And how he was going out of his way to make sure she wasn't bothered. Richie had always thought Ebony was cute but he could never get her to play with him. He noticed how well she was playing and getting along with his 1st cousin Ajay. That was just another thing for Richie to feel inadequate about, when it came to Ajay. He felt like Ajay was always given the special privileges or extra attention, when he wasn't. What he didn't realize was Ajay demanded it, just by the way he carried himself. And when it was something or someone that Ajay wanted, He did what it took to get them or their attention and he made sure he was acting appropriately in order to maintain it. Just as he was doing to stay in Ebony's company. Richie didn't get that part. He had spoken to Ebony several times while they were playing ball. Ajay just watched him. Rich even tried to hold a conversation with Ebony between games but she wouldn't respond to him. She never had before that day either. Richie took it as an insult on that particular day. He was only trying to find a way to get a positive reaction from her but that didn't work. So he figured he would get her attention in anyway possible. Even if he had to annoy her.

Once they were done playing and the skies started to turn to dusk, they all parted off to go inside. Richie Rich followed Tank and Jb inside of Pearl's house. Ajay and June was with them too. Ebony, Nina, T-baby and Rebbie came inside and were about to go up to Ebony's room to play. Lady got next to Ebony's leg, like normal. She was about to follow the foursome upstairs. But suddenly, Richie grabbed her by her collar and picked her up. She started to whimper. She was instantly afraid. Ebony saw the way Richie was hurting her dog and she panicked.

"Don't do that to my baby!" Ebony yelled, "You're choking her!" Richie Rich just started to laugh devilishly and began turning around in circles and swinging Lady while still holding her by only her collar. Ebony burst into tears.

Ajay had gone up the stairs behind Tank, June and Jb. But when he heard Ebony's screams, he ran back down just in time to see what Richie was doing and went straight at him. Ajay grabbed Richie. Richie released Lady and she fell to the floor hard and howled. Her fall was from a height over Ritchie's head or better than 4 feet. Ebony went to the floor with Lady and grabbed her immediately. That's when Ajay lost it. He started punching and wailing on Richie relentlessly.

"What you do that shit for, you punk?" Ajay asked as he continued to punch Richie, who had dropped to the floor and balled up in a helpless knot while Ajay punched and kicked him repeatedly.

"I'm gonna beat the hell outta yo dumb ass," Ajay oozed, "Stop messing with people or things that ain't messing wit you."

Pearl and Jo had run from the living room to see what the fuss was about. They saw Ajay pouring all over Richie mercilessly. Pearl and Jo tried to stop him but they couldn't do it. Not alone. Jb, Tank and June had made it downstairs. They assisted the ladies in getting Ajay off of Richie. But by then, Richie was a bloody mess. He was beaten, very badly. Jo sent Nina to get Anna from their house so they could take Richie to the hospital. During that time, Richie didn't get up off of that floor. That was because as he laid there, Ajay was constantly threatening that if he got up. He was going to get back on him. Richie heeded that warning and stayed in that balled up knot.

When Anna arrived, the men were with her. June had run over at Pearl's request to get big Al and Paul. All of the fathers came when they heard that it was Ajay beating Richie. Chill, Rob, Stoney and Jr had come too, along with Arthur Owens who'd come by Chill's to hang out with the crew. All of the men knew of Richie's psychotic behavior, by that time, so they didn't go in on Ajay at all. Especially not after hearing how Richie had handle Ebony's pet. Al and Paul put Richie in the car and along with Anna and Jo, they took him to the hospital.

Pearl told Chill and the guys to take Ajay over to big Paul's and help him to calm down. All the while, Ebony was trying to tell her mother why the fight had happened and what Richie had done to Lady.

Lady was very subdued after that bout with Richie. Of those who was left in the house, she only allowed Ebony to be near her. She was afraid. Ebony was angry.

"I'm glad Ajay beat him up," she told her girls after they were all in her room, "He hurt my baby and she didn't do nothing to him."

"He was trying to show out for T-baby," Nina said, "He want you to like him, T-baby."

"He *sho* do," Rebbie added.

"Well not like that," T-baby said, "Ajay bust him up. Man, I was scared for him. Ajay is a mad man."

"No he's not cousin!" Ebony yelled, "He's nice and he knew my baby was getting hurt so he stopped him from hurting her and that's all!"

"Okay whatever," T-baby said.

The girls went on playing but Ebony wasn't very talkative after that. She was angry with her cousin for calling Ajay a mad man. Only because he had beat up Richie for what he'd done to her dog. She was happy with Ajay for dogging him out. And she didn't care how much her cousin liked Richie nor how cute she had to say that she thought he was. What he had done to Lady was unforgivable.

Richie had a broken jaw, 3 cracked ribs and a slit all the way down his left forearm which required 100 stitches. He had 2 black eyes, a busted lip and his nose was swollen from a sprain but it wasn't broken. Anna was upset that her nephew had beat up her son and she wasn't the least bit sympathetic to what his reasons was for doing it either. She just saw it as a family trait.

"Richard used his hands on me," Anna said, "Jo you're his sister and that's your son. So what else is he gonna do except use his hands too?"

"He didn't beat on Richie for no reason, Anna," Jo said, "He saw him injuring Ebony's dog and he did what came natural. But Richie was going to really hurt that dog and for what?"

"Being a knuckleheaded boy," Anna tried, "But he never hit it, did he? No he didn't and he should've gotten a whooping from an adult. Not from his first cousin who's his age. That's not gonna fix things."

"I don't know what could fix it," Jo said, "I don't know what would make him want to hurt the dog in the first place."

"He plays rough, Jo," Anna tried.

"That's not rough Anna," Jo said, "That's Ike Turner tactics. Little Richie didn't get that from his blood line, just like my brother didn't. Our father never hit our mother, so that's not from his bloodline. It's from him. That is something that should be addressed instead of you looking for other places to put the blame. He's seen his father doing it with no repercussions, for years. Start looking there."

Anna didn't say anymore after that. Al drove Anna, Richie and 1 year old Ruthie home, at Anna's request because she didn't want to go back to the Easter family get together.

After dropping them at home, Al drove on up the street with Jo, to their home. They wanted to get to Ajay and talk to him. Only to make sure he was over the mood that had led him to beat some reality into Richie. Nothing more.

Ajay and Ebony played basketball everyday after school and most of their crew played with them. Even Richie showed up to watch but he hadn't healed up enough to play yet. He sat off to the side while the others played. It was the last week of April 1983. Stoney's parents Chester Lee and his mother Jackie Coleman had just called to say they were in labor and on their way to hospital. Stoney was about to be a big brother and they already knew it was going to be a girl. Big Paul, Al and John left driving Stoney to meet his parents at the hospital. Chill, Rob, Jr and Arthur went with him. Pearl was at work at the hospital already. Jo stayed at home to keep an eye on the children.

It was on that day that Ajay found out that Marsha had come looking for him during spring break, while he was away at camp. He wasn't particularly interested. He'd had plenty of penetration since her and still none of them held his interest the way Ebony did. Ajay was just looking forward to the end of 3rd grade and the summer. He was going to be 9 years old in July. He had also been invited to play basketball for the 6th grade team as a 4th grader during the upcoming 83-84 season. He was excited about that. He would start practicing at Abe Lincoln Middle school near the end of the school year. He was already telling the older boys that Ebony Brown was going to be in 2nd grade at Beachwood elementary. He also told them that she was his girl and that none of them could say anything to her or they would have to deal with him.

During the last week of school, Ajay got into a fight with a boy from 5th grade. The boy was a friend of a known crew enemy named Jacob, who would be better known as Lil Jake after a few more years. Jacob's friend insisted on making jokes and references to Ebony, as if him and Jacob was going to mess with her. Jacob had put him up to it, even though Jacob wasn't going to that school and Ebony wasn't even in middle school yet. She was finishing up her 1st year at Beachwood Elementary which was on the opposite end of the campus. The 5th grader was saying things about Ebony at Jacob's request, only because he had gotten word that Ajay was coming to the middle school end to practice. He wanted the taunts to get back to Ajay and piss him off. He finally got his wish.

Ajay had been in the middle school's gym shooting baskets with his team and getting ready for the next year. After 5th period, he headed back toward the Beachwood Elementary end to go back to his 3rd grade class. But he made it as far as the 5th grade hallway before he ran across Jacob's friend. That friend started in with the Ebony insults as soon as he saw Ajay. Ajay knew of Jacob and the beef his family had with them. But he didn't know Jacob nor this friend of his, who was toying with him. The friend made 1 more wise crack. Then he cracked up laughing, just before he ducked off into the bathroom. Ajay followed him in there.

"Take it back fool," Ajay said, "Take it back right now and you're gonna stop saying shit about my girl. You ain't gonna say or do shit *to* her either. Do you hear me?"
Jacob's friend just laughed and kept with the insults. Ajay lost it and jumped him right there in the 5th grade boys bathroom.

Jr and Tonya, who were in 6th grade, knew Jacob and they knew his friend too. Jr knew Jacob a lot better than Tonya did. Jr knew what it was about and so did Ajay. Jacob was the grandson of a man named Jacob Johnson who was better known to the crew men as big Jake. Their families had been beefing for decades. Ajay had already heard about this friend of Jacob's and that him and Jacob had been talking shit about Ebony. Only because the word was out that he liked her. But Ajay had never seen either of them, to know them by face. Still Ajay had plans of finding them. Simply because they were kin to big Jake. He was going to search them out anyway, so he could beat both their asses. It just worked out in Ajay's favor that Jacob's friend started *janking* as soon as he saw him heading up the hallway. Ajay started the fight in that bathroom and finished it too. He beat Jacob's friend convincingly while telling him that he looked forward to doing the same thing to Jacob. By the time Chill, Stoney, Rob, Jr and Jb heard about the fight and made it to the bathroom. The fight was finished and Jacob's friend was on the floor doubled up in pain. Teachers had already come in and restored order. Chill and the guys didn't even have to help Ajay because he had gotten it over with, right then and there. The other crew guys vowed to beat Jacob's friend and Jacob too. Every time they saw either of them from then on. They were truly angered with Jacob for sending someone to beef with Ajay and they were going to make sure that Jacob paid for it.

Jacob's friend whom Ajay had beaten went by the name of Carlos Watts. He didn't have to go to the hospital that day but he was still in the school nurses office, 2 hours after school let out. His mother came to get him. She was upset after finding out 5 other boys were already saying they were going to beat him some more when they got back to school next year. His mother took precautions before leaving school that day.

Carlos would transfer to a school in west Cleveland where Jacob would attend for the next school year. But the beef for the 3rd generation was just getting started. Ajay spent the last 2 days in, in-school suspension.

That didn't mean anything to him. He was looking forward to finishing what he had started with Carlos. While at the same time, his plans was to end what Jacob's grandfather had started *decades earlier* with his grandfather.

During the summer of 1983, Chill turned 14, June turned 8, Jb turned 10 and Ajay made 9 years old. The beef with big Jake Johnson and his posse escalated for the crew fathers as well. But there wouldn't be another hands on confrontation with big Jake's posse, right away. Not for another year or so.

Ajay had basketball camps to go to once school was out. In between the camps, he and Ebony played basketball everyday that he was home. He told Ebony she was getting pretty good. Even her cousin T-baby got interested and started to play with them, as did Ajay's cousin Bre. His sister Lynn still tried to play but she was more interested in racing. She could beat most of the boys when she raced them too. Big Al got her into competing city and state wide, just as he had done with Ajay and basketball. Ebony would race too but her game had become basketball. She was determined to be just as good as Ajay was and he really liked that about her. But 1 day in late July, Ebony's world would come crashing down around her and Ajay was right there to try to pick up the pieces.

They had just finished shooting basketball. Everyone was headed home to bathe and get cleaned up so they could attend T-baby's 7th birthday party. Ebony was headed into her side door when all of sudden, Lady ran out of the door at top speed. It wasn't obvious what she was running after. But she was headed straight for the street. Ebony was calling her name. She had even started to run after her but Lady darted right out in front of a Pontiac Bonneville and got ran over.

"*Noooooooooo!*" Ebony screamed as she watched the car tires roll over her Scottish Terrier.

She ran to the edge of the street. The driver of the car stopped instantly and got out. There were 2 other cars on the street, at the time and they stopped too. Ebony screamed her way to where Lady's body was laid out shaking from the last jolts of air which was escaping her body. Ebony was in the middle of the street trying to pick up Lady. It wasn't a busy street but it was after 5pm. That was the time most head of households were returning home from work. The driver of the Bonneville was beside himself with sympathy as he tried to comfort Ebony.

Big John ran out of the house and so did big Paul. Al was at work.

June had run back up the street after hearing the tires screech. He ran in to get Ajay because he knew he was going to want to be there. Ebony broke down. She was crying so hard as John picked her up and hugged her tight.

"It's okay, baby girl," he said, "Daddy will get you another dog."
The driver even offered to pay for her another pet as he patted her back while John tried to comfort her.
"Baby girl he wants to help you get another puppy, okay?"

"No daddy. Get her out of the street," Ebony cried, "Make her wake up before another car comes."

"Baby girl, lady's not gonna wake up okay," John said, "She's gone."

"No daddy no!" she cried, "Please not my baby! Please daddy! Tell her to wake up! Please!"

By that time, Ajay had run out there. He saw Paul pick Lady up and put her in a cardboard box. She was dead. Ajay looked at the shell that was Ebony. She was distraught. He started to cry which was an extremely rare sight for most. He knew this was going to scar his girl for a very long time. Lady was her in-home companion. She slept in Ebony's room and followed her around the house, the entire time that she was awake and moving around. He went to John and Ebony but he didn't know what to say. Chill had run out to help his dad secure Lady. They closed the box that Lady was in and brought it on into the double driveway where John was holding a very fragile Ebony. She wasn't going to be okay. Neither was Ajay because he didn't have a clue of how he could make this one better. Ebony looked at him. Between sniffles she asked,
"Ajay....., if you rub her....., will she..., wake..., up?"
He didn't know what to say, so he asked John should he try it.

"No Ajay," John said sternly, "Lady is in heaven now. We'll just have to find my baby girl another puppy. Lady was with us for almost five years."

"No daddy," Ebony said, "I don't want another puppy. It's..., just gonna....., get ran over. I don't....., want another one. I want lady to wake up. Please!"
She cried and begged but it wasn't going to happen. John carried her inside while Chill, Paul, Ajay, June, Tank and Jb went into John and Pearl's backyard to dig a hole. They were going to have a little funeral for Lady, the next afternoon before Pearl had to leave for work. She was like a member of the family and many of the crew was going to be there too.

It would take awhile before Ebony would get over loosing her first
70

and only pet. She would never have another pet until she was 22 years old, in her own home and married to Ajay. Ajay stepped up his efforts to console her from that day on. He wanted to make sure she knew that she had someone to lean on. Someone to make her feel comfortable and someone who would do anything to make her happy.

****

Rebbie's grandparents Jeb Baker Jr and Jessie Mae Johnson-Baker, who lived in Europe, had come to Cleveland for Allen Sr's funeral and they stayed throughout the end of the summer. Jessie Mae is the sister of big Jake. Her marrying Jeb Baker Jr had only escalated her brother's hatred toward the crew. So during her visit to Cleveland, she didn't even bother to contact him. They hadn't spoken to each other in nearly 3 decades. Big Al was starting to feel like that was going to be the same fate for him and his sister Jessica. Though she still allowed Terrell to come back and visit for the summer of 1983, against her husband Jonathan's wishes. She still hadn't talked to her brother much since she was in Cleveland for the burial of their father and the reading of his last will and testament. That reading had only drove her farther away because their father had left everything to big Al. Jessica had hoped he would've left her the house in The Point since it *was* her 1st home after moving from Boston to Cleveland to attend college. But Al Sr had left that home, his interest in the property which would later become *CrewLand Mall* plus all of his money and assets to his son. Jeb Jr was on hand to sign over his interest as well. Those were the terms that his father Jeb Sr had left in his last will. Their interest in the business property was to go to all of their grandchildren. Chill's crew was the beneficiary of that property and they were expected to make something good out of it, 1 day.

While Jeb Jr was home, he introduced his college buddy and friend Bert Parkwood to the Cleveland crew. Parkwood reminded Jeb so much of his father and he was already pulling strings for the crew through their attorney George Wheeler before they knew who he was. Parkwood was already making plans to get Ajay signed to his alma mater, The University of Cincinnati. Ajay had just celebrated his 9th birthday. He wasn't even out of elementary school yet.

The big Jake beef was on the front burner again as the fall school year started. Ajay was in 4th grade and playing basketball with the 6th grade

71

team and still keeping his eyes on Ebony Brown, who was in 2nd grade along with her 3 best friends Nina, T-baby and Rebbie.

One day during the 1st week of school, a girl tried to start a fight with T-baby but T-baby wouldn't fight her back. She hit T-baby twice with no response. They were out at recess and Ebony's class was outside too. Ebony ran over to her cousin and demanded that she hit her back.

"But I don't know how to fight Ebony," T-baby said.

"I do," Ebony said, "I watched how Ajay beat up Richie. You just gotta start punching her and don't stop until she fall on the ground. That's when you start kicking her and you don't stop until somebody break it up. That way she can't come back to hit you, okay?"

"Okay," T-baby said.

Sure enough that little bully girl came over to where T-baby and Ebony was standing and talking. She was laughing and teasing T-baby. Ebony just reminded T-baby not to say anything to her.

"But if she touch you again, you know what to do," Ebony said.

That girl pushed T-baby 1 last time and T-baby opened up on her and beat her good. It took 3 teachers to pull T-baby off of her. Once the teachers broke it up and got the story. They took the bully to the office and only made T-baby clean the erasers in all of the 2nd grade classrooms, for the remainder of the week. Her status was made from that day. That bully nor anyone else tried to pick a fight with T-baby or her girls, for years after. The word got out that they could fight. Nina had also added that they were going to fight together, from then on. So if anybody messed with 1 of them. They was messing with all 4 of them. Their 2nd grade school year was a breeze afterwards.

But for Ajay, that fight he'd with Carlos Watts at the end of last year, wasn't an issue at school because Carlos had transferred to the west side of Cleveland. But outside of school, it was still as big as the day that it happened because Carlos was with Jacob everyday *this* school year. Jacob's grandfather was the reason for Jacob's problems with Ajay and his crew and he wasn't going to allow any crew win to happen without retaliation.

Robert Jenkins or Lil Rob was in 8th grade when he got initiated to the crew in early October 1983, after he turned 13. There were now 4 official members of the 3rd generation of the crew. Chill, Stoney, Renee and Lil Rob were legitimate crew and there would be many more to come. They would be 18 strong by the end of the decade with 9 adoring couples and absolutely crew tight.

Late fall 1983 was the fighting season for the males in the crew and some of the ladies too. Renee and Chill was expecting their 1st baby and it was due in early December. They already knew it was going to be a boy. Chill and big Paul was extra excited about that part. Chill had gotten out of training school, come home and made a child sometime within the month of March. Renee had moved in with them permanently, shortly after the pregnancy test came back positive. Big Paul and the crew knew they had to keep her near them now. Especially since she was carrying a crew child.

Chill and Renee's son whom they named Kenneth Ramon Payne Jr was born on Christmas day of 1983. That was Ebony's 8th birthday and that was also the 1st Christmas that Ajay had bought Ebony a gift for Christmas and for her birthday. Though his mother had suggested he replace her baby doll that he had destroyed, earlier that year. Ajay opted for buying her a dress and a bracelet. He didn't want her to play with baby dolls anymore. He wanted her to play with him and he wasn't going to play with dolls, with her. He had found 1 of her baby dolls that she'd left in Nina's room and threw it into their fireplace. But that was before Lady was killed. Nobody saw him do it but Jo knew her son and she knew no one else in her home would've done it except him. Al knew he had done it and he also knew why. By then he knew Ajay liked Ebony and even though him and his best friend big John wanted them to be together when they got older. Al knew his son was trying to get it started early. Al and Ajay had a significant talk about it too.

"Ant you are my only son," Al had told him, "Ebony is John's only daughter. We want y'all to marry each other, one day. But you need to remember that Ebony isn't as far along as you are yet. She still likes to play with her dolls so I don't want you to destroy them. She already lost her dog this year and she doesn't need anymore loses. Destroying her dolls won't make her grow up *any* faster. What you like about her is her innocence. That's your trait as a Jackson man. But you can't rush it because then she may become someone you don't like."

"She likes me too," Ajay had said, "I know she likes to play basketball with me. But I want her to know that I like her all the way and not just for playing basketball."

"Okay and that's all good," Al said, "But she'll have to grow into that. For now, you'll just have to keep showing her that you like her. Melting her dolls isn't gonna convince her that you like her. She may start to think that you're mean and I know you don't wanna go that route no more. Just give her time and see if she grows into you."

Ajay said he understood. But he would still destroy more of her baby dolls in the coming months. He wanted her attention on him and him only. That was never going to change for him. Not until they were married and became parents. Then Ajay was okay with being second to their kids.

Chapter 4-The Introduction to *The Chamber*

Lil Ajay loves the conversations he has with his father because Ajay gives him the play-by-play of his life, when they talk. Ajay wants to be the same type of father he has in big Al. Big Al had never sugarcoated anything with him. He always told him and showed him the facts of life because he wanted Ajay to be aware of any pitfalls that could come. Lil Ajay now knows that his father liked his mother since he was the age that Lil Ajay is now.

"That was sad when you was telling me that my great-grandpa died," Lil Ajay says solemnly, "I wish I could've met him."

"He was a great man, son," Ajay says, "I learned so much from him and I'll never forget him or any of the lessons I learned from him."

"I hate that mama's dog died too," Lil Ajay says.

"She was so broken that day, son," Ajay says, "Ah that broke my heart when she asked me to rub lady to see if she would wake up. She was crushed and I knew I was gonna get her another dog whenever she was ready to have another one."

"So Ike and Tina is the dogs you got for her to replace lady?"

"Yes and I didn't asked her if she was ready either," Ajay says, "I just surprised her. That was when she was stressing over not being able to get pregnant. She wanted you and your sister, *so* bad. She was lonely in this big ass house because I was playing in Miami then."

"She was okay with you bringing them?"

"Yes indeed," Ajay says, "Her face lit up. I knew she was ready to have a pet again. I had to get her two of them so she would have twice as many as she had when she was little."

"You spoil my mama good," Lil Ajay says and laughs.

"I love to spoil her too," he says, "You're hearing about her life. Don't you think she deserves it?"

"Yes sir," he answers, "She does. But you liked her since you was my age. But you still haven't told me when y'all got to the kissing part. Do you remember that part?"

"God yes!"

Lil Ajay digs in. He has another question which Ajay welcomes.

"Did you kiss my mama when y'all was little too?" Lil Ajay asks.

"No not the first time I tried too," Ajay says as he smiles, "I asked her one time when all the grandparents and parents took all the kids to a *Eddie Murphy* movie. I could tell she wanted too but she didn't do it. And later on, one day when we had just finished shooting ball. She gave me a peck on the lips then ran in the house. She would give me pecks for a long time but she made me wait almost two more years after that movie. Before she *really* kissed me. It was on after that though, son. I would never kiss another girl in *any* way, after that kiss."

"She made you wait?" Lil Ajay ask as he holds his side and cracks up laughing.

"Yes indeed," Ajay says, "But she was scared when I first asked her. She told me after we got married that she didn't know how to kiss me then and she didn't want me to know that she didn't know how. Because she thought I wouldn't ask her again. But what she didn't know is that I really didn't know how to kiss either. Not with the tongue, I didn't. I can look you in your eyes right now and tell you that your mother is the only woman I ever let put her tongue in my mouth. And her mouth is the only one that my tongue has been in too. And I'm the only man she's ever kissed or even let touch her. Your mother was the most perfect girl I knew. I still feel the same way today as I did when I asked her to marry me. We were born to be together, son. That's what your late great-grandmother, granny Pearline, always said. All of your greats still say that to this day. I agree with them too. We were just made to be together."

"Tell me about that part, pops," Lil Ajay says.

"Sure thing, if you think you're ready for it," Ajay says.

"I'm ready," Lil Ajay says.

"Here's the build up."

}1984{

Ajay was more focused than ever, on who he wanted to be his girlfriend by the time 1984 came in. He'd gotten a Christmas gift from Ebony too. Ebony's mother had helped her to get Ajay a *Dr J* basketball T-shirt with the shorts to match. He had always said he was emulating *Julius Irving* when he made super moves while playing basketball with her. Ajay loved his gifts. He couldn't wait until the spring and warmer weather, so he could wear it while playing ball with her. Dr J was his basketball idol and everybody knew that. He was still a 4th grader playing on the 6th grade team while the 7th grade coaches were already planning to have him on their team, the next year. But Al had already had talks with the 8th grade coaches and he knew Ajay would be playing on the 8th grade team when he made it to 5th grade. He was just that good.

76

****

Ajay would have another encounter with Carlos Watts before he started 5th grade. It was in the late summer of 1984. He would also have his 1st experience with killing someone. It happened after he turned 10 years old. He had hooked up with a 9th grade girl named Malaysia Fields who was suppose to have been the girlfriend of 9th grader Mike Watts. Carlos Watts older brother. It was the week before Ajay would start the 5th grade that he found out about *"The Chamber"* and what exactly went on there.

Ajay, Chill and the guys from the 3rd generation were all at the community gym, playing pick up games against other 5-man teams from the Cleveland area. Carlos, Mike and Jacob better known by then as Lil Jake, showed up with their roadies and home boys. They really didn't come to play basketball. They had heard that the Cleveland crew was there and that they had been running the courts and winning, all day. Lil Jake and his posse was seeking to change that. Mike Watts had already put the word out that he was going to do away with that little young nigga who had laid pipe to 1 of his ho's. So from the moment Ajay saw Carlos walk in, he was ready for part 2 of their fight to commence. Jr, Rich, June and Stoney was on the sidelines watching as Ajay, Jb, Chill, Rob and Tank was playing. Mike Watts called Ajay out while the game was going on. Ajay stopped playing immediately and headed straight toward him. Needless to say, his crew followed him.

"What the fuck did you say?" Ajay asked but not really caring if he answered.

"You telling folks you fucked my bitch," Mike said, "You a little bitty ass boy."

"That Malaysia bitch said I was a man," Ajay asserted, "So what nigga? I fucked her. She sucked me off too. What about it? She came at me and asked me for the dick. I gave it to her. What you wanna do about it?"

"Nigga-"

"If you see a nigga fuck wit him," 10 year old Ajay said calmly.

In an even calmer voice then Ajay had used, Chill said,

"I'm gone let you know right now that shit ain't even about to happen, nigga."

"Get it in, nigga," Jb added, "We right here."

"No shit," Rob said, "Ain't no need to talk about it."

"Be about it," Jr added.

Mike was still standing there but he wasn't talking anymore. None of his boys were either. Carlos hadn't even made eye contact with Ajay while Ajay looked from him to his brother Mike, the entire time. Ajay was in his fight stance. He was ready to throw some blows as soon as either one of them acted like they were going to make an advance toward him.

He added, "It ain't shit between us but air. What the fuck you waitin for?"

Mike and his guys started to retreat but not without a few more negative comments as they were leaving. Chill pulled his crew together for a word. He looked at Stoney and Rob then he said,

"It's about time that we introduce our younger brothers to them *crew thangs.*"

"I'm wit that bro," Stoney said.

"I'm definitely down for some chamber action," Rob added, "Let's get it in."

Chill had some of his faithful street partners to go out and get car descriptions and tag numbers from the vehicles Mike and his boys had gotten a ride to the gym in. Without even 2nd guessing, Chill knew big Jake was their connection because Lil Jake was in the pack. And they always tried to wolf them like the crew was ever going to bow down. Chill readied his crew for combat, just in case Mike, Lil Jake and their boys were still out there waiting when they made it outside.

"I gave up my down and that foul nigga ran?" Ajay asked with a slight rise in his voice, "We had the run of the court."

The crew made it outside where they had rides waiting to take them back to Shaker Heights. Greg Sr, Archie Sr and Brad Sr had brought them to the gym and waited outside to bring them back home. They were already aware of who the rival boys were before they had even gone inside the gym. They had alerted Paul, big Al and big John about the potential confrontation at the gym. By the time Ajay and the crew came outside, big Paul, Al, John and Rich Sr who was home from rehab, were pulling into the parking lot. Chill's father Paul jumped out of his car and met Chill and the guys as they were walking over.

"It's time to set up a chamber meeting," big Paul said without hesitation. "Fuck it. We gone off big Jake's youngsters before they even get grown."

"I just said the same thing, pops," Chill said as they headed to the vehicles to load up.

They left the gym and headed to what the crew call the chamber. It was there that they formulated a plan to do away with the Watts brothers and Malaysia Fields too. They knew Lil Jake wasn't going to push them. But

78

Mike was heated because his girl had fucked Ajay. So his ego was going to make him push the issue, sooner than later. The fathers was going to get them out of the way early. Big Al and John saw it as eliminating future troubles for the crew and more precisely, Ajay and Ebony.

****

It was 2 weeks later when the plan unfolded like clockwork. Ajay was meeting Malaysia for a date at a rave party, is how they had laid it out. She was more than willing and she understood that she wasn't to tell anyone about the date because Mike was already aware that she had fucked Ajay, a few weeks ago. But Ajay had told her to bring Mike along. The excuse he gave her for wanting her to bring him was so he wouldn't be looking for her and catch them together and start some shit with him. If she had really known Ajay. Then she would've known there was something wrong with that entire statement. Because Ajay never shied away from a confrontation. He was more likely to do whatever he had to do to make sure the confrontation happened. He told her they would sneak away from the party while Mike was doing his usual thing of hitting on others girls and ignoring her. He told Malaysia they could get away from the rave and go somewhere where they could be alone. Malaysia bought that lie, all the way.

Big Al and Paul had gotten 1 of the police from their payroll to provide the transportation for Malaysia. The payroll cop used a personal vehicle to do so. He had also provided vehicles to park outside of the fake party to make it look legitimate. Ajay and Malaysia would have their date and it would take place right there at the chamber. Being that Malaysia knew she had to be undercover. She told her mother she was going to the movies with Mike. She had told Mike where to meet her which was apart of the plan to get him there. He was to meet her at her normal bus stop where her ride would pick them both up and transfer them to the crew. The crew hadn't asked for Carlos to come but he did. Mike had brought him along in hopes that he would be able to hook up with some girl at the secret rave party and not be in his way with Malaysia or whatever new chick he would be able to pick up. The 3 of them got into the setup vehicle and the payroll cop drove them to their destiny.

At first glimpse of the chamber from the outside, it looked like it could be a real rave spot. It was a storage looking building which was located in the cul-de-sac on a sparsely populated street in a east Euclid neighborhood. When the payroll cop got there and let them out, it looked very much like there could be a secret party going on inside. Though the scene was very quiet and subdued. Ajay had told Malaysia that the building was insulated and sound proof so that the neighbors wouldn't complain about the noise. She went for that too. Because she was more focused on her real mission. Which was getting these 2 guys to scrap over her.

There was a lot of cars packed inside the cul-de-sac, just as the payroll cop was suppose to do it. No one was hanging outside and as raves go, no one usually did. There was only 1 guy standing outside the door and he was dressed like a security guard. All raves looked like that from the outside as well. That was the way they kept their locations from being exposed. The payroll cop had dropped them off on time. He told them they wasn't allowed to huddle outside. Malaysia, Carlos and Mike told him thank you and headed to the door.

"This party better be jumpin," Mike said.

"It's a lot of cars here," Carlos added.

"I think it's gonna be perfect," Malaysia said speaking on her anticipation of hooking up with Ajay and getting Mike mad enough to claim her.

She would be thoroughly surprised once they all got inside of that fake rave. Malaysia didn't care for either Mike or Ajay. But if she had a choice, she would've preferred the younger Ajay because he had more clout. She had heard about his fight with Carlos, so she knew Ajay was a fighter. She just had no idea of how deadly cold he was emotionally. She had found out about him and went to a crew event specifically to meet him.

She had 1st approached him at this year's 4th of July cookout. That was the 1st day they met. Or rather that was the day she came to him and said she wanted to fuck him. She had been watching him for awhile before she actually approached him. Ajay was okay with the way she came to him and the fact that she said her desire was to fuck him. That was fine with him as long as she knew he wasn't going to date her. But after the fuck session went down. Ajay learned what her real game was. She was suppose to be dating Mike, who was the older brother of Carlos, the guy he had fought at the end of the last school year. She was suspect from then on.

It was well known around town that Mike was fucking around on Malaysia, so she wanted a little payback. That's what Ajay and his crew felt was her reason for approaching Ajay in the first place. She wanted the beef to happen and the fighting to continue too. As a matter of fact, Malaysia was the reason Mike found out she'd fucked Ajay. She knew Mike was nothing but a bully and he would go after Ajay. That was exactly what she'd wanted. She had heard Ajay wasn't the type to back down and she had counted on them having a brawl about her, so she could look like the big girl of 9th grade. Still when he said he didn't want Mike to see them leave because he might try to start a fight. That didn't seem strange to Malaysia. That's how Chill and his crew knew she didn't give a fuck about Ajay and was willing to put him in the crosshairs. The fight she wanted, had almost happened at the gym. But Mike saw that Ajay wasn't the 1 to fuck with because he wasn't afraid, he didn't back down and he had a crew who was ready and willing to scrap. That was why Mike retreated quickly. He had been sending threats to Ajay since Ajay had beat his brother Carlos. Those threats only increased after Ajay fucked Malaysia. The streets had gotten the word that Mike and his boys were suppose to be shooting Ajay, whenever they saw him. That word had gotten to Chill and the crew before Ajay had even fucked Malaysia. Because all she talked about was her boyfriend and how jealous he was. She told Ajay that she wanted to fuck him and if he was down for her. He would beat Mike up anytime she got mad at him for messing around. Ajay saw her just like the other girls. Only she was 3 times worse. She wanted him to be her fool or flunky. That wasn't ever going to happen. His mission tonight was to treat her to what she deserved. Then his crew was going to do away with the brothers because they had plotted to kill him. Malaysia had to go as well because she had instigated the whole thing and plotted to bring Mike and Ajay together in the same place, for her benefit.

From the moment they entered that shed door, they should've known that the outcome wasn't going to be a party for them. There was music playing and there were people dancing too. That was all apart of the stage and it wouldn't last longer than the time it took for Ajay to get Malaysia into the private room where the bed and the 2-way mirrors were located.

Ajay approached Malaysia right in front of Mike and Carlos.
He said, "I've been waiting for you."
Malaysia looked caught up but she tried to smile and play it off. Mike and Carlos looked around and noticed that a lot of the guys they had been threatening to harm for the past month, was in attendance too. There was others there that they didn't recognize. But it was obvious from that point on that Mike and Carlos knew they would have to hold up. They were visibly afraid. Malaysia still hadn't said anything yet so Ajay continued to press her.
He asked, "Are you ready to kick it?"

She looked at Mike. He wasn't his usual boisterous self, at that moment. Usually he would have started with the shit talking and bullying or the selling of wolf tickets. But not at that party. At that party he didn't say a word. Malaysia figured she may as well go for broke and test Mike to his limits. She decided to go on and get some payback. She answered Ajay.

"Yea I'm ready," she said nonchalantly.

"Then let's make it," Ajay said and she followed him into the private area of the chamber while Mike just stood there next to Carlos. Neither 1 of them said a word.

To Malaysia, the room her and Ajay went into looked like a normal but oversized luxury bedroom. There was a huge bed in there, a big screen television complete with a gaming system and VCR. There was even a dresser, chest of drawers and 2 nightstands too. There was a door that led to a huge bathroom. But in the bedroom there was 4 walls. Only 1 of them was all mirrors from the ceiling to the floor. What Malaysia didn't know was *that* was the viewing spot. She even made jokes about the mirrors.

"Wow! We can get real freaky in here and even watch ourselves while we do," she said and giggled in her usual whorish way.

She had no idea that they wouldn't be the only one's who would be viewing them while they freaked. They would actually have a *captive* audience.

After Ajay had taken Malaysia into the room. That's when Chill and Stoney stepped to Mike and Carlos directly and grabbed them by their elbows.

"Don't you even think about resisting nigga," Stoney said, "Y'all *comin* wit us."

"Let's move this thing along," Chill added as they escorted the 2 of them toward the rest of the crew who were already gathered at the far side of the chamber.

Chill, Stoney and the rest of the men escorted the 2 of them to the back of the shed and into a huge opened area known as the killing floor. The fake party was still going on.

From the killing floor, they had a full view of Malaysia, Ajay and the room that they were in. Immediately Chill, Stoney and Rob started to chain Mike and Carlos up. But they never interrupted their view of the 2-way wall. They could see into the bedroom from a huge wall sized window.

"So let me let you fake ass clowns know what the business is, right quick," Jr said, "It's party time. It's time to give y'all niggas the crew treatment."

Ajay and Malaysia were in the bedroom. Ajay knew they were

being viewed from the killing floor of the chamber so he wanted to make sure and give Mike a great show.

That's when he turned to Malaysia and said,

"Take off your shit and let's do this before yo bitch ass nigga start looking for you."

"What?" she asked, "While the party's going on out there?"

"You told me we had a date, right?" Ajay asked.

"With Mike still in there?" she asked but he could tell she was turned on by the thought of her man knowing she was with him.

"He ain't follow you or try to stop you, did he?" Ajay asked with an impatient frown. "He didn't say shit when we was walking off either."

"You're right but it feels weird," she said, "I'm trippin off him. He talks all this shit about how much he loves me and that he'll check a nigga if he find out he fucked wit me. But he didn't say shit when you took my hand and brought me back here, wit his fake ass."

"Well first of all. I ain't no nigga," Ajay said sternly, "And second, that should tell you everything you need to know. Now are we gonna do this or what? Cause I ain't gone waste this night. I can be on somebody else that's ready to get down."

"Nah now," she said, "I'm in here now and he ain't even tried to look for me, so fuck it."

"Then get yo clothes off and let's do this before I have to leave," he said, "I got curfew."

She removed her clothes and he led her to the bed where he removed his clothes also and got on the bed. She joined him. He grabbed a hold of his dick, strapped a condom on it and looked at her. She attempted to kiss him but he wouldn't allow her too. He just pushed her head down to his penis and she started to serve him.

Chill and the crew had left the killing floor. They left Mike and Carlos chained up with a full view of the 2-way mirrored wall. They knew the show should be getting started and they didn't need to see that part. They were just going to wait outside the doors until Ajay gave them the signal. Then they could get to the best part.

Ajay was getting head for 10 minutes. He didn't even want to fuck her but he knew he had an audience of Mike and Carlos and he had to oblige them.

"Lay down," he told her and she did. But not before asking him, "You gonna do me too?"

"I don't eat pussy," he said as he put on another condom and parted her legs. He grabbed hold of his dick and said, "Do you want this?"

"Yes."

"Tell me you want it," he ordered.

"I wanna fuck you Ajay," she said, "You're younger then Mike's ass is and you fuck better then he do. And you got a big ass dick to be so young. Way bigger than his."

That's all he wanted to hear her say. He entered her and started fucking her hard from the onset. He wanted her to make all the noises she'd made on their prior hook up. She didn't disappoint him either. She was very loud and explicit too.

"Oh God! Yo dick is so good!" she yelled, "I want you to be my man Ajay please! I know you know that by now!"

"You do?" he asked just to keep her confessing while he pounded her like it was a night job.

"Hell yea baby," she said, "I told you that the first time we did it! Baby oh you fuck so good! I love the way you make me feel! Oh God!"

He flipped her over and pulled her up on her knees where she was facing the 2-way mirror. He entered her from the back and started to drive his dick into her with maximum force. He was looking directly in the direction that he was told Mike would be chained up. He started to smile while he fucked Malaysia. He knew Mike was watching him while he fucked his girlfriend. That gave him an extra thrill and made his dick even harder. He liked the power that it made him feel to have the guy that had threatened his life over his girl. Watching him while he fucked that girl, who was confessing that her choice was him. Just knowing Mike could see and hear them too, gave Ajay a major feeling of power. It was doing more for his libido than the actual act of fucking. Malaysia was being very vocal about how much she liked him more than Mike. Ajay didn't say anything more. He got up on his tiptoes and pulled her back against him while he rammed her hard. She was loud enough to be heard through that 2-way mirror but they had audio. Ajay fucked her without answering any of the commitment questions she was screaming at him. He just got his nut, finished the job, discarded the condom and pulled his pants back up and fastened them.

Then he told her, "Stay in here until I can go check and see where everybody is. I'll come get you when the coast is clear. Get dressed."

He had told her that, knowing that she was about to die. Ajay was already mentally cold at 10 years old. Knowing that someone wanted him dead before he had even been born, had made him numb to society and others who wasn't in his life in a positive way. So after giving her the last sex she would have. He left her in the room and joined his crew in the hallway where they all had the look of business on their faces.

Big Paul and the father's headed back into the killing floor area where Mike and Carlos were hanging from chains. It was time for them to leave permanently.

Out in the hallway, Chill told Ajay what the next move would be.

"We're about to do them clowns in," he said, "And the girl is gonna have to go too. We don't leave no witnesses."

"That's a fact," Jr added.

"Okay," was Ajay's answer.

Up until that point, Ajay had only been involved in very decisive fights in which he'd won. But he'd never taken a life. He was *just* told that the whore he had *just* finished fucking was going to die and he didn't care if she did. He was 100% crew and down to do whatever was deemed necessary to remove any threat to him and his family. So what if he hadn't killed anybody before and he'd had many fights that he'd won? Being part of his crew meant always being ready to handle whatever he faced. He had heard about how killing was done, from his forefathers. He had been trained to shoot and how to use a boa knife too. He knew that when the time came for him to do crew *thangs*. Then killing would most likely be apart of it.

"Are you ready to get your wings, Ajay?" Stoney asked.

"I'm ready Stoney," was Ajay's response.

"Bring that bitch on back here," Rob said.

"Yea she had plans of helping you to get knocked off," Chill said, "It's time for her to know with no doubts, she was on the wrong team."

Jr went back into the bedroom with Ajay to get Malaysia. She was dressed when they entered the room.

With a bright smile, she asked, "Is it safe to walk out?"

"Yea come on," Ajay said solemnly and she followed him.

Ajay led her to the killing floor where all of the crew males were waiting. As soon as she saw Mike and Carlos in chains, she panicked.

"What is this?!" she asked Ajay, "What did they do?!"

Ajay didn't respond and he barely looked her way. He just looked at his crew to find out what he was to do next. That's when Malaysia noticed the 2-way wall. She knew instantly that Mike had seen and heard her fucking Ajay. Their sex act was now being played back on 2 TV screens, just in case she had any doubts about if Mike heard what she had confessed too.

At that time, was when big Al handed Ajay a .357 Magnum. It was the very same magnum that had been left to him by his recently deceased

85

grandfather Al Sr. Malaysia didn't see big Al hand Ajay the gun because she was to busy asking questions of everyone else about why her sex scene had been taped. And why was her man and his brother harnessed in chains and hanging from the ceiling. The door was blocked in case she had any ideas that she would be able to run away.

Big Al looked at Ajay.

Then he said, "Son it's time to let these clowns know that their troubles from this female will die right along with them."

"Just in case they have any hopes that she'll be alive to tell anybody what happened to them," big John added.

"Get your stripes Ajay," Chill said.

Ajay pointed the pistol at Malaysia and she started screaming. He aimed and pulled the trigger. His 1st shot hit her in the shoulder. She fell to the floor. She was still screaming, only then in immense pain. Mike and Carlos struggled in the chains. Their mouths were taped so all they could do was make noises that sounded like moans and mutter. Malaysia wasn't fatally shot. She was only wounded as she continued to scream. Al looked at her with no expression. The only way he viewed her, was as this girl who had plotted the death of his only son. He wanted her done before she started begging. He turned to Ajay who was still holding the gun as he stared at Malaysia. He had no expression either and Al knew he wasn't phased by it at all. Ajay had a lot of practice with shooting guns and he was never afraid to shoot 1 either. Al wanted him to get it over with.

He said, "Finish her, son."

Ajay stepped closer to Malaysia and stood over her to get better aim. He cocked the hammer back and put a bullet into the center of her forehead. That loud annoying screaming stopped. Ajay watched as the contents from her head spilled out the back of it. He stood there numb and his face still held no expression. At that moment, he didn't know what to feel. He knew Malaysia wanted to set him up and she was a link to this whole beef plot with Mike and Carlos that he'd found himself in. That helped him to feel at ease about doing away with her. She didn't care about him anyway. She only cared about what she could use him for and the name she could get after using him. With her brains on the chamber's killing room floor, he could now put that worry to rest. She wouldn't be starting anymore shit for him. It was then that John spoke and after him, Paul spoke. While the rest stayed quiet and waited for their next job.

"It's time to get my sons some stripes too," John said, "Ajay I guess these *bitchass* negroes thought comin at you meant they'd only have to beef with you. But that bastard big Jake knew it was a whole lot more than that and still he let them walk into the valley. That's why our parents saw no fit for his disloyal and worthless ass, in this crew."

"Sure he did," big Paul said, "That bitch ass nigga don't care who he set up and send to their deaths. He keeps sending all of these misguided ass fools to fuck with my crew. But he fails to tell them how thick we roll and when you go after one. You're going at all of us."

"And you won't be making it back," Al added.

"Ajay you don't mind if John junior and Tank get some of this payback, do you?" big John asked as he reached for the .357 Ajay was still holding snug in his basketball shooting hand.

Ajay said, "No sir I don't."

But he was still holding onto the gun very tightly, not looking like he wanted to give it up. His stare was fixed on Mike. Shooting Malaysia had given him a certain kind of calm that he'd never felt before. It was almost as exhilarating as sex was for him. He actually liked killing and he wanted to do it some more. But he knew the father's had planned for this to be a team effort and a changing of the guards too. The 2nd generation was passing the crew torch to Chill and the 3rd generation. Tank and Jb were only 2 of the 4 males left in the 3rd generation who had never killed anyone, since Ajay had just gotten his rank. June and Richie were the others. They were present too but they would have to get their stripes later.

Ajay doubted if his 1st cousin Richie would ever be able to do what he'd just done to a human. He only went after defenseless creatures or those whom he knew wasn't a challenge for him. Ajay knew Richie was scared of everything and everybody including him. Because they had argued a lot and fought a couple of times too. But only when Richie was disrespecting him or someone he cared for. Ajay was 6 and Richie was 5 years old when Ajay had beat him up the 1st time. That was because Richie was always going into Ajay's room and messing with his property. Ajay had kicked his butt for going in there without his permission. Richie had cried and tried to get his parents to make Ajay's parents whip him. But that didn't happen then either. That had only made Richie angrier. He wasn't as mentally strong as Ajay was and Ajay knew that bothered Richie. That's also how he knew that Richie wasn't ready to kill anybody and live with it. He knew that their fathers had to know that too.

Jb and Tank were different. Ajay knew they could do it and so did their fathers. Mike and Carlos was going to be Jb and Tank's, 1st kills.

"We promote the protection of our families in the crew," Al

started, "And in this crew, everybody is family. As long as you uphold our crew creed. Then you will all be seen and treated equally. You fuck over the creed and we will deal with you the way we see fit. Now do all of you understand that?"

"Yes sir," the guys from the 3rd generation responded.

Still Ajay felt a thirst for more. He had started to rock from side to side like he would do on the basketball court, right before he would do a cross over and leave his defender with broken ankles. He was still clutching the pistol as John still stood in front of him. John had to get his attention, all over again.

"Are you gonna let me have the gun or shoot me wit it?" John asked and chuckled as Ajay, who seemed to have gone into a death stare, finally acted like he had heard John's voice.

He snapped back to the reality that was before him as he handed the pistol to big John. Then big John brought Jb and Tank forward. He placed the pistol in 11 year old Jb's hands and said,

"Just like I taught you. Spread your feet for balance. Extend your arm and lock your elbow. Aim and shoot."

Jb followed his instructions to the letter. He shot Mike straight through his right eye and didn't even blink when the deposits from Mike's head splattered out of it and sprayed all over the far wall behind him.

"Damn good shot, John junior," big Paul said, "You got your daddy's poise, son."

Then it was Tank's turn. He was shorter than both Ajay and Jb so the fathers pulled a desk up for him to stand on. 9 year old Tank climbed up on that desktop like he was about to write on a chalkboard. He repeated his father's instruction to make sure big John knew he hadn't forgotten what to do. He shot Carlos in the center of his forehead like he had done it before. He didn't blink either. But he did smile slightly. Then he turned to his father and asked,

"Do you got somebody else for me to shoot?"

The fathers laughed and so did Chill, Stoney, Rob and Jr. They found it amusing. At the same time, they were proud because Tank, Jb and Ajay was going to be in their crew. They knew that if it came down to them having to shoot to protect them or themselves. They would be able to do it. After he chuckled, big John said,

"There will be more son. Just not today. That's all for today."

Al said, "No traces can be left after a kill. So let's go crew. White gloves."

"Yea come on second generation and let's show these young bucks how to *clean up* after a cleaning," big Paul said as all the fathers laughed again.

They started to clean and clear away the bodies and all of the evidence from the area. Richie and June helped but Ajay could tell they were mesmerized by everything that had just happened. The fathers noticed that too and made the 2 of them stick close to their sides. June's father Brian Sr was there but Rich Sr wasn't present. Because since the day of the planning meeting, he had gotten caught with drugs again and was serving 1 of many bids in county jail for drug possession. The latest sentence was for 6 weeks but he'd had several, with more to come. That was something that played out in Rich Jr's life from very early on. It continued to plague his ability to function with confidence and normalcy. Even though his crew gave him the same opportunities and protection as they did the rest of his age group.

After everything was cleaned, they took the bodies to be disposed of. Then headed back to Shaker Heights in the early hours of the morning. Ajay knew the actions of that past evening would never leave his mouth. But more importantly, the tactical skills and knowledge he'd learned about how to do away with family troubles and get away with it, would never leave him either. That was the 1 thing his father, the entire 2nd generation and the older boys in his own generation of crew had counted on.

By mid-August 1984, 2 other males and a female got initiated into the 3rd generation of the crew. Bradley Wilson Jr or Jr turned 13 on the 14th of August. He had his initiation party at big Paul's house. Tonya was his date for the party. She was officially inducted to the crew as well. She wouldn't turn 13 until September 30th but Jr wanted to share his party with her. Plus Chill, Renee, Stoney and Rob shared a yes vote with Jr to make her a member. They inducted Arthur Owens at that same party because he had proven himself to be loyal. The 3rd generation of crew was 7 strong.

"I'm official now cousin," Jr said to Ajay as they hung out at the night party.

"It's all good," Ajay said, "I wish all the females from our crew could be at the night party though."

"Cousin you're sweet on Ebony, ha?"

"Yea cuz," he said, "That's gonna be my baby."

"That's alright Ajay," Jr said, "You got my vote too, cuz. I think y'all would be a perfect couple."

"I know we will," Ajay said.

Chill and Stoney joined them and they continued to kick it as they smoked weed together. Jr started to tell them about the trip to the point earlier that day.

"Hey man y'all know we took food to Freddy Kruger's family again today, right?"

They all laughed and Chill added, "That Lil dude always wearing the mask and glove too. We gotta keep a eye on him. He might put in some work, one of these days."

"And they live on Elm street too," Stoney added and laughed more.

"Damn that's like *Nightmare on Elm street,* for real," Ajay added and they continued to laugh.

"And the movie don't even come out till November," Jr said, "But that bootleg video Arthur got, they got one from the same hustler."

They all laughed again.

Tonya and Renee came over to get Chill and Jr so they could slow dance. That left Ajay and Stoney standing alone.

"I gotta get me a crew lady," Stoney said, "I need a girl I can bring to the crew events."

"I already know who I wanna bring," Ajay said, "I just gotta give her time to get a little older."

"Ebony, ha?"

"You know it."

"It's gonna be a minute before the foursome gonna be able to come," Stoney said, "They're the youngest girls for our crew. The parents are gonna stick to the code with them. They gotta wait until Nina and Ebony turn thirteen before either of them can come to the night time parties."

"That's the part that's fucked up to me," Ajay said, "Me, Tank and Jb up in here and we're not thirteen but then that's because we're males."

"Jan and Bre gonna start being able to come when Lynn gets crewed up because that's three the hard way," Stoney said and laughed. "Those three ain't gonna be separated just like the foursome is already. They do everything together too."

"That's how it's gonna be for T-baby and Rebbie," Ajay said, "Because they in the foursome with Ebony and Nina. I wish Ebony was wit Tonya and Renee, *shit.*"

They laughed hard before getting back into their party groove.

****

90

It was less than a month after Jr's party when Richie Rich had requested to be called Rich Jr instead of Richie. The crew agreed that they would shorten his nickname to Rich for his 9th birthday, which was less than a week away. But after getting something that he wanted. Rich saw that as a power boost and he decided to strike again.

It was the day after his 9th birthday party. Rich Jr was an honor student since Kindergarten. He had been able to skip a grade which put him in the same grade as Bre, Tank and June when they had entered 1st grade. He just didn't have a lot of common sense when it came to how he moved outside of his books. His mother had to go to work on that early October morning. His father had finished his 6 week sentence. But him and Anna were still not living in the same house since their separation after his last domestic violence incident. He was living with his older sister Deb, at her and Brad Sr's house. No one felt he was ready or responsible enough yet to be in charge of his young children, so Jo had offered to watch Rich Jr and Ruthie. That way Anna could make her shift.

Once again Rich Jr decided to partake in the meddling of Ajay's things and the testing of his patience. They were all adjusted to the 84-85 school year by then. It was after school and football practice when Rich Jr would do 1 of the many things he was known to do that really worked Ajay's last nerve. He had gone into Ajay's room and messed with what was his most prized possession at that time. Rich Jr messed with Ajay's basketball card collection. But even worse than just messing with it. Rich had stolen Ajay's *Julius "Dr. J" Irving* rookie basketball card.

When Ajay went into his room, he knew immediately that someone had been in there meddling. Some of his things were moved around. His card collection box was on the floor by his closet. Instead of on the top shelf where he usually kept it. He knew it was Rich Jr because that was what he was known to do. Ajay knew without a doubt Rich had done it because his sisters never went into his room without him being in there or without asking for his permission first. Ajay also knew why Rich Jr had messed around in his room.

At the start of Ajay's 5th grade year, he'd made the football team but football wasn't his top sport. Basketball was the sport he would be destined to leave his mark on and football was Rich's best sport. Rich was tall and lanky. He wasn't as tall as Ajay but he had quickness and agility which made wide receiver the perfect position for him. When Ajay had made the team, he was put in the wide receiver position also. During that particular week, Ajay had caught more passes than Rich and he'd made

91

more touchdowns in practice as well. Tank and June teased Rich about it. Ajay didn't nor did he laugh at their jokes. But still Rich was upset. He felt like Ajay was going to do better than him in football, just as he had already done in basketball. So to get back at Ajay, Rich went into his room after practice on that October evening of 1984 and stole his Dr. J rookie card. Ajay had calmly asked him for it back but only once and Rich had denied having it. Ajay beat him down quickly. During this fight, Ajay had bloodied his nose and nearly broken his wrist before Rich would own up too it. But he finally did.

"Then get my shit right now and give it to me," Ajay said, "And it better not have no damage or I swear I'm gonna break your fuckin arm."

"Okay Ajay," Rich said, "I gotta go get it."

"Then let's go," Ajay said as he followed closely behind Rich because he thought he might try to run and hide like he'd done after previous fights, where he'd left him able to walk away.
That was the reason Ajay had started beating him down when he fought him, the last few times. That was going to happen again if Rich didn't hurry up and get that vintage card back in his hands. Rich had hid it at Chill's house and before Ajay would even allow him to call his mother to go to the hospital. He had to get Ajay's card back. Rich got the card and gave it back to him. Ajay inspected it and made sure it was still in mint condition. It was. So then and only then, did Ajay allow Rich out of his sight. That fight must've drove the point home with Rich Jr. Because he learned to leave Ajay's property alone and stop doing things that got Ajay fired up. Thus Ajay wouldn't have to beat his ass again for another decade and a half.

Subsequently Ajay's basketball coaches and Mr. Parkwood had all contacted big Al and Jo about Ajay even playing football. They were afraid he would get injured and that could interfere with his ability to go all the way in basketball. Al and Jo talked with Ajay and found out that he didn't even like playing football. He'd only gone out because the football coaches had begged him too and also because he could be around his crew brothers Tank, June and Rich. Al and Jo let Ajay know he could quit football, if his heart wasn't in it. He left the team before the season was 4 games old. That made Rich's life and Ajay didn't even miss it. He already didn't have much time as it was. With basketball and all of the extra press he had started to get for it. Football and practice after school was interfering with his chances to play basketball with Ebony. He quit the football team in mid-October of 1984 and never even looked back.

The 5th grade Ajay and Ebony who was in 3rd grade, played on the half court everyday after Ajay made it home from after-school basketball practice. He had told Ebony that it was their court and that really made her excited. She had really gotten the hang of the game by then and had even learned most of the regulation rules. She could dribble well enough to play 1 on 1. She couldn't stand to lose which was just like Ajay, so he would play her and go easy on her most of times. She didn't like that at all. It made her upset instead of happy.

"You're not even playing hard!" she would yell to him.

"You're gonna get mad if I beat you," Ajay would say and chuckle, which would only make her more angry.

"You playing me like I'm a punk and not like you play when the boys are out here!" she yelled and he would laugh and swear he would play hard but he still didn't.

"You're not a boy though, Ebony," he said, "You're a cutie pie. I can't go off on you, out here."

"I can't stand you!" she would yell at him, only because he had been correct with what he had said.

He would crack up laughing and steal the ball from her, then go on and score a hoop. Often times grabbing the rim and swinging on it while he laughed. That made her madder.

"You make me sick!" she would yell at him again and poke her lips out.

Jo and Pearl would come outside and make them behave or just stop playing, all together. There were many days that Ebony would leave angry and stay angry until the next day. That's where their mothers got the impression that they didn't get along. Thing was, Ebony had started to like Ajay and she knew why she liked him. She also knew that he liked her and why. Her grandmothers would discuss it every time she helped them out in the kitchen. She had learned that a person who loves you and wants to make sure you do your best. Would surely bring you their best. She knew Ajay wasn't doing that and that angered her. She wanted his best because, if she was ever going to beat him playing basketball. She wanted to be able to say she knew that it was because she was just that good. He didn't get that part, back then. He was just trying to go easy on her, in hopes that she would know he liked her because he wouldn't allow himself to beat her. *Wrong*! He still wouldn't learn that before the first snow of the fall of 1984.

For most of that fall, Ebony and Ajay argued and that would drive their mothers crazy. She wanted his best and he wanted her to feel like she was better than she was, by taking it easy on her. That only made her more furious. It would be years later before he would figure that out. Chill knew what it was because Ebony would always complain to him about it.

"He plays me like I'm a baby," she would complain to Chill, "I wanna be good at basketball, just like him. But he won't play hard when we play. If he play me hard like he play when y'all play and I beat him. Then I'll know that I'm good. But he want even play right."

"Baby girl he likes to protect you and your feelings," Chill would tell her, "He don't wanna do anything that he thinks will make you not like him. He just don't know what kind of a soldier you are yet. Give him time. He'll learn it."

"Well he better hurry up," she would say, "I ain't no baby. I'm a big girl and I wanna beat him on the court, so he'll know I'm not a baby."

"How about if I talk to him about that," Chill said during 1 of those talks, "I'll let him know that you don't want him to take it easy on you when y'all play, so you can get better. But any other time, he has to treat you like a princess. Would that be okay?"

"Yes," she said, "Tell him that, so he can play his best. I like when he style and profile on the court. Not when he play like he's sorry."
That made Chill laugh hard. He knew Ebony and Ajay wanted the best for and out of each other and he was going to see to it that they both knew that about each other.

Chill would try to tell Ajay to play hard when he was out on the court with Ebony. But Ajay was stubborn and set in his ways. The 1 thing he didn't want to do, was to make her angry. He had his mind set on how he was going to get Ebony to be his girlfriend but he was doing it all wrong and wouldn't take Chill's advice to heart. He wanted her to like him as more than just her basketball buddy. He knew she liked to play basketball with him. But that wasn't enough for young Ajay. His problem was that she wasn't smiling at him when they were in each others presence and that was driving him crazy. Still he didn't realize that he had to perform at his best, at everything because that was what gave Ebony the biggest thrill. That was what would make her happy and keep her smiling.

Chapter 5-The Kiss for a Lifetime

"Richie Rich is the one who killed himself?" Lil Ajay asks.

"Yea son," Ajay says, "He decided to end his life because he didn't like who he was. That's the way I see it."

"He sounded like an ass to me," Lil Ajay says, "What kind of a person would kill little animals?"

"He definitely had a serious self esteem problem, son," Ajay says, "And it started early."

"Do you think he wanted to kill lady?"

"I wouldn't put it past him," Ajay says, "As we have our talks. I'm gonna tell you more about him and the things he did before he got it over with. And to be completely honest with you. I don't miss him. Not the bad shit. Because I feel like he hated me and he acted on it several times throughout his life. But we'll get to that later, if needed."

"Did he ever go into the circle?"

"Oh hell yea," Ajay says, "We'll talk about that when I get on into the years. But yes he had to be checked, several times."

"Is the chamber still there?"

"It is," Ajay says, "And there will always be a chamber until it comes a time where there is no threat left to this family."

"Can I see it?"

"Yes you can," Ajay says, "And you will. That's coming sooner than later too."

"I wanna see it," Lil Ajay says, very enthusiastically.

"Bet."

"My mama was mad at you for *not* beating her in basketball?"
Ajay laughs and says, "Oh yea. She use to get heated out there on them driveways. But it was so cute to me. Ebony could never do anything to make me *not* like her. And the only thing she could've done to make me mad, would've been talking to another boy or just talking about talking to another boy."

"Mama is a good woman, pops," Lil Ajay says suddenly, "How did you get her to be like that?"

"She was raised in this crew. So she already knew how to behave and how to carry herself. There's a motto from my grandpa Saul who was killed before I was even born. He started this motto for how a man in this family had to be the man, no matter what. He felt like the biggest asset to being a man was the way he handled his relationship with his woman.

The motto was, '*The test of being a real crew man is to have the type of control and dominance in your relationship and household, if you're in the same house, where you don't have to give your girl a reason for why she shouldn't do something. Just her man telling her not to do it, is suppose to be enough to insure that she doesn't.*' That was it for me. But at the same time, I had to behave as a man who deserved to have a woman who was loyal to me. And who didn't need another man to chastise her or tell her what she was to do. Your mama learned everything there is to know about how a man and a woman are with each other, from me. And she was such a good pupil too," he laughs and continues, "Ebony was never a whorish type of girl. She had demands. Things that she would absolutely *not* compromise on and I had to get my shit together and keep it that way. Because she wasn't going to deal with me being anything other than the best man for her. I knew she was the best woman for me, so I got my shit together."

"But y'all still haven't kissed yet," Lil Ajay says and laughs, "When did that happen?"

"It took awhile to get to that sort of thing with Ebony," Ajay says, "Because one of the things I loved and still love about your mom. Is that she wasn't fast. She was a nurturer. She wanted me to be the best I could be. Plus she didn't know anything about sex or being intimate. So she wasn't in a rush to do something she didn't know a damn thing about."

"I know girls that want me to kiss them but I don't wanna kiss them," Lil Ajay says, "I like to feel on them and they let me do it too."

"None of them will be your girl," Ajay says, "A virtuous girl wouldn't allow you to get to that point without knowing she was someone special and that's how you know the difference."

"I like Kimmie, pops," Lil Ajay says suddenly, "I don't feel on her because she don't even talk about that kind of stuff. She just want me to talk to her and smile when I do. That's how my mama was, ha?"

"Yep."

"I wish she lived here all the time and not just for holidays and stuff," Lil Ajay says, "I just like seeing her and watching her."
Ajay smiles and says, "That's how it starts. And you have butterflies when she talks to you but you don't even know why you do."

"Yep."

"Treasure that and keep it that way," Ajay says, "If it starts off that way. Then it will stay that way."

"I can't wait for her to come back," Lil Ajay says, "But Alan can stay in Chicago. He likes my twin but she's not ready to have no boy talking

96

to her yet. He needs to stay in Chicago if he thinks he gonna talk to Lannie. I want him to like her though but not right now."

Ajay cracks up laughing. He can hear every bit of himself in his son.

He clears his throat and says, "Eric junior and me already talked about them coming to live here and going to school with y'all."

"For real?!" Lil Ajay says very excitedly.

"For real," Ajay says, "We'll see to that happening, okay?"

"Okay," Lil Ajay says, "Now I need to learn how to make sure she keeps liking me and *just* me. Because she do like me and she told me she wants me to be happy and not mean."

"Well that sounds a lot like your mother," Ajay says, "This is how she moved with me."

}December 5, 1984{

It was less than a week into the last month of 1984. Twenty days before Ebony's 9th and Kenny Jr's 1st birthday. All 3 generations of the crew were going to see the new movie with *Eddie Murphy* titled *Beverly Hills Cop*. By then, Chill knew that several members of his crew were already liking each other. Chill was in 10th grade. Renee, Stoney and Rob were 9th graders then. They were all in high school and it was time for them to be in *crew* charge. Chill and Renee was the 3rd generations lead couple. Jr and Tonya were a couple and they were in 8th grade. Stoney and Rob was still single but they were already crew, so they were going to the movies without dates. They were already getting eyes from the younger Breanna and Janice, by that time. Janice or Jan was in 5th grade with Ajay. Breanna was in 4th grade. It would be a few more years before they would be a couple with Rob and Stoney. But the girls were already making plans to have Stoney and Rob as their crew men.

Ajay was going to the movies and he was happy to know Ebony was going to be there too. But he wanted more. He wanted her to sit next to him *at* the movie. The 4th grade boys crew of Tank, June and Rich were going and so was the 3rd grade girls of Nina, Ebony, Rebbie and T-baby better known as the foursome. Ajay had gone to Chill's house *early* to pitch his wishes. He needed Chill's help. He wanted Ebony to be seated with him, instead of with the mothers. He knew his crew leader would assist with getting him those ideal seating arrangements.

"Chill I want Ebony to sit with me," Ajay said, "I wanna buy our snacks too. Can you hook that up for me?"

97

"For sho," Chill said and chuckled, "Tonight will be my first time being in charge of my *whole* crew. So I'll make sure you and baby girl sit next to each other. You just make sure you be on your best behavior though. She's a special kind."

"I know she is and I will be," Ajay said and smiled. He added, "She knows I like her. I can tell that she likes me too. She's gonna be like my mama and her mama when she get grown. That's the girl I want and I know that already. Just help me out, big brother."

"I got you, Lil bro," Chill said as he still chuckled, "Don't you even sweat it. I'll even get Arthur to take pictures, if you want."

"Cool," Ajay said and readied himself to head home and get dressed. He got to the door, turned to Chill and said, "I'll see ya."

"In a minute crew," Chill said, "But that crew part ain't official until you're thirteen."

"I got ya," Ajay said, "But I'm doing crew thangs now, so I'm gonna get around that age thing, just like you did."

They laughed loud and Ajay headed home. He had a huge smile on his face. He saw that upcoming movie night as his 1st date with his future.

Ajay wanted to look nice for their movie date. He wore a pair of Levi jeans with heavy starch and creases sharp enough to cut paper. With his jeans, he wore a *Cuugi* golf styled shirt underneath his *Cuugi* sweater. Both gifts given to him by Rebbie's grandparents while they visited for his birthday. It was a clothing line which originated in Australia and the name would change to *Coogi* by 1987. Ajay was the 1st person the crew knew to even wear the brand. But it would become popular with rappers by the late 80's and early 90's. Jeb and Jessie Mae Baker had given him a sizable head start. He accessorized his outfit with a Kangol hat to match and a pair of *Britishers a.k.a. British Walkers* sneakers. He wanted to impress Ebony and he was dressed to kill. He went to his parents room to get some cologne. Al smiled at him as he took him into the master bedroom.

"So you're trying to smell like a man tonight, ha?" Al asked as he chuckled.

"I wanna smell good, pops," Ajay said.

"Well you're looking good, son," Al said, "Shit I might have to change my clothes."

They laughed together as Al pulled out his bottle of *Stetson* cologne and showed Ajay how to properly apply it. After they were both smelling irresistible, they headed downstairs where Jo and the girls were ready and waiting.

"Ajay you take longer to get dressed than we do," Lynn said as she giggled.

"Yea but I look better," he retorted and they all laughed as they grabbed their coats from the foyer closet, then went out to load up in their van.

Ajay was hoping to see Ebony then but her family was already loaded into their car. Within minutes, the rest of crew families pulled up in their cars and they all convoyed to the movie theatre.

When they got to the movie, Chill did his part and sat Ebony next to Ajay. Tank and Nina sat together too. Richie and T-baby sat next to each other, as did June and Rebbie. Chill's crew was seated in the upper tier with the 1st generation sitting around them. Their parents or the 2nd generation sat in the tier just below them, so the fathers could watch everything that moved around them plus in and out of the doors too.

Ajay had gotten a huge tub of popcorn, 2 boxes of Whoppers and 2 large drinks in their favorite flavors. Ebony liked Strawberry soda while Root Beer was his favorite. Before the movie started, he could tell Ebony was happy to be seated with him. She smiled every time she put her hand in the tub of popcorn and their hands touched. He had always found it difficult not to look at her when she smiled. He thought she was the prettiest girl he'd ever seen. And when she smiled, it did something to him that made him feel all tingly inside. She was smiling while Nina whispered something to her. Then she looked at him and found him looking back at her. She blushed and turned away shyly. He figured he'd better say something to her, so she'd know he wasn't upset that she'd looked at him.

"I heard this movie is suppose to be *real* good," he said.

"Me too," she said, "Eddie Murphy is so funny on his tape. My daddy and big Al listen to it in our living room, after we go to bed. I be sneaking to the top of the stairs so I can hear it. He cracks me up."
She giggled and Ajay felt those butterflies in his stomach again. He felt almost nervous, just to be this close to her and there not be a basketball involved. But he liked the feeling he had and he never wanted it to go away.

"You smell good," she said.

"Thanks," he said, "My pops let me wear some of his cologne."

"I like how that smells," she said, "And your clothes are sharp."

"You look real nice too," he said. Then he added, "I hope you're not still mad at me."

"I'm not," she said, "But I do get mad at you when you don't play your best, Ajay. You be trying to let me win. That's not good and I don't

99

like that. Because you're suppose to be teaching me how to play good, just like you."

"I know but I don't wanna beat you," he said and cracked up laughing.

"You can play real good Ajay," she said.

"You can too," he said, "You're getting real good Ebony. I'm gonna help you get good enough so you can try out for the school team when you get to fifth grade."

"That would be the bomb," she said, "Then I can be on the team just like you."

"That's right," he said and smiled at her.

She smiled and looked away. Something told him that she liked him for more than just playing basketball, at that moment. But he wasn't going to ask her. It took her a minute or 2 before she looked back at him.

But when she did, she said, "I don't want you to let me win. Teach me how to play like you play. And you play to win when you play with Tank and them."

"I just don't feel right if I play hard because when I beat you, you're gonna be mad," he said, "And I don't want you to never be mad at me. That's why I don't try to play hard. Cause I don't wanna beat you."

"You might not beat me," she said and cracked up laughing.

He couldn't help but laugh too. He liked that a lot. She had fire and she wasn't a pushover. She spoke her heart and she wanted him to play his best. Even when he played her. She was smiling a lot that night. He had never seen her so happy. He knew she was having fun on their 1st date. He didn't even know if she saw it as a date or not. But he certainly did. He looked over and saw Nina drinking from Tank's soda. He already knew they liked each other and Tank was planning to ask Nina to be his girlfriend. Ajay wasn't nowhere near that point with Ebony. He had to study her for awhile longer to find out everything she liked, before making that move. But she surprised him when suddenly, she asked,

"Can I taste your drink?"

"Yea," he said as he held his cup for her and smiled.

When she sipped through his straw, she was looking into his eyes. He was looking into hers too and his stomach was in a huge knot.

Then she asked, "What kind of drink is that?"

"Root beer," he said, "It's my favorite."

"It taste strong," she said, "You're real strong and you already got muscles too. I guess that's why you like strong drinks."

She giggled. She was enjoying herself. He looked over and saw Tank kissing Nina. Ebony saw it too. She looked at him, then to the movie screen. She had a look on her face that he couldn't read. He didn't know if she wanted him to ask her for a kiss or not. But he wasn't going to pass on the opportunity. He went for broke and whispered in her ear.

"Can I have a kiss?" he whispered.

She looked down at her drink cup. Her face held what he thought was a sad look. She didn't say anything. She just kept staring at her cup. He didn't know what to say after that, so he just started to watch the movie. She didn't answer him.

After a few minutes, he looked back at her and she was watching the movie. Neither of them said anything else about kissing throughout the rest of the movie and they only talked about the movie when they did say something else. He felt bad. He thought he had said something wrong and he didn't know where to go from there. He felt as if he had scared her off. They continued to share their popcorn and watch the movie while they witnessed Tank and Nina kiss several more times. But Ajay didn't dare asked Ebony again.

When the movie ended, she thanked him for the snacks and asked, "Did you like the movie?"

"Yes," he said, "I liked it a lot and I liked it even better that you sat by me too."

"Me too," she said as they filed out of the theater.

Pearl was calling her to come on so they could load up and leave. She turned to Ajay and said, "I had fun. I had a lot of fun."

She smiled. He smiled back and said, "Me too. Sit by me the next time, okay?"

"Okay," she said and rushed to her mother's side.

She watched him the entire time until their car pulled away. He didn't want that night to end. He felt good about the movie date but he didn't know where to go from there.

As soon as they got home Ebony, Nina, Rebbie and T-baby went to Ebony's room so they could talk about their movie experience. Nina's whole talk was about kissing Tank. She also told them that Tank asked her to be his girlfriend and she had told him yes.

"I knew he was gonna ask you," Ebony said.

"I think granny saw y'all kiss *one* time," T-baby said, "But she smiled and told papa to look. Then they both smiled at each other."

"He kissed me *four* times," Nina said as she giggled.

"I saw y'all kissing too," Ebony said, "Ajay asked me to kiss him but I didn't."

"He gonna be mad with you," T-baby said.

"I don't know how to kiss," Ebony said, "That's why I didn't do it."

"I'll bet you Ajay know how to kiss," Rebbie said and the 3 girls giggled but Ebony didn't.

"Yep Ajay know how to do it," T-baby said, "He knows how to do everything. He be wit the big boys all the time and all of them big girls like him too."

"I hope he don't be mad at me," Ebony said as she looked worried, "I don't want that. He didn't seem mad when we left. He asked me to sit by him next time we go to the movie."

"What did you say?" Nina asked.

"I said okay," Ebony answered.

"He's gonna asked you again and next time you'd better say yes," Rebbie said.

"So he won't be mean to you," T-baby said.

"Jeremy like me and my brother like Ebony," Nina said while her, T-baby and Rebbie giggled but Ebony still didn't.

Ebony didn't say anything else after that. She didn't believe he would be mad at her. He had smiled at her before they left. The look on his face did not indicate that he was upset at all. His look said the opposite and he had already told her that he didn't want to do anything that would make her angry with him. She sighed as she pulled out her baby doll and began combing her hair. Her and her girls played in her room until it was time to go to sleep. They were all sleeping at Ebony's house that night.

}Spring Break 1985{

The Johnson beef always seemed to surface when the weather got warmer, so the crew fathers always prepared themselves during the winter. They had been hearing threats from their street contacts. Word was big Jake Johnson was planning to send his gang to Shaker Heights to try and catch 1 of the crew men or their sons, off guard. The fathers knew that wasn't going to happen and big Jake wasn't going to come anywhere near their community. He just liked to sell wolf tickets to anyone who would buy them. But as a precaution, big Paul and the rest of the fathers got their sons together and made sure they knew to stay crew tight, be ready for wherever and stay close to their blocks.

Once the snow started to melt and it was warm enough to play outside, Ajay and Ebony got back to playing basketball together. She had turned 9 years old at Christmas while Ajay was looking forward to his 11th birthday in July. They had seen each other nearly everyday at school, church and home since that movie date. But they hadn't really talked, mainly because Ebony didn't know what to say to him after not giving him a kiss. But he still smiled at her and she smiled back each time. Ajay was still curious about how she felt about him after he asked her to kiss him. He knew she wasn't mad at him though because she still spoke whenever they saw each other. But he had to know if he'd upset her when he asked her to kiss him. So he found a way to ask her while they were playing basketball, 1 spring break evening.

"Did you get mad when I asked you to kiss me at the movie?" he asked.

"No," she said, "Did you get mad at me cause I didn't do it?"

"No way," he said, "I thought you was."

"No," she said, "I wasn't."

"Okay," he said, "I don't ever wanna make you mad at me. Please remember I told you that. Please remember that, okay?"

"Okay," she said and they continued to play ball.

He played a little harder today but still he didn't play his best. And once again, she took him to task about it. He just laughed because he knew he wasn't going to play her like a boy and he liked the way she fussed. She didn't fuss at him like she use to when he didn't play hard. But she had to let him know she wanted his best.

"You still didn't play like you do with the boys, Ajay," she said.

"I know but my mind won't let me," he said, "I always say I'm gonna do it. But when we start playing, I just can't."

She just smiled this time and let him go with that. She was just happy that he wasn't upset with her for not kissing him. She didn't know how to tell him that she didn't do it because she didn't know how.

When they finished with their last game, she just stood there. She wanted him to asked her to kiss him again but he didn't say anything. He just stood there looking back at her.

Finally she said, "Come here Ajay."

He came over to her. Then she moved over by their car sheds, so they would be out of sight of their mothers if they happened to look out of their kitchen windows. She called him over to her again.

"Come over here," she said and he went to her, "Lean down."

He did. When he did, she kissed him, lips to lips. Afterwards, she didn't even look at him. She just took off running and hurried into the side door of her house and left him standing out there alone.

He was caught off guard but he was smiling from ear to ear. He was thrilled by that move. That kiss made his day. She had kissed him and even though she ran away. He knew it wasn't because she was mad. He stayed on the driveways shooting basketball alone, for another half hour. He was hoping she would come back outside but she didn't. He looked up at her window several times but he never saw her there either. Eventually he went inside of his house, smiling the entire way.

He went up to his room and grabbed some clothes, then headed to the bathroom to take a shower. He knew Ebony liked him and most likely, the same way he liked her. That's all he'd ever wanted to know, for nearly 5 years. Now he knew the girl he wanted, most probably wanted him too. He made up his mind that day that he was going to do whatever he needed to do, to make sure she became his girl. He wanted to kiss her again and again and he didn't want her to feel like she had to run away the next time. But it would be another year and 2 months before they would *really* kiss. She had left him yearning to know what a real kiss from her would feel like. That peck on the lips had stirred something in him that he had never felt before, with *any* other girl and he wanted to know more about that feeling.

From that day on, each and every time Ajay was available to play basketball and she could come out and play, Ebony did. Her girls wanted to be where she was, so they were always somewhere around them and so was Tank, June and Rich. The 8 of them officially became a pack with Jb and Lynn in the spring of 1985.

It was also during that same time that Terrell's visits slowed down tremendously. They had been slowing since the death of Al Sr and the argument between big Al and Jessica. Terrell's visits would eventually stop due to the beef Jessica had with Al. And also because of the pressure which was put on Jessica from her husband and Terrell's father, Dr Jonathan Layton. Terrell was devastated by the separation and so was Lynn. But Ajay didn't care, either way. He was still angry with Terrell and he wasn't trying to get over it. Lynn and Terrell had still written each other letters for the last 2 years. But that would eventually stop too. Again largely because of his parents interference.

Dr Layton wanted Jessica to break off her communication with her only sibling, long before their father died but he used the fight between Ajay and Terrell as his reason for insisting on it by 1985. He wasn't going to allow his son to be beaten on by his *thugged* out cousin. That was how Dr. Layton had said it. When in reality, Dr. Layton saw Al and his whole crew as less than him. He'd sought to separate Jessica from her roots from nearly the first day their courtship had begun, back in the late 1960's. Dr. Layton was successful that spring and it would be 11 years before they'd speak again.

By the end of the school year, Ajay was focused on a courtship of his own. He had made it his priority to see Ebony, as often during each day as possible. Though they would sometimes still argue when they played basketball because he would intentionally take it easy on her and let her win. The arguments didn't interfere with their admiration for each other anymore. Ajay knew already that she was his ideal girl and even though Ebony still didn't recognize her feelings and why she felt she had to make sure he was doing his best at everything. She knew she liked him to be around her now. Whenever she had to water Pearl's flower garden. She would ask him to help her with the hose. When she drew pictures in her room or wrote a poem. Ajay was the 1st person she showed it too. He was very proud of that statistic because now she was seeking him out for his help whenever she had outside chores. Or she wanted his approval of something she had done. He felt honored. Before him, Tank had that honor. But Tank didn't mind being 2nd in that line because Ajay was his best friend guy and Ebony was like his twin. Ajay, Ebony, Tank and Nina had started to spend all of their home time together. The 4 of them were inseparable because they lived next door to each other. If Ebony and Tank wasn't at Jo's house. Then Nina and Ajay was at Pearl's. It was the beginning of a beautiful and learning summer break. But all things couldn't stay perfect in the crew's lives.

On the last day of school there was a horrific F 5 tornado in Niles Ohio. It happened on May 31st. One of big John's coworkers lost his home, shed and his entire family of 4, who was inside of the house when the tornado hit with no warning.

All 3 generations of the crew got supplies and food together and loaded it up in John's rig. Al rode in the rig with John. Paul, Greg Sr, Rich Sr and Brian Sr all trailed them in Greg Sr's car, as they went to be hands on support for the town of Niles.

****
105

The beef with big Jake would be back in the forefront before the summer. Big Jake's son Jake Jr had started to send threats, right after the 1st thaw just as his father had always done it. That told the crew that Jacob Johnson III or Lil Jake wasn't going to be any different in the future. But unlike Lil Jake, Jake Jr's threats were directed to big Al and the fathers of the crew. And the father's were inviting him to bring it on, just as Chill and his crew had done with Lil Jake, that day at the gym. The beef was now 3 generations deep, on both sides. Any time a chance to confront the Jake's presented itself. The 2nd generation was always willing to take it on, just like the 1st generation of crew had done it when the beef first started. Al and the fathers were ready to give it to Jake Jr, his father and the grandson too and they made sure the streets knew that. That way, the word would surely get back to the Jake's and their posse. Those loyal to the crew did the duty and made certain that Jake Jr and his boys heard all of the comments from the crew. But even if the crew hadn't heard a word back. They knew that the Jake's knew they were equipped to annihilate them. The crew as a whole had done away with over 50 of Jake's group, over the decades. But somehow big Jake still carried on like he was succeeding. It was almost comical to the crew for him to continue to take loses. Yet he still hadn't given up his vendetta and left them alone. Big Paul had even changed Jake Jr's name in the streets to *Joke Jr* and the rest of his crew picked up on it and carried it. That was especially insulting to the Jake's, partially because it was true. Big Jake was putting together a plot to attack the crew and he was determined that they would loose lives from that new mission.

The weekend of Father's day 1985 wasn't in anyway a typical 1 for the Cleveland crew. It was a weekend where they would take a temporary lose. John was home from the road, for 2 weeks and Pearl had a special day planned for them to spend some alone time. Their youngest son Jesse or Lil man was going to stay at John's brother Greg's house. Jb was going to stay at big Paul's with Chill, which was ideal for him. Tank and Ajay would usually beg to stay at Chill's house but not this time. This time Ajay had told Tank to spend the night at his house so Ebony could spend the night with Nina. Instead of going to her uncle Greg's to spend the night with T-baby.

"I'll get Lynn to go spend the night with Jan," Ajay told Tank, "Because you know they're gonna end up hanging out with Renee and Tonya anyway. And they'll keep them there so late, that they'll have to spend the night. Lynn will be happy with that cause Jb will be over there."

"And Rob will too and that's gonna work out for Jan," Tank said finishing his sentence, "And since Ebony's gotta stay somewhere else besides home…."

"She can spend the night wit Nina," Ajay said, "Because her favorite big brother will be right there to make sure she's okay."

They both laughed and Tank ran back home to let his parents know that he wanted to stay at Jo's and he was going to take Ebony with him, so she could still be as close as possible to home and her room.

Pearl said it would be fine if they spent the night next door. She got their overnight bags ready for a weekend stay while John spent father-daughter time with Ebony.

"So my baby girl is getting pretty good at basketball, ha?" John asked Ebony as she sat on his lap in the living room.

"I am daddy," she said, "Chill use to coach me but now Ajay does. He's really *good* too daddy. But when we play a game. He won't play hard like he do when Tank plays."

"Well he's gotta be a gentleman, baby girl," John said as he chuckled, "He's not gonna make my princess feel bad by beating you. Everybody knows my baby girl don't like to lose, just like her daddy."

"But he don't like to lose either," she tried.

"Baby girl, nobody likes to lose and I sure don't," John said, "Unless it's to your mother. She can beat me anytime and I would still be smiling."

Ebony smiled only because her father was. But she didn't understand what her father meant. She just thought of the image of her parents playing basketball and her mother being able to win. Her and John talked for more than an hour before Pearl came down and said she had the overnight bags ready and was ready to walk with them to Jo's house.

"I'll be right back, daddy," Pearl said to John as she gave him her bedroom eyes, then giggled before she headed out the side door.

"I can't wait," John said as he answered her with seductive eyes.

Pearl took the bags over to Al and Jo's and squared things away with Jo for Tank and Ebony to stay with them for a night or 2. While her and John spent some time catching up on the romance they'd missed out on during his last 2 week excursion. Tank was staying at Jo's house and so was Ebony. They were spending the night with Ajay and Nina. Only in Ajay and Tank's mind, they were planning to make sure Ebony and Nina knew that they wanted to be more than just neighbors.

By 5pm, everybody was done with dinner and settled at the homes where they were staying for the evening. Tank was in Ajay's room while Ebony and Nina were in Nina and Lynn's room. Lynn was already at Chill's house with Renee, Tonya and Jan. Ajay was working on plan 2 and Tank was all for whatever he came up with because he knew Ajay always knew how to get what he wanted. Tank just wanted to make sure he got something out of the deal too.

"Alright, you know they're in there playing with them damn baby dolls," Ajay said, "I can't wait to get rid of them damn things."

"Good luck with that," Tank said, "Every since lady got killed. That's all twin like to do, besides playing basketball wit you."

"It's gonna be my job to change that, just a little bit," Ajay said as he laughed. "But Tank, I'm gonna take my time and you have to take your time too. We can't move to fast for them, cause if we do. Pops and big John will kick our ass and you know it."

"Yep that's true," Tank said, "So what can we do now?"

"Just follow me and remember," Ajay said, "Don't try to do nothing that Nina don't wanna do. Don't even talk about it, if she don't understand what you're talking about. Because if she gets confused about something you asked her. She's gonna ask mama what it means. Then our mama's will know what's up."

"Yea and shut our shit down, for real," Tank said as he laughed.

"Correct," Ajay said, "Let's do this."

Ebony and Nina was playing with their dolls when Ajay knocked on the door.

"Who is it?" Nina asked impatiently.

"Ajay," he said trying to keep his voice low, "Let us come in."
Nina smiled as she went to open the door. She knew Tank was with her brother and she wanted to see him.
"What y'all doing?" Ajay asked as him and Tank entered the room.

"Playing," Nina answered Ajay, "What does it look like we're doing?"

"Y'all playing with baby doll's again, ha?" Ajay asked as him and Tank chuckled.
Ajay and Ebony's eyes met and he smiled at her. She answered him.

"Yes we're playing with our babies," Ebony said to Ajay and smiled back.

"I know I don't wanna play wit no baby doll's," 10 year old Tank said suddenly, "I wanna play wit Nina. Twin why don't you go and play wit

108

Ajay and let me and Nina stay in here and play together, for a little while."

"Well what are we gonna play then?" Nina asked as she smiles. "Because I don't wanna play wit no Ninja Turtles."

But she was obviously interested in whatever game it was that Tank wanted to play.

"I don't wanna play wit no ninja turtles either," Tank said, "But I'll tell you what we can play, if twin go to Ajay's room and let us stay in here and play by ourselves."

Ajay was still looking at Ebony and he was still smiling. But Ebony wasn't smiling anymore.

"Ebony go play with Ajay and let me and Jeremy play together, for a little while," Nina suggested with a giggle, "It'll be okay."

Ebony looked like a deer in headlights. She had never been alone with Ajay before unless they were outside on the basketball courts, playing basketball. Plus she figured Tank and Nina was going to kiss again and she wanted to see them. She wanted to see them, so she could learn how to do it correctly too. Before Ajay asked her to kiss him again. Nina had told her she could watch them kiss and learn how to do it, by watching what they do. Ebony still didn't know that Nina and Tank had already tongue kissed. But Nina was the oldest of the foursome, so she had always insisted that she had to be the first 1 to learn new things. She also felt like she had to be the teacher of Ebony, T-baby and Rebbie. Ebony was okay with Nina's demands where kissing was concerned. She already knew her 1st real kiss was going to be with Ajay, just like the pecks were. She just wanted to know how to kiss him, the right way. But now that Nina was sending her away to play with Ajay, she knew she wouldn't be able to see how a kiss was to be done. Still, she stood up and followed Ajay to his room. Tank stayed in the room with Nina as Ebony and Ajay headed out the door.

Once inside Ajay's room, Ebony sat in the chair next to his lamp table and Ajay sat down on his bed in front of her.

"Are you okay?" he asked.

"Yes."

"I don't want you to be scared to be around me when nobody else is around," Ajay said, "I'm not gonna do anything to hurt you, Ebony. I promise, okay?"

"Okay," she said and she tried to smile but she was nervous.

"I like you Ebony," Ajay said suddenly.

"I like you too," she said.

She didn't really understand the context in which he was speaking of and she always shut down, if she wasn't sure of what she should say. But Ajay tried to explain himself.

"I'm not just talking about because we play basketball," he tried, "I mean, I like you all the way."

Ebony didn't respond because she surely didn't know what, *"all the way"* meant and she was afraid to ask for clarity. But again, Ajay continued to make his point.

"I know we're too young to go together, right now," he said, "But I like you being around me, all the time. Is that a bad thing?"

"I don't think so," she said and smiled. She added, "I have fun when we play together, just like I do with my girls."

He knew she still wasn't getting his point. He wanted to be closer to her, than she was with her girls and he wanted to be more to her than what her girls were to her too. So he went for broke.

"When you kissed me by the shed that day," he said, "I liked it. I liked that a lot. A *whole* lot and I need to know something. Why did you do it?"

"I don't know," she said, "When we was at the movie, you asked me to kiss you but I didn't do it at the movies. I thought you would get mad at me and I didn't want you to be mad at me and start being mean to me. So I just did it."

"I would never be mean to you Ebony," he said, "You're my cutie pie. I always told you that. Even when you wasn't even speaking to me. Can you remember when you didn't ever speak to me and you wouldn't even look at me?"

"I think so," she said.

"Do you remember how I use to show up every time you was around Chill?"

"Yes."

"It was because you always talked to Chill and I just wanted to hear your voice," he said, "I wanted to hear you talk because you never talked to me. Then at Chill's party at the detail shop, you talked to me and you let me play with Lady. I liked that a lot, Ebony."

"You liked Lady too, didn't you?" she asked.

"Yea I did," he said, "But I liked Lady because of you and because I knew she was gonna be around you. She was your dog and you liked her, so much. I wanted to make sure she liked me. Because then you would let me come around you, so I could play wit her."

Ebony smiled. She liked remembering Lady and Ajay scored major points

110

by saying good things about her deceased dog. Ajay just liked that she was smiling.

He continued, "Then when I souped up your bike and you got mad at me. I was so mad at myself because I had messed that up. You stopped talking to me again."

"I know," she said and giggled, "Now I know that my bike wasn't broken. You just made it go faster."

"Ah man that bugged the hell out of me," Ajay said, "Because after that, you use to just stare at me but wouldn't talk again. Why was that?"

"I don't know," she said and she was becoming confused.

She didn't know if he really liked that she kissed him. Or he had felt like she'd invaded his space. To her, he seemed irritated even though he had just said he liked it a lot. Ajay was known for not wanting anyone to push anything on him or toward him, that he didn't like or initiate. He wasn't a very patient person and his entire crew knew that. But she would learn later, that was not ever going to be the case, when it came to her. Ajay was the only person who could ever convey that to her and he was trying too. He wanted her in every way possible but still he was afraid to say that to her. Because her level of maturity on private or intimate matters, was nowhere near his level. He didn't want to say too much or make her feel rushed. He knew Tank was treating Nina like a girlfriend while he was in her room. Ajay wanted Ebony to be his girlfriend that day too. But he knew he had to tread light.

"I just need for you to remember this one thing, okay?"

"Okay."

"I would never be mean to you or hurt you unless you hurt me," he said, "Even when you was mean to me. I couldn't be mean back to you. So remember that for me, alright?"

"Okay," she said with a sigh as if she was relieved, then she smiled.

He saw that she was relaxing a bit more, so he decided to step into some unthreaded water with her.

"Do you think I'm cute?" he asked suddenly.

She definitely thought he was cute but she had never said it to him or anybody else. She had kept that to herself. Now he was asking her if she thought it and she didn't know if she wanted to tell him. She was alone with him and not in public, so she didn't answer him honestly.

"I think you play basketball real good and I don't think you're mean like everybody else was saying," she tried.

"Okay thanks. But do you think I'm cute?" he pressed.

111

"Why do I have to say that?" she asked and he could tell she was beginning to feel uncomfortable again, so he decided to let it go.

"You don't have to say anything or do anything until you're ready too," he told her, "You don't have to answer that question either, okay?"

"Okay," she said and she relaxed again.

Ajay wasn't superficial at all. He never cared about someone liking him because of how he looked. He wanted them to respect him for who he was and who he was raised to be. He knew Ebony was the type of girl who could do that and her opinions were always going to matter to him.

After that exchange, she sat quietly while he still sat across from her and stared at her. She was nervous and he could see that. It was because she liked him and he could see that, as well. She just wasn't ready to like him and show it. Not in the same way that he was ready to show that he liked her. He was ready to be all the way open about it, right then. But still he remembered what Chill had always said to him.

'She's still a little girl mentally too. She's not advanced like you are. So just give her all the time she needs. Y'all were born to be together and I know it's going to happen, one day. Just be patient with her.'

So again he said, "You don't have to say or do nothing you don't wanna do and I really mean that, okay?"

After he said that, she didn't answer but just looked at him. She found him giving her a huge smile. She was 9 and he was about to turn 11 and already they were learning to understand certain things about the other ones mannerisms. He realized they had time to get to the point of where they could both express their inner feelings about each other. He knew he wanted her to be completely relaxed around him and never feel like she had to be afraid.

He decided not to pressure her for an answer about how she thought he looked or in what ways she liked him. But he did want her to kiss him again, so he asked.

"I do wanna know if you will ever kiss me again though," he said.

She leaned into him and gave him a peck on the lips, the same way she'd done out by the shed, weeks back. But this time, she didn't run away. She sat right there in that chair. He was shocked but he liked it.

"Do it again," he said and she did.

He kept asking her to kiss him and she did, each time he asked. At that point, he was the person who was confused.

He smiled and shook his head. Then he said, "I can't believe you'll kiss me

112

that many times but you can't tell me if you think I'm cute enough for you."
She didn't say anything. She just sat there. That was just young Ebony's
way. Whenever she wasn't sure of what to do or say. She just shut down
and didn't respond. She figured he had to know that she would never kiss
an ugly person. Ajay was only beginning to learn that about her. But he
wanted to know everything it was to know about her. He also wanted her to
know that she was the 1 person who motivated him to voice his feelings and
not let anyone gather the wrong conclusions about him. On that day, he
became determined that he would be the same thing for her.
"I know you don't wanna say anything right now and you don't even have
too," he said though he wasn't going to give up until she told him.
"I think I know how you feel and I know how I feel and that's a fact."
Suddenly she kissed him again. Still just lips to lips but she held it there for
5 seconds or longer before she released. During the kiss, Ajay put his arms
around her, pulled her up from the chair and closer to him. He wanted to
try a tongue kiss. While they were still lips to lips and he was hugging her,
he opened his mouth and let his tongue touch her lips. She pulled away. She
had a very confused look on her face. He had to say something right then.
"I'm sorry," he said, "I just wanted to know what a real kiss felt like. I've
never had a real kiss before either."
She didn't say anything. She just continued to stare at him with a confused
look on her face. He wasn't sure what to do, at that point. He didn't know if
he'd frightened her, angered her or what her emotions were at that
moment. But she was still there. She still hadn't run away. The problem for
Ebony was that she knew she didn't know how to tongue kiss and she
figured if she tried to do it and it was wrong. He would know it and not ever
try to kiss her again. She didn't want to disappoint him with a bad tongue
kiss. She would rather him be disappointed that she didn't do it at all. But
she remembered he had said, she didn't have to do anything until she was
ready too. So she finally said, "I don't wanna do that right now."
"Okay. That's okay," he said.
Right then, she figured Tank and Nina must had already graduated to
tongue kissing since the movie because Ajay and her brothers were always
in some sort of competition with each other. She figured Ajay wanted to
tongue kiss her, so that her twin wouldn't have anything over him. But she
didn't know how too and she wasn't willing to risk doing it wrong.
Something else she didn't know, was Ajay didn't know how to tongue kiss
either, not from experience. He had never kissed a girl that intimately. He
had never even wanted to be that intimate with any of the girls he'd had

113

sexual contact with. He was saving that first for Ebony, the only girl he saw as worthy of him giving his intimate side too. But now he had to figure out how to get her back to kissing him, lips to lips.

"I won't do that no more until you're ready too, okay? Just please don't stop kissing me," he pleaded.

"I won't," she said quickly.

That was a relief to him and he wasn't going to push her any farther, that day. He just wanted her company and her attention and he already had both. He decided to leave well enough alone, at that point. He figured he would find something else that the 2 of them could do in his room, to give Tank more time to spend with Nina. He was going to take his time with Ebony because he knew without a doubt, she was worth the wait.

"You wanna listen to some music?" he asked suddenly.

"Yes," she said, "I like the one you play all the time. I can hear it when I'm in Nina's room."

"The Isley's Brothers?" he asked in surprise, "Are you trying to tell me that you like them too?"

"Yes I like them," she said, "They sound good. My daddy play them too, just like big Al do."

"Well alright, so what's you're favorite song by them?" he asked, "Cause I'm gonna play it right now."

"I like the one where they be singing, "I'll always come back to you," she said and smiled.

"That's Voyage to Atlantis and I love that song," he said, "That's my favorite one too."

He forwarded the tape until he found the song and then he let it play. She smiled as soon as it came on and he smiled too. They had just found out that they had a favorite song in common, to go along with basketball and Lady.

Suddenly she said, "My mama and daddy always dance to this song."

He figured he would see where she was going with that statement, so he asked, "Do you want too?"

"I don't know how-"

"Don't worry," he said as he interrupted her, "I don't know how to dance either. But we can practice it in my room. One day, we'll both know how to dance real good. Then we can show everybody else how to do it."

She smiled. She thought that was a great idea. It was on that day that her and Ajay started to slow dance together in his room.

From that day on, they would start meeting in his room every chance they could get, so they could practice and perfect their slow dancing.

114

That was the same way they had done outside on the court with basketball. They would eventually graduate to not only a real kiss with tongue. But they would get to the intimate side as well. Including what Ajay would later tell her was, *"The Real Thing."*

Chapter 6-Passing Of The Legacy

Ajay and his son sits down for their talk today. Lil Ajay is still anxious to know more about how his daddy's life had been, from a sexual standpoint because he knows his mother wasn't the source of his intimacy relief, in his earlier years. He has heard about several girls, so far. But not those that Bruce's crew talked about. Ajay assures him right away that he isn't going to leave anything out. He's going to fill him in, year by year or day by day, if that's what it takes. Because he's determined they'll have the same bond that he has with *his* father. Lil Ajay loves hearing about how his parents relationship started and grew. He also loves how open and honest his father is being with him about his childhood too. But he still has many questions.

"So uncle Tank and auntie Nina started before you and mama did ha?"

"Hell yea," Ajay says as he laughs, "They always have been faster than me and Ebony, when it came to getting to shit with each other. Your mama and me, we moved slower than they did. But we got it completely right along the way. At least, *we* feel like we did and so does the first and second generations."

"Nana Jo and Nana Pearl didn't even know you liked my mama," Lil Ajay says and laughs, "Why you didn't tell them?"

"Because certain things in this family are set up to go a certain way," Ajay says, "The fathers are the ones who we had to take our orders from, when it came to the girls in this crew or any girl that we wanted to bring into this crew."

"So did papa Al and papa John know you liked her?"

"They knew I would and they wanted me to like her, son," Ajay says, "They just made sure I was moving according to *their* plan. Which was hard as fuck to stick to later on, when Ebony wanted to be with me and be open and free about our relationship. But we're gonna get to all of that. Let's just take it one year at time, so I can make sure that you get the full picture. I want you to get this right the first time, son. Because I know you're about to start getting with girls, a lot. I just wanna make sure you know the signs to look for and what to avoid, like I said before. Because the girls always seem to think they're in charge. But if it's not the girl that you want. Then she won't be in charge of shit. Only my Ebony gets her way and that started from day one."

"I like how you treated my mama," Lil Ajay says, "You was taking care of her when y'all was little. You was always like that, ha pops?"

"I made some mistakes a long the way and that's for sure," Ajay says, "But I always gave Ebony *her* way. As long as she wasn't headed for danger, I let her have her way. Because I knew she was a prize, way back then. I had to have her, just for me. I knew I had to find a way to let her know and understand the way I looked at her, what I saw in her and that the way I felt about her was a *totally* different feeling then I had for anybody else in the world. She was like magic to me. Everything she touched was brighter or golden. Even me. Your mama made me wanna be my best, son. And at the same time, she made me demand the best from her. We just clicked."

"And that was a slick move, the way you got her to start dancing wit you."

"It *was* pretty smooth, now that I look back on it," Ajay says and smiles, "But I wasn't even trying to run no game. I just didn't want her to leave my room. And son, if any girl was going to get me to take an interest in dancing. It was gonna be your mother."

"Did y'all learn how to dance?" he asks as he starts to chuckle and sounding just like Ajay did, at his age.

"Oh yea we got it right," Ajay says as he chuckles too, "You see us dancing around the house. We perfected it. I wanted to learn how to slow dance. That was the only way I felt comfortable trying to touch her, back then. And she let me touch her when we danced. Hell, she even asked me to hold her tighter after awhile and you know I was *to* honored to do that."

They both laugh hard before Lil Ajay starts to ask more questions.

"So when did you get her to kiss you with tongue?" he asks.

"That was still another year away," Ajay tells him, "Your mom was very innocent and I loved that about her. I still love that about her, to this day and I don't ever want that to change. I want all five of your sisters to be exactly like your mother, when it comes to holding onto their innocence. Ebony played with baby doll's a lot but I wanted all of her attention. I didn't wanna rush her at all son because as I said, I could already see us where we are right now. With a nice home and a big family. I just had to figure out how to get myself to the status where I deserved her and where I wouldn't feel guilty after she gave in to me and wanted to be with me, all the way."

"That girl Malaysia, she deserved what she got," Lil Ajay says, "She was about to get you killed over her."

"Yea she did deserve it," Ajay answers quickly, "Son, the Johnson beef is real and I'm gonna make sure you know about it and that you know to be careful whenever you're out and about."

"He wanted to kill you and my mama?" Lil Ajay asks.

"Oh yes but that started with your great grandfathers," Ajay tells him, "Basically because they wouldn't take care of him and his household. Son, the only way you can ever call yourself a man. Is if you're doing what a man is suppose to do and that's being responsible for your family. You are not a man until you can feed your mama. Never look for anyone else to do that for you. You have to *be* the man. You can't just claim to be a man."

"I'm glad the chamber is still there," Lil Ajay says.

"Yes it is," Ajay said, "And it's been upgraded so much since I was your age. Every time we made more money. We invested it in ourselves and our families safety *first*. The chamber will always be there until there are no enemies left. And I'm gonna keep telling you that until you stop asking because I'll know that you got it."

"There's always gonna be enemies, pops," Lil Ajay said, "I know that already."

"You're exactly right and it's up to the men in this family to be protectors of everybody and everything that we hold dear," Ajay tells him, "You come from that, son. Strong men, who don't take no shit and we don't spare any lives when it comes to keeping our women and children safe. That is the first thing I want you to commit to your memory."

"Okay and pops, I wanna take big Jake out," Lil Ajay says suddenly, "I'm not gonna let him hurt my family. He wanted to kill you and my mama. I could kill him, right now."

"You sound just like I did, back then," Ajay says, "But Chill and me, we said when we had sons. We was gonna teach y'all and make sure that big Jake don't live pass y'all childhood. Kenny is already an adult, so it's time. Kenny has been waiting on you."

"Big Jake caused his grandmother to die and his grandfather too, didn't he?" Lil Ajay asks.

"Yes he did but big Jake won't live to see you turn thirteen and get initiated into the crew," Ajay says, "That's already set and it will happen before you reach double digits. We were just waiting for you to get some age on you."

"I'm six and I'll be seven this summer," Lil Ajay says, "You taught me how to shoot already and I'm getting real good at it too."

"Yes you are," Ajay said, "And soon, you'll be experiencing sex too and you know what I've already told you about that."

"Don't love them ho's," Lil Ajay says and they crack up laughing before he says, "I listen to everything you tell me, pops. Hearing how your life was, makes it easy for me to understand and know how to move."

"Honesty is the best quality in a man," Ajay says, "If you're not honest. You can never have a woman like your mother. No matter how bad you think it is. You always have to tell your main girl the truth. If not, it'll just come back later on and cause major problems. My grand daddy drove that point home with me. Big Al senior didn't play no lying shit from *nobody*."

"I wish I could've met him," Lil Ajay says, "But I can promise you this. Big Jake will not take you, my grandpa big Al or no more of my family. Lil Chill can't wait to get him because he took his grandma and grandpa."

"He did," Ajay says sadly, "And he's the reason Orian and her twin brothers great grandparents haven't moved back stateside yet."

"He's a snake," Lil Ajay says.

"He's less than a man," Ajay says, "After he caused Chill's mother to wreck her car. Your grandpa Al and his crew took out fourteen of his crew. That still wasn't enough for him to back the fuck off. He still came back. He tried to kill five of our fathers at one time, in nineteen eighty eight."

"That's when Kenny's grandpa got shot up and he died later?"

"Yes, sort of," Ajay says with anger showing on his face. He says, "But it started a few years before that. He had more than twenty guys to jump both your grandfathers and your uncle Richie. They got him back though. His son died and several more of his posse. I went on that run."

"Tell me about that," Lil Ajay says.

"Fasho."

Summer 1985

It was 1 of Big John's weeks to be home. Ebony always loved when her daddy was home because she got a gift, every time. He spoiled her like a princess and she loved it. She was his baby girl. He was the person who *gave* her that nickname and that was what he called her. He rarely called her by her name. John would take Pearl shopping each time he was home. And every time he bought her mother a gift. He bought Ebony a gift as well. He raised her to know and believe that her mother was a treasure and so was she. He had long told her that 1 day, there would be a man in her life that was suppose to see that in her and take her, as his own. And John always

119

told Ebony he would see to it that *that* guy treated her the same way that he treated her mother.

"You are a gift to us," Big John said, "And that is how I will always demand that you be treated, baby girl. No boy is going to call my daughter his girlfriend or his wife. Unless he can treasure you the same way that your mother and I do, okay?"

"Yes sir daddy," she said and smiled.

John had a special weekend planned for him and Pearl and it would start on the following night which would be Friday. They shared a special weekend or 2 nights alone, every time John was home from the road. For their alone time *this* trip, Tank was going to stay with Ajay. But Ebony was going to spend the night at her uncle Greg's house with T-baby. Their mothers had already planned for Nina and Rebbie to go over there too. Though Ebony and Nina wanted to stay at Nina's house again. Pearl and John had already decided the sleeping arrangements and it wasn't going to be compromised.

That afternoon prior to date night, John was going to hang out with Ajay's father Al and Al's brother-in-law Richard Sr. He was Jo's younger and only brother. They were going to a little spot off of Brook Park road called *The Landmark*. John and Al had planned to have a few beers while they talked with Richard about the way he had been treating his wife Anna. Richard had been suffering from a drug problem which had started in his teens and lasted for over a decade. Over that time period, he was both domestically and verbally abusive to Anna frequently. That was something that none of the men in the crew was ever going to be okay with. Al had taken the initiative and talked Richard into going to rehab once and he went. Al saw that it had worked then, so being the brother-in-law and the closest to Richard, he had asked John to come along to assist in trying to talk Richard into going back into the treatment for a longer stay.

Al drove his car with John riding shotgun. They picked up Richard from Debbie and Brad Sr's house, around 2pm and headed out. Poppa and big mama was flying in from Houston in a few hours and the 3 men were going to pick them up on the way back to Shaker Heights. They got to The Landmark and went in. Before they could even sit down and order the 1st beer, they already had the females attention. John and Al were okay with being cordial to them. But Richard was conversing with them like he was ready to take it further than just drinks and talking. John and Al warned him about his activity and that he was a married man, still even though they was separated. But Richard became defensive after Al and John told him

120

not to lead any of the ladies on. While they was trying to settle that confusion, more than 20 men rushed in the front door and ran straight for them.

At Jo's house, Tank and Ajay was on the phone to T-baby's house. Rich and June had come over to Jo's and joined them and they were all talking to the foursome. The boys were making plans to go visit all 4 of them. T-baby only lived 2 blocks away. So the 4 of them headed out the side door and down the street.

At T-baby's house, the foursome was giddy from both nerves and excitement. Ajay and the boys was on their way and all 8 of them were going to play outside together. T-baby had her own basketball goal on their driveway by then and she had her own basketball too.

"So we're gonna play them?" 8 year old Rebbie asked.
Her and T-baby wouldn't turn 9 until later that summer. T-baby already loved to try and play basketball. But Rebbie and Nina wasn't interested in that side of the sport at all.

"Yes we're gonna play," T-baby answered, "And it don't matter that y'all wanna be cheerleaders. You can still play wit us, so we can have four on each team."

"Rich and June can't play either," Nina said and laughed, "Ajay can play and Tank too. Ebony know how to play, so T-baby y'all four can't be on the same team."

"Okay," T-baby said, "I want Rich on my team though."

"Good cause I don't," Nina said and her and Rebbie laughed.
Ebony hadn't said anything yet because she knew her and Ajay wouldn't be on the same team. Only because she was the best girl player and he was the best boy player.

"Ebony and Ajay should be captains," Rebbie suggested, "And they can pick who they want on their teams."

"That's cool I guess," Ebony said.

"Let's go outside and get some practice in before they get down here," Nina said and all 4 of them headed out the door.

Within a few minutes, the 4 guys were there and ready to play with the foursome.

"So all four of y'all are gonna play basketball?" Rich asked as he laughed.
He was trying to crack wise on the girls but Ajay stepped right up and said, "Ebony and T-baby play better than you cousin. You can't rip on them."

121

Everybody laughed and Rich looked dejected. But he didn't dare try to challenge Ajay because he had learned by then, not to ever try him.

He just said, "June can't play and Nina and Ree Ree can't either."

"I play better than you," Nina snapped before Tank stepped in to moderate.

Tank said, "Then we'll split y'all up. I'm picking a team and T-baby get to be a captain too. Ebony and Ajay *gotta* be the last picks to keep it fair."

It was settled. Everybody agreed with Tank's plan and T-baby stepped up to pick first. She picked Rich. Tank picked Nina. T-baby picked Rebbie next and Tank picked June. T-baby picked Ajay. Ebony went to Tank's team and they got the ball first. Before Ebony could take the ball out, Ajay had something he wanted to say.

"Ebony they made us go last because we're the best players," he said and smiled.

She smiled and said, "I know we are."

They started to play the 1st game and only got a chance to score a basket each before Greg Sr came rushing out of the house. He told them to pile into his car with him and Sandy, who had already put her young sons Greg Jr and Steven in the car, on the front seat. She was locking up the house so they could all leave while Greg Sr got the 8 bigger kids seated in the back of his Caprice Classic.

"I want the girls to sit on the boys laps," Greg Sr said, "It's a short drive to John's house. But I don't want anybody walking right now."

Of course each of the foursome sat on the lap of the boy that they liked while Greg Sr and Sandy got in, secured the young boys in the front and they all headed down the street.

"Where are we going daddy?" T-baby asked.

"To your uncle John's house," was Greg Sr's answer.

Sandy didn't say anything but all 8 kids could tell that she was on the angrier side of upset. The boys knew instantly that something had happened in their crew. All 8 kids could tell that was going to be a long day, longer night and an even longer weekend.

They arrived back at Jo and Pearl's homes. At first glance, Ajay could tell by the look on the grownups faces that something really bad had happened. Something which would require some male action and he was *too* ready.

Greg Sr and Sandy grabbed their baby boys and hurried into Pearl's house. Tank, Ebony and her girls went inside too. When they first pulled up, Chill and big Paul was already outside in a *patrol* stance. Chill had told Ajay that his mother and father was inside of Pearl's house. Ajay could tell by his expression that Chill was angry and so was his father big Paul. They were pacing around outside and already discussing a plan of action. Ajay went on inside where he saw John, his uncle Richard and his father big Al. He took 1 look at his father and the other 2 men and his blood started to boil.

He said, "I know it's time to ride."

And though he didn't raise his voice, everybody in that house knew he was upset. Ajay knew instantly that they had been in a fight. The women took the girls on into the dining room and left the males in the living room alone. Ajay couldn't hold his thoughts.

"I'm ready for whatever," he said to his father, very impatiently.

"Good because we're gonna do whatever it takes to send them fools to meet they *muthafuckin* maker, *this* weekend," Al said in his usual calm.

He was bruised and bloodied, as was John and Richard. But John was so upset, he wasn't even his usual calm like he and Al were both known to be. John was pacing the floor and pounding his fist into his other hand. He was using language he had rarely used and surely not with hearing distance of their females. As the other fathers and sons filed into the living room, Al and Paul was trying to convince John to calm down long enough to get a plan together for the next day. John wanted to retaliate immediately.

"We're gonna put together our strategy here and now," Paul said, "The same way we always do it. And we'll move at a specific time, tomorrow afternoon."

"Ain't no fuckin *way* I'm gonna sleep on this shit tonight," John said, "You can kill that noise."

He wasn't yelling but it was obvious to everyone in the room that he was highly pissed off. Paul told Chill to get his crew together on their part of the plan and make sure they all knew not to leave their block until it was time to hatch their plan, the following day.

"Okay I gotcha," Chill told his father before gathering Ajay, Tank, Jb, Rich and June and heading to his house across the street where Stoney, Jr and Rob was already arriving with Arthur.

The females had taken the girls and gone to Jo's house at Al and John's request. The ladies knew it was going to be chaotic for the next few hours and they had to be somewhere else while the men and boys talked. Before they left, Paul had assured Pearl that they would make sure John didn't leave home.

Ebony was upset after seeing her daddy plus Al and Richard

123

bloodied and with cuts and lacerations. She was in tears before they could even get inside of Jo's living room for the talk the mothers was about to have with them. Ajay had seen her crying. And though he had to go to Chill's house for their meeting. He made sure she knew he would be back to talk to her until she felt better. She told him thank you, then watched from Jo's window as he walked to Chill's with the guys.

Later after all the plans and talks were done and everyone had gone home. Or in the men's cases, taken shifts to guard the crew homes. Ajay, Tank, Ebony and Nina were seated in Jo's living room having a talk of their own. Ajay felt very affected when he saw Ebony upset. He didn't even understand why he felt like it was his job to make her feel better. But he did. He sat next to Ebony in their living room and gave her a chance to tell him how she was feeling.

"Are you okay now?" he asked while Tank and Nina carried on their separate conversation.

"Kind of," Ebony said, "Why would somebody beat up on our dads?"

"Because they wish they could be them," Ajay said quickly, "Our daddy's are bosses and they have a lot of power. That makes people jealous of them."

"That's just dumb."

"I know it is. But we're ready for 'em," he said, "I just need to know you won't cry no more. It bothers me to see you crying because it makes me wanna go off. So don't cry unless you want me to fight somebody. Our dads are gonna be just fine and this won't ever happen again, okay?"

"Okay," she said and she smiled at him.

"You're already cute to me," Ajay said suddenly, "But when you smile you look like a princess. And I want you to smile, all the time. I was already mad when I saw what happened to our dad's. But then when I saw you crying. I was ready to kill somebody."

"You wouldn't do that," Ebony said innocently.

"Only if I have too," he said quickly and his face was blank.

She had no idea that he had already killed someone. And when the plan for the next day hatched out. He'd be adding another 3 or 4 to that tally. But he wasn't going to put her up on that side of him because he felt like that would surely scare her away again. Besides, that was the men's business and not something they shared with their females. They just did whatever was necessary to make sure the Johnson beef or any other problems, didn't reach their women or their children and homes, in anyway.

"I don't think you're mean enough to kill somebody," Ebony said.

"Nah I haven't killed nobody today," Ajay said in a joking manner. That was enough to satisfy Ebony and to be honest with her, at the same time which was good for him. She laughed at that comment and just assumed that she was right. Ajay left it at that.

"Are you gonna spend the night with Nina again?" he asked with a smile.

"I don't know," she said, "We was suppose to stay over T-baby's house before all that fight stuff happened. Now I don't know if my mama and daddy still gonna have their date night or not."

"If you stay with Nina, then we can have our date again," he said and he was still smiling.

"We can practice our dancing again too?" she asked excitedly.

"Yep."

"Okay," she said, "I'm gonna call and ask my mama."

"Okay cool," he said, "And if she say no. Then you can asked her to let you stay tomorrow night. Our dad's are mad tonight about that fight, so they might want the girls to stay home."

She called to asked Pearl if she could spend the night and sure enough, her mother said she had to stay at home. Pearl told her that both sets of her grandparents were coming over for dinner and an evening of talking.

"It's gonna run late and it'll be past your bedtime before we're done talking," Pearl said.

"Okay mama," Ebony said, "Then I wanna stay the next night, if that's okay."

"I'm sure it'll be okay but baby girl, we have to ask your daddy first and make sure he says it's okay. And make sure he doesn't have other plans for us, okay?"

"Okay mama," she said and they hung up.

She relayed the info to Ajay, Tank and Nina. Ajay nor Tank seemed surprised. Ebony and Nina didn't know the men's plan would be unfolding, early the very next day.

"I have to stay at home tonight," Ebony told Ajay.

"It's okay," he said, "Just ask her tomorrow until she say you can stay."

"Okay," Ebony said.

It wasn't long before Pearl called back and told Jo to send her kids home and to prepare for the crew talk because the 1st generation was on the way.

The next morning, the men and boys were out of the house early and assembled at Paul's home. They were ready for battle as they double checked their arsenal and handled all last minute changes and preparations.

Renee and Lil Chill was at Jo and Pearl's with the females. Big mama, granny and the ladies were all making a huge family dinner so the entire crew could eat together, after the men were done taking care of their business. All of the girls were helping while the smaller children napped or watched cartoons at either Jo or Pearl's homes.

Ajay was helping Chill and the rest of the young men make homemade tire strips. They also had the job of loading all of the weapons and the extra clips too. The crew men expected more than 30 of big Jake's guys to show up at The Landmark, looking to finish what they'd started. They had caught John, Al and Richard off guard yesterday. But since then, the crew had put the word out on the streets that John and his crew would be back in that bar looking to finish off big Jake and his gang. Just by putting the talk out there in that way, the crew knew big Jake's gang would show up with weapons and plans of shooting them up without ever leaving their vehicles. But the crew was a step ahead of them, as they usually were. Yesterday was a fluke, as far as the crew men being caught off guard was concerned. They had a family issue with Richard and felt they needed to have him in a bar where he'd be more comfortable. Big Paul had told them that soon, they should open their own bar and have security. That way they would be secure day and night and know who's coming, as well. Big Jake had caught them slipping but that wasn't going to be the case today. Today the crew was on point, like normal. Their plan was to wait at the rendezvous spot, 100 yards above the point where big Jake's gang was to meet up. It was several blocks west of the bar. The crew was going into big Jake's side of town to handle this matter and they were prepared to leave every member of his gang dead, before it would be all over.

After everything was prepped for their attack, the men went to their homes to change into what they called their *battle gear*. After John had changed his clothes and was heading down the stairs preparing to leave, he was met at the door by Pearl and Ebony. Ebony had expected him to take her and her mother shopping because that's what he'd always done within 3 days of being home. Pearl was more concerned about the temper he was known to have about matters like his assault, the day before. She was also wondering if they would still have their full weekend date which was suppose to have started that evening. She knew John had been in an

126

impatient mood, all night. He didn't even make love to her because he knew he would've been way too aggressive. Especially after the fight which had already left him bruised and sore. He barely slept and he wasn't in the mood to calm down about the big Jake situation. He was still impatient, as he grabbed his bag and headed to the door. That's where Ebony caught his attention.

"Are you still gonna take me and mommy to get a dress?" 9 year old Ebony asked.

"Baby girl, daddy will take you to the store when I get back," he said, "I've got something to do right now. I'll take you and mama shopping for some nice dresses and shoes too, when I get done. Right now I just have something I need to take care of first. You're gonna stay here and help all the ladies make a big dinner. Then we can all eat together when I get back and the whole crew can go to the mall."

Then he turned to Tank and Jb, who were waiting just off the short hallway which led to their living room.

"Let's go sons," he said.

"Yes sir," both Tank and Jb said as they headed out the door in front of John.

"I wanna go with you too daddy," Ebony said after seeing that her brothers were going with their father, right then.

"I can't take you with me on this trip, baby girl," John said, "You, your mama and your little brother can go with us to the mall, once I get back."

His voice was impatient as he leaned down and gave her a kiss on her forehead. While he was hugging Lil man and giving Pearl a huge hug and a kiss. Ebony went and stood in their doorway. She was watching Tank and Jb. They were already outside by then. They had gone to Jo's side door to meet Al and Ajay, who were coming out to meet up with them. John went around Ebony and on outside of their door. Ebony was now watching Ajay, who had just come out of their house with Al. He looked at her and noticed her watching him. The look in his eyes told her that he liked that. Though he was focused and ready for today's mission, he couldn't wait to get back so they could play ball, dance or talk some more. Or whatever it was she wanted to do with him. She noticed a bulge under his shirt, near his waist but she had no idea what it was. Within minutes, all of the fathers and sons who were going on the caper was there and ready to roll out. They got together at big Paul and Chill's house to cross their T's, dot their I's and make sure everything was fool proof. They loaded up in the vehicles and left

127

shortly after. They were heading out to the rendezvous point to clean up.

They arrived at the cut off point, then laid in wait with a plan to catch big Jake's gang while they were in route to their meeting place. Before their supposed *surprise* ambush at the bar.

In less than a hour, big Jake's gang came down the road. When they got to the mark, the crew hit them with persistence and did major damage. Their plan worked like a charm and they took out a dozen of big Jake's gang on that late Friday morning. They knew they had dealt a major blow to big Jake because his son Jake Jr was 1 of the 12 who was left dead at the scene. That was a huge score for the crew and an even bigger lose for big Jake because 1 of the dead was his *only* son.

Ajay had shot Jake Jr in the legs and left him crippled. Then he watched as his father and big John beat him until he had no breath left in his body. That was exactly the way the crew had planned it. John, Al and Richard was suppose to be the one's who took big Jake's son. Because they were the ones attacked, the day before. They had wanted to take out big Jake's son on that mission, even if they hadn't gotten anyone else. But as it turned out, they got 11 more along with his only son. The mission was completed and the crew man headed back to Shaker Heights victorious. But they knew it was only a matter of time before big Jake would put together another strategy and try again. They planned to be ready.

Ebony was in the kitchen with the mothers and grandmothers, doing the finishing touches on the huge family meal when her father returned. Tank, Jb, Al and Ajay had followed him inside of their house. Ajay was looking to locate Ebony from the time he walked in the door. He saw her standing next to big mama. That was the ideal location as far as Ajay was concerned. Big mama and granny were Ajay's strongest female allies when it came to him and Ebony. Ebony could tell that her dad was in a much better mood, then he was when he left home. When he walked in and peeked into the kitchen, he was smiling which was something he hadn't done since that morning before he was attacked. Tank asked the mothers permission to enter the kitchen and he was asking for him, Jb and Ajay.

"We need to sample some dishes to see if they right," Tank said as he chuckled.

"Come on in here," big mama told him, "I need my young crew to let me know if this macaroni and cheese is ready."

"Oh we can do that, big mama," Jb said as he entered the kitchen with Tank and Ajay and headed straight to 1 of the 3 large roasters of southern styled homemade macaroni and cheese.

Ajay looked at Ebony and smiled. She smiled back.

Then he asked, "You learning how to cook?"

"Yep."

"I want you to ask them to teach you how to make chocolate cake too," he told her, "Then when you learn it. I want you to make one for me."

"You like chocolate cake?" she asked and she was still smiling.

"It's his favorite cake," his mother Jo said, "Ant would eat the entire cake, if I didn't make him save some for the rest of us."

They all laughed.

"Ajay we got *three* chocolate cakes, over there," Ebony said with excitement in her voice, "Me and my girls getting ready to put the frosting on them."

"Cool," Ajay said, "Did you help make those too?"

"Yes."

"I know they're good already then," Ajay said.

Him and Ebony stood there smiling at each other for a few seconds before he walked with her over to where the cakes were sitting. She got started with adding the frosting. Pearl and Jo looked at each other in shock. This was 1 of the first times they could remember Ajay and Ebony being in the same space and they wasn't arguing with each other. It wasn't long before her girls joined her and they added the chocolate frosting to all 3 of the cakes.

After allowing Tank, Ajay and Jb to have samples of some of the foods, the women ran them out of the kitchen so they could start setting up the tables at both Pearl and Jo's homes. Big mama kept Ebony close to her while they did the set ups. She wanted to put a bug in her ear.

Big mama and Ebony always had a very special relationship. Big mama had that same type of relationship with Ajay too. She advised them both and both of them always came to her for advice about what to look for and what to do, to insure that they were on the right path to the best future possible. Big mama was determined to make sure that each of them got it right. She wanted them to find each other. Because she already knew there was something special about each of them that only the other 1 would be able to find.

"You're going to help me today, little Eloise," big mama said to Ebony and she smiled.

"Okay big mama," Ebony said, "I love to help you and granny, every time. I just like to listen to y'all when y'all be talking. Y'all are so

129

smart and y'all know everything. I'm gonna be smart just like y'all."

"Some folks call it wisdom and they say it comes with age," big mama started as she smiled, "But I don't believe age automatically brings wisdom. I think it's the living and the experiences you go through when you're growing up. You have to learn something from everything you go through. And not only that. If you experience something bad in your life, then you'll have to learn what you need to do to make sure you don't have that same experience again, okay?"

"Okay."

"I think the people in your life are some of the best teachers," big mama said, "You can learn a lot by simply observing and being aware of those around you. Like Ajay, for instance. There is something so absolutely right about him. But it takes a very special and acute person to be able to see that."

"He calls me cutie pie, all the time," Ebony told big mama as she smiled.

She wasn't exactly sure what acute meant. But big mama was about to make her aware of where their conversation was headed.

"Well you *are* cute," big mama said and smiled, "But when I said acute. I meant intelligent. It takes a smart person to recognize what's best for them. You and Ajay are very smart and I want the best for both of you. I want the two of you to chose partners in your lives, who want what's best for you also. The only way a person can know what's best for you. Is they have to really know you first. They have to know who you are and what you come from. They have to take the time to learn what you like as an individual too. Then they would have to want to embrace that and nurture it. There's never gonna be another boy who will know you better than Ajay does, baby girl. So remember what I said to you. The only way that a man can ever really love you. Would be that he knows you and what you're about. Then and only then, can he understand what it really takes to make and keep you happy."

"He knows I don't like him to let me win when we play basketball," she said, "He promised me he wouldn't do that anymore. But he still does it. He thinks I'll get mad at him, if he beats me."

"Do you smile when you're winning?" big mama asked.

"Yes ma'am."

"Then that's what he's trying to see," she said, "He wants to see you happy, first and foremost. And that's important. I'll bet that's a very special thing for him to know that he can make you smile. He'll learn how

130

to accommodate you, as he gets older. But for now his worse fear, is of making you angry at him. He doesn't wanna do anything that will make you not wanna be around him or not smile while you *are* around him."

"Okay," Ebony said and she smiled.

She remembered Ajay always talked about her smile and he always said he wanted her to smile. She figured big mama must be correct. That put her in a very good mood. Ebony loved the talks she had with her grandmothers because they could always make the most confusing things or even things she thought she had already figured out, make sense.

****

By the next morning, the police were at all of the crew's homes arresting the fathers and grandfathers. The plan was to charge each of them with multiple murders. Their attorney George Wheeler had been with the family for over 8 years and was a very vital part of the crew, by now. He met the wives at the jailhouse and brought all of the husbands home on bond. None of the boys were charged. The police didn't even believe the crew men, *black men*, could've pulled off such an elaborate caper. They thought surely some rogue cops, on the prejudice side of the law, had killed those 12 men. Big Jake had sent the police to pick up the crew which was something he was always doing. So the police figured this was just more of the beef that's been on record for decades. Though big Jake had started the action with the bar fight, 2 days prior which the crew men had never reported. He still turned around and gave the police the crew names, just like he always did when he lost. He had also told the police that the crew men were dealing drugs. The police had shown up with dogs and search warrants but found nothing. Big Paul was very heavy in the game. But him nor the other men *ever* kept anything in their homes. The chamber was their stash house, as well as their killing floor. Plus they had warehouses in The Grove that was still under Jeb Baker Jr's name by design.

There were many charges brought and most were dismissed for lack of evidence. However, 2 of the crew charges held. Richard Williams Sr was held on an outstanding warrant for robbery and he would have to serve 8 months. Attorney Wheeler was able to swing a deal to get him drug treatment and anger management while he served his time. Chester Lee, Stoney's father, was held on a murder charge for Jake Johnson Jr only. He would receive a 20 year to life sentence of federal time. He would serve out his sentence in a California federal prison. But the fact was, Chester Lee

131

hadn't killed anyone and everyone knew that, even the police. They had fabricated it and then presented the evidence to the district attorney per George Wheeler and the crews specifications. The officer that put the case together was the very same officer who had helped the crew to get Malaysia Fields and the Watts brothers to the chamber, a couple of years back. No other crew men received any real charges behind the melee in Lorain. The police never even showed evidence that they were at the scene. That was because the cop on the crew's parole had it fixed before the mission was ever carried out. Even though Jake Jr had been killed and Chester was headed to prison for his murder. The crews beef with big Jake was nowhere near over.

****

In the late summer of 1985, Ajay and Jb attended their usual basketball camps. Ajay received MVP honors for the 11-15 year old division and he was only 11 years old. That was huge and it officially put his name on the basketball map. That was when he started to gain the attention of not only high schools in the Cleveland area. But he was getting attention from college recruits as well. That's also when big Jake decided he needed to get rid of Ajay.

His grandson Jacob or Lil Jake had informed him that Ajay had beat up Carlos because he was making fun of Ebony. So big Jake figured out that Ebony must be Ajay's girl for the future. Big Jake knew the Watts brothers were dead and gone. He knew the crew had most likely did them in too. But he couldn't prove it. He couldn't even prove they had been near them nor when they actually died. Their bodies still hadn't been discovered, some 2 years later. But big Jake was off on another tangent by then. He wanted to ruin Ajay and he was going to go after his future, in order to do so. Before Ebony was even 10 years old, there was already a plot started to ruin her virtue. Big Jake knew the pride the crew men took in their women being loyal and only for them. So he figured he would start with the next prize of the crew which was Ajay and ruin his future before he could even get started. But once again, big Jake in his haste to sound bad. Had underestimated the crew and their strength. Even though big Jake was still going to go after the fathers. He had now decided that the kids weren't going to be off limits for him either.

"If I'm ever gonna get rid of those muthafuckaz for good. Then I need to start knocking off their next generations," he had said, "That way

132

they'll be weaker when those snot nose bastards get of age."

****

Ebony, T-baby and Rebbie spent the night of Rebbie's birthday with Nina. Since the girls was there, the boys were sure to follow. Rich, June and Tank spent the night with Ajay. Jb and Lynn was at Chill's house with Jan and Rob, who was getting closer to dating each other every week. Ajay didn't even care who else was at his house, as long as Ebony was there. He told Nina to take Rebbie and T-baby into the basement to play. She did just that. Then Ajay sent Tank, June and Rich down there with them. That way, he could have Ebony in his room alone with no one upstairs in Nina and Lynn's room making noise that would get his mother's attention. He didn't want Jo to come upstairs to warn them about too much noise and discover that he and Ebony wasn't in that room with the rest of them. He figured if they went into the basement, then Jo would just yell down at them from the basement door like she normally did it. The other 6 went to the basement to play while Ajay and Ebony was in his room alone.

"Finally we get to be by ourselves, cutie pie," Ajay said.

"I know," Ebony said and giggled, "We haven't danced in two weeks and three days."

"You're keeping up wit it ha?"

"Uh huh," she said, "But I wanna ask you a favor."

"Okay, what is it?"

"Can you call me baby girl and not cutie pie?" she asked.

"But that's what your dad calls you," he said, "Do you think it's okay for me to call you that too?"

"He won't mind," Ebony said.

She was thinking about what her father always said about the boy who was going to be with her and how he would have to treat her. She already saw that Ajay was very protective of her. Because he had beat up Carlos and Rich for bothering her and her dog. So she figured if Ajay addressed her the same way that her father did. Then he would look out for her the same way as her father did too, in all areas. Ajay liked that she wanted him to call her the same name that big John did and he agreed that he would call her baby girl. But he had a favor that he wanted to ask her too.

"Everybody calls me Ajay but I don't want you too," he said.

"Then what do you want me to call you?"

"Well it's like this," he started, "My pops name is Al and

133

everybody calls him Al except for my mama. She calls him Allen. Then with my mom, everybody calls her Jo except for my pops. He calls her Joanna. They call each other by their real names. So for you, I want you to call me Anthony and not Ajay."

She smiled and said, "Nobody calls you Anthony. Not even the news on TV. Not your coaches or nobody. Your mama and daddy call you Ant but not Anthony."

"So will you call me Anthony?"

"Okay Anthony," she said and giggled hard.

"You sound good when you say it already," he said, "I like how you say my name."

"Thanks. So are we gonna dance?" she asked suddenly.

He didn't even answer her. He just smiled really big as he got up and walked over to his boom box and turned on that Isley Brothers tape. He had Voyage to Atlantis already *Qued* up to play. The song started and he reached his hand out to her.

"Come here," he said and she came.

They started to slow dance. He gave her a lips to lips kiss and he held his lips against hers for more than 15 seconds. He was hoping she would part her lips but she didn't. He didn't try to force it either. He just held her and repeated the lip to lip kisses, every few minutes. Finally she spoke.

She said, "I like when you dance with me too. Just like I like when you play basketball with me."

"I like it too, baby girl," he said.

"I like how you say that," she said and smiled very big.

He was trying to keep his answers short at that point because he wanted her to do most of the talking. He was where he wanted to be and doing what he wanted to be doing and that was anything that Ebony was apart of. And the best part about all of it was she was talking and she was comfortable.

"This is my favorite song," she said, "Is that weird?"

"No."

"I asked you that because the Isley brothers are old men and I'm not even ten years old yet," she said and giggled.

"It's my favorite song too, baby girl," he said, "So what if you're just nine. I'm only eleven."

"You seem older than that Anthony," she said, "You act like big Chill to me."

"Why do you say that?"

"You treat me like a big girl," she said looking up and into his eyes.

"I don't see you like a baby," he said, "I told you before. I really like you and in a different way then it is with anybody else that I've met."
She smiled and said, "I'm not a baby but I don't know a lot of stuff yet. I'm just glad you're nice to me and you don't try to make me feel like I'm slow. Everybody act like I don't know anything. I do know some things."

"I like you just like you are, baby girl," he said, "I'm just trying to learn how to make sure that I show you that. You don't have to change nothing about yourself. You don't have to try to be bigger than you are now or older either. Just be you. Because that's who I like."
She smiled and held onto him until the song ended. He didn't want that moment to end so he rewound the song and they started to dance and kiss lips to lips, all over again. They did a lot of smiling and she still did most of the talking. Ajay didn't want that time to end. He thought about introducing her to a different type of touching. But he had just told her that she didn't have to change anything about herself. So he decided to just move at her pace for the entire evening.

They had a great time until they heard the other 6 crew coming back up the stairs. He knew it was time for bed. In his mind, he wished Ebony could sleep in his room with him but he wouldn't dare say that. He knew he wouldn't be able to control himself, if she was laying next to him. He wanted to progress into that slowly and give her mind and body time to get to that point as well. He knew right then that their special time would come eventually. Because he was going to spend every moment he could with her. He was going to make sure she knew he wanted to be with her in ways he had never been with anyone else in his life. He wanted to love her the way his father loved his mother.

By the fall of 1985, Ajay was in 6th grade and playing basketball on the 9th grade team. That was also about the time that big Jake went into overdrive with his focus on taking his young life, as revenge for the lose of his own son. It surely wasn't hard for big Jake to get news on Ajay because he was making the local news, 3 days a week. Also with Ajay being a 6th grader and playing for the 9th grade team. That brought on a bigger influx of 9th grade girls and females even older than school age. But there would be 1 older woman who'd come into Ajay's life during this time that would never seem to find her way out of it. Her name; Darlene Casey.

Darlene was a substitute teacher at Abe Lincoln middle school during Ajay's 6th grade year and it wouldn't be long before Ajay would make sexual contact with her, even though she was 10 years his senior. But the situation that would eventually happen between Darlene and Ajay didn't exactly start with her having interest in Ajay. Darlene was going after big Al initially. But Al made it clear to her before the school year was even 3 weeks old that he wasn't interested in fucking around with her nor was he going to fuck her either. He let her know that he was happily married and he was only going to fuck his wife Joanna. But what he did do was put 16 year-old 11th grader and 3rd generation crew leader, big Chill in charge of Darlene and her advances. Al figured if she was that ready to fuck a married man. Then she would fuck a teenager too. He also had no doubts that she would eventually fuck his 11 year-old son because if she was going to be near Chill for long. She was going to honor his crew. Big Al was absolutely correct. The way Darlene's eyes lit up when he told her he was only there that day to check on his son who was in 6th grade. Left him pretty sure she would be willing to fuck an extension of him. After all, Ajay was single and Al wasn't. Ajay wasn't legal but he was fucking like he was and he had been consistent in his sexual progress for more than 3 years.

When Darlene learned about big Chill, she set her sights on him immediately. Chill was only 16 but just like Ajay, his maturity level was years beyond his age. Darlene was 21 and she had already heard a lot about Chill through the Cleveland street scene and from many of the students at Abe Lincoln. The students who had spoke on him, spoke very highly. Most of them was infatuated with the whole crew movement. They knew it wasn't gang life but more of a family thing. They also knew the crew was making moves daily which even those in gangs admired and respected. That was enough to let Darlene know that the crew thing was the move she needed to make. She had to find a sure fire way to be connected to it. Whenever she heard a student speaking about the crew, she got in the conversation and she would ask for more details. Before long, she knew the names of all the students at Abe Lincoln who were members of the crew. And still, just on their impressive reputation alone, Darlene wanted membership. But according the girls she asked. The only way to get into the crew was to fuck the guys who were in the crew.

"That's the only way to be in the crew, Miss Casey," a student named Tamara told her.

Tamara was in 8th grade and she had already been with Jr. Though she wasn't in the crew, she always bragged to others that she was. Only because she had been sexed by a crew male. The fact was Tamara wasn't crew. She was a *crew thang* and many girls held that title at Abe Lincoln, MLK, Smith

136

High and every other school in the city and the Tri-State area. Darlene didn't feel her ability to fuck a crew male was going to be a problem. She was older than Tamara and the other students. And she felt like she had more to offer because she had a job, a car and an apartment too. However, she wasn't very smart because she let on to some of the girls that she was about to throw her hat into the crew ring.

Lynn, who was in 7th grade, found out about Darlene's talk. As soon as she found out Darlene was planning to get involved with Chill. She passed that info on to Renee, who was a 10th grader at MLK.

"She's a sub at Abe Lincoln and she talking about she's gonna fuck big Chill," Lynn told Renee.

"And I'm gonna fuck her ass up too," Renee said, "Every which way but loose."

"Just let me know when we get to stomp that ass," Lynn said.

"Fasho," was Renee's reply.
She was use to outside girls who may or may not have fucked Chill and his crew. But they were always staking some kind of claim on them. She was ready and waiting for Darlene to surface, so she could get what she really had coming to her.

Darlene started to ask around for information about how she could get in contact with Chill. She was already familiar with a female staff member at MLK high school where Chill was attending and she was sure that staff member would know him. If she didn't know Chill, then Darlene figured that Chill wasn't anyone to know. The staff member whom Darlene knew, was a teacher named Debra Wittman. Wittman was into her student teaching phase during that time which would last for 2 years. Afterwards she would be on her way to becoming a full fledge member of the faculty. Darlene contacted Debra immediately to learn more about Chill. She found out that not only did Debra Wittman know Chill but she knew him well. She was already sexing him and she liked it a lot. She also made Darlene aware of Renee who was his live-in girlfriend. But she still told Darlene that she would hook something up for her.

"The best way to get your name into their heads is to go to their events," Debra had told her, "They're known for their parties and cookouts and they have a lot of pull and know a lot of people. More importantly, they are known for being powerful and some damn good fucking dick layers." Darlene squealed with laughter and yelled, "Get me in!"

"Bet," Debra told her and that's exactly where her work started. The first thing Debra did was brought Darlene with her to a crew party.

Renee and Tonya knew Debra had been sexual with their guys but crew parties was always the place where those types showed up, no mater which generation was hosting it. Debra, just like many of the *crew thangs,* used that to her advantage. Crew parties and cookouts were damn near open to the public because many people made plans to attend them. Darlene was happy to finally be apart of the mix, as she started to quickly introduce herself to those she thought were crew affiliated. Renee and the girls never allowed her to get near them. They just watched and took notes. It was from that point on that things would start to get very hairy for Darlene Casey. She felt like she could get inside of the crew circle. She wanted to be all the way down with them. She was already proclaiming that she would be attending every function they would have and bring her younger cousin Gloria along, since she was Chill's age. That was probably her 3rd blunder.

She showed up for her 2nd crew party, the Halloween party in 1985, and that's where the shit first hit the proverbial fan for her, as far as the crew females were concerned. And things would only get progressively worse, from that point on. Big Paul hosted the house party. Debra, Gloria and Darlene attended. That was when Darlene decided to make her move on big Chill. She did it in sight of everybody.

"They call you big Chill, right?" Darlene had asked.

"Yea they do," Chill answered.

"What's the name about?" she asked, "Is it to let women know that you're gifted?"

She giggled and before long, Gloria who was standing right next to her got in on it too.

"That could be seen as bragging, you know," Gloria said with a flirtatious giggle and eyes to match.

She knew Chill from the high school scene and she knew he was very popular. She had always wanted to get with him but she knew he had a girlfriend who was *bout it,* so she had kept her distance. Chill was only vaguely interested in them and only for money purposes.

"My grandfather gave me that nickname," Chill told both of them, "It's gonna stay. You can take it to mean whatever you want it to mean. But I handle mine though. Business or personal. Just make sure you know that."

"I would like to know more about the personal," Darlene asserted, "I've heard some good things about you and yes. I did check around after hearing them. The word is that you are the one to get to know better."

"Well what the fuck you waiting on?" Chill asked, "I see you got

138

Wittman with you plus this new chick here. Go get a room and let me know the room number. I'll fuck the shit outta all three o y'all."

"We already got a room," Darlene told him, "Debra told us to have one on standby, in case we scored some crew dick tonight."

"What's the room number?" he asked.

"One thirty nine."

"Where's the extra key?" he asked and Debra Wittman gave it to him. Then he said, "I'll be there in an hour and I'm bringing some of my crew brothers wit me. If y'all truly want some crew dick. Then you've gotta be willing to get all that's available."

"Bring it on," Darlene said.

"We'll meet y'all there in an hour," Chill said and he walked away leaving the 3 of them standing there giggling seductively.

Lynn and Tonya witnessed the key passing but they didn't hear the room number. They went straight to Renee and told her what they'd witnessed. Renee knew she wanted to foil their attempts. The first thing she had to do was find someone to drive her to the motel and she knew who she was going to call.

Renee called Brenda and Rena, the youngest 2 mothers from the 2nd generation. They had been telling her since the day they knew she would be inducted into the crew, that whenever she needed assistance with *crew thangs,* not to hesitate to call them. Brenda picked up on the 1st ring and told Renee not only would she drive her to the motel. But she would pick up Rena and bring her along too.

"You just be ready," Brenda told her, "Get Tonya and Lynn to come with you. It's three of them, so I want three young ladies. And don't you worry Renee. Whatever the three of y'all can't handle. You can best believe Rena and I will."

"Okay," Renee said, "We're ready and we're waiting."

Chill had gotten Paul's car. Him, Stoney, Jr and Rob was already at the motel and they had brought Ajay with them. They were an hour and 45 minutes into the session before Renee and the females had even left Shaker Heights. Chill had done all 3 and shared them with the guys. Ajay had gotten head from all 3 but he hadn't fucked either 1 of them. He didn't want too either. Gloria acted as if she didn't know he was 11. But both Darlene and Debra Wittman made it known that they were aware.

After seeing the size of his dick, Darlene wanted to fuck him just to see if he knew what to do with it. Debra did also but she was already having the older boys on the regular. She had plans of getting to Ajay too, once he got to high school. Darlene wanted him then and she made her advance.

"I wanna know what you can do with this," Darlene said after she was done sucking him off. She asked, "Have you ever fucked a real woman before?"
Ajay didn't answer her. He just stared at her. He had never fucked a female who was a decade older than him, so he was a bit nervous. At the same time, he was thinking of what all he could get her to do for him, if he was to allow her the fantasy that her eyes was telling him she obviously had.
"Well have you?" Darlene pressed before Chill stepped in and told her to back off.

"If he ain't ask to fuck you. That means he don't want too," Chill said, "Believe me. If he wanted to fuck you, he would've."

"Well anytime he wants to fuck," Darlene said with seductive grin, "Make sure you bring him to me."

"We'll see about that," Chill said, "But we about to get up outta this bitch."

"No shit," Jr said before there was pounding on the door.
Stoney peeped through the peep hole and then started shaking his head and chuckling before he said, "Too late."
He had just looked out, saw Renee and company and he could tell they were ready for war.

"Open the fuckin door, Kenny!" Renee screamed, "I know you're in here!"

"You too Brad junior!" Tonya screamed, "We know y'all got them old ho's in there! Open the damn door, so we can get ours too!"

"I'm ready to kick some ass!" Lynn yelled, "I know my brother is in there too. Open the door! I know y'all ain't scared crew!"
Inside of the room, the older teens were laughing but the ladies wasn't. Ajay just stood back and waited to see what Chill would do. To his surprise, Chill opened the door and stood back out of the way. Renee, Tonya and Lynn hurried in and went straight to work. They tied up with Debra, Darlene and Gloria. The 2 older women were only slightly too much for them but Rena and Brenda evened that up quickly. The 5 of them kicked ass until they were out of breath and energy.

Finally Chill, Jr and Stoney brought the fight to a halt. Renee and Tonya wasn't nearly ready to be done and neither was Lynn.

"I know y'all ho's didn't think we wasn't gonna get up in that ass!"
140

Renee yelled as she pointed at Chill and said, "This man right here is mine! So you best know anytime you're fucking him. You're fucking wit me!"
She was still trying to get around Chill but he wasn't going to allow that to happen. He already knew he would have to find someway to smooth this over with his girl and it was going to take something major.

****

After that night at the motel, things were tense between Chill and Renee plus Jr and Tonya, for a few days. Chill and Jr was doing everything possible to and for Renee and Tonya, just to stay on speaking terms with them. They had to find the calm and that was the only demand big Paul made. Them not getting along would've left the household in unrest because Renee lived with Chill and Paul and so did Tonya. Jr was there so much it was like he lived there too. The 4 of them did manage to get things settled and back to normal but that took a couple of weeks. Once things were calm, Chill swore off of Debra, Darlene and Gloria forever. He didn't want to ever see that look on Renee's face again. He really loved her and planned to marry her, one day. It would've been extremely difficult for Chill to claim he cared about Renee, if he had ever fucked with any of those 3 women again. So he made up his mind that he wasn't going to go there anymore. Renee's happiness and respect meant way more to him than any crew thang. She was the mother of his son and he knew he had to be an example for his junior. That was the end of it for him.

It was less than 2 weeks before the Thanksgiving holiday when Darlene made another move. Her, Gloria and Debra showed up at another crew event but neither of them dared to go inside. They just hung around outside in their vehicle and waited for some unsuspecting guest to walk by. They was going to send them to get Chill. While they were seated in the car, they spotted Ajay. The event was at his house this time, as well as at Ebony's house next door. Ajay was going from his side door to Ebony's side door when Darlene put down the window and called his name.
"Ajay!!" she screamed.
Ajay paused and looked out toward the street to see who was calling him. With all of the problems the Johnson beef spawned, he wouldn't just walk out to a car he didn't know. However he did know the car. He knew it was the same car that the 3 females came to the motel in, just over 2 weeks ago. Still he didn't walk out there. It was chilly weather and light snow on the

141

Ground too. He waved his hand and continued on into Ebony's side door. He was going to make sure he got a chance to talk to Ebony before her bedtime. Afterwards, he would see if he could get some of his crew guys to go out there with him.

Darlene and the 2 females still sat and waited while Ajay went inside, found Chill and told him the ho's was out there. Chill told Ajay about his decision.

"I'm not gonna fuck with them because Renee just started back talking to me," he said, "We got a kid together and even though we're not married. She lives in our house. My pops told me he didn't want me to go there again because that would leave Renee in a position of having to stop fucking wit me or be played for a fool. I can't do that to my son's mother. Me and junior gotta chill on those three. But you, Stoney and the rest of the brothers are good to go."

"Do you think she got some money?" Ajay asked, "Cause that's all she can do for me and let me drive her car."

"She get a little check and she got two little kids that she get welfare and stamps for," Chill said, "You got enough game, Lil bro. You can get it. That bitch wanna be down with the crew *so bad,* you can run a wheel on her. Get something out the deal but by no means do you ever let her think she's your woman. Do you feel me?"

"Yep," Ajay said, "I don't want her like that. I just wanna get whatever her dumb ass got to give. She was talking about all the shit she could do for me and give me, when she was sucking me off. That's all that stayed on my mind."

"Alright cool," Chill said as he snickered and said, "I'll get Stoney and Rob to swing something and y'all can do what it do."
Chill did just that. He told Stoney to deal with that situation and take Rob with them too. Stoney was ready and willing to make it happen. Him and Rob was still single. He got Rob and their newest crew brother Arthur Owens. The 3 of them got Ajay and they headed out to the car. Stoney told Ajay to do the talking to Darlene while him, Rob and Arthur was going to talk to Debra and Gloria. Darlene put the window down as they approached the car.

"So what's up?" Ajay asked Darlene.

"You're what's up young man and whatever you wanna do," Darlene said with a smile.

"Let's go back to the motel but I want you to get your own room,"

142

Ajay said per their plan, "I'm not trying to share no room with all these muafuckaz."

"Alright," she said, "I can do that."

The 4 guys crowded into the car with them and they headed to the motel.

Chill got with Al and let him know Darlene had shown back up. He told him she had called Ajay and that he was gone to the motel. Al knew this because he had witnessed it. Him, Greg Sr and Brad Sr was on his porch smoking when Darlene had called out his son's name. Al and Chill had a previous discussion on exactly what he wanted Chill to advise Ajay on when Darlene came back for him. And how he wanted him to handle the Darlene situation where Ajay was concerned.

"You handled it just right," Al told Chill, "I talked to Ant before she came and since the first night. He knows how to handle her."

"She knows his age because she subbed at his school," Chill said and laughed, "But he's taller than the normal eleven year old and he looks like he could be my age."

"It ain't his age that got that bitch's attention," Al said, "It's the legacy and the size of his dick."

They laughed and went on enjoying their party with confidence. They knew the males plan for tonight's motel trip would be executed to perfection.

Once they got to the motel and got 2 rooms, Ajay went into the room with Darlene. She striped immediately and laid on the bed. Ajay took off his shirt, shoes and his corduroy pants. He kept on his socks and boxers. Darlene started to talk to him as she waited for him to join her.

"I know you go to Abe Lincoln cause I saw you there," she said, "But you look like you should be in high school."

Ajay didn't say anything to that. He just grabbed a condom from his pants pocket, reach down in his boxers and pushed it onto his dick.

"You gone give me some head?" he asked.

"Are you gonna take the boxers off?"

"I want you too," he said.

She obliged him immediately. Then he laid on the bed, flat on his back and pulled her head toward him. She went to work on him while he laid there staring at the ceiling and knowing what his next request was going to be. He was 11 with a dick that was getting close to 9 inches. Darlene was loving it and she wanted to give him more head but she had a request.

"Can we try this head job without a condom?" she asked.

143

"Hell no," Ajay said quickly, "You don't get no parts of this dick without a shower cap."

"Oh a safety man ha?"

"Fasho," he said, "Let's do this or get me the fuck back to Shaker Heights."

She started sucking his dick like she was on a mission. She got him off and then he fucked her, for over an hour. They fucked in many positions. He wasn't willing to fuck her in her ass but she told him, he could if that was something he wanted to do.

"I don't want no ass," he said, "I'm all man."

"I hear that baby," she said, "You damn sho got a man sized dick. That's a fact."

She gave him head again and again. After he was sure she thought she had him sprung out and mesmerized. That's when he started to make his pitch. They laid on the bed and she laid her head on his chest. He had to channel someone else to even have a conversation with her that sounded serious. But he was on a crew mission.

"Do you watch basketball?" he asked.

"I do but I don't know all the rules," she said, "I know you're good at it though. You're playing for the ninth grade as a sixth grader. I see your name in the paper, all the time."

"I love it," he said, "I play a lot and I wear out a lot of shoes too."

"I bet you do," she said, "That's a lot of running and jumping. Is it hard on your feet?"

"No," he said, "Just on my shoes."

"Do you go through a lot of them?" she asked.

"Yep," he said, "My mom and pops have to buy a lot of them. It's hard on them."

"So what kind do you like?"

"Converse and Nike's," he said, "But I only play in the leather ones. Why? You gonna get me some?"

"Well I can," she said, "I'm a grown ass woman. I'm not like those little teenagers you're use too. I don't have to wait on my mama to give me money or to buy me things."

He had her right where he wanted her. She was ready to spend money on him and he wasn't going to stand in her way. But it was time for him to make a quick getaway. He had to let her think about him some more while he ignored her for a week or 2. He was sure that would get him not only shoes for basketball but pocket money, gear and most likely something very

144

nice for Christmas and eventually the use of her ride too.

Ajay had learned something since becoming sexually active. He knew he was never going to allow a female to use him or make him anything or anybody that he wasn't. But he had learned to make them think they could because that could get him more than just a nut.

Darlene had set her sights on the son of the man she had no chance in hell with. She moved her scope and set her sights onto the younger Ajay. He didn't have a girlfriend who was hunting her down to stump a mud hole in her ass either. Though he was younger than her by a decade. She still wanted him. She figured she could reel him in and he would fall for her. And that would be her path into the infamous crew. But she was wrong on every aspect of her plan. Darlene had no idea that the ass whipping's for her had *only* just begun. She also didn't know that Ajay already had his eyes on his girl for life too. It would take another 5 years or so, before Darlene would realize that she had no chance in hell with Ajay either. And even though he would tell her and show her too. She just never went completely away.

CHAPTER 7-Man With a Child's Face In A Man's Place

Ajay and Lil Ajay have made these father and son talks a weekly thing by now. Lil Ajay's sex invites had tripled before his school let out for Christmas break 2005. This Christmas break has blessed his family with a set of triplet girls named Ariel, Arianne and April to grow up in his household. Just like his father, Lil Ajay feels like it's going to be on him to make sure that all 5 of his little sisters grow up *without* incident.

Lil Ajay and his pops have just sat down in Ajay's office at Allen Saul's Recreation center, so they can pick back up where they left off last week. At last week's talk, Ajay told his son how Darlene came into his life. He still has to finish telling him about that phase, though he really hates to think about it. He's still not proud of that portion of his life. But he wants to make sure his son knows everything he went though, good and bad. So he'll be able to navigate through and across the bridge he's very close to crossing and those which are still to come. Lil Ajay isn't fond of Darlene, just on what he's heard so far. He knows her sons are working there at the Rec center and they're on his pops good side. But he's already got plans of making sure they know to keep their mama away or she's not going to leave breathing well.

"That woman was ten years older than you," Lil Ajay says with an unpleasant look on his face, "And she was dumb as hell too."

"Yes," Ajay says, "Most of the females I messed around with was older than me. Except for your mother and two others. But Darlene wasn't a woman and neither was the other two. Which I'll tell you about when we get to that part of my life. But Darlene wasn't a woman. Not in a real woman's sense. Not like your mother."

"She *sho* wasn't like my mom," Lil Ajay adds quickly.

"Nowhere near it, son. Your mama was raised right. She knew at a young age that she was a prize and she was suppose to be treated like one. Darlene thought her age was gonna make me want her. But she wasn't no different than the other girls who was teenagers, when I was eight. And she wasn't gonna have any more of my attention than they had."

"Is Darlene still alive?"

"Yea she is, for now," Ajay says, "She still comes around the chill spot and she still tries to push up on me. But that's a wrap and she knows it's a wrap. I'm in love with your mother and I have been, for a *very* long time."

"Do she try to mess wit my mama?" Lil Ajay asks, "Please just let me know that much, pops. Because if she's still messing wit my mama. She can get it today. She's gonna have to go, if she's bothering my ma."

Ajay chuckles and says, "She *will* get it, if she ever tries to come at my baby and she knows that. She knows me *well enough* to know how to stay in her lane, by now."

Lil Ajay laughs and says, "Cool because if she mess with my mama. That's gonna be my first chamber action."

"And I would gladly take you there for that one too," Ajay says.

"Do her sons know their mama is a ho?"

Ajay laughs harder before saying, "A son knows his mother. You know what kind of a woman your mother is, right?"

"I sure do."

"Then there you go," Ajay says, "There's a reason why her sons look up to your crew. They saw role models over here, in both the males and the females. That's why Rodney and Jamal wanted to be down. They came to the fourth of July event in nineteen eighty six and got some home training before that day ended."

"What happened?" Lil Ajay ask as he laughs.

"We'll get to it in a minute. But lets just say they didn't have a real mom," Ajay says, "She was trying to spend quality time with me, instead of raising them. She was taking money she got for them and trying to buy me."

"She bought you stuff?"

"Every week, I got a new pair of shoes, gym clothes or both," Ajay says, "She even bought jewelry for me. But I gave it to your mama or your nana Jo. She gave me money too. I was just learning how to drive a car when I was eleven and she would let me drive hers. I could go get it and drive around by myself. But of course, I had to have some of my crew wit me, you know that."

"She sounds like she was stupid."

"She was and still is," Ajay says and laughs, "But she was doing whatever I said I wanted her to do. She did it too. So long as I came back and fucked her or just spent some of my time around her. I didn't even *have* to fuck her. It wasn't even about that for me. She was trying to fuck your papa Al from the beginning, like I told you. And he told me about that before I ever went wit Chill to the motel, the first time. So she was ass out before anything ever happened between us. She was trying to be in this crew and that was never gonna happen."

"That's not the kind of girls and ladies we like, is it pops?"

"No way son," Ajay says, "But you will meet more of those types

147

than you will, the kind we *do* like. Girls like your mama are rare. But that's the kind of girl I want you to have."

"You said it was nineteen eighty six before my mama gave you the first *real* kiss, right?"

"Yes. It was the Fourth of July and it was great," Ajay says as he reminisces and smiles.

"So when did you know that my mama liked you?" Lil Ajay asks, "Because you had to know it before she gave you the first real kiss."

"I knew she liked me as a friend and someone who would look out for her, already," he says, "But it wasn't until her tenth birthday which was Christmas eighty five. That's when I knew she liked me, as a boy. The boy for her."

"She told you?"

"Not exactly. Not right away."

"So how did you know?"

"Here's how that went," Ajay says and he begins to tell Lil Ajay how he knew that his lifetime with Ebony was going to happen.

}*December 1985*{

It was the week before Christmas and Ebony's 10th birthday. Kenny was going to turn 2 years old. Ajay had started his shopping early. He wanted to make sure the gifts he got for Ebony this year, was something appropriate. Something that would let her know without any doubts that he liked her for more than just a friend, a basketball buddy, a dance partner and a neighbor. He had to make sure the gifts were right. So he went to the men in his crew for advice. He started off with his father Al and Ebony's father big John, as they sat in John's living room.

"Hey pops. Hey big John," Ajay started, "I wanna get Ebony something for her birthday and Christmas. But I don't know what to get her. It's gotta be something special and something that she won't forget."
Al looked at John and smiled. He knew what this was about and so did John. They knew Ajay was sweet on Ebony already. They figured Ebony wasn't there yet and it would be another 8 years before she *would* be. But they both knew they wanted them to be together, in the future. John started first.

"Ajay I'm gonna tell you like this," he said, "She's my only girl and you're Al's only son. Al and I have been best friends every since he moved here from Boston. We were around the same ages that you and Ebony are right now."

"Once we became teens and started thinking about the day we would be fathers," Al said, "We said we wanted our kids to date and marry each other. But it's gonna be awhile before Ebony is thinking about a boyfriend though."

"But when she does. I want him to be someone that comes from my crew," John added, "*This* crew. And he has to be a young man who knows what I want for my baby girl. I know Al knows what that is. And I know he's raising you to be *just* that. I don't know what to tell you to get her as a gift though. She only asked me for dolls, ovens and clothes."

"You'd have to ask the ladies about that one, son," Al suggested.

"How about big mama?" Ajay asked, "She always knows what everybody likes or needs to do."

"I'd say that's a damn good start," John said and laughed.

"And you could ask Ebony too," Al said as he chuckled, "She's the only one who can *really* tell you what she would want from you."

"But I don't want her to know what it is," Ajay said.

"Then ask her big mama and she'll find it out for you," Al said, "But you just make sure you understand that she's got three years before she will be in the crew. And a lot more than that before she'll be able to get permission to have and date a boyfriend."

"Okay," Ajay said, "That's no problem. I can wait for her. I want her to tell me what she wants to do. I'll do it for her."

"I have a feeling this is going to happen sooner than we planned on," John said suddenly, "Baby girl is a lot like her mother. Once she gets set on something. She's not gonna back down."

Ajay looked at John. He had something to ask him and he wasn't sure if he would be okay with it. But they have to live on the honor system, so he went for it.

"Big John, I need to ask you something," Ajay said slowly.

"She's too young to get married, so I'll have to say no, at this time," John said and him and Al burst out laughing before Ajay caught on and eventually laughed too. Then John asked, "What is it son?"

"She told me she wants me to call her, *baby girl*. Is that okay with you?"

"Well *damn*," John said with surprise, "Obviously my only girl has already picked out her prince charming, it *sounds* like."

"I told her you was gonna be mad, if I called her that," Ajay tried.

149

"No way," John said, "I'm not mad at all. I think it's cute actually. So long as you remember not to take my daughter down a road she isn't ready for. Can we agree on that?"

"Oh yes sir," Ajay said, "I'll wait as long as she wanna wait, for *whatever*. I just don't want her to like no other boy, that's all."

"As a father of four girls. That's the day I'm dreading," Al said as he shook his head. "But I'm seeing it already. I know Lynn likes John junior already. I guess they think we don't know. But men know what to look for because we were boys *before* we were men. It's the mothers who don't know the game right away. I just want Lynn to tell her mama and not let her find out on her own. Because that's gonna be like an *Eff* five tornado around here, when Joanna goes off."

Ajay knew Lynn and Jb had already had sex last year. Before JB had turned 11. He knew their fathers already knew it too. Because Jb had told big John and surely big John told Al shortly after finding out. Jb told Ajay that big John told him he would rather him go outside of his crew for sex. Until after they got to high school. But Ajay also knew that Lynn was against him doing that. Ajay wasn't going to admit anything he knew about it and he knew the fathers didn't expect him too. So he changed the subject back to him.

"So it's okay if I call her, baby girl?" he asked John.

"Sure. As long as you treat her like a princess," he said, "That'll be fine with me. I'm the only one she can call daddy. *Before* she's married."

They all laughed before Ajay revealed 1 other thing.

"I asked her to call me Anthony because my mama calls my daddy by his government name," he said, "I want her to call me by mine."

Al and John looked at each other again and smiled proudly. They knew what that was about. Ajay was already planning on Ebony being his wife, one day and they were both in agreement.

"I like that a lot," John said, "Because now I know exactly what your plans are for her. That's okay with me too."

"Just take your time though, son," Al said, "And move at her pace. Whatever that pace is. Are we clear?"

"Yes sir," Ajay said and he smiled before shaking hands with the men and then going on his way.

He was going home to call big mama. He had to get her advice of what gifts would be best for his *baby girl*.

After he was out of sight, Al and John poured themselves a shot of cognac as they smiled and did a toast and said, "To the future of the crew."

Ajay was rushing from Pearl's side door to his own because it was cold, there was snow on the ground plus more coming down. Before he got to his door, he heard a females voice calling his name. The voice was coming from behind their shed and behind Pearl's back fence. He stepped back toward the voice and peeped around the shed. He saw a female standing on the other side of the fence and she was looking directly at him. Though she was cloaked in a Parka jacket and gloves for protection from the weather. He knew who it was, instantly. And he wasn't interested in talking to her, at that time.

"Ajay," Marsha said again.

"What?"

"Can I talk to you for a minute?"

"It's cold out here," he said, "What you want?"

"I wanted you to come over," she said, "My aunt Lou's gone to work and-"

"And you want me to come over there and fuck you again?"

"Well yes," she said, "It's been along time, I know. But we never got to finish the first time. It's been more than three years. But I never forgot you. Every time I came back to visit, you were always gone to basketball camps. I know because I asked your crew and they always said-"

"That day turned out bad," he said as he stuffed his hands in his pockets to keep them warm, "That probably means I shouldn't have done it."

"I remember that," she said, "I came over to talk to you, every time I was here but you was never at home."

"I had stuff to do," he said, "Hey, it's cold out here and I need to get inside."

He started toward his mother's door but then he remembered he never told her which house he lived in. He turned around and she was standing right behind him.

"I told you I got something to do right now," he said without any patience in his tone.

"Will you come see me when you're done? Aunt Lou is working a double. She won't be home until tomorrow morning at eight o'clock."

"I don't know," he said, "I got stuff to do."

"Call me when you're done."

"I might," he said and he left heading back into John's door and Marsha hurried back to Lou's house.

Ajay made it back inside John's door, where John and Al were still

151

seated in the living room with cigars lit. Ajay wanted to call big mama immediately and he knew John would allow him to call from there. Besides that, Ebony was upstairs in her room and he would have more of a chance of seeing her, if he stayed around her house. He asked John to call big mama and John did just that.

"Hello," big mama answered from her home in Houston.

"Hey mama Eloise. It's John."

"Hey son-in-law. How are you and the family?" she asked.

"We're okay and looking forward to seeing you all real soon."

"I know and we'll be there in four days," she said, "It must be something urgent, for you to call me today."

"Well yes it is urgent," John said as he laughed, "It's for Ajay. He needs to ask your advice."

"Okay. Put him on."

John passed the phone to Ajay and went back in the living room and took his seat. Ajay took the phone into the hallway so he could talk privately.

"Hello big mama. How are you?"

"I'm good Ajay. How are you doing, young man?"

"I got a problem and I need your help."

"What's the problem?" she asked.

"I wanna get a Christmas and birthday gift for Ebony. But I wanna make sure it's something that she won't forget. I need you to help me figure out what to get for her. Do you know what I could get her? Two things, that she'll *really* like?"

"I'm gonna asked her so I can be sure. Because I know you probably want it to be a surprise, right?"

"Yes ma'am," he said, "I don't want her to know what I'm getting for her. But I wanna make sure I get something that she likes. Something she would want from me. I want it to be a gift that she's gonna remember."

"You sound *really* determined to get the perfect gifts."

"I am," he said, "They gotta be perfect."

"Well one of the things I know she would love to get from you, is her very own basketball," big mama said, "She loves that you're teaching her how to play and to be as good as you are. But I will check with her for more, okay?"

"Okay. Thank you big mama. I love you," he said and smiled big.

"You're welcome and I love you too," she said, "Is she there?"

"I think she's in her room."

"Of course she is," big mama said and laughed, "She's always in

152

that room, writing something or practicing a song or something similar. When she's not playing basketball with you."

"Do you want me to go get her for you?"

"You want too, don't you?"

He chuckled and said, "Yes ma'am I do."

"Okay. Just let John know I wanna speak to her and I asked you to go and get her to the phone," she said as she giggled playfully.

Ajay was still smiling as he asked John if he could go get Ebony for the phone.

John chuckled at him and said, "If it makes you *that* happy. Then I guess I'll have to say yes to that too."

Ajay laid the phone down and ran up the stairs. He knocked on Ebony's door and waited for her to answer. He could feel his heart pounding. He knew he was nervous and he knew why. He liked that he was about to see her face and her eyes. She opened the door and looked shocked to see him standing there.

She smiled and said, "Anthony! Hi!"

There was major excitement in her voice and he knew she was happy to see him too.

"Hey baby girl," he said as he smiled back, "Big mama is on the phone. I just talk to her. You know she's like my big mama too. She wants to speak to you and she told me to come and get you."

"Okay!"

She hurried down the stairs with a huge smile and he went right behind her. He made sure to let her see him smile at her once more. Before he headed into the living room with their dad's, while she went into the kitchen to answer the phone.

That felt like the longest wait ever, as Ajay sat in the living room and pretended to be interested in what their fathers were talking about at that moment. He was more interested in watching Ebony. He watched her through their server window as she talked to her big mama. She had hopped up on the kitchen counter which gave him a clear view of her. She glanced at him often, while she talked on the phone. He figured it was because she wanted to keep her eyes on him too. He couldn't hear what she was saying. But her facial expressions told him the conversation was a good one for her. Because she smiled and giggled a lot. She looked at him a lot too.

Ebony and big mama's conversation was about what gifts she wanted from everyone. But the first person Ebony mentioned and wanted

153

to talk about, was Ajay. Big mama smiled and listened as Ebony had her say.

"Big mama he is *not* mean," she said, "I don't know why everybody always saying that. He's nice. He plays basketball with me everyday when he's home and it's warm enough outside."

"Well that's *great*, little Eloise," big mama said, "He's nice to people who make him feel special and people who he feels are special to him."

"Big mama, he thinks I'm special. Do you know how I know?"

"How do you know that?" big mama asked.

"He told me to call him Anthony," she said and giggled, "And he said can't nobody else call him that but me."

" I think that's very special *indeed*," big mama said as she giggled.

"He said he wants me to call him by his real name, just like mama Jo do with big Al," she continued, "And I'm glad he thinks I'm special, big mama. I told him to call me baby girl, like my daddy do. And when he came to get me for the phone. That's what he called me."

"I love that, little Eloise," big mama said and continued to giggle, "I love that a lot."

"Me too," she said, "And I'm gonna tell everybody that they can't call him mean, no more. Or I'm not gonna be they friend."

"That's a good idea," big mama said, "But I wanted to know something."

"Yes ma'am?"

"Have you thought about what gifts you want for your birthday and Christmas, this year?"

"He bought me a present last year and it was a pretty dress!"

"Are you talking about Ajay?" big mama asked, "Because I do still have to call him Ajay, I suppose."

"Yes ma'am. He bought me a dress," she said and giggled, "And yes you have to call him Ajay. I'm the *only* one who can call him Anthony."

"Got it. Okay so you like getting dresses from him?"

"Yes. My daddy always buy me dresses too," she said, "And *he* bought me a dress. That was so cool."

"Is your favorite color purple?" big mama asked with a grin.

"Yes."

"Do you know I think that's his favorite color too?" big mama said.

"It *is*?!"

"Uh huh and that's something else you two have in common," big mama said, "You like basketball and your favorite color is purple. You are the only girl in your family and he is the only boy in his."

"His favorite Isley brothers song is voyage to Atlantis, just like mine, big mama," she said, "Do you like that song?"

"I love that song and anything else Isley," big mama said and laughed, "Honey that is my generation right there. What do you and Ajay know about the Isleys?"

"I don't know," she said, "But we like that song."

"So that's something else y'all *both* like," big mama said, "That's very sweet."

"I hope he buy me a purple dress," she said, "If it's his favorite color and it's my favorite too. Then that would mean he knows I'm his favorite."

"Do you wanna be his favorite?" big mama asked with caution in her voice.

"I do and I don't even know why but I do," she said.

"Well something's were just meant to be and we don't always understand and know why they're like that. Not right away," big mama said, "But I think it's a sign of things to come."

"You do?"

"Yes I do," she said, "I think you might be his favorite person. He doesn't go looking for anyone else to play basketball with or to hang out with but you. That's very special."

"That's cool to me," Ebony said while still giggling.

"Is he your favorite in your crew?" big mama asked and hoped her answer would be a positive one.

"Yes ma'am," she said and laughed hard.

"Oh that's so sweet," big mama said, "He's cute, smart, talented and raised by the strongest of people. Not bad for a favorite."

"Big mama, he asked me if I think he's cute but I didn't say nothing."

"Do you think he's cute?"

"Yes he is," she said and laughed hard.

"Didn't you tell me he called you cutie pie?"

"He was calling me that but now he calls me, baby girl."

"Well that means he thinks you're cute," big mama said, "And I would bet my last dollar that you're his favorite person in your crew too."

"Well he's my favorite and I'm his favorite," Ebony said in a matter of fact tone, "That's cool, right?"

155

"Absolutely," big mama said, "And you can talk to me about your favorite person and things, anytime. Okay? And don't forget that."

"I won't, big mama," she said. Then getting back to the gift talk, she said, "I'm gonna get him a present again this year too. I'm gonna get some Los Angeles Lakers basketball stuff. Their colors are purple and gold. Will you help me pick it out when you get here?"

"I most certainly will and I'm gonna love it," big mama said, "I'll be there, three days before your birthday. We'll get there early in the morning and after I rest up and see everybody. Then we can go shopping. How's that?"

"Perfect," Ebony said, "Thanks. I love you so much, big mama."

"I love you too, namesake," big mama said, "Now put my daughter on this phone, so I can see what's all on the menu for Christmas. I'm getting the boxes ready to ship. I wanna make sure and mail all my seasonings that I can't find in Cleveland."

"Okay I'll get her now. Bye big mama."

"Never say bye to those you love, namesake," big mama told her, "Always say something that means you plan to see them soon, Okay?"

"Okay. I'll see you soon."

"Okay sweetheart. Tell Pearl to get the phone because I still have to call Pearline before I finish these boxes."

Ebony laid the phone down, hopped off the kitchen counter and ran upstairs to tell her mother to pick up the phone in her room. She was giddy about her conversation with her big mama.

Ajay was still in the living room with their fathers. He never went to see Marsha nor did her call her. Not that day nor the next one.

3 days before Christmas was Nina's 10th birthday. Jo and Pearl had a party for her and Ebony together. Which was the way they'd done it since the girls turned a year old. Marsha was invited and she came. It was a cold December day in Cleveland. The party was at Pearl's house and of course, Ajay and all of the guys from the crew was there. Ajay reminded Rich Jr of their last episode in that house.

"I know you should feel bad now, after how you treated lady," he said, "Because now she's dead."

"I do, cousin," Rich said, "I told her I was sorry but she didn't say nothing back to me."

"Good," Ajay said, "She don't have too. You was mean to her pet. Now that pet is gone. She ain't gonna forget how you treated her either."

Other then Rich feeling bad and knowing he just had to take what Ajay said and heed it. The party was great. But it wasn't long before Marsha approached Ajay.

"Hey Ajay," she said.

"Hey."

"So this is your sister and her best friend's party?"

"Yep."

"They're very pretty," Marsha said.

Ajay was very short with her. He didn't like her talking to him at Ebony's house nor while Ebony could see them. So he made haste in getting her out of his face.

"I'm about to go kick it wit my crew," he said and left her where she stood.

He continued to avoid her for the remainder of the party and before long, he saw her talking to 1 of the neighbors named Marcus Carr. They called him Mark and he lived several blocks away. The crew guys knew him from school and the courts too. Ajay was happy to see them talking. He hoped they would hit it off and she would spend her time in Cleveland with him from then on because Ajay was no longer interested in her.

By the end of the party, he would get his wish. He saw Mark walking with Marsha back to her aunt Lou's house. He was glad to see it too. He wasn't planning to fuck her anymore. And now, after seeing her allow another boy to spend time with her. He had a legitimate reason to give her, if she came back to him again.

Big mama and poppa arrived before sunrise the next morning. All of the females in the crew went shopping together that afternoon and got all of their Christmas and birthday shopping finished. They headed to granny and papa's house in The Point to do all the gift wrapping and to start Christmas dinner preparations.

Later that evening, as the men were hanging the decorations on all of the crew homes. Darlene showed up looking for Ajay. The men were finishing up Paul's house when Darlene pulled in across the street. Tank spotted her first.

"Ajay there go Darlene pulling into y'all driveway, man," he said.

"Let's go see what she wants," Jb suggested, "We need to get the car for tonight, so we can go collect money in the grove."

Ajay didn't say a word. He just walked with Jb and Tank and they met Darlene at her car.

"Hey Ajay. Hey guys, what's up?" she asked in a jubilant tone.

"Hey what's up wit you?" Ajay asked.

He was working his game early because not only was he going to get her car tonight. But he was going to get her to commit to giving him some Christmas money and buying some gifts too.

"I came to pick you up," she said, "Are you ready?"

"If my boys can come too, then yea," he said.

"Of course they can come," she said, "Crew are always welcome at my place."

"Cool then, let's go," Ajay said and he got in the front seat while Jb and Tank jumped in the back.

Ajay wanted them to hurry up and leave while Ebony and the females was still out at granny's house. He didn't want her to see nor learn anything about Darlene. Before they could pull away, Stoney and Rob ran over and jumped into the car with them.

"Crew rolls deep," Stoney said and the rest agreed.

"Let's roll," Rob added and Darlene pulled away.

"You got some drink at your place?" Jb asked.

"No but I can get some," Darlene answered quickly.

"Then let's do this," Stoney said, "And get some of your women friends over there too. Unless you can entertain all five of us."

"For real, cause I get bored easy," Tank said and they all laughed.

"That can be arranged," Darlene said, "Gloria is already out there with a friend named Anita."

"That's enough," Ajay said, "Let's just get there."

Darlene headed to Maple Heights on Ajay's order because, even though there was 5 young men in her car. He was the 1 whom she wanted to pacify.

They arrived at her place and got right into it. Darlene wanted to suck Ajay off before he could even get a buzz. He told her to go into her bedroom with only him first and she gladly did.

"I like that you want some alone time with me," Darlene said to Ajay, "That turns me on *big* time."

"You got me some gifts under your tree in there, don't you?" he asked, "Why wouldn't I wanna spend time wit you? Get naked while you tell me what you getting me for Christmas."

"I can't tell you what your gifts are, baby," she said seductively as she stripped out of her clothes.

"Cool," he said, "But I need some money so I can buy gifts too. You got me?"

sexual experience had been with Ajay's older sister Lynn and it was her 1st experience too. She had turned 11, just 3 months before he had in April of 1984. They were an official couple and the third one of Chill's crew. But their crew was still the only ones they thought knew about them. They hadn't made 13 yet and they couldn't announce their official union. But they planned to do it next April on Lynn's 13th birthday. The guys knew their fathers was aware of them but still no one was going to announce it until they were official crew because that was the rule of the family.

But for tonight, Jb was ready do what the single crew men were good at doing. He wanted to sow his wild oats. He wanted to fuck this older woman and that was about to happen. Darlene just had to hear the okay from Ajay.

"You heard my crew say he want some o' that ass," Ajay said, "What you waiting for?"
Jb went to Darlene and bent her over her recliner and started fucking her from the back. Stoney moved around to Gloria's mouth and told Ajay to take the rear. He did after applying another condom. Tank was fucking Anita while Rob was getting her mouth. They all switched up at least twice that night. It was only Tank's 2nd time having penetration. But by the time that night would end. He was a lot closer to 10. Anita seemed especially fond of Ajay's dick when he fucked her. He finally fucked Darlene too. Afterwards, he took her back into her room.

"I need to go get this money so you gotta take me back to Shaker," he said.

"I wanted you to stay all night," she whined.

"I'm not staying by myself because crew stays together always," he said, "Stone man told you that before we left."

"All of y'all are welcome to stay," she tried.

"We gotta get our paper. So we're gonna need to go to Shaker to get some wheels," he said, "But if you want us to come back down here. Then you need to let us use yo ride. If you do that, then we can come back here when we're done. But that's up to you."
Without hesitation, she handed the keys to him with gas money. Then she rolled over onto her pillow very seductively and said,
"I'll be waiting to fuck and suck some more, when you get back."

"That's cool. But I told you I need some cash for some Christmas shopping that I need to do too," he said, "And I need to know how much I'll have, so I don't stay out there hustling no longer than I have too. So how much you got for me?"

She reached into her wallet and pulled out 3-$50 bills and handed them to him and said, "That's all I can give you baby. I still have to get some toys for my sons."

"This good," he said and smiled, "You're not gonna kiss my cheek?"

She jumped up and gave him a kiss on the cheek. She tried to kiss his lips immediately after but he said, "I'm not there yet."

She knew not to force it.

Ajay and his crew left to go collect their money in The Grove.

After they were done with all collections, they went to Chill's house and munched out on all of the leftovers that the females had brought over for the men to eat while doing decorations. Then they crashed out on the floor and left Darlene's car parked in Chill and big Paul's driveway. Ajay had never planned to go back to Maple Heights and neither did the other 4 guys.

Christmas was a great day for the crew. Ebony turned 10 and Lil Chill celebrated his 2nd birthday. Ebony had gotten Ajay a *Lakers* warm-up suit, a purple *swatch* watch to match, as well as *a Michael Jordan #23 Chicago Bulls* jersey. *Michael Jordan* was quickly becoming Ajay's favorite player. Big mama had helped her get the warm-up suit which they got in a size large because Ajay was over 6 feet tall by then. Big mama had also helped Ajay get Ebony's gifts too. He'd gotten her an NCAA women's basketball, a beautiful purple dress with the socks and hair accessories to match it. He'd also given her a pair of gold door knocker earrings which Darlene had purchased. Darlene thought she was getting them for his mother. Jo still hadn't found out about this older woman who was messing around with her only son yet. It would only be a matter of time before she did.

}1986{

The tensions between Darlene and the crew girls would escalate several more times after the new year began. By the end of February, Lynn had found out about that night out in Maple Heights when Darlene had fucked Jb. That happened for 2 reasons. One was because Darlene ran her mouth to students at Abe Lincoln. The second reason was because of Darlene's persistence. She had picked up her trips by Jo's house, looking for Ajay. But he was into his basketball season, his crew life, Ebony and everything else except her. But when Darlene pulled her car into Jo's driveway on the last day of February in the snow, as Lynn was getting off the school bus and asked for Ajay. Things went to a fevered pitch instantly.

"Is Ajay home yet?" Darlene asked.

"Who the fuck is yo grown ass and why are you looking for my Lil brother?" Lynn yelled into Darlene's car window.

Lynn was well aware of who she was. But she wasn't going to give her the benefit of her recognition.

"Oh I'm Darlene-"

"You ain't nobody but that old bitch that's been fucking all the crew," Lynn said because she wasn't able to hold it any longer. "I guess we gonna have to whoop yo *stanking* ass again ha?"

"I don't have time for this," Darlene said.

She put her car in reverse, backed out and pulled off down the street where she decided to park and wait awhile longer. She thought that spot was going to be much safer for her. But the crew lived in about every 3rd house down that street. Darlene had parked where she could still have a visual of Ajay's house but not be close enough to hear Lynn, if she continued with the verbal assault. But she just happened to have parked directly in front of Jan's house. It wasn't long before Jan and Bre came walking up behind her car to inquire about why she was sitting there.

"Why are you sitting in front of my house?" Jan asked in her usual calm tone. "And don't act like you don't hear Lynn talking to you. Is that why you pulled down here?"

"You know it is," Bre added, "We don't want you down here either. Take yo ass back to Maple Heights. You don't live in Shaker."

Lynn came running up the street to meet Jan and Bre and they all made their way closer to Darlene's car.

"Get yo ass out bitch!" Lynn yelled, "Yo old ass fucked my boyfriend and I know you did! I wanna beat yo ass!"

Soon the high school buses was turning onto the street and Darlene saw Renee and Tonya get off. She knew they would join the 3 middle school girls in a matter of minutes. Because Lynn was already alerting them that she was there. She decided to start her engine and get the hell out of there while she still had the chance. That's exactly what she did. She threw it in reverse and backed her way to the next corner, put it drive and sped away.

"Them young bitches crazy," she said to herself as she drove away.

Renee and Tonya had run down to meet Lynn, Bre and Jan who filled them in on what had just transpired.

162

"That bitch stay looking for Ajay now," Renee said, "She think he's gonna be available for her ass but she's wrong."

"My brother ain't bringing no ho like that up in this crew," Lynn said, "He got his eyes on Ebony anyway. That's the only girl he's gonna date. So Darlene can keep her washed up ass in Maple Heights."

"Cause if she come back around here. We kicking her dumb ass," Tonya added.

Ajay had gone to the 9th grade gym for his after school practice, as they were preparing for their district tournament. It was very apparent that he didn't keep in close contact with Darlene or she would've known his schedule. Lynn was still heated by Darlene's impromptu visit. She rushed home to tell her mother about the visit and why Darlene had started coming around their home, all of a sudden.

"She's sleeping wit Ajay," Lynn told Jo.

"What?" Jo asked, "She's a substitute teacher and I know she has to know she's too damn old to be messing around with the students."

"Renee told me she tried to go wit daddy first and he told her she had no chance," Lynn said, "That's when she went after Chill. And mama since then. She has slept with like five or six of the guys in our crew."

"I don't allow no whores around my house," Jo said, "Your brother knows that. I'm for certain your father does too and has told him just that. Listen Lynora. Boys at that age are most concerned with how much they can get sexually. And in every other way. Ant knows not to have her around here and I don't think he told her to come here today and no other day."

"She gives him money and she lets him drive her car too."

"That explains all the new pairs of shoes he has, that I know I *nor* Allen bought," Jo says, "She'd best not let me run into her.. Or that's an ass whooping that can already be recorded in the books."

"Me and my girls gonna get her *for* you, mama."

"I want you to keep on building on your track status Lynora," Jo said, "You've moved up to the high school team and you're only in seventh grade. That's much more important to me, than you focusing on a whore."

"I know ma but I got reasons to wanna whip her."

Lynn wanted to tell her mother more about her and Jb. But she couldn't find the courage. She just let her mother talk until her heart was content. Jo was set on telling Lynn what her reasoning was. Instead of allowing Lynn to come completely clean.

"And that reason is because you always protect your *only* brother,"

163

Jo said, "Or at least, that's the only one that should matter at this point. You'll be thirteen in less than two months. And you're going to be official crew. You and John junior both. I just hope y'all don't rush anything else."

"We're boyfriend and girlfriend but you already know that, right ma?"

"Yes I know," Jo said, "Pearl and me talked about that on the phone, just this morning. And we know that didn't just start either, did it?"

"No ma'am," she said, "He asked me almost two years ago. I told you the same day he asked me."

"I know and I'm glad you did," Jo said, "But I don't want you all rushing into anything. You are a seventh grader and you're already joining the high school team for track. I know how much you love to race and there is no telling how far you can go with that gift. I want you to stay focused on that dream, sweetheart. You have four siblings coming behind you and they're watching you for guidance. You will always carry yourself as a role model for them and that's how me and Allen know you'll be just fine. Just remember that John junior is a crew young man. So he's going to be vibrant with the females. But he's raised by parents *just* like yours and he knows what's going to be allowed and what isn't."

"Darlene slept with him too," Lynn said and Jo could tell she was heated just from having to say it.

"The males in the crew have always shared women," Jo said, "The females in this family are the only ones they're partial too. It didn't just start with your crew. They all did it. But once they start looking toward marriage. They usually get rid of that notion. It's best if they're gonna sow their wild oats, as the first generation says it. Then it's much better they do it prior to marriage, then it would be to do it afterwards, okay?"

"Okay mama," Lynn said, "But I'm still gonna get her."

Jo left it at that. She knew her daughter had *her* mentality when it came to any other females having any type of time and attention from the guy that she liked. Jo wanted to beat Darlene's ass too and for more reasons than her oldest daughter did. But she didn't go into it any farther, that day. She just left Lynn with a simple thought.

"Every dog has his or her day, Lynora," Jo said, "And when that day comes, that dog gets bitten. Darlene will have more dog days than she's had years on this earth. Because she's fucking with the wrong family of men and trying to get some stature. Her type will never get any tenure of a genuine kind from a male in our crew. Rest your mind, honey. Every parent in this family lives by the same guidelines. Pearl and John would never

164

allow anything but the best for their kids. Same as myself, Allen and all of the rest of the men and women in this crew."

Lynn was fine with that answer. She went on up to her room to do her homework. But she wasn't off of the idea of kicking Darlene's ass. Not that easy.

Ajay's basketball season had been great again this year. Him and the 9th grade team were still undefeated as they went into the conference tournament. All of the crew was there for their 1st conference game which they won.

After the game ended, they all went to eat. Ajay sat next to Ebony and they had some great conversation once again, while Jo and Pearl kept watchful eyes on them.

"You played a good game, Anthony," she said, "Your crossover is the bomb."

"Thanks baby girl," he said.

He liked that she enjoyed his game but his mind was on her being his girlfriend and he wanted to make sure their entire crew knew that too. So right then and there while everyone was together. He decided he was going to let them know what his future plans were as far as a girlfriend was concerned. He let them know that although everyone else in the crew called him Ajay. He had told Ebony not to call him that. He told them all, how it was going to be for him and Ebony, from that night on.

"Y'all know I use to call Ebony, cutie pie. And that was because she's cute to me," he said. "But I'm gonna call her, baby girl from now on. That's what she asked me to call her. So I went and I asked big John if I could call her that and he said I could. He said he knows that one day I'm gonna take care of her, just like he does. She's not gonna call me Ajay, like y'all do and I already told her that too. She's gonna call me Anthony. That's why she called me that tonight. So I don't want nobody else looking at her all weird because she's calling me Anthony, alright? She's gonna call me by my real name. Just like my mama do with my pops."

Pearl and Jo looked at each other. Not so much in shock but more like it was a revelation. Al and John had told them about the talk they had with Ajay and what he had told them. Jo and Pearl knew they wanted them to be together when they got older. But Ajay seemed determined he was going to lay his mark down right then. He was making his point clear, just in case there was any other guy in their crew who was thinking of having Ebony as their girl. Which could've only been Rich Jr because he was the only 1 not

related to her. Or in Stoney, Rob, Jr and Arthur's cases. They already had someone picked out or they already knew Ebony was his choice. Pearl and Jo smiled at each other as they continued listening to Ajay make his pitch. He turned to Ebony and said, "So now they know what we talked about before and what each one of us wants. I'm gonna call you baby girl from now on, okay?"
Ebony smiled and said, "Okay."
She knew he liked her a lot without a doubt, at that point. And she knew she liked him too. But now everybody in their family knew it. This was a new feeling for her and 1 she wanted to know more about. So she could make sure she didn't mess it up. Still, Ajay had more to say.

"And just like I just told them. I know they all call me Ajay," he said, "But I want you to call me by my real name. Call me Anthony."

"Okay," she said and smiled again.

"Now everybody know it," he said, "And we said it in front of them. That should take care of any other questions that anybody else might have. Now let's eat."
Rich was looking suspicious. He liked Ebony too. He thought she was cute but she never talked to him. He had apologized to her several times for hurting Lady. Mainly because of his fear that Ajay would beat him up again. But even when he apologized, she never answered him nor looked at him. Rich wasn't going to get Ebony and he knew that. He had his mind on T-baby. She seemed to like him. He knew Ajay was going to do his thing in stages, so it would still take awhile before he would asked Ebony to be his girl *officially*. Rich was determined he would beat Ajay to that punch. He was going to have a girlfriend on the books before his high and mighty 1st cousin did. He had too. It was the only way he felt like he could upstage Ajay, after tonight's dinner. He was going to asked T-baby to be his girl before Lynn's crew party. But from that night on, Ebony was going to call Ajay by his government name. He was planning on making her his girlfriend soon. And later on, he wanted her to be his wife. Rich could play him and T-baby's whole courtship up like a competition, if he wanted too. That was up to him. But Ajay wasn't thinking about anyone else and their situation. He was only thinking and acting like a man who had found the woman whom he was going to spend his life with and Ebony was all smiles.

By the end of the week, Ajay and the 9th grade team had won their conference and finished the season undefeated. Ajay had already been invited to play for MLK high school basketball team for the 86-87 school year. He was nearly 6 feet 2 inches tall but he was only going to be a 12 year old 7th grader. Jo was concerned about him moving up to high school but Al wasn't. He knew his son was ready for the advancement, both physically and mentally. So him and Jo met with the high school coaches and let them know they would allow Ajay to move on up.

It was spring break, April 1986. Marsha was back to visit her aunt Lou. She wanted to fuck Ajay, even though she had fucked Mark from 7 blocks over, during her last visit. Ajay knew about it but he didn't care. That was leverage for him and an easy way to make sure she stayed in her place. He knew if he ever fucked her again. He would make sure she knew that he was aware of her and Mark. Therefore she could never be anything more to him than a fuck. He was going to make sure she knew that if she ever came back to him saying she wanted him as her boyfriend.

A week ago, Lynn had turned 13 and was initiated into the crew. Arthur who hadn't had the chance to have an official crew party for his initiation, was invited to celebrate along with Lynn. The guys told him, he could have his party with Lynn or just do the male initiation side of it only. That part was done in secret and was what would make him legit. It included some chamber action. Arthur quickly chose the chamber action.

"Let Lynn have her coming out party alone," he said, "That's only right. I shared the party with junior and Tonya already. I wanna get to the killing floor."

"I figured you'd say that," Stoney said as they all laughed and it was settled.

They would take care of another ne'er-do-well between the start of spring break and Lynn's party. That chamber stop included Arthur. He was able to fuck the doomed man's girl while the doomed man watched. Then of course, they both died afterwards. Arthur was all the way in, from that point on. He even took a greater interested in film and video afterwards. He wanted that to be his contribution to his crew. They were all for it and saw it as a good tool to have, as they moved into the future.

Friday night toward the end of spring break, big Paul and Al gave Lynn a crew party at Paul's house to celebrate her induction. The 3rd generation was 8 members strong, *age* wise by then. Chill, Renee, Stoney and Rob along with Arthur Owens, Jr, Tonya and now Lynn were official crew. Jb was going to be 13 when the 4th of July holiday came. But him, Ajay, Jan, Bre and Tank always went to anything where Chill was going to be. So of course they attended the full party. Everybody younger than Tank could attend the daytime party. But they had to go home before the night party guest arrived and things got into the full swing.

At that party is where Darlene showed up again with Gloria and Anita in tow. Lynn wasn't going to pass on giving the ideal birthday present to herself either. She wanted to get in Darlene's ass and the other 2 ho's, as well. Because she knew they had all fucked Jb by then. From the time those 3 stigmatic females arrived, Lynn was plotting on a get back. She got with Renee, Tonya, Bre and Jan and they put a plan together on how they would whoop their asses.

"Let's just lay back in the cut and act like we squashed it," Renee said, "Once everybody get they buzz on and stop checking us about staying cool. We're gonna get them bitches locked in a corner and get that shit done."

"I hate ho's wit a passion," Tonya said, "Especially the kind that act like they're so proud of being a damn ho."

"That's all they know how to be," Lynn said, "That's what my mama told me. So ho's should expect to catch a beat down and we're gonna give it to all they stank asses."

Bre laughed hard at Lynn's statement but she was with it, nonetheless. Bre was 11 and born in 1974, just like Jan and Ajay. But Bre was in 5th grade. Only because her birthday fell after the 1st day of September. She was born on September 9th and missed being classmates with Ajay and Jan by 8 days. Bre, Jan and Lynn were collectively called *3 the Hard Way* because they did everything the guys did except fuck around outside of the crew. They had learned things about the street game through Renee and Chill which would make them even more valuable as they got older. But that night, all Bre was thinking about was fighting because she had her eyes on Stoney as her crew man and those 3 ho's each had a sample of him too.

"I'm doing whatever y'all wanna do," 11 year old Bre said.

"For real," 11 year old Jan agreed, "I'm fighting too. That's all I gotta say. I'm strong anyway and y'all know I can hit softballs to the outfield on a good pitch now. So I'm definitely ready to see if I can knock a ho out too."

The 5 girls laughed hard as they broke up their little plotting circle and started to mingle because the fathers was watching them and knew they were plotting.

Pearl and Jo showed up shortly before dark to take Nina, Ebony, T-baby and Rebbie to Pearl's house where they were spending the night.

Brian James Sr picked up June and Rich Jr to take them home before the party switched gears for the night time. Marsha was at the party too and she was hoping to spend some time with Ajay. That was the exact same plan Darlene had. Only Darlene was planning for Ajay to go home with her for the full night, as if that had worked the last time.

Up until that point, Darlene and her girls felt like they were on safe ground. No one had approached either of them. Nor had anyone given them any mean or threatening looks. But that was all about to change. Once Darlene approached Ajay in the kitchen. Things went down hill for her, Gloria and Anita, from that moment on.

Ajay had gone into the kitchen as a diversion, just for Darlene to bite and follow him like he knew she would. She was on some outstanding shit, as of late. Like she could approach a crew male without an invite. That shit would never go over smoothly. Ajay knew his older sister and the females were plotting on getting in their asses by that time, so he had gone into the kitchen knowing she would follow him in there. And he was absolutely right. No sooner than he got in the kitchen and grabbed a 12 ounce beer. Darlene was there to close the refrigerator door.

"Hey Ajay baby," Darlene said, "You didn't even speak. Are you mad at me?"

"No," he said, "I'm just kicking it wit my crew."

"So do you wanna drive me home and keep my car tonight?" she asked seductively, "Then you'll have a ride to come see me later."

"Hang on a minute and let me see if I can leave," he lied.
He knew he could go, as long as he took his crew with him. But he wanted his crew females to get theirs in while he still got to keep Darlene's car for the night too. He was going to do whatever he could to assist them. He had Darlene to wait in the kitchen until he came back. He went to find Lynn. "Hey sis. What you got planned for that ho?"

"I'm beating her down, that's what," Lynn said, "I'm just waiting on Renee to give me the word. Why? What's up?"

"She wants me to drive her home and keep her car, so I can come back and spend the night," he said, "But I don't wanna do that before you get yours in. Cause I'm not spending the night with that bitch. Besides that. Marsha bugging me to come fuck her too. So shit. I'm gonna go with Marsha to miss Lou's house and get that. But I wanna keep the car too. So let me do this shit wit Marsha and get back. And while I'm gone, y'all can move something."

Lynn said, "Cool. Stall her ass out before you leave and give us time to get it

169

in. I gotta let Renee and the girls know you're gonna help keep her here. We're gonna whoop all they asses tonight."

"Bet," Ajay said, "I got it. I already told her I gotta go handle some business. I'll just get her keys and tell her to wait here until I get back. Y'all get that shit done while I'm gone. But Jb and Tank gonna be look outs for me anyway. So they can let you know when I'm bout to come back."

"Word," Lynn said.

Lynn went to let Renee know Ajay was going to assist them with their caper. While Ajay headed back into the kitchen to stall Darlene.

He told her he would drive her home after he was done with his crew business. Jb and Tank had taken Marsha outside to wait for him while he set things up with Darlene.

"I gotta go handle this first," Ajay said, "I want you to wait for me. Give me your car keys. That way, if one of yo girls get wit crew and wanna leave. You can tell them you can't go *nowhere* because I got your keys and you're waiting for me. Got it?"

"Okay," Darlene said with a smile, "That's a good idea."

"Jb and Tank waiting on me, so I need to go," he said.

She gave him her car keys and he allowed her to give him a kiss on the cheek to seal the deal. He walked out of the kitchen and headed for the front door.

Jb and Tank was waiting on the front porch with Marsha. The 4 of them walked across the street and onto the driveway on Pearl's side. Ajay and Marsha headed to Lou's house. He was going to signal Jb and Tank when he was ready, by flashing the bathroom light on and off several times. When they saw that, they would get the word to Lynn so her and the girls could handle their business. Ajay would arrive back in time to rescue Darlene and her friends. Then drive them home. He was hoping that somehow that plan would be altered slightly to something which would get Darlene out of his hair for the rest of the night while he still kept her car.

Ajay and Marsha went inside Lou's house while Jb and Tank went into Al and Jo's side of the utility shed to smoke weed. They were going to watch for Ajay's signal through the shed window.

Marsha took Ajay straight to her room and he could tell she was happy to have some time with him. She complimented him on his hair.

"Your braids are getting so long," she said, "They look great. If you ever want me to braid it for you, just let me know."

"I'm cool on that," he said, "My mama do them or my cousin's girl. So I'm good. I thought you wanted to fuck me. You talking about doing my

170

hair and shit. All you need to do is get on this dick and let's get this done, alright?"

She didn't waste anymore time with the idol chatter. She unzipped his jeans and went down to her knees. He was happy she stopped talking and he was even more pleased that she hadn't tried to ask him to hang out. She got his jeans undone then looked up at him. He knew she was about to ask if she could suck his dick raw. But he didn't even give her the time. He put on a condom and let her do the job he came there for her to do.

"Mmmm," he moaned as she took him into her mouth, "You're good at this shit, ha Marsha?"

16 year old Marsha looked up at him from her knelt position and attempted to smile while she sucked his dick. He put his hands behind her head and helped to guide her in the rhythm that he liked best.

"Suck that dick, girl," he demanded, "Take it to yo throat for me."

He coached her on what he liked most about her skills and she did as he demanded, over and over. She moaned and kept at it. Ajay was loving the sensation he was feeling. She was about the same as Darlene or any of the other girls who had given him head, over the past 5 years. He was still 11 and wouldn't be 12 for another 3 months. But his sexual experience rivaled that of a 21 year old man. His basketball skills was already being ranked with high school players and his mentality was far more mature than any other 11 year old. He had a child's face but his body mirrored that of a man. And in a man's place is where he often found himself. He had no problem with that positioning either.

"You like it don't you Ajay?" she whispered as she kept going and he could tell she wanted to please him.

"Hell yea I like it," he grunted, "Stop talking and keep sucking this dick. I want this nut girl."

She did as he told her to do. It wasn't long before he got his nut. Afterwards she got undressed and he fucked her once. Before telling her he had to go.

"That was straight but now I gotta go handle some business," he said, "You know that right?"

"Ahhh you always leave as soon as we finish," she said, "You did that the first time. I don't ever get to talk to you, Ajay."

"Look all we ever gonna talk about is fuckin," he said, "That's how it was the first time *and* this time. Both times we got straight to it and that's good for me. I tell you what. You can talk to Mark about whatever you need to talk about and have him hold you afterwards. That ain't my job. You fucking other motherfuckahs Marsha. So let them niggas talk to you.

171

But I ain't wit that. Can you handle that? Cause if you can't, just tell me that right now. So I'll know not to come around you no more. This is how it started from day one. All you said you wanted to do was fuck me. You fucked me, so don't try to change shit on me now alright?"

"But I want you to be my boyfriend Ajay," Marsha said sadly. "I wanted that from day one. That's why I keep coming back to Cleveland. So I can be with you. The only reason I left with Mark after your sister Nina and Ebony's party was because you was ignoring me."

"So if I ignore you from now on. Then you'll fuck wit Mark?" Ajay asked, "Is that what you're saying to me?"

"I don't like Mark," Marsha said, "I like you."

"I don't want a girlfriend right now," he said, "Not before I'm thirteen and I'm gonna pick who that's gonna be. I gotta go handle my business. Stop talking Marsha cause it's getting on my damn nerves. And if you get on my nerves. I swear I won't even speak to you no more. Do you understand that? Don't get on my nerves. The head was good. The pussy was good too. But if you wanna fuck me again. Then stick to the same shit you started wit. Cause that's what I saw then and that's all I'm looking for now. I'm outta here."

He left her on her bed and headed into the hallway bathroom to discard the condoms. He washed his hands and flickered the lights for Jb and Tank. He looked out of the bathroom window and saw Tank running to Chill's house to alert Lynn. He saw Jb heading into the path to miss Lou's house to meet and signal him. That way he would know it was safe to come out and no one else was outside watching to see him leave. He went back to Marsha's room to put on his pants and shoes.

"Please don't leave," Marsha tried.

He looked at her impatiently. He knew that would be the last time he visited her there. If he ever fucked her again. She would have to come to him. He gave her a half smile as he tied up his newest pair of shoes that Darlene had bought for him. When he was done, he turned to Marsha and said,

"I'm out. Are you planning to get on my nerves?"

"No."

"Then we might fuck again," he said, "Later."

He left her room a second time and descended the stairs quickly. He looked out the back door window and saw Jb standing by the wooden fence. Jb signaled for him to come on out. He did and met Jb, just at the back of mama Pearl's fence. They headed back to Chill's house where they were sure a fight was either happening right then. Or 1 had just finished.

172

CHAPTER 8-Just To Breathe Again

"*Man*. Pops you was slick, ha?" Lil Ajay ask as he laughs.

"I didn't see it as slick though, son," Ajay says, "I was always loyal to my family and my crew *first*. I knew your mama was gonna be my girlfriend or I was never gonna have one. It was just a matter of me waiting until *she* was ready and could have a boyfriend. I use to tell girls I was waiting until I turned thirteen. When in fact I was just waiting on Ebony."

Lil Ajay laughs and says, "But you still haven't got that real kiss yet. I know you told me one time when we was talking, that you went to *Juvie* before you was twelve and before you got that first real kiss."

"Yes I did," Ajay says and chuckles, "I went to Juvie *three* times."

"When you went the first time, it was about my mama?"

"Yes it was and the second time too," Ajay says, "It was about me protecting her from an asshole who wanted to disrespect her. I was never gonna have no parts of that kind of shit. Not then and definitely not now."

"The first time you went, how long did you have to stay?"

"A month."

"So after my auntie Lynn and them beat up Darlene. The police made you go the *Juvie*? Why? You didn't do nothing wrong and that wasn't somebody messing with my mama."

"No son. After that fight we all went home and things were cool for awhile," Ajay says, "It wasn't until we were back in school, long after spring break, when I got that Juvie charge. School was almost out. Actually it was my last week of sixth grade and fourth grade for your mom."

"Tell me what happened."

"Here goes," Ajay says.

}*Conclusion of Lynn's party, April 1986*{

Ajay and Jb arrived back at Chill's house just in time to see the tail end of the melee. Renee, Tonya, Lynn, Bre and Jan together, had whooped Darlene, Gloria and Anita *pretty* damn good. The thing was, Lynn didn't want to stop there. She had Darlene in a choke hold and she continued to punch her, about the head and face. Her father Al was having a hard time getting her to let go of Darlene. Even though Darlene was nearly 9 years older than Lynn, Lynn had beat her convincingly and wanted to continue with that beating.

"Lynn calm down and sit in this *damn* chair," big Al ordered.

Once he got her hands free from Darlene's throat. He added, "And don't you even think about getting up again."

Lynn saw the look in her father's eyes and she knew she had to either calm down or she would have to deal with him later. She calmed down almost instantly. That's when Ajay came to her side to check on her and make sure she was alright.

"Sis, are you good?" he asked.

"For now," she said and she was still pretty winded. "But every time I see her. I'm bringing it to her. She tried to kick me in my knee, *Ajay*. You know I'm a track star. She could've ended my career. She know I run. She work at our school, so you *know* she knows. That just tells me without a doubt that she's *scandalous*."

"She did what?" Ajay asked as he looked over to the corner where Paul and John were shielding Darlene, Gloria and Anita from anymore punishment from their crew girls.

That when he added, "She'll get hers, sis. I'm gonna break that ho and buy you something wit her money. Don't sweat it."

By then, John was signaling for Ajay to come to him. Immediately Ajay went to see what he wanted.

"Do you have her car keys?" John whispered, speaking of Darlene.

"Yes sir."

"You're trying to keep her car, *right*?" he whispered even lower.

"Yes sir," Ajay answered with a slight smile because he knew right then, the fathers were going to help out his mission.

"I got this," John whispered before he got the attention of the entire household.

He said, "The crew sons got some business that *must* be done and finished tonight. So Paul and I are gonna see to it that these ladies here, get back to Maple Heights. John junior, Tank and Ajay need to get with Chill, junior, Stoney, Rob and Arthur and get about y'all goddamn business. Right now!" The guys in the crew knew the only reason big John cursed or yelled was for the affect that it would have on the none crew, who were still present. More precisely Darlene and her girls, so they would think that was the reason Ajay wouldn't be available to drive them home. Al came in right after John.

"Ant, y'all get the hell on out there and do what you know you're suppose to be doing," Al said, "You said you had a ride before. Do you still?"

"Yes sir. I was gonna keep Darlene's car," Ajay said, "I was gonna drive them home and meet her there later. My crew brothers was going over there with me though."

That was convincing enough for Darlene. She just wanted to get out of that house and away from those crew girls before they got lose again.

"I'll see you later, Ajay," she said, "Be careful and call me when you're on the way. I'm going home and ice my face. Okay?"

"Alright," Ajay said without so much as a glance or going over to check on her.

It was taking everything in him *not* to burst out laughing. He was loving how well his crew and his pops crew could gel when needed. Darlene should've known better than to try the actions she'd tried with the crew. Being that she was older than *all* of them. But her longing to be a member of the crew and wanting to feel important, didn't allow her to think logically. Her, Gloria and Anita followed John and Paul out to Paul's car.

Two police cars were arriving as they got outside. The police took statements and basically, charted things up to a random party fight. Since the girls who had gotten the best of the altercation were the minors.

But just the sight of the police cars outside on their street. Got the attention of Pearl and Jo. They came out of Pearl's house to see what was going on. The foursome was still up, as well. They followed the ladies outside. The Foursome wanted to know what happened with their crew at big Paul's house. That was the night when Ebony would *first* hear Darlene's name. She didn't yet know what part Darlene had played in the fight ever starting. Nor did she know the part she would play in her future life. That night she only found out Darlene had gotten into a fight with Lynn, Renee, Tonya, Bre and Jan. And that Darlene had lost the fight. That information was okay with Ebony, as long as her crew sisters wasn't hurt.

After the police left, Pearl took the girls back inside her house and Jo went on home. Al had told her he was allowing Lynn to finish her party and he would be there to make sure she was okay. Darlene, Gloria and Anita were already in Paul's car by then. John got in the front seat and went with Paul to take them home.

Inside Paul's house, Chill and the rest of his crew got right back to party mode.

"Good that bitch gone," Chill said as he laughed. Then he turned to Renee and said, "Baby, you off the rip. I told you I ain't fucking with that ho no more."

"Yea I know that baby," Renee said, "But see the problem now is, that she's working her way through the crew, Kenny. Those are my little

175

sisters men. So she best to be knowing that she's *still* gonna get it from me. On everything I love. That's on principle. *Crew* principle."

"I feel you," Chill said, "That's exactly what I expect from you. But they're gone, so the party can continue now. *Right*?"
He cracked up laughing which made Renee laugh too. Then everyone else joined in as they got back to the party.

Al, Brad Sr, Greg Sr and Brian Sr were all still there as parental figures and Al allowed Lynn to stay at her own party past 11pm. The rest of the party went on without incident.

It was nearing the end of the school year before Ajay had any more trouble with anyone who was getting on his nerves. They were in the last week of school at Abe Lincoln middle and Beachwood elementary. With only a half day left before school would be dismissed for the summer. Ajay had just finished his last test of the day and the school year. He was relaxing in class and waiting for the bell to ring to go home. He had plans of playing basketball with Ebony and his crew, once they got home.

Ebony's last class of the day in 4th grade was PE. Her class was outside on the playground when 1 of her classmates named Billy Marshall decided he wanted to taunt her. She was on the swings along with Nina, T-baby and Rebbie when Billy came over and grabbed the chains of her swing. He started to yank her around.

"Stop it!" Ebony yelled.

"*Stop it*," Billy mimicked her but he continued to yank the chains.

"Stop before you make me fall!" Ebony screamed.
1 of their teachers witnessed it and was on her way over to correct the problem. Before she could get there, Billy yanked both chains hard and Ebony fell to the ground.

"You stop it and leave her alone!" Nina yelled and pushed Billy in his chest.
T-baby kicked his knee cap while Rebbie threw a handful of dirt on him. They were ready to fight, right then and there. But by then, the teacher had gotten there and grabbed Billy.

"You are going to the office, young man," she said, "You are not to bully your classmates and you should never taunt anyone. Especially not a little girl."
She took off with Billy, on their way to the office while a second teacher along with Nina, T-baby and Rebbie helped Ebony up and brushed the dirt for her legs and her clothes. Ebony started to cry. Not from fear. But from

anger. Nina, T-baby nor Rebbie liked the fact that Ebony was crying. They thought it was because she was afraid. They were mad because they hadn't gotten a chance to hit Billy *more* before he was taken to the office. That when Nina got an idea.

"Stay with Ebony," she said to T-baby and Rebbie. "I'm gonna go find Jeremy."

Nina took off running. The 2nd teacher thought she was going after Billy and started calling for Nina to come back.

Nina ran right past Billy and the 1st teacher and into the building. She ran until she got to the 5th grade hallway. She needed to find Tank and tell him what had just happened to his little sister. She ran straight to his class. The classroom door was opened so she darted right in and went straight to Tank's desk while his teacher was trying to get her attention.

"Billy pushed Ebony off the swings," Nina said, "She's crying."

Tank took off out of his classroom without permission but yelled back to his teacher, "My Lil sister is hurt! I gotta go see about her!"

Nina ran to try to keep up with him but he was a lot faster than her. He went on the 6th grade hallway to get Ajay. Tank had 1 thing on his mind and that was beating Billy's ass, so he'd know not to try anything like that again with his sister. He got to Ajay's classroom and flung the door open.

"Ajay come on," he said, "Somebody hurt twin."

Ajay grabbed 2 pencils from his desk and took off behind Tank. Nina was in a distant 3rd then, as they headed toward the 4th grade hallway.

By the time they got to the 4th grade hallway, the 2nd teacher was bringing the class in. Ebony was at the front of the line with the teacher. Ajay and Tank could tell she was upset. Before they could console her, that's when the 1st teacher came out of their classroom. She had stopped in there to get a discipline form before taking Billy to the office. Billy wouldn't make it to the office for discipline on that day. His punishment would come at the hands of Tank and Ajay. More so, from Ajay.

Tank and Ajay started to hit him simultaneously and Billy fell to the floor. He tried to cover himself up but that didn't work at all. Tank and Ajay beat and kicked him continuously. Before long, Ajay had him completely covered and Tank couldn't even find an opening.

"That's my girl, *muthafucka*," Ajay said to Billy in a chillingly calm voice. "Don't you ever touch her and don't say shit to her. Do you *hear* me bitch?"

Ajay had him smothered and Billy didn't stand a chance of getting free. Tank got in several more kicks and stomps but Ajay was out of control.

Suddenly he pulled the 2 pencils from the back pocket of his jeans and started to stab the *already* beaten boy. Billy was alive but he wasn't moving. 2 male teachers and coaches, who had coached Ajay from the 8th grade team, finally brought the beating to an end.

"Ajay *please* son," 1 of the coaches said in an almost begging tone. "Whatever he did. He's gonna be punished for it. Trust me. I don't want you to end up killing him. Let the teachers handle this one."

"He pushed my girl off the swings," Ajay tried to explain. "Don't *nobody* touch her. I ain't gonna let nobody fuck wit her. That's my word."

"I understand," his coach said, "And we will make sure that he's properly punished. I just need for you to come with me."

"Call my daddy," Nina told the coach, "He can talk to Ajay."
1 of the teachers ran to the office to call big Al while the coach tried to escort Ajay to the gym and calm him down. But Ajay wasn't willing to lose sight of Ebony.

"Bring her too," he told the coach and the coach did.
He brought Ebony, Nina, Tank, the 2 assistant coaches and 1 of the male teachers too. Ebony's teachers had gotten the office to call an ambulance for Billy. Ebony could hear the sirens coming as she walked into the gym with Ajay holding 1 of her hands. Tank was holding the other one. Jb and Lynn left their 7th grade class and found them in the gym.

"Are you okay, baby girl?" Jb asked.
Ebony shook her head yes. But Jb could see that she was still upset. The look on her face was terror because she had witnessed Ajay and Tank come to her rescue. She witnessed what kind of mess they'd made out of Billy Marshall too. She had never seen that much blood in her life. It frightened her. Ajay could see that she was still upset, so he tried to calm her down. He put an arm around her shoulders.

"You don't have to be scared of nobody, baby girl," Ajay said, "I'm not gonna *never* let nobody mess wit you. And if they do. I'm gonna beat they ass good. Okay?"
She shook her head yes but she wasn't over that sighting of Billy yet. Not right then.

Before long, Al was at the school and so was Jo and Pearl. Billy had been taken to the hospital for the puncture wounds in his arms, legs and stomach. He would require a tetanus shot and some stitches too. He would get demerits which would be applied to his record for the next school year. But the fate for Ajay was going to be much worse. He was going to family court. The principal told Jo and Al that he wouldn't apply an expulsion to

Ajay's 7th grade school year. But appropriate punishment was mandatory. Everybody knew Ajay didn't get expelled because of his basketball abilities. The school district was looking out for itself as well.

"But I will have to have a police report because the other student went to the hospital," the principal said, "And it's mandatory that family court is notified."

"I understand that," Al said, "Let's do what we have to do while it's summer time. That way it won't affect his upcoming school year."

With that said, the principal notified the police and Ajay was turned over to family court and the Juvenile division.

Three days later, Ajay had to go to a hearing. At that hearing, he was sentenced to 30 days in training school. He would have to leave on the 4th day of June and he would not be released until the day before the 4th of July holiday.

Ebony couldn't manage a smile after finding out Ajay was going to be gone for a whole month. She played basketball for only a couple of days with T-baby and the crew. They all agreed it wasn't the same without Ajay. They all stopped playing and headed to Chill's house. They wanted to know how he felt about Ajay being gone and what advice he had for them to help pass the time.

They made it over to Chill's house. He, Renee, Tonya and Jr were all sitting in the living room together. They were already discussing Ajay's departure.

Chill said, "I know what he's dealing with but Ajay can handle it. He called last night. He told me he wanted to talked to Ebony. I'm gonna make that happen for him tonight."

"Yes. Mama Pearl said she could bring Lil Man over to play with Kenny," Renee said, "So she'll be here when he calls."

"Can we talk to him too?" June asked.

"I'm gonna be over here," Jb said, "I can yell in the background. I don't care."

They all laughed before Chill said, "I want all my crew to be here tonight."

"Good man. Cause he just left two days ago and it feels like he's been gone for a week," Tank said, "Damn I miss my homeboy."

"Ebony will be holding the phone," Chill said.

Ebony smiled as he continued, "She's the one he asked to speak too. I know how it is in there. When I went in there, I had no idea what it was gonna be like. But the worse part was being away from my girl and my family."

"That's what he said the first night he went," Nina said, "He called home and said that was gonna be the only thing hard about it."

"But he said it was some boys in there that knew him from playing basketball," Lynn said, "And he said they was gonna play ball the whole month."

"Chill said he played yesterday, right Chill?" Jr asked.

"Yea he's gonna stay on them hoops while he's in there," Chill answered.

"I just wish he was here," Ebony finally said, "It don't feel right to play basketball without him."

Chill smiled and said, "I know he misses you, Ebony. He said it about four times during that fifteen minute call."

"She misses him too," T-baby said, "She don't even wanna play basketball wit us cause Ajay not out there."

They all laughed before Ebony said, "I *don't* though. He's my coach. So I don't feel right playing if he don't tell me what I need to try next, so I can score on y'all."

"We're gonna hold you down until he get's back, baby girl," Tonya said, "Or at least until you go to Houston."

"Big mama's gonna let him call you while y'all down there," Rob said, "I know that already."

"Yep because she's like that for all of us," Jan said, "She always trying to make sure that the girls get a guy that's right for us."

Bre added, "And if big mama cosigning him. Then you know he's the one for you."

"She told me she would be okay with my pick too but she said I have to wait about two more years," Stoney said and laughed, "I was worried about that for a minute."

"That's because you're in the tenth and Bre in the fifth," Chill said.

"You're fifteen and she's eleven," Renee said, "Same as Rob and Jan. Y'all got to get crewed up first because of y'all age difference."

"Well we all do. Even though some of us didn't wait until we made thirteen to get together," Chill said as they all laughed.

"Yea but we're gonna stay together though," Nina said.

"That's right," Rebbie agreed and they all laughed again.

"So June you're liking Rebbie by now, right?" Chill asked.

"Yep," he answered and chuckled.

"Rich, how about you?" Chill said, "You like T-baby don't you?"

"I sure do," Rich said.

"This crew ain't gonna never stop," Jr said.

Then Rich stood up and said, "T-baby I wanna know if you'll be my girl?"

T-baby smiled and said, "Yes but we have to wait until I turn thirteen before you can ask my daddy though and you have to call me Trisha."

"That's alright," Rich said, "I'll ask him then and I'll call you your name too. I just wanna make sure you know I wanna be your boyfriend."

"Okay," T-baby said, "I will."

Just like that, Rich got his girlfriend before Ajay and he felt like he had finally beat Ajay at something.

"I already asked Nina boo," Tank said, "She'll be eleven this year and I'll be twelve when my birthday come. We can announce it later too. But we're already a couple and Ajay knew it before he went in and he was cool wit it too."

"He told me he was too," Nina said and smiled.

Ebony just looked at them. She knew they were a lot more advanced in their intimate time than her and Ajay. She felt alone sitting there in big Paul's living room with Ajay not present. What was worse is he was gone to juvenile detention and she was leaving to visit Houston in 4 days. She was happy for all of the couples who had just declared themselves for the future. But she felt incomplete without Ajay and that was all she could think about at that moment.

Pearl and John sent their kids to visit big mama and poppa in Houston during the 2nd week of June. They were going to stay for 2 weeks. Jb, Tank, Ebony and Lil man flew to Houston for Father's day weekend. Big mama had food ready for them to eat, as soon as Poppa got them to the house from the airport. Poppa was still on the police force but he was planning to retire in another year. Big mama had just retired from the hospital where she was an RN. Pearl had taken after her mother and became a registered nurse as well. Ebony was happy to see them both but she still felt alone. She couldn't wait to talk to big mama.

After they finished dinner, poppa took the boys fishing while big mama and Ebony put the food away and cleaned the kitchen. Ebony was looking forward to talking to her grandmother about her feelings and about Ajay.

"How are you doing my little namesake?" big mama asked.

"I'm okay," Ebony said but big mama could tell that she wasn't. She asked, "Are you sure? How do you feel about Ajay being sent away?"

"I don't like it," Ebony said, "It don't feel right with him gone."

181

"Well that's because you two have become so close, sweetheart," big mama said, "I know he misses you too. And don't worry because he already knows he can call us down here."

"That's what Rob said when we was at Chill's house," Ebony said as she smiled.

"Our number is on his call list and he knows he can call us."

"I talked to him at Chill's house, one night," Ebony said, "Then I talk to him at mama Jo's house last night. He said he misses me."

"He's knows you're here, right?"

"Yes ma'am," she said, "I told him we was coming today and he said he was gonna talk to me soon."

"That means he'll call us, for sure," big mama said and smiled.

Big mama and Ebony finished in the kitchen. Then they unpacked all of her and her brothers clothes and put them away in their rooms. Once that was done. They worked in big mama's flower garden and talked a lot more. Big mama told Ebony that her and poppa was coming to visit for 4th of July and they would be flying back with them. So they could be there for their 3rd grandson June's 11th birthday on June 26th. Ebony was excited to know her big mama and poppa was going back with them and she was happy that her 1st cousin June would be having a birthday party too. But what she was most looking forward to was Ajay. He would be coming home 1 week after she got back. She couldn't wait to get back home. Which was a new feeling for her too. She use to love going to visit Houston and staying with big mama and poppa. But things had changed since her last trip south. She had Ajay on her mind and she couldn't wait to hear his voice again.

Ebony, her brothers and their grandparents returned to Cleveland on the early morning of June's birthday. Ebony was just excited to be back at home. She had talked to Ajay 6 times during the 2 weeks while she was in Houston. She still missed playing basketball with him. But she was looking forward to dancing with him again too. And she was also ready for them to have their 1st *real* kiss. Rebbie and T-baby had both moved into the tongue kissing ring with Nina while Ebony was in Houston. It wasn't even like a competition for her. She just wanted to kiss him because that's all she had thought about while she was away and while they talked on the phone. She knew that last week in waiting would be dreary. The days before she left for Houston had seemed long and dreary too. She realized the biggest part of what her days fun was over the last year, was having Ajay around. Now he'd been in training school since the summer vacation began, so things were just ultimately boring and really out of sync for her. She was just anxious for that to change.

Her and Pearl went to lunch after June's party. John had insisted they go as soon as Ebony returned. He had gotten Paul, Al and Greg Sr to go along to make sure they were secure. Ebony and Pearl had lunch together at least once a week, on 1 of Pearl's off days. They would always get some shopping in while they were out too. Ebony had Ajay on her mind today and she wanted to talk about it with her mother.

"So baby girl, did you enjoy your trip to mama and daddy's?" Pearl asked as they enjoyed their lunch.

"It was fun but I was ready to come back home," Ebony said.

"Really?" Pearl asked in surprise, "That's a first. You usually never wanted to leave when you got down there."

"I missed playing basketball," she said, "I wish Anthony was here, so we could play."

"You miss him don't you?" Pearl asked.

"I do mama," she said, "Nobody can play basketball like him and I learn so much more when I play with him. But he won't play hard when we play and that makes me sick."

Pearl laughed and said, "Well honey. He's got manners and he doesn't want to beat his girl neighbor. It's different when he's playing with your bothers. They have an all out war, out there."

"I know but if he play hard. I'll play harder too."

"He thinks you're special, baby girl," Pearl said, "You see he asked your daddy if he could call you baby girl and he asked you to call him Anthony instead of Ajay. That means he really wants you to think highly of him and not be so mean when y'all play together."

"Well I won't be mean to him but I am gonna fuss if he don't play his best, mama," she said, "He said he wanna go pro when he gets big. So he's got to play hard every time. That's how he said doctor jay did it and that's how Michael Jordan and Dominique Wilkins do it now."

"I think he wants to be more than just your coach, when y'all get older," Pearl said with a sweet smile, "I know it will be much later on. But Jo and I have been noticing a difference in you and Ajay's friendship. We don't hear y'all yelling and fussing, like y'all use too."

"I know because he's not gonna play to beat me. So I just stop even trying to say it," she said," But he's not mean either, mama. Everybody use to say that about him. He was never mean to me."

"That's because you're special to him," Pearl said and smiled.

"Big mama said the same thing," Ebony said.

"She told me he called down to her house too," Pearl said, "I knew he would want to talk with Tank and John junior. He's gotta be missing them like crazy."

"And me too," Ebony said.

"Yes but Ebony he's missing your brothers for a lot more reasons. Because they hang out together, party and everything else," Pearl said.

"But he talked to me the most," Ebony said and giggled.

"Well he knows you're spoiled and of course, your brothers were gonna let you have your way," Pearl said, "And if you demanded to have the phone. None of them were gonna tell you no."

Pearl giggled but Ebony was persistent. She wanted her mother to know that Ajay was calling to speak with her, first and foremost.

"But I'm the reason he called," Ebony said, "He asked for me when he called. He didn't asked for twin or Jb. He asked for me, mama."

She giggled and her mother laughed. Pearl didn't understand or she wasn't ready to *believe* that street tough Ajay saw Ebony as a priority. She would have to learn that *much* later. They finished their lunch then hit up the stores. When they finished their shopping, they headed home along with Paul, Al and Greg Sr.

When they got home, Ebony's girls were at Nina's house waiting for her. She joined them and played with her baby dolls while they talked. When they were alone, her girls were only talking about Tank, June and Rich and all of the new things they were experiencing. They really didn't pay the baby dolls much attention, though Ebony still enjoyed hers. It was fun listening to them talk about their boys. But she wanted to do the same. She just didn't have as much to talk about as they did and she really wasn't ready to share her and Ajay's private talks with them, at that point.

It was July 1st and they were playing at Rebbie's house during the day. There was 2 days left before Ajay would be home and Ebony was so excited she could barely keep still. She was with her girls and they were about to start discussing their boys again. But Ebony cut them short that day. All she wanted to talk about was Ajay and how much she wanted him to come home.

"I can't wait until he comes back," she said and smiled, "I missed him so much, it feels crazy to me."

"He likes you Ebony," Nina said suddenly, "Every time when we go visit him. He always ask about you and he wanna know how you're doing.

He said he talked to you a lot and he missed playing basketball with you too."

"I like him too," Ebony said, "I like him a lot. I didn't really know that before. But when I was in Houston. Big mama told me to write him letters and I did. I hope he liked them."

"Did you tell him you liked him on the letters?" T-baby asked.

"Yes I did," Ebony said with caution in her voice, "And I told him that when I can have a boyfriend. He's gonna be him, so he don't have to worry about that no more."

"He liked them letters then," Nina said as she laughed, "Because he told Lynn that he wants you to be his girlfriend and he said he's gonna asked you too."

Ebony liked that statement a lot. She was all smiles as they played with their dolls and tea sets. Well, she was the only 1 really *playing* with them.

"That's gonna be cool," Rebbie said, "Lynn and Jb are already boyfriend and girlfriend. Then Tank and Nina are too. So when Ebony and Ajay start being boyfriend and girlfriend. That's gonna be all sisters and brothers going together."

"And y'all are gonna be going wit our cousin's," Ebony said.

"That works for me," Nina said.

"Me too," Ebony said shyly, "But I have to give Anthony a real kiss so he'll know that I really like him."

"You should do that when he comes home," Nina said, "That will make his day."

"I am," Ebony said, "And I'm gonna tell him that I like him and that he is going to be my husband, one day."

The girls laugh and have fun talking about boys and kissing before they head to Jo's house were they're staying for the night. They help Nina and Lynn get fresh clothes packed for Ajay, so they can take them when they go pick him up. Ebony wishes she could go but she knows her mother won't allow her to go near anything that resembles jail. She'll just say she isn't old enough to understand that sort of thing yet. And with the conversation she had with her mother 5 days ago. She knows Pearl will say no because she'll think Ebony is getting confused about Ajay's intentions. But Ebony wasn't the 1 who didn't understand what was happening. It was Pearl.

It's the day before Ajay comes home and all the mothers are having another card party at Pearl sister Brenda's house. They had done the same thing on the evening of June's 11th birthday. The fathers aren't cooking on the grill. Today they're frying fish. They're going to barbeque in 2 days

185

which will be 4th of July. Tomorrow the ladies will be prepping for it while waiting for Al and Paul to return with Ajay. The foursome had stayed at the card party with their mothers but Ebony wanted to go home. She wanted to be at Nina's house actually. Because she knew Ajay was going to call. And even though he would be home the next day. She still wanted to talk to him. But for that evening, her and her girls hung out at Brian Sr and Brenda's house. The foursome actually liked when their moms got together because they always had really detailed discussions. The foursome would always find a good hiding place so they could eavesdrop and hear everything their mothers talked about. When their mothers talked openly, they were often times very graphic about the sex lives they were enjoying with their husbands. Being that it was a changing time in their lives, the foursome paid attention and took notes. They wanted to know what to expect when that day came, so they could be ready to take the plunge into sex too.

}July 3, 1986{

Ajay was returning home this morning. Al and Paul had gone to pick him up. All of his crew was there waiting for him to get back. All of the mothers were already at Jo and Pearl's preparing for the families big 4th of July event and the younger girls was yet to join in. The mothers gave them the morning off so they could greet Ajay outside when he arrived. The father's were marinating the meats and enjoying beers and more. That was always a special time for the entire crew. Big mama and poppa had arrived from The Point with granny and papa. Renee's younger brother Wesley had come back to visit and spend the holiday with her. The foursome was upstairs in Ebony's room playing together as usual. But Ebony was more excited that Ajay was on his way home, then she was about playing with her girls. She had no doubt in her mind anymore about whether she liked Ajay as more than just a basketball buddy. She liked him period and she had missed having him around.

"I'm glad my brother is on the way home," Nina said and the other 3 girls agreed with her.

"I'm glad too," Ebony said and smiled.

"So are you gonna kiss him?" Rebbie asked, "Because you told him in your letters that you was gonna kiss him."

"Are you gonna do it, Ebony?" T-baby asked, "If you don't he's gonna be mean, I'll bet."

"I don't know," Ebony said.

She had planned to kiss Ajay once he returned. But she didn't want to share that part with her girls anymore. Because she was feeling suddenly nervous and a bit shy too and she wanted that to be her and Ajay's secret.

"He's gone wanna kiss you, cousin," T-baby said.

"He sure is," Nina said, "I told you the only girl he asked about when we went to see him is *you*."

Ebony blushed openly and said, "That's good."

Her girls started to tease her about how much she was blushing but she didn't reply anymore.

Within minutes, they heard Tank and Jb run in the side door downstairs. They were yelling loudly and making rough house noises about the news they had run in to share.

"Ajay's home!" They both yelled and cut up.

Ebony heard them and felt butterflies, all of a sudden. She was frozen in her tracks. Her girls jumped up and ran downstairs to greet Ajay on the driveway but Ebony stayed put.

Ajay hopped out of the car to cheers from his crew. He hugged everybody and gave dap to his boys while he surveyed Nina, T-baby and Rebbie. The most important person in that quartet was missing. He didn't panic because he knew she was shy. He went on inside his house to put his things away and freshened up.

Ebony was still in her room. She was still playing with her baby doll and wondering what Ajay looked like after 30 days. But still she didn't go outside to try and find out. She remembered what he said on 1 of their phone conversations.

He had said, "You'll know how much I look forward to seeing you when I come home. Because I'm going to come to wherever you are. I don't even care if it's in the kitchen with the ladies. They're gonna have to left me come in there so I can watch you."

That made her smile during that whole phone conversation.

As soon as Ajay had showered and changed his clothes. He was back outside. Still, Ebony wasn't there. Not to be denied, he called Tank over to where he stood after he'd separated himself from the pack.

"Let's go in your house," Ajay said, "I need to go get Ebony."

"Cool," Tank said and they went in through Pearl's side door.

Before going up the stairs, Ajay spoke to all the women who were in Pearl's kitchen doing prep. Then he followed Tank on up to Ebony's room.

187

Nina, T-baby and Rebbie had gone back in there with her, by the time Tank and Ajay arrived and Tank knocked on the door.

"Who is it?" Ebony asked.

"It's me, twin," Tank said, "Let me come in."

Nina hopped past Ebony and opened the door for Tank, as she smiled big. Ajay spotted Ebony and he smiled. She smiled too.

"Hey baby girl. Why you didn't come and tell me hey?" he asked.

"Cause I knew you would come and get me," she said innocently.

"Oh okay," he said, "You remembered what I said ha? So you ready to catch up on our games?"

"Yes," she said with excitement as she hopped up, put her doll on her dresser and grabbed her sneakers.

"You still wearing the sneakers I got for you?" Ajay asked.

"Yes," she said, "These are my favorite ones."

Tank laughed. He knew Darlene had given Ajay the money to buy those shoes. She had also put money on his books while he was in Juvie. He signed money off to Al so he could give it to his boys in the crew. And they could buy things for Ebony while he was locked away. His only stipulation was that they couldn't buy her any new baby dolls.

"I'm ready," Ebony said.

"Let's do this," Ajay said, "I wanna see how well your game improved while I was gone."

"Okay. I wanna see how much better you play too," Ebony said.

Ajay was only looking forward to spending time with Ebony. But when they got outside, the rest of their crew wanted to play too. T-baby had followed them out there, as well as Tank, Nina and Rebbie.

"Okay," Ajay said, "We'll all play. But Ebony is gonna be on my team and I'm not changing that. Y'all better put Chill and Stoney on y'all team to keep it even."

They played basketball until it was getting too hot to stay outside. Ajay wanted Ebony to come home with Nina. But their mothers had other plans. Pearl came to the side door and called the girls in.

"You girls are ten or almost ten and you have to start helping us with food prep for holidays, for the whole day," Pearl said, "So let's go."

The foursome headed inside immediately as Ebony looked back at Ajay with a sad look on her face. Renee and the older girls was already inside helping. Ebony felt disappointed as she continued to look back at Ajay, who was standing with the same disappointed look on his face. Ebony went on into the kitchen to help out.

Ajay and Tank had followed them inside and they were hanging around the kitchen, just as Ajay told Ebony he was going to do when they talked on the phone. But his mother had other plans for him.

"Ant, y'all are not suppose to be in here in the way," Jo said, "Allen is suppose to be taking y'all to work at the detail shop. You still have your job down there to go to *whenever* you're not doing something with a basketball team or a camp. You need to let your father know that you've changed clothes."

"Yes ma'am," Ajay said but he was even more disappointed.
He knew if they left for the detail shop, then they would be down there until after dark because the day before the 4th was always an *all day*, work day. He went back to his house where he found his father and Paul waiting. His crew brothers were all outside and prepared to go to work too. All of the males left heading to the detail shop.

In Pearl's kitchen, Ebony felt suddenly sad. She knew she wouldn't see Ajay again until the next day for the 4th of July holiday.

But as soon as they got to the detail shop, Ajay did call back to Ebony's house to talk with big mama. He had to let her know how much he'd missed being home and seeing Ebony.

"Well I think she missed you too, Ajay," big mama said.

"I could tell by how she looked at me, big mama," he said, "She likes me, like I like her. I can tell."

"I think so too. But you know it's gonna be awhile before she can act on those feelings though, right?"

"Yes ma'am I know," he said, "I'll wait for her to tell me when she's ready. So long as it's me that she likes. That's all I wanted to know, for a long time."

"Good to know," big mama said, "Pearline and I are going to take Ebony out to her house with us tonight. We're going to make the pies before we come back out here. We'll see where her head is at, right now and just see if she has any questions for us. Okay?"

"Okay and be sure to tell her again, how much I missed her," he said, "And how I couldn't wait to get home. And the only person I really wanted to see and play ball with today, was her. Will you tell her that for me, big mama?"

"Of course I will," big mama said as she giggled, "I'll make sure she knows how much you look forward to seeing her *daily*."
That made him smile and they hung up. After the prep work was done, just as big mama had told Ajay. Ebony went to The Point to spend the night.

189

Before the sunrise, big mama and granny was in the kitchen making sweet potato pies, pecan pies and sweet tarts. Ebony got up and joined them.

"Good morning baby girl," granny said with a smile, "Are you ready to show us you've perfected the crinkling of pie crust?"

"Yes ma'am," Ebony said with a smile.

"Well come on in here and let's get this finished, so we can get back out to Shaker Heights for the celebration," granny said.

"I'm glad we do them at me and Anthony's houses now," Ebony said, "I like having them at home because everybody can come to our house."

"That may be a sign of the future, baby girl," granny said.

"Ma'am?" Ebony asked for clarity.

"What she means is, one day you and Ajay may have your very own house to invite everybody too," big mama said as she giggled, "Since you two have turned out to be each others favorite people."

Ebony just smiled. Big mama was all smiles too. Ebony knew her and granny had a game plan for that pie crinkling session. They wanted the heads up on exactly what was on their oldest granddaughters mind, on the morning after Ajay had returned home.

"You're pretty good at basketball already, aren't you baby girl?" big mama started.

"I can make all my shots now," Ebony said with excitement.

"Ajay has been a good coach for you, hasn't he?" granny asked.

"He sure has and he's so good at basketball," Ebony said, "And he makes sure that I play good and that I know how to play in a game too. That's why I didn't even like to play when he wasn't here."

"That's sweet, isn't it?" granny asked.

"Yes," Ebony said and giggled.

Granny and big mama continued to talk about Ajay and how much they thought of him while they made the pies. Ebony was listening and taking notes. She didn't know that both her grandmothers already knew that the 2 of them liked each other, as more than friends. And that each of them were already planning to be a couple, very soon. She thought they were unaware of that part of it. But she would learn years later that they both did know and they were all for it.

By late morning, all of the pies were finished and sitting on the window seals cooling. It was time for granny, big mama and Ebony to get dressed. Papa and poppa had been dressed and was just waiting on the ladies.

"Well don't you look pretty this morning, little Eloise," poppa said to Ebony.

"Thank you poppa," she said, "This is new. My brothers bought this for me."

"I'll just bet they did," papa added and chuckled.

Her grandfathers knew that money had come from Ajay through Darlene. Darlene had put money on Ajay's books while he was in Juvenile detention. Ajay had made sure every penny of it was taken off and put in big Chill's hands, so the guys in the crew could use it to get Ebony some nice things for the summer.

Once everyone was dressed and all of the pies were in the car. The 5 of them headed to Shaker Heights for the celebration.

As the celebration commenced, all of Chill's crew stuck close to each other. Debra Wittman, Gloria and Darlene showed up for the event and Darlene had even brought her 2 sons. Rodney, who was 8 and Jamal, who was 7 years old were a hand full. They were already big Ajay fans, even though he was only a few years older than they were and already seeing their mother. It was time to get started on the family entertainment portion of the day and all 3 generations was ready to compete, this year. This was actually the first year the entire 3rd generation participated.

That was the foursome's 1st year presenting an act. They song together and danced. Ajay watched Ebony the entire time with a huge smile on his face. He loved what he saw. Then Lynn, Jan and Bre did a rendition of *Salt & Pepa* with Jan doing the *Spindarella* deejay part of the act. They were great too. Ajay, Tank, June, Rich and Jb did raps by *Jazzy Jeff & the Fresh Prince, Slick Rick & Dougie Fresh* and *L.L. Cool J.* They even added in some of their own original raps. That's when the family party went into overdrive. Marsha, Monica and Anita Davis showed up later and so did Tamara, another girl named Juanita and several others girls who went to MLK with the high school crew. They were all very vocal during the entertainment as Chill, Jr, Rob and Stoney did raps by *Heavy D & the Boys*. They even sang songs by *New Edition.* Renee and Tonya sang *Whitney Houston* songs and rocked the party with hits by *Klymaxx* like *Meeting In The Ladies Room* and *The Men All Pause.* After the 3rd generation had completed their portion, their parents and grandparents knew they had their work cut out for them. It was the 2nd generations turn next and when

191

they all took hold of the microphones. They brought the house down. They sang and danced too. The 1st generation performed songs from the Jackson-Jones Revue bands touring days while papa played the piano and poppa played guitar. Granny and big mama sang lead while Sally and Annabelle did background vocals. At the end of the performance portion of the event, the entire family sang gospel songs and it was very moving. They stopped traffic. *Literally*. Folks were pulling their cars over to park and get out so they could witness and be apart it too. When the singing was done, it was time to eat and the crew fed everyone in attendance. Darlene and her posse were mesmerized. They had never seen such a display of togetherness.

"They got it going on," Darlene said to Debra.

"I told you," Debra said, "The crew is the shit."

While the 2 of them was scheming and plotting on how they would get the crew guys to spend time with them later. Darlene's 2 sons were running rampant around Jo and Pearl's yard. They had broken 2 of the American Flag sticks that were lining the driveways and was on a mission to pull the rest of them up and snap them in half too. Mama Sandy got after them.

"Hey, where is y'all mama?" she asked, "You can't take the flags out of the ground. We want those there for decoration."

The 2 boys started talking back to Sandy while they still headed toward the other flags. Sandy warned them again and this time, with mama Brenda's insistence. At that point, Rodney started using curse words toward both of the mothers. Sandy and Brenda were shocked. That wouldn't last long because granny Pearline heard them and went to break some switches, right then. She got some good ones and twisted them up. By that time, Jamal had joined in on the cursing with his brother. Granny gave Sandy and Brenda the eye. She didn't want them to say another word, just deliver them to her.

"Bring them to me, right now!" granny yelled.

She wasn't going to tolerate a disrespectful nor disobedient child in her presence. Sandy and Brenda tried to grab the boys by the hands so they could deliver them to granny but the boys wasn't going without a fight. They used the "F" and "B" words several times until the fathers got wind of it. The men came over, yanked them up and took them to granny.

"You'll be better off letting her whip your behinds," big Paul said, "But if it were me. I'd punch you as hard as I could. Right in your chest and watch you cough up everything inside of your body."

The look on their faces said it all. Having a man take a stance with them had put fear in them. Paul and Al took them to granny, who whipped both of their butts good while Darlene wisely held her tongue. Once the

192

whippings were done, Rodney and Jamal went to Darlene crying like they were about to die. She told them to sit down by her and be quiet.

"Shut up," she said, "Y'all know better then to be tearing up other people's stuff. Now sit there and be quiet."

Grandma Sally and Annabelle had some advice for Darlene as they turned to her. Sally spoke first.

"If you don't get a hold on them, right now," Sally said, "They won't live to get to your age."

"They don't have any respect for you," Annabelle said, "Boys have to see examples in their mother, so they'll know how women behave. You can't have boyfriends that's nearly their age either, miss."

"They haven't had any male discipline," Sally said, "They was already crying before Pearline got hold of em. That's because they were afraid when Paul went to them."

"They won't learn it from here because I don't think you'll be in the mix around here, from too long," Annabelle said, "See our sons know better than that. They would never keep nobody that far from what they were raised on."

"We're gonna all gather around those tables," Sally said as she pointed to the tables and chairs, "And we're gonna sit and eat like a family of respectable people. It's okay to talk at the table. But there won't be any showing out. Make them dry up that fuss and come on. They got the one thing they needed, for carrying on like that."

Darlene and her posse brought Rodney and Jamal to 1 of the guest tables so they could all eat. The 2 boys didn't cause any more disturbance for the rest of that day, after getting a whipping. Darlene didn't say a word to Sally nor Annabelle about what they told her either. But she felt like she knew better than what they said. She had Ajay pegged as a thug. A black hearted careless young man who didn't have any home training, so he wasn't going to care about any female because he wasn't interested in love. Not from her or anyone else. She thought she had a hold on him because she was paying her way to be in his space. But she was wrong. He treated her and other females that way because they allowed it. And even if they wanted more. They wouldn't get it. If those who were not on his list of worthy of his best, would've made demands. Then Ajay would've just left them alone completely. He had already left Marsha and the rest on a long leash. That would eventually happen to Darlene as well. Ajay was only killing time with Darlene and all of those other females in his life. Because he was already grooming his grand prize and just waiting for her to show him how to give

193

his attention, love and heart to a girl who was worth all of the above and more. The intimacy for Ajay and Ebony was going to start in a matter of hours and he didn't even have any idea that it was going to happen that day. He had told Ebony that she was on her own time and that he was going to be there waiting. Waiting for her to let him know whatever it was *she* wanted to do next. Because he knew she was worth it. After all, all of the folks whom he looked up to, had always solidified her.

After the eating and entertainment, it was time for the crews to have their separate celebrations. Paul and the fathers went to his house. Pearl and the ladies went to her house while the grandparents went to papa and granny's in The Point. Chill's crew got together at Ajay's house and no one liked that more than Ajay.

They started off hanging out in the yard. They played kickball and tag for an hour or so before they all did raps and songs together while some of them even danced. They played basketball for another hour or so. They were having a great time but Ajay was ready to be in Ebony's company. He wanted to talk to her alone, so he made his way over to her.

"You having a good time today?" he asked.

"Yes. Are you?"

"I am now," he said and smiled at her.

"Me too, now," she said and smiled back.

"Nina told me what you said."

"What did I say?" she asked.

She knew what he meant. Nina had told him she'd said she was going to kiss him when he came home. And though she did say it. She started to feel suddenly shy but she wasn't going to back out, if he asked her.

"Do you like me as a boy now?" Ajay asked her first.

He wanted to hear her say it before he would even dare asked her for a tongue kiss or accept and agree to it, if she were to ask him.

"I do like you and it's sad around here and boring too, when you're gone away," she said, "Big mama and granny said you think I look at you, like I'm scared of you. I'm not scared of you and I don't think you're mean. Not to me, you're not. But I just don't know how to.....you know."

"Tongue kiss?"

"Yep."

"I don't know how too either," he said, "I ain't never did it before. I want you to be first girl I kiss like that. To keep it real with you. I want you to be the only girl that I kiss like that because I like you a lot. It's different than the way I like *any* other girl and I always knew that

194

somehow. I don't even like any of those other girls that I've been around. I even told big mama that too."

She smiled. That was all she needed to hear him say. He liked her. That was huge in helping her to relax and just go with what she was feeling.

"I do wanna try it," she said, "But not in front of nobody else."

"Me either," he said, "I want it to be just us by ourselves, when we do it. So this is what I'm gonna do. I'm gonna go up to my room and just wait for you. When nobody ain't looking. I want you to just come inside and come on up to my room. I'll tell Tank to look out for us and let you know when to come in, okay?"

"I can just come to your room like that?" she asked, "You don't ever want nobody in your room. I remember when you beat Rich up for going in your room."

"I didn't want him in my room because he always messing with my stuff," he said, "But I want you to come in there. I don't mind if you go in my room."

She smiled again because that was also huge for her. Ajay doesn't just see her as *any* other girl. He sees her in that special way that her mother and grandmothers always told her about, when they talked about that special boy that would be in her life, one day.

"You're special to me," he said all of sudden, "I wanna make sure you know that, okay?"

"Okay."

"But you do like me, right?" he asked again and he chuckled.

He just wanted to hear her say it again. It gave him Goosebumps the first time she said it.

"Yes I do like you," she said, "I knew you liked me too. Especially after my granny said that's why you want me to call you Anthony and not Ajay."

"She's right and that's right," he said, "And you are the only girl or person that I want to call me by real name, okay? I'm gonna go inside now. I can't wait to see your face again and your eyes. You have some pretty brown eyes, baby girl."

"Thank you," she said and blushed hard.

"I'll be in my room," he said.

"Alright," she said.

He backed away slowly, never taking his eyes off of her until he got inside of their side door. She was watching him too.

Once he was inside and out of her sight, she felt suddenly alone.

195

It was weird how she had started to feel empty when he wasn't around her. It was like it was hard for her to breathe normally or to be excited. She still didn't understand that feeling nor why she was having it. But she was glad he was back from training school because the past month had been horrible for her. But now they've talked privately and he had told her how he felt. She had those butterflies again and a lot of excitement to go along with them. That was the affect that *only* Ajay had on her. He made her feel like she was a big girl and not like a baby, the way everyone else except Chill seemed to treat her. She's going to go through with what she'd first said to her girls. She was going to kiss Ajay and she was going to kiss him today.

The rest of their crew was still in the front yard playing or just having a good time, when suddenly Tank approached her.

"Twin, go on up to Ajay's room," he said, "If anybody asked for you. I'll tell em you went to use the bathroom at mama Jo's house, okay?"

"Okay," she said.

"And if mama wants you. I'll run in and come tell you, so they don't come to the house."

She said okay again, then started toward the side door as she glanced back at Tank. He was watching the parents. Some of them were still outside in Paul's front yard but they were into their card games. They had 4 different tables set up and loud music playing. They wasn't paying attention to her, for a change. She went inside of Jo's side door, hurried up the stairs and made her way down the hall to Ajay's bedroom door.

The door was open which was unusual. He never left his door open but it was, that day. She stopped in front of his door. He was in his room sitting on his bed and he had his boom box playing. It was that familiar tape, *The Isley Brothers* and he was playing his favorite song, *Voyage To Atlantis*. The same song she told him was her favorite. The same 1 they had always practiced slow dancing too. He looked toward his door and saw her standing there. He smiled, then got up quickly and made his way to her. He stood in his doorway and reached out his hand to her.

"Come on in," he said.

She took his hand and he guided her into his room and closed his door behind them. Alas, they were all alone.

"You're playing our dancing song," she said as she smiled.

"Yep. Do you wanna dance to it?"

"Okay."

He put his arms around her and they started to slow dance. It was great, just like the times before. But this time was a bit different. He was looking

196

down at her, the entire time. Her shyness wouldn't allow her to look back at him. Not into his eyes anyway. When she did look up at him. She just looked at his mouth. That made him feel anxious and a bit turned on. Which was something he only felt around her. That was how he first knew she was the girl for him and for his future. Because no other girl had given him those feelings. He could tell Ebony was nervous because she was trembling. He knew he needed to get her to say something, so she could calm down and he still wanted that first kiss.

"'Are you ready to kiss me?" he asked and his face darned a very serious look.

He was so handsome to her. He had a baby face but his body was not baby-like, at all. He had been promoted to 7th grade but he was the size of the boys in high school. He had been taller than big Chill for along time but now he was the same height as Stoney. He was over 6 feet 2 inches tall and very built. Even though Ebony was still only 10 years old, she knew he was fine and she knew he had the kind of look and body that all of the older girls talked about too. She still hadn't answered him.

"Are you ready?" he asked again which brought her attention back to that moment.

"Yes."

"Okay look up here," he said as he put his index finger under her chin and raised her head up.

She looked into his eyes and those butterflies she'd had earlier, turned into small birds. She was very nervous. She had talked with her mother and big mama about what it would be like when this moment came. But still she was trembling a lot because she wanted to get this right. He started to give her instructions.

"I want you to push your lips out just like you do when you give me a regular kiss."

She did. He put his lips to hers. They kissed regular, the first time but then afterwards, he had more instructions.

"Okay. I want you to do the same thing. But this time open your mouth up *just* a little bit and your teeth too."

She did. He put his lips back to hers and this time, he put his tongue between her lips and into her mouth. He started to move his mouth over hers. That felt so good. He paused and looked at her.

"Close your eyes and suck on my tongue."

He put his mouth back to hers and gave her his tongue again. She sucked on it and it just felt natural. He moaned and that sent major chills throughout her body. At that moment, she knew that was something she was going to like and want to do, a lot.

He paused again and said, "This time I want you to put your tongue in my mouth okay?"

She shook her head yes and they put their lips together again. She gave him her tongue. He started to suck on it as he moaned even louder. Suddenly he took her head in his hands and they really got into it. They started to swap tongues automatically and that felt very natural as well. It was getting very warm in that room to her. Ajay was caressing her face and the back of her neck while they kissed. They kissed very hard and long for more than 30 seconds. It was the best feeling she'd ever had in her life. When they finished, she looked up at him. He was still staring into her eyes. He looked so handsome to her and she wanted to tell him that. But she couldn't.

He asked, "Did you like it?"

"Yes," she whispered, smiled and looked back into his eyes.

She was breathless after that long kiss but her body was tingling all over. She wanted to do it some more.

"I liked it too," he said with a slight rise in his voice and she could tell he was excited. He said, "I liked that so much. Oh my God."

His face was very serious, at that point. It held a look she had never seen his face hold. It was gorgeous and his eyes seemed to sparkle as he stared at her. She looked back at him and he moved in for another kiss. That 2nd kiss led to another and another. They were standing still in his room while they kissed and both of them started to breathe harder. He paused, then put her arms up on his shoulders and asked her to keep them there. She did and they kissed again for more then 30 seconds. She could feel a hard object in his pants and though she wasn't experienced in the sexual department side of things yet. She knew exactly what that hard object was. There was no doubt in her mind what part of Ajay that was. Suddenly he started to grind against her while they kissed. She loved how that felt, even more. He was caressing her body and moaning a lot while he kissed her. He was grinding and then, he started to slow dance with her again while they still kissed. He was making this moment *maximum* for her. She started to have a feeling which was very new. Her body felt very warm by then but she liked it. His touch felt so gentle and so perfect. It made her feel like the only girl in the world and a big girl, at that. Ajay was very gentle with the way he touched and caressed her. His fingers touching her face made her feel so protected, so safe, so interesting and so endearing. Ajay was running his fingers through the back of her hair which was in curls, for the holiday. He kept

198

moaning and he was breathing very heavy by then. He kept kissing her. It had been over a minute and he didn't show any signs of coming up for air. He was enjoying the moment, same as her. But at that point, she was finding it hard to breathe. He sensed that and paused.

"Mmm that was so good," he said and smiled, "You're having a hard time breathing ha?"

"Yes."

"You gotta breathe through your nose while you're kissing me, okay?" he said, "And don't worry. I just learned about all that during the other kisses. Because I didn't wanna stop kissing you."

They both laughed. His music was still playing. It was a mixture of slow songs. But there was a lot of *Isleys* on that tape too.

Suddenly a song came on with a woman singing it and she had a heavenly voice. Ebony had heard that song before. She had heard her mother playing it but she didn't know the name of it or the woman who was singing it.

"What is this song?" she asked.

"Out on a limb," he said and smiled.

"Who is that singing?"

"Teena Marie," he said, "She's white but she's got a black voice."

"My mama play her a lot but I didn't know her name," Ebony said, "I like her song. Mama got the album."

"The album is called *starchild*," he said, "It came out last year. You and your girls was just dancing to one of her songs when we did the entertainment today."

"Lovergirl?" Ebony asked, "That was her too?"

"Yep," he said, "This was on the same album."

"T-baby picked the song for our dance," she said, "She like her a lot. So you like her too?"

"Yes," he said, "This is the same lady that's on fire and desire with Rick James. She's bad."

"I knew you liked the Isley brothers but I didn't know you liked ladies who sing too," she said and smiled, "You like a lot of music, Anthony. And you know a lot about music too."

"I love music," he said, "All kinds of music. You know I learned to play the piano from your papa. He always had the best music to listen too. My grandpa use to play songs when we was over there and papa would teach me how to play some of them on the piano."

"That's so cool," she said.

199

"But do you know what made me like this song?" he asked.

"What?"

"When I'm trying to tell myself how I feel when I'm around you," he said and smiled, "This song says it all. *I feel so insecure but yet I never felt so sure.* I ain't never been insecure about nothing that had to do with females. But I do get nervous when around you and I like that. So if you feel nervous when you're around me. You're not the only one. I am too."

"I do," she said, "But I figured out why."

"Are you gonna tell me?"

"It's because I like being around you," she said, "I like you Anthony and yes. I do think you're handsome. Not cute but handsome."

"Wow," he said, "You just made my day. You're the prettiest girl I know, baby girl. I like you a lot and I'm gonna ask you to be my girl too. I just wanna do it right and you know I have to go through the men in the crew, right?"

"Yes," she said, "Twin and them didn't do that. They just asked my girls to be their girlfriends. Then went to the men after that and they told them that they can't be saying that to nobody until they get in the crew."

"I know and that's why I'm gonna do it the right way," he said, "That's our tradition and I'm gonna do it the way I was taught too. You're a traditional type of girl. So I wanna do everything the right way."

"Out on a limb," she said and smiled at him. Then she said, "That's a good way to say how I feel too. I don't know anything about this kind of stuff, Anthony. But I feel like I should be doing this with you. Does that make sense?"

"Yea it make sense," he said, "I've done a lot, as you know. But not like this. I didn't wanna do this part with no other girl. I told you I was waiting for you. I don't wanna do nothing wit you until you say you wanna do it. Just remember that okay?"

"Okay," she said, "I wanna kiss again. You said to breathe through my nose?"

"Uh huh."

"Okay I can try that," she said and blushed, "Let's do it again."

He smiled and quickly obliged her. Within seconds, she had found a comfortable breathing pattern. That bulge in his pants got even larger and harder. She figured she must've been kissing him correctly. He was swaying to the music, as Al Green was playing by then. He held her head in his hands and kissed her *so* passionately. She knew this was something he was enjoying.

Ajay wanted that day to be extra special to her. One she would never forget and would want to repeat often. He sure as hell wanted it to last forever and so did she.

They held that last kiss for over a minute before they heard Tank coming up the stairs. They pulled themselves from each other but still, they stood there just staring at 1 another as if they were both is a trance. They both felt more relaxed and more comfortable than either of them ever had. They knew it was right. They could breathe easy. They felt comfortable in each others presence. And at the same time, they were both nervous about not doing something correctly for the other. The only thing bad about that last half hour was that Tank was at the door and they knew their alone time was about to end. Just like the music tape just ended.

Tank tapped on the door. Ajay heard him whisper his name. *"Ajay."*

Ajay sighed.

"Yea," he answered but he stayed there in front of Ebony while her back was to the door and she was still looking at him and the music stopped.

"The mamas are looking for twin to help cover the food up while they play cards," Tank said.

Ebony frowned as she continued to stare at Ajay. She didn't want their alone time to end but she knew she had to go or her mother would come looking for her.

"I guess I have to go," she said sadly.

"Yea but Chill is having Jb's party tonight, so he can be initiated into the crew," Ajay said, "That's where I'm gonna be. I hope you get to come too."

He was hoping she would try to find a way to be there too. He was about to hear her say something he had never thought he'd hear from her innocent lips.

"My girls are staying with me tonight," she said, "When it gets dark. They're gonna move the card tables over here to y'all house. I'm gonna see if my girls wanna sneak over there. I know I'm sneaking out."

"You're gonna sneak out?" he asked in surprise but he was hoping and smiling.

"Yes," she said, "Tank and Jb do it all the time and they don't get in trouble when mama and daddy find out they're gone. I might as well try it too."

"I don't want you to get in trouble, baby girl," he said, "But I do wanna see you again. I'll be waiting on you, if you can come," he said as he stared deep into her eyes.

He had a longing look in his eyes. It was almost like he was sad. She assumed he was just sad because she had to leave. But it was much more than that. Ajay had acted from his heart. That was a first for him with a female and the first time he had ever wanted too. He was more afraid of not pleasing her, than she was about being mature enough for him. He has known for nearly 6 years that this was the girl he wanted to impress. The girl he wanted to be a major part of his life and the only girl that he saw himself being happy with.

"I will surely be waiting to see you again," he said, "I don't even wanna leave now."

"I don't either, Anthony," she said innocently.

He gave her 1 more short kiss and took her tongue into his mouth. It was short but still sweet. When he released her tongue, he stepped back and smiled. Then he said, "We'll finish this as soon as I see you again, baby girl, okay? Whenever that is."

"Okay."

He finally scooted around her and opened his door to find Tank still standing there.

"Here she come," Ajay said and he still wasn't smiling.

Tank couldn't pass on the opportunity to be nosey though. It was too tempting.

"So did y'all cross that tongue kissing bridge yet?" he asked Ajay as Ebony made her way out of the room and into the hallway.

Even though Tank is her closest sibling, a part of her didn't want to share that milestone with him. Not at that time. Ajay seemed to sense that she wanted to keep their happenings private. So he took the liberty and answered Tank's question.

"Nah we just slow danced again," he said to Tank, "I want her to take her time. Ain't shit gonna happen until she wants it too. I'll be here waiting for her *whenever* she gets ready though. That's a bet."

"Damn twin," Tank said, "You been up here for thirty minutes and you still didn't get it in? Girl you're gonna have to grow up, one damn day. It's time out for them baby dolls."

"Leave her alone man," Ajay said suddenly and they both could tell he didn't like Tank chastising her. He said, "She's on her own time. She ain't gotta rush shit for me. Like I said before. I'll be here."

Ebony smiled to herself. She liked the way Ajay took up for her. Even more, she liked how Tank didn't try to push him for more details like he would've done had it been just her. She turned and looked at Ajay and they smiled

202

at each other. He winked his eye at her and licked his lips. She caught another chill from that, as her body quivered. She turned and went on down the stairs, smiling all the way.

She headed on out of Jo's side door and blended right in with her girls, who had waited for her to come out. The foursome headed into Pearl's house to get lids and foil to cover the food. Ebony just couldn't stop smiling, no matter how hard she tried. The time she had just shared with Ajay was monumental. It was so honest, so intense, so sensitive and real and it was all theirs.

CHAPTER 9-Every Little Bit Of My Heart

Ajay and Lil Ajay are as close as Ajay is with big Al. Lil Ajay trust his pops *completely* and he knows his father takes pride in that fact. They've just finished lunch at *Crew's House of Soul Food* and are heading to Ajay's sports complex to shoot basketball and talk some more. Lil Ajay is already making shots on his own and he plans to be the best male basketball player in the crew, when he gets to high school. Even better than his father had been. He feels his mother is the best basketball player of all the females in his crew. Just on her records and her stats alone.

Ajay and his son just had the discussion about the 1st kiss. Lil Ajay likes hearing that his father loved his mother so much that he was patient with her. He also shows he understands this is how he is to behave whenever he chooses a girl to be his one and only. But he wants to talk about the first kiss, just a bit more.

"I think it's so cool that my parents taught each other how to kiss, pops," he says with an Ajay chuckle. He adds, "That's off the chain."

"I agree with you son," Ajay says and smiles, "Do you know I still get butterflies when I see your mom?"

"Ah man," Lil Ajay says as he chuckles more and sounds *even more* like Ajay did, at his age.

But Ajay takes him to task immediately, "Do you think that's weak?"

"No sir, I don't," he says, "I just never imagined you would be afraid of anything."

"Son, I was scared to death of your mama not liking me," Ajay confesses, "I wanted her so bad that I asked all the elders what I needed to do to get her. And I kept them involved on every step. They knew I would love her, just by me wanting to know what steps to take. That's what love does, son. It's a beautiful and the most *priceless* thing. When you truly love someone. You have fears of messing it up. But I'm not afraid of anything anymore, as far as Ebony goes. I was then and I told her I was. That way she knew it was okay to tell me that *she* was afraid too. I learned that from your great-grandfather Al. Then the men in this family including your papa Al junior, made sure I followed the protocol because Ebony was worth it. Love is the best thing that happened to me. And Ebony *is* love. Love *unconditional*. What it is, is excitement. It's exhilarating to see your mom with a smile on her face. It is now, just like it was from day one. She's my air. She's still beautiful, still fine, even smarter and she's still going to make sure I do my best at whatever I'm involved in. Including being her husband, the head of our household and being you and your sisters father."

"Was she always like that?"

"She was," Ajay says, "But I wasn't always on my best behavior. She always loved me and respected me. But she wasn't going to tolerate no bullshit from me."

"Did she sneak out to come see you?" Lil Ajay asks with a smile.

"What do you think?" Ajay asks with a smile.

"She did."

"Of course she did," he says and laughs, "The only time your mama ever did anything disobedient, was to get to me. And I had to fix that because I was the one who was gonna lose, if she ever came to any harm while misbehaving."

"Did you have a lot of girls?"

"I had a lot of ho's on the side," he says and laughs again, "But no one was ever gonna move Ebony out my heart. I made sure whomever the ho was that I was messing with. Or that was trying to get with me. She knew about Ebony. They all knew your mother was my heart and she was the only female I was going to look out for and take care of. Every single one of them knew from the start of whatever we had. But that still didn't stop a few of them from taking things too far."

"After the kissing started. Was there anymore girl problems?"

"Plenty of them," Ajay said, "Let me put you up on that part of it."

{Jb's 13th birthday party}

Ebony's girls questioned her about what happened and what she was doing inside of Ajay's room, for so long. She just told them the same story Ajay had given to Tank.

"We just practiced on our dancing again," she told them.

"Girl you wasting time," Nina said and frowned, "Ebony you gotta get with the program. You should've got to that tongue kissing part. Instead of just dancing. You're just so *slow*, Ebony."

"I know but I can take my time if I want too," she said as she heard Ajay's voice in her head, "I'm on my own time."

"Whatever," Nina said as she laughed.

It was at that time that T-baby had to add her advice and she didn't try to be nice about it either. She went straight in on Ebony and in the wrong direction at that.

"You better get Ajay before that old ass bitch Darlene come back over here," T-baby barked, "She went to take her bad ass kids home. But she was telling them other girls that was wit her. That they was all coming back for Jb's party. She on her own time too, cousin. *Ajay's* time."

"For real," Rebbie added.

The 3 of them cracked up laughing but Ebony just looked at them and smiled. What they were saying wasn't bothering her at all. And she quickly let them know.

"She can stay on her time then," Ebony said as she stacked lids on the counter to take outside. She said, "My time is what matters to Anthony. Not hers."

"Okay then, Ebony," Nina said, "You're gonna have to grow up if you're gonna be Ajay's girlfriend. He's already doing the real thing. The sex thing. You do know that, don't you?"

"I know my time is what matters," she said before turning to her girls and handing them stacks of lids. Then she said, "Now can we go cover this food up so our parents can get along with moving their card party to mama Jo's house? Thank you very much."

"Oh yes ma'am," Rebbie said, "She sounds like a mama *now*."

They all laughed as they headed outside and over to Paul's yard. They began covering all the leftover foods and preparing to take them to 3 separate homes. Renee and the older girls were waiting there to help them. They got everything covered and then carried some to Jo's house. Some stayed at Paul's house for Jb's party which would start in 2 hours. They took the rest back to Pearl's house.

Afterwards the older girls headed down the street to Jan's house to get dressed for the party. The foursome stayed outside and played until the parents got all of the tables moved into Jo and Al's home. Then they had to go inside Pearl's house where they were going to stay for the night. The grandparents had taken all the youngest kids including Lil Kenny with them to The Point and took enough food for them as well.

"I kind of wished I could've baby sat for Lil Chill tonight," Ebony said all of sudden, as she started to make her pitch for sneaking out.

"He's at papa's house, cousin," T-baby said and laughed. "Nina told you, you're slow. You do know Chill is having a party tonight, right?"

"Yea and Lil Chill is too little to be at home when they have a party," Rebbie said and she laughed too.

"That's because they be getting buck wild over there," Nina said and laughed.

"Sometimes he be there," Ebony said, "I wish we could go."

She thought it was funny how her girls thought they knew everything and talked to her like she was clueless. That was all the better for making sure her plan worked. She was working her way into making her girls want to go to that birthday party. And she was going to let them think it was *all* because of their guidance and leadership. And that it was all their idea too.

By 9pm the parents were in party mode at Jo and Al's house. The foursome was at Pearl and John's house alone. Jb's party across the street at Paul and Chill's had started an hour and a half ago. Ebony was still on her mission to get over there. She knew Nina saw herself as the leader of them. Ebony had already learned how to be a master at feeding her ego too. She started talking about Nina and Tank. She started reminding Nina of how much more advanced she was than the 3 of them. Ebony knew if she could get Nina started on talk about Tank. Then Nina was going to want to *see* Tank and she also knew Nina would come up with a way for the 4 of them to get out of that house and over to Jb's party too.

"Nina have you and Tank started being boyfriend and girlfriend yet?" Ebony asked, though she already knew that answer.

"Yes girl. How did you know?" Nina asked with a smile.

"Y'all been kissing for a long time," Ebony said, "And he's always talking to me about you and trying to get me to tell you to spend the night wit me. He act like he wants you to live over here. Because he's always telling me to call you and tell you to come over here and stay with me."

"And I come right on over here too, don't I?" Nina said and they all cracked up laughing. Then she said, "We kiss everyday and he be rubbing on me. I have already let him touch my kitty cat too. Y'all probably don't even know about finger fucking yet, do you?" she asked suddenly.

"Ewww," Rebbie said in disgust.

"Yes," T-baby said, "I do know about it. But I don't let Richard do that yet. We just kiss and he rubs on me but that's all."

"Brian kissed me too," Rebbie said, "And he rubs on me now too since Tank told him what to try. But not under my clothes, he don't."

"Y'all know I have to learn it first because I'm the oldest," Nina said boastfully. "Then I can tell y'all about it and y'all will know what to do and what not to do."

"Nina you've got a chest already too," Rebbie said.

"They're called breast Ree Ree and I know," Nina said as she batted her eyelashes, "I let Jeremy suck on them. He goes crazy on them."

"Do that hurt?" Ebony asked.

207

"Nope," Nina said, "It feels good."

"I don't have a chest yet, so that ain't gonna work," Ebony said, "You and T-baby got them already. Rebbie's is coming in too. But me? I've still got a flat chest."

"Well Ebony you need to kiss first though," Nina said and T-baby and Rebbie agreed.

"Yea cousin you need to start out with tongue kissing before you go any farther," T-baby added with a flat tone to her voice.
The 3 girls seemed to be enjoying talking down to Ebony. But Ebony knew that meant her plan would work perfectly.

"Y'all making me feel like I'm still a baby," Ebony said for the affect of it, "All 3 of y'all have kissed and even more than that. Nina and Tank already boyfriend and girlfriend too."

"Me and Richard are too," T-baby said.

"And Brian asked me today," Rebbie said.

"What I wanna know is when did y'all start calling them by their real names?" Ebony asked, "Y'all copied off of me and Anthony."

"So what?" T-baby said, "We *should* be calling them by their names before *you* do. Because we go together and y'all *don't*."

"Kiss my brother, Ebony," Nina said suddenly, "He likes you. I know he does."

"Did he tell you that Nina?" Rebbie asked, "Because Ajay don't like nobody. He got all of these big ole girls looking for him and coming around here to be with him. I bet *they* be kissing him."

"A grown woman too," T-baby added, "Don't forget about her."
Ebony laughed inside. She knew no one had kissed Ajay but her and she wasn't even trying to hear either of those last 2 comments. She felt like she knew where Ajay's head and heart was. And it was on her. After all, they had kissed today and still no one knows about it except the 2 of them. She knows Ajay had probably told Chill since the party started and Chill would tell Renee. Ebony had to get her girls minds off of her and Ajay and onto sneaking over to the party. So she could see Ajay again. She got back to it.

"I bet you Tank, June and Rich having fun at that party," Ebony said, "I hope they're not kissing on no other girls over there."

"I know Jeremy better not be or I'm gonna go off on him," Nina said as her voice started to rise. She said, "I wanna go over there."

"Me too," T-baby said.

"I wanna go too," Rebbie adds, "We *always* have to stay home. Bre and Jan not that much older than us and they get to go and stay late now."

"I wish we could go too," Ebony said, "But our parents at they own party. By the time they finish and come home. It'll be way to late to ask them."

"We should go over there anyway," Nina said, "I can call Jeremy and tell him to come and walk us over there."

"You think he will?" Rebbie asked.

"He will," T-baby said, "My cousin will come get us and I know he will. Call him, Nina."

"Ebony go get the phone for me *please*," Nina said in her usual bossy way.

"Okay, if you want me too," Ebony said as she poured on the innocence.

"I want you too," Nina said forcefully.

Ebony went into her mother's room to get the cordless phone. She brought it back into her room and handed it to Nina. Then she sat on her bed and watched while her girls called Chill's house and sealed the deal.

Within 15 minutes, there was 6 of their crew members at Pearl's house. Tank and Jb had brought Ajay, June, Rich and Bre home with them, to walk the foursome to the party. Ajay smiled as soon as his eyes met Ebony's. She smiled too. He knew she wanted to see him. He also knew she was the reason her girls had made the call. He just knew that in his gut. Ajay saw Ebony as the true leader of the foursome. Even though he knew his sister Nina was more boisterous. But he also knew Ebony had a persuasive edge. She was the kind of person that people liked to please and be allies with. After all, she got him and his undivided attention. No other person had been able to do that, prior. He saw her as being just as important in his life as his crew legacy and basketball. And 1 day she would most likely trump the latter 2. She made him want to smile and be in a good mood. That took skill. He knew she was the kind that would fight for him and fight to be with him. He knew she would also be ready to fight him, if he didn't do his absolute best in life. She was more like him, then she was different and that's what made her the perfect girl for him. He was so ready to get back to that alone time they'd had earlier, as the 10 of them headed back out of the side door and over to Chill's house for Jb's party. Ajay walked right next to Ebony, the entire way.

Renee saw the foursome when they came in the door. She went straight to them and insisted that they hang out upstairs in Lil Kenny's room. There were older teenagers there. Darlene and her pack was there too and Renee didn't want anyone to bother them. Let alone try to talk to 1 of them. So she walked them up the stairs and into the room.

"Y'all can keep the door open and watch from the stairs. But I don't want y'all to come downstairs," she said, "Not without one of us coming up here to get you, okay?"
They all said okay. They were just glad to be there and be able to see what their older crew was doing. They also wanted to see the affect their crew had on non-crew folks. They had heard lots of people talk about how much they revered the crew. Nina, Rebbie and T-baby seemed angry that they had to stay upstairs but Ebony wasn't. She wasn't worried about going downstairs at all. Ajay was down there and he knew she was upstairs. That was good enough. She knew for sure he would make his way to wherever she was before long. It was just something about the way he smiled at her that assured her of that.

Sure enough, another 10 minutes later, Ebony and Ajay was in Chill and Renee's room alone. Ajay didn't waste time letting her know how happy he was to see her again either.

"I'm so happy you came over here, baby girl," he said, "The only thing that's been on my mind is the time we spent in my room today."

"Mine too," she said, "And I was missing you. Does that sound crazy?"

"No. It sounds good to me," he said and he moved in and started tongue kissing her right away.
She put her arms up on his shoulders, the way he had shown her earlier and kissed him right back. When they released, she looked at him and smiled.
"You kiss so good," he said, "I'm glad you started kissing me and I'm glad you like it too."

"I do like it," she said, "And I'm glad that it's our business too."
He asked, "So did you *really* miss me?"

"Yes I always miss you when you're not around me, Anthony."

"Same here," he said, "I remember when all I wanted was for you to talk to me. Now you're kissing me. You just don't know how bad I wanted this to happen."

"I was glad when you started playing basketball with me," she said, "That's what made me want to be around you, all the time. You always called me cutie pie but I think you're handsome. I use to think you was mean like everybody use to say. But you was never mean to me and now I know why. And when you beat up Billy for messing with me. I knew you had my back."

"Yea I do," he said, "I ain't gonna let nobody fuck wit you, Ebony. I promise you that. You don't *ever* have to be scared of nothing or nobody. Because if somebody mess wit you. I'm getting in that ass, okay?"

"Okay and I know that now," she said, as they started their kissing session again because she knew she wouldn't be able to stay long.

They spent another 30 minutes in that room kissing and talking. Ajay knew Ebony couldn't stay long and he didn't want her to get in trouble with her parents either. He got Tank, Rich and June to go with him to walk them back to Pearl's house. He managed to pull her away from the eyes of the others, long enough to get 1 more quick kiss before they said goodnight. It was easy for them to get private time because the other 3 couples were having it too. Soon, the guys headed back to Chill's house.

The foursome got back to Pearl's house before any of the parents could come check on them and know they'd been gone. It was a great night for all 4 of them. They had new kisses to add to their diaries and more stories to tell. Ebony still didn't tell them her and Ajay had kissed yet. She just didn't want to let go of those private moments. Not so soon. But she would tell them by Ajay's 12th birthday which was a week later. And they were all supportive and happy to hear that she had crossed that bridge.

By T-baby's 10th birthday, her and Rich were an official couple in the 3rd generation. Only they couldn't announce that to the family. Jb and Lynn were both thirteen and crew by then. Everyone in the family knew they were dating. Jan and Rob were liking each other and so was Bre and Stoney. The crew started to take on a couple form before the fall school year began. Chill had daytime crew party's so all 18 *potential* crew members could be together, at the same time without incident. That was something Ajay had asked him to do. They were bonding and everybody was learning what the loyalty of their family was all about. But even though the crew's bond was tightening and growing. The outside women wasn't backing off any. Namely Darlene. But she wasn't *even* the biggest hindrance. The beef's outside of the crew with big Jake wasn't going away and neither was the crew's insistence of getting rid of him and his posse for good.

{Fall 1986}

By the time the school year was in full swing again, Ajay was in the 7th grade and being driven to MLK high school to practice basketball with their high school team. That was exposure that money couldn't buy.

His exposure to all the division 1 colleges was building for sure and so was his exposure to the high school girls. He was on a younger teacher's radar by then too and she was already familiar with Ajay, from the past.

Debra Whitman was still there. Her and Darlene wasn't as tight by then. Because ho's who fuck the same men usually don't manage to remain *good* friends. But Debra and Darlene still communicated and partied together. Debra knew Darlene had a romantic interest in Ajay. She didn't give a damn because at that point, so did she. Only she had planned to wait until he was at least a teenager which is how she'd played it when she met Chill, Stoney, Rob and Jr. She had just recently started to bed down with Jr, who had turned 15 in August. But since Ajay was coming to the high school everyday. She decided to make her move on him. Debra knew about the size of his penis because she had sucked it at the motel. Plus Darlene, Gloria and Anita had shared that information *braggadociosly*. They even invited Debra to join them when the crew guys visited Darlene's apartment but Debra had never taken them up on that offer. She decided when she *did* get the chance to get some of Ajay. She wanted his 10 inch dick, all to herself. She was of the same mentality as Darlene when it came to Ajay's age. Debra figured she was older than him and she would be able to control him with the things that older people had.

She made her move on Ajay by the middle of September, 1986. However Ajay wasn't interested in her at all and definitely not at that time. The experiences he'd had with Darlene left him feeling like, being with an older woman really didn't have any advantages. He wasn't going to double up by messing with Debra Wittman too. But everyday he came to MLK. The high school girls were flanking him as he made his way from the office where his ride would drop him off. To the gym where he spent his time while he was there. He would eventually fuck several of them before the basketball season even started. But he never showed Debra Wittman any interest. Many of the high school girls tried visiting him at home too. But that effort was foiled by Lynn, Nina and mama Jo. And after several complaints from his mother, Ajay got a handle on all of those uninvited girls who had took it upon themselves to start hanging around his street and his neighborhood. They didn't miss a crew event either. Ajay told them not to come around unless he called them and he knew he wasn't going to call them. But he didn't want them looking for him either. Especially not dropping by his house or any of his crew's houses. Ebony was the only girl with personal interest in him that he wanted to be visiting his mother's house and he made sure that those other inquirers knew that too.

He made Debra Wittman aware of it very early and her only recourse was to pass that bit of information on to Darlene and that posse. That didn't matter to Ajay because Ebony was his air and he'd told all the other girls that, from the start of whatever it was that they thought they had with him.

"My girl is Ebony Brown," he had said to one and all, "She can come to my house whenever she wants too. And she's the only one that's gonna come there. She's the only girl I'm gonna have feelings for because she's the only one I wanna feel for. She's the one who keeps me relaxed and on my best. She's gonna be my future too."
He was definite in his delivery and they knew not to cross him, if they ever expected him to even acknowledge them again. Ebony was his priority and as long as she was happy and smiling. He could breathe easy.

One day in that same week, as Debra Wittman suffered another failed advance toward 7th grader Ajay. Down at Abe Lincoln middle school, 5th grader Ebony Brown had made the basketball team. She was so excited and she couldn't wait until Ajay got back down to their school so she could tell him the good news. As soon as he returned from practice at MLK, he saw the list of those who made the cut. He asked the principal to allow him to go congratulate Ebony. The principal sent for Ebony to come to the office. She came and saw Ajay in there. She didn't know if he was in trouble or not until he smiled at her. She knew then that he was the reason she was called to come to the office.

"Hey baby girl," Ajay said with a huge smile, "You made the fifth grade team ha?"

"Yes I made it. Can you believe it?"

"Yea I can believe it," he said, "You're a superstar, just like me."
They laughed and she said, "T-baby made it too and Nina and Rebbie have cheerleader tryouts after school today."

"They'll make it," Ajay said with confidence, "My crew don't fail. We always rise to the top."

"They're nervous about it," she said, "But me and Tee told both of them that they'll make it."

"I'm happy you made the team," he said, "Now when we get back on the court. We'll be getting you ready for your season."

"Okay," she said, "I'm ready and you have to play me hard too. The girls on the other team ain't gonna take it easy on me. So my coach can't either."
They laughed and soon the principal told them they had to get back to class.

Nina and Rebbie made the cheerleading squad with ease and all of their crew had stayed after school with them. When they all got home, Ebony was ready to play basketball and so was T-baby. But Ajay had other plans. He had something he wanted to show Ebony before they could start even 1 game.

"Baby girl, come inside my house for a second," Ajay said, "I need to show you something."
She looked at him and blushed. She thought surely he wanted to go to his room so they could celebrate her making the team with a kissing session. He smiled at her because he knew she thought he was trying to be slick. But he had to let her know it was really something he had to show her.

"I really do wanna show you something," he said, "I'm gonna go up to my room. When the coast is clear. I want you to come on up, okay?"
She smiled and said, "Okay."
She still believed it was about kissing. But either way, she wanted some of his private time so she watched for an escape after he had gone into his house. Ebony watched the other 6 to see if they were paying attention to her. Nina and Rebbie was practicing cheers while T-baby and Rich shot basketball with Tank and June. They were doing their own thing, so Ebony quickly made her move to mama Jo's side door and went inside. She ran up the stairs. Ajay was standing in his bedroom door waiting on her.
He smiled and said, "Come on."
She went on into his room and he closed the door behind them. First of all, she had to know if he was trying to be slick and she asked.

"Did you trick me to come up here?" she asked and smiled.

"I always want to spend every little bit of my time wit you, baby girl," he said quickly, "So I know you think I was just trying to be slick. But that wasn't it. I would've just said let's go to my room so we can kiss. I told you. I'm not a liar, okay? I really got something I wanna show you. It's something I started drawing."

"Okay, let me see it," she said and took a seat in the chair next to his lamp table.
He went to his closet and pulled a sketching tablet from the top shelf. Then he laid it on his bed and opened it up. Ebony stood back up so she could see what he'd drawn.

"I know you like to color stuff," he said, "But I've been drawing this mansion that I'm gonna build when I go pro."

"You're drawing it already?" she asked and giggled.

"Yea," he said, "It's got three floors and a big garage, so far."

214

"I can tell how it's gonna look too," she said, "You can draw *really* good, Anthony."

"Thank you," he said, "This is a mansion but it's on a Ranch style. A French Country Ranch style. I want it to be on a lot of land too. So I can put my own ponds on it and a full court. That's for when I have kids. So they can learn how to play at home, just like me and you."

"Kids," she said and giggled more, "You talk like a man."

"I'm gonna be a man," he said, "I already know what I want when I get grown and I know who I want too."

"You do?" she said as she gave him a shy look.

"I told you, baby girl," he said, "I want you to be my girl by the time you're thirteen. And one day I'm gonna ask you to be my wife. We're gonna live in this house together and have our own family."
She giggled a lot but she liked what he was saying. She smiled at him and he smiled back.
Then he said, "You do know I'm gonna ask big John can I be your boyfriend when it's time for you to be in the crew, right?"

"I didn't *know* you was," she said and continued to smile, "But lately. I've been hoping you was."

"I am Fasho," he said, "Big mama and granny already told me they want me to keep talking to them and they're gonna make sure I make the right decisions. So I can get it right."

"Well okay," she said as she gazed at the pictures he'd drawn. Then she asked, "Are you gonna draw the pond too?"

"I'm gonna draw everything I want for this mansion," he said, "I want a big garage so we can have all kinds of cars and a pool and big yard too."

"I didn't know you was drawing a house for me too," she said.

"Yes I am because I want you, baby girl," he said and he looked so sincere that she knew he was serious. She knew he meant it. He continued, "That's why I told you I want you to call me Anthony. I want you to be my girl. I was for real about that. But I'm not gonna try to make you move too fast. I just want you to know that I want you to be with me. My girl and I don't want no boys trying to come visit you or talking to you either. And they better not mess wit you or try to hurt you. Because I'm gonna hurt them. You feel me?"
She looked confused. She didn't know what that expression meant yet, so she just sat quiet. She knew he had already beat up Billy Marshall for knocking her off the swings. So she knew he would protect her. She knew he
215

had her back without a doubt. She just didn't know what he meant by, "You feel me?" He picked up on that right away too and he changed the way he asked her.

"Do you understand what I mean?"

"Yes," she said and smiled with understanding.

"Okay," he said, "So from now on, I'm gonna call you baby girl and you're gonna call me Anthony. I made sure the crew knew what we was gonna be calling each other too. But I still have to ask big John first, before I can ask you to be my girlfriend. Okay?"

"Okay Anthony," she said and smiled.

"I love the way you say my name already."

She blushed. She wanted to kiss him. He sensed that too and moved in quickly.

"You wanna kiss, don't you?" he asked.

"Yes."

He kissed her instantly. She held onto him while he held her too. There wasn't any music playing from his boom box but she could hear music in her head. She started to move her body as if she was slow dancing. He moved right with her. They spent another 30 minutes together before they headed back outside to play basketball with their crew.

Nina looked at Ebony and smiled. She knew her and Ajay had been kissing. All of her girls did and his boys did too. Their kissing sessions was old news now. Ebony and Ajay were well on their way to being the next couple in the crew. They had danced, kissed and tongue kissed. They would spend every available minute together during the fall of 1986 and Ajay made sure to keep her updated on the mansion he was designing for them.

By late October, it was basketball season. Ebony was starting her first season along with T-baby while Nina and Rebbie were on the sidelines cheering. The entire crew attended their games and so did Ajay. He was so happy that MLK played their games on different nights and much later then hers. So he could come and watch her play.

At 1 of her games during early November, an 8th grade girl named Brittney Blank pushed her way through the crew to sit next to Ajay. He looked at her like she was crazy.

"What are you coming up here for?" he asked before she was even settled in her seat.

Chill and the rest of the guys laughed hard because they knew Ajay was about to go in on her. Big Al and Paul chuckled because they knew it too.

"I wanted to sit by you," Brittney Blank said.

"Well you're not gonna sit by me," Ajay said, "I'm wit my family and we're here to support our crew. You're gonna have to get at me some other time but you can't sit here."

"Please Ajay," Brittney begged, "You're so fine. I've been wanting to say something to you at school. But you always leave for the high school during my free class. I just wanna talk to you about something."

"Do it later," Ajay demanded, "But you need to move right now."
The look on his face was serious and his crew knew he was about to get upset. Chill, who was a senior at MLK that year, knew he had to step in.

"Miss lady you need to move and move now," Chill said, "This is a family thing. You heard the man. So move."
Brittany got up and moved after she saw the look on all of the men's faces. Al cracked up laughing at Ajay as him and Paul shook their heads and gave each other dap. Ajay didn't even smile. At least not until Ebony scored her 1st basket of the evening. When she hit her first jump shot, Ajay was the loudest fan in the stands and he bragged a lot too.

"She's the truth!" he yelled as Ebony scored 4 baskets in a row.
She got 3 steals which led to 2 of those baskets and T-baby scored as a result of the 3rd steal.
"Baby girl is gonna be a superstar! Y'all better recognize! She's gonna be way bigger than me!" Ajay yelled.
The crew had a blast as Ebony scored 15 points, got 11 rebounds, 7 assist, 4 steals and 2 blocked shots in that game. While T-baby added 12 points, 13 rebounds, 8 assist, a steal and an offensive foul.

"My crew is red hot!" Chill yelled as he cheered along with Nina, Rebbie and the cheerleaders.
Nina and Rebbie had the cheerleading squad yelling crew, as they all headed out of the gym and to their cars. Ajay walked Ebony to Pearl's car.

"You did so good, baby girl," he said as he smiled and hugged her.

"Thank you," she said, "My daddy is gonna be mad that he missed this game."

"He'll be here for the next one," Ajay said, "And Arthur got pictures, so big John will be able to see those. You know I'm cutting the article outta the newspaper tomorrow right? Baby girl you kilt it. You and T-baby. Shoot y'all scored twenty seven points out of the forty total points y'all team had. You must think you're me now?!" he asked as he chuckled but he was very excited too.
Ebony laughed hard and said, "You *was* my coach, you know. You and big

217

Chill. Just make sure you remember that. After seeing how much better I played. Aren't you glad you started playing me a little harder?"

"Not really," he said and laughed.

"I meant instead of playing soft and trying to keep me smiling," she said and giggled, "Because we both know that didn't work too good."

"Yea I did step it up, didn't I?," Ajay said, "But you was trying to beat me."

"And I'm gonna beat you, one day," she said and laughed.

"If I let you," he said and laughed even harder than she had.

Their parents and crew were loading into their vehicles so they could all go grab a bite to eat and then head home.

"Let's ride wit Chill," Ajay suggested suddenly.

"I want too," Ebony said, "He got his own car now. I can't believe he's almost out of school. He's gonna graduate in May."

"Uh huh and he's gonna start working on opening another business too. Big Paul is gonna help him put up the money for it and all the other men are too."

"I'm gonna ask mama if I can ride with Chill and Renee," she said.

"Okay," Ajay said, "I'm bout to tell him to wait for you."

Pearl allowed Ebony to ride with Chill. Everybody loaded up and headed to eat. While on the way, Ebony turned to Ajay.

She said, "Do I get a kiss for my good game?"

He kissed her for more than a minute while Chill and Renee smiled at each other. Lil Kenny was in his car seat next to Ebony. He even laughed out loud.

"They don't waste no time, do they?" Renee asked Chill and they both laughed.

"Ajay and Ebony already see their future," Chill said, "And we are gonna make sure they get there too."

Ebony smiled as she leaned on Ajay. He put his arm around her and they rode like that all the way to the restaurant.

{Thanksgiving 1986}

The family celebrated at big Paul's house this year and he hosted the all male party, after all of the females left for Jo and Pearl's houses. Ebony was missing Ajay and wondered why the men were meeting, so late. Her and her girls didn't know it was an all male party because the men always had separate meetings. The older women knew it. It was a long standing tradition that Ebony wouldn't find out about until her and Ajay was living in that mansion that he was still drawing daily.

}1987{

Ebony and Nina had turned 11 in December and Lil Kenny made 3. Tank turned 12 in January and he was already declaring that he was official crew, a year ahead of time. The kissing games between the foursome and their boys were still very active and had gone into overdrive. Ajay and Ebony were still the only foursome couple who wasn't feeling each other up but that would start soon. June and Rebbie had become an official couple by March of 1987 but their parents didn't acknowledge it. Per the crew rule. By April of 1987, all of Ebony's girls had boyfriends. Ajay still hadn't asked Ebony to be his girlfriend yet. Even though he already considered her to be. Bre and Stoney had started working toward a relationship and so had Jan and Rob. Lynn and Jb were official on all accounts but her dedication to her track team was wearing Jb thin. He wanted her time, *all* the time. They were in 8th grade. And just like Ajay, Lynn was on the high school team but for track and field and it was very demanding.

It was nearing Lynn's 14th birthday when Ajay and the males in the crew caught on that big Jake had a new plot in the works for them. Chill was going to graduate high school, the next month. He would be turning 18 when the month of June rolled around. By this time, Chill had adopted big Paul's street game and he was running it so sufficiently, his name had become well known. He was known not only for his crew ties but for his street reputation and his power as well. He was known to get rid of enemies, just like the crew men before him did. And just like the crew men prior to him, Chill wasn't leaving any evidence that he had even been at the scene. His crew of Stoney, Rob and all the way down to Richie Rich were all onboard and doing things the crew way by then.

But while Ajay had the Johnson beef to watch out for. He also had to be on the look out for the girls and women who were vying for his time. Darlene was becoming more persistent and Debra Wittman seemed to be pushing Darlene to demand more of his time. Simply because she couldn't get it. Debra had even asked Darlene to arrange a ménage with Ajay included, so she could get some of him.

Marsha had come back for spring break and started to hang around Pearl's house, just to get a sighting of Ajay. Monica had stayed behind to attend school. Only she went to a different school than the crew.

219

She would show up at all of their events along with Brittney from 8th grade and the girls from MLK, who'd had a turn with him at some point. Still Ajay never allowed them to approach him in sight of his family and definitely, not with Ebony around.

It was the day of Chill's graduation when Brittney Blank decided she wasn't going to be denied an opportunity to be in Ajay's company. She showed up at the pre-graduation party at big Paul's house. All of the other crew thangs was there as well. But Brittney didn't act like she knew how to stay in her place. All of Chill's crew was there including the foursome. And Ajay was happily spending his time with Ebony. They were laughing and talking about the fact they had won basketball titles that school year. Her 5th grade team had gone undefeated. Ajay and MLK high school had finished in 2nd place in the state tournament but he was named to the All-State tournament team as a 7th grader. Many said his ticket to the NBA was punched right then and there. He had just been promoted to 8th grade and already he was being added to basketball polls with high school players. Ebony had passed to the 6th grade and she maintained her straight A average again that school year. All of their crew had passed which was a normal thing in the crew family. But that was the first year that 1 of the 3rd generation was completing high school, so it was a big day.

Ajay and Ebony was standing together and talking. Rob was the Dee-Jay and Jr was helping him. They played *Head To Toe* by *Lisa Lisa* and Ebony started to dance where she was standing. Ajay liked what he was watching. Her girls were already dancing, so Ajay called Tank, June and Rich over to him.

"Why don't y'all take Nina, Rebbie and T-baby to the dancing area and dance with them," he said and they did.

He was about to bring Ebony to the dance area too. That was when Brittney stepped to him. She stepped between him and Ebony with her back to Ebony. She was facing Ajay with her hands on her hips.

She said, "I know you not gonna leave me standing over there by myself. Like you don't even know me."

Ebony was shocked. She had never seen this happen and especially not to Ajay. She moved around to where she could see Brittney's face and looked at her. Then she looked at Ajay. She didn't like that move at all. The look on Ajay's face was mean and Ebony could tell he wasn't happy with the intrusion either. He didn't waste any of that precious time getting his point across to Brittney.

"Get the fuck away from me," he said, "Don't you ever push my girl away or step into her space again. Move now."
He wasn't talking any louder than a normal speaking voice. But she could tell by his expression that he was ready to rip her a new one. She moved back to where she once stood and Ajay escorted Ebony on over to the dance area.

"Who was that?" Ebony asked.

"Some girl from eighth grade," he said, "She did that same thing at one of yo games in the fall. I told her to leave me alone then."
They started to dance together and Ebony said,
"I thought you was about to pop her in her mouth because you was looking so mad. Your lips was trembling."

"I don't hit girls," he said, "But I was about to put Lynn on her. And I still might do that. She better not push me."

"You told Lynn I was your girl," Ebony said and giggled.

"I told you as far as I see it, you already are," he said, "I just have to wait on our folks to be okay wit it."
She smiled and continued to dance. She was completely over that intrusion by Brittney Blank but Lynn wasn't. She was still watching her. She was watching Darlene, Gloria, Anita and Debra Wittman as well. Before they could break from the daytime festivities to go and get dressed for Chill's graduation. Lynn went to Renee with her woe.

"That bitch Brittney ran her ass up in Ajay's face a little while ago," Lynn said, "I was just waiting to see that vein pop up in his forehead and I was gonna grabbed that ho."

"She did?" Renee asked, "Is she a crew thang too?"

"Hell no," Lynn said, "Ajay ain't never even gave her the time of day. But she keeps running up on him like she done lost her mind."

"Well it won't take but a minute to dust her ass off," Tonya added, "These ho's on Ajay, worse than they on his older crew. I think it's because he's so good in sports and he's always on the news and in the newspaper."

"And he's damn good looking like his big sister," Lynn said and she wasn't laughing.

"Yea okay and that too," Renee said as they all laughed. Then Renee added, "Let's get our crew to their houses so they can get dressed and go see my man graduate. Him and Lil Kenny gonna be wearing the same suit."

"Ah man that's hot," Lynn said.

"Mama's Belinda, Rena and Sandy hooked them up," Renee said.

221

"Them is some sewing ass ladies too," Lynn said, "They can make anything you wanna wear."

"For real," Tonya agreed.

"Big Paul already told Kenny he wants to help them to have their own store, one day," Renee said, "Y'all know we're all going to open up our own shops, clubs and have independent businesses once the first set of couples in our crew get out of high school. Chill hasn't decided if he's going to college yet but the rest of us are gonna go."

"That'll work," Lynn said, "I know I'm getting a scholarship for Track."

"I'm going for cosmetology," Tonya said.

"Yes you are so come on and get our hair right for tonight," Renee said as they laughed and headed inside Paul's house.

Chill graduated and they had a bigger party that evening. The foursome snuck over to that party too. As soon as Ajay saw Ebony come through the door. He wasted no time getting to her and then finding them a place to have privacy. They went to Chill and Renee's room while once again, her girls hung out on the stairs and watched the party from there.

In Chill and Renee's room, Ajay and Ebony was already engaged in a very heated kissing. He was moaning a lot and so was she. Finally they came up for air.

She asked, "When you kiss me. You move your hands a lot. I like that but I don't know if I'm suppose to do that too."

"Do you feel like you want to?"

"I do but I don't know how I should or what to touch," she said.

"You just do whatever comes natural," he said, "I feel good when I kiss you and I just wanna hold you tight. What I'm doing with my hands is just a natural thing. It goes with how I'm feeling."

"My girls said twin and them be rubbing all over them and touching they..." she paused. Then she said, "Well, you know."

"They touching they pussy, ha?" he said with a straight face.

He didn't expect their conversation to go there but it had. He knew Tank and Nina was experimenting with intimate touching. Rich had said him and T-baby had done it a time or two. But he wasn't going there with Ebony yet. She was still along way from that point. He wanted to kiss her and get her body use to his touch before he would go toward her vagina. Only because he knew he wouldn't want to stop, at just touching it.

"I think we should work on getting your breast to grow first," he

222

said, "What I mean is. One day I'm going to suck on them. That will make them start to grow."

"It will?" she asked in surprise, "So that's why my girls are getting them and I'm not."

"I'm gonna help them grow but not yet," he said, "You're not ready for that stuff yet, baby girl. You don't know what that kind of stuff will do to me. So I don't wanna do that to you until you understand all of the stuff that leads up to that. And what else that will lead too. I told you before. You ain't gotta rush a damn thing with me. I'm gonna take my time wit you. Because I wanna get this right. I wanna make sure you know what the next move is before I make a move with you."

"I do want my chest to grow," she said, "I always gotta be the last one of my girls to know everything that we don't learn in school."

"But when you do get to it," he said, "It's gonna be a move that will last and then grow to something else. I'm just telling it to you the way I was taught by my pops and my grandpa. They told me if it's the girl I want. Then I have to take my time. They said I don't only have to learn what she likes. But I have to make sure that I do it the way that she likes me to do it too. That way she'll want me to do it all the time because I'm gonna wanna do it all the time. Do you understand?"

"I think so," she said, "We're gonna wait before you do it to me?"

"Yea," he said, "I'm having fun with the kissing and rubbing, right now. One day when I have to teach my son. I'll have to tell him to take his time with the girl that he likes too and don't rush her. Because boys usually do that just to get to the good feeling. To the real thing. But once they get the real thing in a rush. They're usually done exploring. It's nothing new left and they didn't even find out what she liked. If it's a girl that you want to keep around. Then you gotta know what she likes too. My pops been telling me that for like eight years. Since I was getting ready to start Kindergarten. I have to do this right. I wanna get to the real thing with you, baby girl. So don't think that I don't. I *really* do. It's just that I want it to be right when I do. Cause I want it to last forever, for both of us. The only way for me to do that is to make sure you know what you want and I know what you want too. And see, I'm gonna make sure you know what I like because you can hear me moaning and all that. You don't do that all the time. Sometimes your body is real tensed. Like you're not really feeling what I'm doing. That's when I have to change up and rub and stroke you while I'm kissing you. I like to play in your hair too. It's so soft."

He smiled a lot during that spill. She was in a trance just listening to him.

She knew she liked Ajay all the way, at that point. She was sure she wanted to know everything he liked too and what he wanted her to do to him. She wanted to learn what he could teach her and she wanted only him to teach her, whatever it was to she needed to learn. She was curious about what that real thing was that he was speaking of too. But she knew if he wasn't ready to make her breast grow yet. Then he certainly wasn't going to show her what the real thing was yet either. She figured she'd better get him back to the kissing and rubbing so he would be absolutely sure that she was loving that. She never wanted him to stop anything they had done up until that point. She was already sure of that. He seemed to sense she was working it out in her mind.

He asked, "Do you like everything we're doing, so far?"

"Yes," she said and smiled big.

She was so happy she didn't have to tell him that she wanted him to keep on with what he was doing. He was going to keep it up because after she said yes. He knew she liked it. And he had just said once he knew what she liked. He would make sure he kept doing that and just add more to it, as they moved things along.

"So let's get back to the kissing before you have to leave," he said.

He didn't wait for her answer. He just moved back in closer to her and took her in his arms. He started tongue kissing her very hard and very intense. She moaned loud and his whole body shook. He thought to himself.

Oh she really likes it when I kiss her hard. Damn that's so good!

"I like this a lot Anthony," she said, "I like you a lot too. I feel like I'm the only person that really knows you. I'm so glad you like me and I don't have to be scared when I'm with you. And I'm not scared either."

"It sounds so good to hear you say that," he said, "I'll give you anything you want from me, baby girl. Even my heart. Just stay innocent. Just like you are for me. Stay the way you are right now. Baby girl I'll teach you what I like when I know you're ready to learn it. I wanna give you everything, starting with my heart. And then I wanna give you every little bit of my heart from then on. And do you know why?"

"Why?"

"Because until I started liking you like this," he said, "I didn't care if nobody liked me. Cause I didn't like nobody. And when it comes to girls. You are the only girl that I like in this way. I want you to remember that, *please*. I wanna be good to you because I know you deserve a man that's good. A man that's good enough to be with you. I'm gonna be that man."

CHAPTER 10-Older Really Doesn't Mean Wiser

For today's talk, Lil Ajay and his pops are hanging out in the male sanctuary of their home. Ajay figures it's time to introduce his junior to their lair because he knows he'll spend a lot of time there with him and in their basement as well. Lil Ajay is more ready for this talk than ever because in their last talk, he'd found out how his parents had taken the biggest step toward the relationship they have now. His mother had told his father that she liked him and she wanted to be with him. She'd also told him, she wanted him to teach her what he would expect her to do to be with him. Lil Ajay is beside himself today because he knows his parents first time is going to be talked about *very* soon. But there's something else he has to know first.

"Pops, you really started drawing this house when you was still little?" Lil Ajay asks.

"First of all, son. I was *never* little," Ajay says and laughs. He adds, "But yes I was in the seventh grade when I first started to draw out my dream house."

"Do you still have the drawings?"

"They're in the safe," Ajay says as he still laughs. "How did I know you would asked me that? You are *definitely* my son."

"I wanna know everything it is to know about you and mama," Lil Ajay says, "I want my life to be *just* like yours and my papa too. Y'all are just cool. My whole crew is but it's something way real about a Jackson man. We don't take no loses. I like that, the most."

"None whatsoever," Ajay agrees.

"So the girls haven't let up on you none," he says, "That Brittney girl was out of pocket too."

"I think she had a baby, the next year," Ajay says, "I don't even know what happened to her really. But she pretty much left me the fuck alone after Chill's graduation. It was one more time that I saw her and she did step to me. But it was some pressing shit I had to handle on that day."

"So you never fucked her, ha?"

"Oh hell no," Ajay says, "She came at me *all* wrong. She tried to come in between my time with Ebony. Come on now *son*. You know that shit don't work for you and your sisters. How would a ho get away wit it?" They laugh hard.

"Yea you're right pops," Lil Ajay says, "I'll never try to interfere with y'all time again. I know you told me I walked in y'all bathroom on y'all. I can't remember that far back and I'm glad I can't. Because man, that's messed *up*."

"Yea but you thought I was hurting your mama," Ajay says and they both laugh again. Then he says, "I knew then that you wasn't gonna take no shit about your mama being uncomfortable. I was alright with that. But trust me son. She was comfortable. She was loving it. I spent all of my young life figuring out how to please her, in every way. And son that's the *only* way to get to a relationship that works on every level. I wasn't the perfect man always. I hurt my baby along the way while I was growing into the man that I am now. But do you wanna know how we got here?"

"Yes I do," Lil Ajay says, "How?"

"I always owned up to what I did or what I was trying to do," Ajay says, "I saw us like this, back then. And I have my forefathers to thank for that. I've never been a liar and I will never be a liar. If I had started this off by lying. Ebony wouldn't be with me now. So remember this. Whatever you do. You have to be man enough to accept it, acknowledge it and if it's wrong. Then you have to learn from it and then fix it."

"Wow pops," Lil Ajay says, "You *are* the man."

"And you're going to be a better man because you're gonna do what me and my daddy and his daddy did. *Plus* you're gonna add your own flavor to it. That's what my pops told me. I wanted what he had with your nana Jo. When my mama looks at my daddy. Her eyes sparkle. Even if she was mad about something. I never had a doubt that my pops was the man. That he was in control of his household. And just like him, I'll do any damn thing within my *power* to make sure that your mother is smiling. I don't want her worried about *shit*. Because to me, that would mean I'm not doing what I'm suppose to be doing and that's to take the burden off of her. I'm going to be the man. So that way, when I get home, she's stress free and ready to relieve whatever stress I have. That's when we get to the real thing. The *best* part. And *now* that you know what's going on when we're alone. We don't have to worry about yo ass creeping up in our room talking about you hurting my mama, no more."

They laugh. Lil Ajay still feels embarrassment about a moment he doesn't even remember.

Lil Ajay says, "I'll just call from my cell phone."

They crack their sides laughing before Ajay stands up and heads to the pool table.

"Let's see if you've sharpened your skills up enough to beat me," Ajay says.

226

"I might not be there yet, pops," Lil Ajay says, "But I'm still six. I'm learning it all now. Give me another year."

"Or five years, you mean," Ajay says, "You'd better have it and beat me when you get to double digits or I'm gonna feel bad as hell."

"I know right," Lil Ajay say as he grabs his cue stick. He asks, "So that older woman was still around after Chill's graduation. When did she finally accept that backseat?"

"Hell fuck yea, she was and she still ain't gone completely out of sight," Ajay says, "She just gets a new group of ho's and shows back up."

"Did you ever go after the other teacher or the girls from the high school that was coming to the crew parties?"

"Oh yea," Ajay says, "Debra Wittman thought she had position. She had Darlene fighting teenagers or anybody she thought liked me. But she wasn't dumb enough to come after Ebony. She knew the crew would dead her ass. But Ebony got in Darlene's one night and handled her too."

"That might be a good way to set Darlene up," Lil Ajay says suddenly, "Since she was fighting other girls too. Set her up. You know, with the devil you said is getting out in a couple more years. Set her up."

"I told you, you are definitely my son," Ajay says and chuckles, "I thought about that too. Me and your papa Al and the men folks talked on that, a few years back."

"Tell me some more about Darlene," Lil Ajay says, "Because I'm thinking of a master plan for when I get my chamber action. When that Angel bitch gets out. I'll be the same age you was when you first went to the chamber. Is it okay for me to call her a bitch?"

"Of course it is," Ajay says, "So long as your mama don't hear you using bad language. If she hears you. I'm gonna play shocked. You got it?"

"Got it," Lil Ajay says, "I won't let mama hear me saying nothing bad. Okay, you was getting ready to be official crew by this time, right?"

"I was gonna turn thirteen in a few months," Ajay says, "And it was getting better and better with Ebony."

"So how was Darlene acting, at that time. Like after my mama let you know she wanted to be with you."

"She was still that same ole nagging ass bitch," Ajay says, "Playing herself for some power, she was never gonna get."

"We're gonna get that over wit, pops," Lil Ajay says as he makes his first shot. Then he turns to his father and says, "Now that I know my mama had to fight her. I can't wait. Motivate me to put a plan together."

"Well here goes," Ajay says, "Here's how I got crewed up."

227

{June 1987}

Darlene hadn't gone away and she wasn't planning on leaving. She was very persistent when it came to Ajay. She had stayed in touch with Debra Whitman, only to keep tabs of Ajay. MLK had gotten 2nd place in the state that March and Ajay was a big of part of their success. Darlene had attended every home game too. She witnessed all of the attention Ajay got from the high school girls. She didn't like that part though. She'd even asked to be a substitute teacher at MLK but that never happened. By 1988, she couldn't sub at Abe Lincoln anymore. So she had gone into retail and waitress work, to pay her bills and to pay Ajay. She would still visit Debra Wittman every chance she got. She started to confront the girls whom she'd seen with Ajay and the ones Debra told her was messing with him, as well. Darlene had 7 fights with high school girls, from March until June. Still Ajay wasn't paying anymore attention to her, then he had before. She was around only for what she could give him and that was all she would ever be.

As soon as it warmed up, Ajay was back to playing ball with Ebony and getting her ready for her 6th grade team. She wasn't going to have to tryout. She was a shoe in. Her *and* T-baby. Ebony wasn't on Darlene's radar yet. Darlene didn't know Ajay had feelings for her. She saw Ebony as Ajay's neighbor whom he played ball with everyday. She witnessed them playing several times when she rode by his house for a sighting of him, after calling many times and not getting him on the phone. From the start, she could tell they were good friends. She could see that Ajay enjoyed being out there with her. But Darlene thought she knew Ajay's preferences. She thought Ajay preferred older girls and that he was only playing with his *little* neighbor. She would find out later, she was *all* wrong.

But Darlene wasn't the only one spying on Ajay during those driveway basketball sessions with Ebony. Big Jake Johnson was watching also. He had spies watching both Ajay and Ebony. He was already plotting on a way to end the camaraderie they shared. He wanted to end Ajay's life and he was willing to try to infiltrate them as a couple. He was planning to get to Ajay by planting someone on the inside of their crew. That was his latest tactic.

By the end of that school year, a boy named Eddie Washington came into the lives of Chill's crew. He pretended he wanted to work for Chill. From that week after Chill's graduation party in May of 1987, Chill had started to play him off. Eddie kept sending messages to Chill saying he wanted to be down with him and he wanted to work for the crew too.

228

He'd sent that message via everybody big Jake told him could get word to big Chill. And even though Chill had gotten nearly every message. He wasn't in a hurry to meet with Eddie. Instead of taking a meeting with him. Chill started searching his background because he knew that was crew protocol *anytime* someone from the outside wanted to join or be brought into crew business. And once again, that would prove to be the smartest move for the crew.

By 4th of July 1987, Chill had turned 18 and was looking forward to his 1st year as a registered voter. Big June turned 12 and Jb celebrated turning 14 at big Paul's house. Just like last 4th of July holiday, the foursome found a way to sneak over and see their guys. They had done that at most of the crew parties, throughout the past year and the kissing sessions for Ajay and Ebony had gotten even more intense.

Ebony was beginning to feel like Ajay when it came to them seeing each other. She wanted to see him all of the time. When she turned 11, she started to baby sit 3 year-old Lil Kenny. That helped her get permission to be there when the parties were going on too. But most of the time, she would get permission to watch him when Chill and Renee was going on a date. Paul worked nights, as did Al and several of the fathers. So Ebony would be alone in the house with Lil Kenny. While Sam Sr and the other fathers who wasn't at work, would watch all of the crew homes. And the mothers would check on them by visit and phone, at least once per hour. But for the most part, it was just Ebony and Lil Kenny. Until Ajay showed up and he *always* did. That gave her and Ajay even more time together. He would come to Chill's house and help her watch the baby. Unless he was gone to a basketball camp. Ajay liked it better when it was only the 3 of them. Lil Kenny called Ajay his uncle because his daddy Chill had raised him too. He called Ebony his big sister and he loved when she came to keep him. Ajay liked when it was only Ebony doing babysitting duties. But often her girls would come too. Still Ajay would always find a way to keep them busy with Lil Kenny, so he and Ebony could sneak away to another area in the house and be alone. They still hadn't progressed farther than the tongue kissing and rubbing. But at that point, Ebony had told him several times about the things her girls had admitted to experiencing. She had told him she wasn't ready for him to see her chest yet. He knew it was because her breast hadn't started to form and her girls were either at or nearing the need for a training bra. Ajay wanted to add touching to her experiences and he wanted it to happen for his 13th birthday. But he knew he had to wait for her to want it too. And it couldn't happen if she wasn't allowed to

229

attend his party *with* permission. So everyday since the talk of his party began, he had been trying to come up with a way to make sure Ebony would be at his party and with her parents permission.

It was July 9th and the crew were preparing for Ajay's crew initiation which was the talk of the area. He would be turning 13 on the 11th which was 2 days away. There was at least 8 girls who were vying to be his date. But Ajay wanted something else for his crew induction. He'd figured out how he could insure that Ebony would be at his party with permission but he was going to need the help of his parents to make it happen. He and his father Al had a great relationship and Ajay was sure his dad would assist him with his wish. He went straight to Al for a serious talk.

Ajay told Al that he wanted to have a date for his birthday party but he didn't just want it to be just *any* girl. And definitely none of the ones who had been dropping by and calling repeatedly. Without giving away too much as to how he really felt. He told Al, he wanted his date to be Ebony. Al tried to act shocked but he didn't do to well with his deception.

"You do?" Al asked him and he was smiling.

Al and John had planned for them to marry one day but they didn't see them becoming involved for another 5 to 7 years. Ajay knew not to tell his father about the kissing. But he did tell him that when big John allows Ebony to have a boyfriend. He wanted to be him.

"I'll put in a good word for you, son," Al had said, "She's a special girl and she's definitely the type of girl that your mother and I approve of. However, she isn't as advanced as you are. So you will have to wait awhile before you can talk to her about anything more than basketball and crew parties. Okay?"

Ajay wanted to tell his father the real story but he didn't. Not at *that* time. He just shook his head and said, "Okay. But if she tell me she wants to be my girlfriend. I'm not gonna say no."

"I don't want you to say no," Al said, "But I do want you to make sure she knows that she has to wait until her father gives her the okay. Got it?"

"Not really," Ajay answered honestly.

"She's still very innocent," Al said, "And I'm sure she's not gonna be as open to physical touching from a boy. Nr anything that resembles affection. Not at the age she is now. It'll probably take her longer than the other girls her age. She may still be confused about those types of things. I want you to take your time with her and let her tell you what she's ready for. Do you understand?"

230

He was alright with that part because that was what he was doing already. He answered, "No problem. I want it like that anyway. She ain't the type of girl who tries to act like she's gonna make me somebody that I don't wanna be. She's more like me. She want let nobody force her to do nothing she don't wanna do. She won't even let me lose to her when we play basketball. She tells me to play my best. So that she knows she's getting better. Pops, she said she's gonna beat me one day."

They both laughed and Al said, "Well if she does. I'm getting her into these camps *with* you. She'll get more money than you will in the NBA, if she's beating you."

"She's the one, pops," Ajay said suddenly. "And I promise you I won't try to make her do anything that she don't wanna do. I just like being around her. Can she be my date?"

"I'll talk with John about it tonight," Al said, "We'll make it happen. How's that?"

Ajay said, "That's cool. I gotta be clean for that date too."

"So is Darlene offering to buy your birthday clothes?"

"She already bought two outfits and she's been trying to get me to come look at em," Ajay said, "I ain't had time too. But she's bringing them by Chill's house today. I'm gonna get some money from her and that money is gonna be for Ebony's outfit. I want mama and mama Pearl to take her shopping for the outfit that she's gonna wear as my date. Do you think they'll do that?"

"Yes I'm sure they will," Al said, "But you give me the money and I'll give it to Joanna. If you give it to her. She's gonna know it came from somewhere it had no business coming from. Because she knows you're tight with your cash. One hint of Darlene and your mother's gonna beat her brains out. Your oldest sister will be ready to help her do *just* that too."

"I know but tell them *please* don't mess up the bank though," Ajay said and they laughed.

"I don't know if I can convince either of them not to take her out. But I'll do my part to make sure you get your birthday wish, son," Al said and chuckled. "You just make sure Ebony feels special and respected, at the end of that date. That's my only demand. You got me?"

"I got you, pops," he said, "I give you my word. I won't do nothing she don't ask me too. Okay?"

"Cool."

"Thanks man," Ajay said.

"Anytime."

Ebony was already looking forward to Ajay's party. She felt like if she missed his party. It would be the worse thing that could happen to her. Her whole family would be leaving for visit Houston this year and they were leaving next week and staying for 2 weeks. She knew she would miss Ajay again and he would be going to camps, a week after she returned. She knew she would be looking forward to getting back to Cleveland to spend that week with him before he had to leave too. But if she could attend his party, they could create some new memories for her to take on that Houston trip with her. She was racking her brain trying to come up with a way to let her mother know how bad she wanted to attend. But she was still only 11 years old and knew Pearl would throw that crew rule up in her face.

Nina called her on the phone while she was still in her room trying to come up with the perfect reason to give to her mother.

"Hey Ebony, what's up?" Nina asked.

"Nothing much," she said, "I wanna go to Anthony's party. Can you think of a good plan to get mama Jo to let you go? If she let you go. Then mama will let me go. Then Rebbie and T-baby can go too."

"I'm gonna start on my mama right now," Nina said, "I'll get Lynn to help me, okay?"

"Okay."

"I'll call you later," Nina said and she hung up.

It was less than an hour after Pearl was done with the breakfast dishes, that she went to her only daughter with the news that would change Ebony's whole outlook on things. Ebony found out that morning, not only would she be going to Ajay's party. But also Ajay wanted her to be his date. Furthermore since her and her girls were inseparable. Her girls would be allowed to go too. That was going to make them happy, as well as Tank, June and Rich too.

When Pearl came into her room to tell her about the invitation. Ebony found it hard to conceal her excitement. She felt all giddy inside, like she wanted to burst.

She asked, *"Really*? He wants me to be his date? That's nice, mama. Why does everybody always think he's mean? That's not mean."

She had already started trying to change everyone's perception of Ajay. Because she'd seen whom he really was and she wanted the others to take notice and admit it too.

"Well baby girl. This is just a birthday party and really, you're the only girl that he plays basketball with," Pearl said as she made light of the invitation.

Probably because she still viewed Ebony as just her little girl and she didn't feel that Ajay's invitation for her to be his date, was because he liked her as his girlfriend. Pearl was thinking he didn't want any of those *many* other girls to try to be his date, once the party started. But Pearl was wrong and it would be another 2 years before she would find out that Ajay and Ebony was already planning their future as boyfriend and girlfriend. Pearl told Ebony to get dressed so they could go shopping for an outfit. She told Ebony that Jo and Al was buying the outfit, as a gift for her doing this for Ajay. Ebony knew it wasn't a favor at all. She was honored. Mama Jo had told Pearl that Al gave her money for them to shop with. But that was the money which had come from Darlene Casey, last night.

"Get dressed and let's go to the mall," Pearl said, "We're gonna get you decked out. This is your first party, so I want you to look nice. But you won't be going from here on. You will still have to wait until after you turn thirteen before you can attend crew parties. And John junior and Tank will still have to take you and make sure you get home, *even* then. But for Ajay's party, this is a special invite. So I want you to understand that's the reason you are being allowed to go, okay?"

"Okay," Ebony said.

She didn't care what her mother's reasoning was for allowing her to go. The fact was, she was going and she was going as Ajay's date. That was all that mattered to her. She already knew she was going to have the time of her life. *Again*.

She got dressed quickly and hurried downstairs. Jo had Nina, Rebbie and T-baby with her when she came to Pearl's door to let her and Ebony know she was ready to go. Nina smiled at Ebony, then shrugged her shoulders. Because when she'd gone to ask Jo about the party an hour ago, Jo had said, *"Yes you can go and I was gonna tell you that today. Now get dressed because Sandy is dropping T-baby and Rebbie here, any minute. And going home to park her car and ride with us. We're going shopping for outfits for the four of you."*

So once the foursome was together to go shopping, they were excited. Ebony and her girls were all smiles as they headed out the door to load up.

"We're picking up Sandy and Rena on the way," Jo said to Pearl, "We're getting outfits for all four girls. *Matching* outfits. Allen felt real generous this morning. He said buy something for all of them. But Ant said to make sure *his* date looks the best."

Jo and Pearl laughed and Pearl said, "That sounds great. Let's do this then."

The 6 of them loaded into Jo's brand new van and took off on their shopping trip.

Almost as soon as they left, Darlene pulled up to Chill's house. She must've been waiting down the street when the ladies left. She was looking for Ajay. Still she wasn't going to Jo's door, even though she knew she had just left the house. She got out and went to Chill's door, as if she had forgotten she'd got her butt whipped there, twice in the past year. She was hoping Ajay would keep the girls off of her since she did anything to and for him. But she wasn't going to fair any better at Chill's house either. Ajay wasn't about loving Darlene. He never was and never would be. She was just a fuck, for convenience. Still Darlene stepped up to the door and knocked.

Renee answered the door and was soon joined by Tonya. As soon as Darlene saw the 2 of them. She ran back to her car, jumped in and locked the doors. Renee nor Tonya gave chase. They just stood on Paul's porch and made their point from there.

"Don't even think about coming back here looking for our crew, you bitch!" Renee yelled.

Tonya added, "And not for the parties either. You must want your ass stomped again!"

Ajay was inside Chill's house but he didn't bother to make himself seen. He peeked out the window and watched as Darlene hurried back to her car. He laughed at Renee and Tonya, as they closed the door and laughed too.

Renee said, "Some ho's just don't get the point and that's one ho that don't seem to realize. The *only* thing she's gonna get when she comes dropping around here, is an ass whooping. Definitely as long as she come here looking to talk to a man in this crew." She turned to Ajay and said, "Ajay you ain't studying that ho for real, *are* you?"

"No way," Ajay said.

"I know that's right," Tonya said, "Ajay you done already picked out your crew girl, ha?"

"I have," he said and smiled, "And she done picked me too. I just gotta take my time. That's what big Chill, my pops and every other man in this family told me to do. Big mama and granny said the same thing. Ebony is *so* smart and she's pretty too. I'll be glad when she stop playing with baby dolls though. And just spend *all* of her time wit me."

"Ajay you're way more advanced then Ebony is, homeboy," Renee said, "She's still doing things that girls do, at her age. You're doing shit that Kenny does and then some."

"For real, Ajay," Tonya added, "You've been out there with Chill and Brad for years."

"I know and Chill told me to let Ebony tell *me* what she wants and when she's ready for whatever," he said, "I'm cool wit that. I know she likes me. So I'm just gonna do what I have to do to make sure I keep her attention on me."

"I'm so glad you was raised in this family, Ajay," Renee said, "You are smart enough to know what's good for you. Darlene is older and she thinks she can buy you into her life with money and her car. Or her having her own place."

"That bitch is older but that shit don't mean wiser," Tonya said, "Ebony is smart and she's gonna be a perfect match for you. Y'all are going to cosign each other, all the way through life. I can see that already and I wasn't always here."

"It's *like* you was always here though, Tonya," Ajay said, "You and junior just clicked. He happy as hell since you came into his life and the crew. I just can't wait to have that same thing. I know I'm gonna have that with Ebony. We're already best friends."

"I like that," Renee said and smiled.

"So do I," Tonya said, "That's crew right there and y'all are gonna be the prince and princess too. We got y'all backs."

"Yea we do and I ain't gonna let no ho's get in Ebony's way either," Renee said with a matter of fact tone to her voice. "I'm the queen of the third generation of this crew and Tonya is my assistant. Ebony and all the girls in our crew are our little sisters."

"And nobody's gonna fuck with my little sisters," Tonya said, "And one day when I'm older. My little sister Venitia is gonna come and live with me and Brad junior too. Get her away from that hell my mama is putting her through."

"Word," Renee agreed, "When she gets of age and we all have our own homes. She's gonna be crew, just like her big sis."

Ajay loved hearing them say all of that. They were genuine girls which his crew leaders had brought into the family. They knew the vision too. Ajay knew Chill and Jr had his back and they wanted him to be with Ebony too. Renee and Tonya had just given him their blessings and he knew his sisters Lynn and Nina wanted him to date Ebony. As well as Jb and Tank, who are Ebony's older brothers. They want them to date too. Ajay was really looking forward to his birthday party, that year. He wanted to make it something that him and Ebony would never forget.

235

The foursome and their mothers were done shopping and headed back to Shaker Heights. Ebony loved her new dress, shoes and accessories for the party. Her and her girls sat in the back of the van and whispered, so they couldn't be heard by their mothers.

"I'm gonna be sharp," Ebony whispered as she giggled.

"Yes, we all are," Nina whispered, "You're the first one of the foursome to have a date. But we all have our boyfriends already."

"Ebony, you gotta get your boyfriend too," Rebbie whispered.

"Maybe Ajay is gonna ask her to be his girlfriend at his birthday party," T-baby whispered.

"That would be cool," Nina whispered, "Then we'll all know that he likes you."

"For real," T-baby said.

Ebony didn't comment. She still liked keeping her and Ajay's business private. She knew he liked her. But she still didn't know just how much yet. She was looking forward to his party, even more now and she was hoping he would ask her to be his girlfriend. She was planning to say yes.

}July 11, 1987{

It was Ajay's 13th birthday and the party was going to start in about 3 hours. Darlene was at her apartment in Maple Heights. She wasn't going to go near that party. But she was hoping Ajay would call her and ask her for her car or something. *Anything* just so she could hear from him and try to wheel him into her clutches for his birthday night. She would be sorely disappointed because that would not be happening tonight. Chill and Stoney was going to provide the transportation for their crew that night. If anyone had to go anywhere. They had been on the Ebony and Ajay team forever and they were going to do whatever they had to do to make sure their first date went perfect. That would include keeping any of the other hopeful ho's out of Ajay face, for the entire evening. They didn't want anything to happen to discourage Ebony from liking him. They knew if some of those wild ass high school girls got to close to Ajay. They would certainly make a scene and probably scare Ebony away from the party completely.

Ebony and her girls were getting dressed at Pearl's house while Tonya was helping the mothers to curl hair for all the girls in the crew.

"This is gonna be a *big* party," Tonya said to Lynn.

"It sure is and this will be the first party that *all* of our crew will be at for the whole time," Lynn said, "Our crew is gonna be complete tonight and I'm *so* glad."

"Y'all can thank Ebony for that," Renee said to all the younger girls as the mothers laughed.

Then Jo said, "I'm kind of proud of Ant for asking Ebony to be his date. I never thought I'd see the day that he asked a girl out."

"I know that's right," Debbie said, "They always ask him."

Debbie or mama Deb is Jo's younger sister, Jr and Bre's mother and the auntie to Jo and Al's kids. She was very proud of Ajay's date choice and she let that be known when she said,

"Y'all can call Ajay mean or stubborn or whatever else you want too. But you can't call him dumb or blind. Look at Ebony. She's already a beautiful little princess at eleven years old. My nephew is putting down on his future tonight, ladies. That's all this is."

They all laughed while Ebony blushed. All the girls were dressed and ready for the party. They all planned to walk over together.

Suddenly there was a knock at Pearl's side door and then her doorbell rang. Pearl went to the door and looked out the peep hole to see Ajay standing outside. He was dressed very nice in his Cross Colors outfit with the shoes to match. He looked so handsome. Pearl opened the door, smiled and complimented him immediately.

"Well you look so handsome, Ajay," she said with a bright smile.

"Thanks mama Pearl," he said, "Is Ebony ready?"

"Oh you're gonna escort her to your party, *are you*?" Pearl asked in surprise.

"Yes ma'am. If that's okay," Ajay said as he darned a huge smile, "She's my date and I wanna make sure she gets there safe. I'm gonna walk her back home too."

"Oh that's just so sweet," Pearl said as the other mothers joined her at the door, "He came to escort my baby girl on their date."

Jo smiled proudly and yelled, "That's my son!"

All the mothers laughed hard as Pearl invited Ajay inside. He stepped into that house full of females and felt right at home. But as soon his eyes met Ebony's, his jaws dropped.

"Whoa, you look really cute," he said instinctively, "And like a little lady."

"Thank you," Ebony said as she blushed.

"Uh oh I see the magic," Pearl's younger sister Brenda said, "This is the future of the crew right here. And where are the other boys? I don't see June over here to walk little Rebbie over there," she laughed and added, "I need to get on his daddy, right now. This third generation better be on point. That's all I gotta say on that. All of them are gonna be at their first crew party together tonight!"

"That's what I'm worried about," Jo said sarcastically, as she looked at Lynn and Nina and everybody laughed.

Nina and Lynn squirmed because they knew what they're mother was hinting on. Ajay decided he would bail all of them out.

He said, "I told them to stay over there because it's my party and Ebony is my date. I wanted her to be the *only* one with front door service. She's my date, so she gotta be treated special all by herself."

"Well okay then," Pearl said as she smiled and motioned for Ebony to step up to where Ajay was standing.

Ajay was ready to get this date going. His eyes had not left Ebony's since he walked in. She couldn't stop looking at him either.

Finally she said, "You look nice, Anthony."

"Thank you."

"Oh and she calls him Anthony," Brenda said, "This is the *stuff* y'all."

Pearl could see that her baby girl had eyes for Ajay. But she wasn't ready to think of it as anything more than puppy love. She had no idea that the light lipstick she was allowing Ebony to wear. Wouldn't make it though the first hour of that party.

"So are you ready to go?" Ajay asked Ebony.

"Yes."

"Okay, let's do this," He said as he bent his arm and pointed his elbow toward her.

She put her arm through the loop he'd made and they stood next to each other, arm in arm.

"I gotta get a picture," Sandy said as she hurried to get her camera.

They had been taking pictures of the girls, all day as they got dressed and dolled up.

"Why come the other boys didn't come with you *anyway* so they could walk us over?" Bre asked Ajay because she was sweet on Stoney.

"I really didn't want them to come, cousin," he said, "They all wanted too. But I just wanted to come and walk Ebony over because she's my date and it's my party. It's her first party, so I wanted to make sure she got there safe."

"He's a man already," Belinda said as her daughter Jan snickered. Jan and Ajay are the same grade in school. They'll both be in 8th grade this year. She knows Ajay likes Ebony as do all of his crew. But the parents don't really see it yet. Or if they do. They're not ready to acknowledge it. They would just rather think of it as cute.

"Well Ajay you can walk all of the girls over there," his aunt Anna says, "How's that?"

He didn't want to do that. He wanted he and Ebony to walk alone. But he knew the mothers weren't going to understand it, if he said no.

"That's cool," he said, "Y'all ready. Let's go."

He walked out the door with Ebony on his arm as the other girls followed and flanked them. Jo stood in the door with the mothers and watched as they all strolled toward the street.

"Ajay looks comfortable with all of those girls around him, don't he?" Rebbie's mother Rena asked as she giggled.

"Too comfortable," Jo said, "And that's the problem. I'll be glad when he's old enough to settle down. I'm so sick of all of these fast ass girls and women too, calling my damn house for him."

"He's gorgeous, Jo," Debbie said.

"And he's got those eyes and that look too," Brenda added, "And hell, he's already the size of a twenty year old."

"Uh huh with a twenty three year old bitch running in behind him," Jo said, "Buying him clothes and shoes. That woman is letting him drive her car too."

"Well it's a good thing we ain't raising no damn fools like that," Debbie said, "The girls in this family are growing up to know how they're suppose to be treated. It won't be no caking going on, from our daughters and that's for sure."

"And from our sons either," Brenda said, "They know only the girl they wanna be with, gets special treatment. And Ajay is getting a jump start tonight. I really think he likes Ebony, in the crew way," she said and smiled at Pearl.

"Oh Brenda, it's just a party date," Pearl said as they went back inside her side door and closed it. She added, "He's just becoming a teenager. It ain't that serious yet. Ajay probably just don't wanna be bothered with all of that other trash that's gonna show up over to Paul's house, trying to get into his britches."

"Well I'm glad he picked Ebony as his date," Jo said, "Because at least tonight. I know he'll stay in them damn britches, for once."

239

They all laughed and Jo continued, "I am so over all of the girls calling my house and Ant don't even take the calls. But they keep calling. And that one that's twenty three? Ant's mother is gonna kick off in her ass way sooner than later. Do y'all hear me? You see she didn't bring them bad ass kids of hers back, *this* fourth of July. I told Allen to make sure Ant told her not to come to anything else that our family has. Even with Renee and the girls whooping her ass twice. That still don't stop her from coming after my son. It's gonna take a grown up woman, just like her ass is, to put a beating on her the right way."

"We'll damn sho be ready to help you, when that day comes too," Belinda said.

"She should know better than that anyway," Sandy offered.

"Well Sandy, older doesn't always mean wiser now does it?" Rena asked as they all laughed and headed into Pearl's kitchen.

The mothers gathered the extra foods they had on reserve for the party and placed all of it on the counters. It was already wrapped and waiting for Renee and the girls, for when they started to run low. It was going to be a perfect night for Ajay's initiation. It had started perfect for him and Ebony.

Ebony and Ajay arrived at his party, still arm and arm as Chill and the men folk applauded. The men had handled his initiation into the crew, prior to the females arriving. All that was left now was the party.

"Do you wanna dance?" Ajay asked Ebony.

"On a slow song?" she asked.

"Whatever you want," he said.

"I don't wanna dance, right now," she said and the look in her eyes said she wanted to talk to him alone.

"Do you wanna go somewhere so we can be by ourselves?"

"Yes," she said and smiled.

She wanted to kiss him. She didn't want anyone to see them and she didn't want to waste anytime getting to it. They went into the dining room but that wasn't private enough.

"Let me ask Chill to hook us up," Ajay said, "He can get us to a private spot without anybody else seeing anything."

"Okay."

Ajay went to find Chill, who was in the backyard where the fathers were around the grill.

"Hey Chill," Ajay said, "I need a favor."

"What's up, Lil Bro?"

240

"I need some privacy for me and baby girl," he said.

"*Already* Ajay?" Chill asked as he laughed, "She just got here."

"I know but that's what she just asked me," Ajay said, "She said she wanted to go somewhere so we can talk in private. Do you think I'm gonna say no to that?"

Chill smiled and said, "Y'all wanna play the kissing game again, ha?"

"I think so," Ajay said, "She didn't tell me. She just looked at me and smiled. Then she looked around at all the people in the front room and frowned. That's what she do when she don't wanna be around other people. I've learned that about her."

"Go ask her and be sure," Chill suggested and Ajay went back to where he'd left Ebony standing.

"Do you wanna go to a empty room so we can kiss?" Ajay asked her and smiled.

"Yes," she said without hesitation.

"Okay," Ajay said, "Cause Chill told me to ask you to make sure."

"I do wanna be by ourselves," she said, "Because I don't know how long mama's gonna let me stay. Even though I am your date."

"Bet," Ajay said, "I'll be right back."

He went back to tell Chill what Ebony said. Chill didn't waste anytime escorting them to the private living room. That was a room that no one went into except for holidays.

"Will this do?" Chill asked Ebony and Ajay.

"Yes," Ebony said in excitement and before Ajay could even answer him.

"Alright," Chill said, "I'll watch out for y'all. If somebody asked for either of you. I will come and get you, myself. Okay?"

"Okay," they both said and Chill left them alone.

Ajay looked at Ebony in her brand new digs that he knew he had gotten money from Darlene to buy for her. He couldn't stop smiling.

"You look so pretty," he said.

"Thank you. And you look handsome," she said, "You look like a man already. I wish I looked like a big girl."

"I like you just like you are right now," Ajay said, "Ebony I have a lot of girls who come around me with make-up on and hoochie mama clothes on. The whole nine. I don't like them. I don't like girls who are ready to do anything just cause they think I want too. Or those who go out of their way to get my attention when I don't want theirs. You never did that, baby girl and I like you. I came after you. That's because I like who

241

you are and what you're about. The things that make you feel comfortable. You don't have to change nothing about you. Not for me. I have always saw you as the perfect girl for me. I just wanna be good enough for you. I want you to feel special because I feel special when I'm with you. Does that make sense to you?"

"Yes," she said and she smiled.

Ajay could tell there was something else on her mind. Something else she wanted to say.

"What is it?"

"I want my breast to grow," she said without a smile or any hint of shyness.

"You want me to help them grow?" he asked as he looked into her eyes.

"Yes," she said.

"So are you telling me you're ready for me to suck on your nipples," he asked and he was already feeling the knot in his pants rise.

"I do," she said, "I just wanna know what it's all about. I like you, Anthony. I like how you treat me. I always liked that. When you use to come in Nina's room while me and my girls was playing. You always spoke to me. Just me and nobody else. I knew it was something about that. I knew you liked me. But I didn't know what I was suppose to do or say. So I use to just snap at you. I didn't wanna be mean to you or make you sad. I never wanted to make you feel sad and I still don't wanna do that now. I love when you smile at me. You was doing that then but I was scared to smile back because I didn't know what you would say next and if I would know what the answer was. That's all that was. You are the first boy I've ever liked like this and I feel so special. I can say things to you and do things with you that I would never say or do wit nobody else. I just want you to know that. It's your birthday and you're thirteen. You're crew now and plus you're gonna go pro in basketball because I'm gonna make sure you play your best, every time you play. If I don't see you doing your best. I'm gonna say something about it."

"That's what I want from you," he said, "Cause I know I'll do what I need to do to get it right. And I'll do what I'm suppose to do, if that will make you smile for me and be happy."

"Doing your best *will* make me happy," she said, "And I can tell by the way you hold me when we dance, that you like me in the same way that my daddy likes my mama. That makes me very special and I want to keep on learning from you. I wanna know what you like and what makes you

242

happy too. Because Anthony, I want you to be happy. I want you look out for me like you already do. All of that makes me feel special. So I know if you're touching me. You're gonna do that in a way that makes me feel special too. Because you care about how I feel."

"I sure do," he said.

"So can we try it?"

"Okay."

He stepped to her and started to kiss her hard, like he knew she liked it. He held her tight and she held him the same. They were caressing each others bodies while they continued to kiss. After a few minutes into it, Ajay unbuttoned the top 3 buttons on her dress while he looked into her eyes. She was nervous and he could tell. But she did look back into his eyes and she gave him a smile. She could tell he was unsure if she was still willing to go through with him seeing under her clothes. She assured him.

"I want you too," she said.

He put his mouth on her right nipple and started to suckle it. She moaned pleasantly. It felt very good to her. He got into it and started to alternate nipples. She liked it and she liked it a lot. She moaned and rubbed through his braids. He started to moan as he kept at his pace. They were feeling each other 100% at that moment and neither of them wanted to stop.

In the party room, the crew were having a great time. Everybody was dancing as couples and nobody was asking where was Ajay and Ebony. Well the crew wasn't because they all knew they were having alone time, by then. But there were some outside girls there and they were inquiring as to when Ajay would be arriving for his own party. They didn't get any answers from the crew.

About an hour into the party, Renee's brother Wes showed up. Their aunt from Akron had brought him to visit his favorite sister. Wes was happy to be there and he hadn't forgotten T-baby either. Wes was born in 1975, the same year as Tank, June, Rich, Nina and Ebony. His birthday was in July. He would be celebrating his 12th birthday in 15 days, on the 26th which was 2 days after T-baby would be turning 11 years old. He wanted to talk to T-baby while he was at Ajay's party. But Rich was hogging up all of her time. Wes could tell Rich knew he liked T-baby and he could tell she knew it too. Wes asked Renee if he should approach her anyway and Renee advised him not too because Rich was her crew.

"He is the one the grandparents picked for her to be with for her first choice, Lil bro," Renee told him, "That's how things are in this crew. There is a certain order that they all follow. It's how they keep things going

243

smoothly and it helps their parents keep up with them and who they're seeing and hanging around with. I would love it if you could be in this crew with me. But all the girls your age are already spoken for."

"If he don't treat her right," Wes said, "I'm gonna come to the rescue. She is so cute to me and I like her style. She don't take no mess."

"She's gonna be a strong woman, that's for sure," Renee said, "She will be smart enough to know if she's being treated like she should be. And hey, if it don't work out. I'll be the first one to tell you and I'll tell her about you and how you feel. Okay?"
Wes said okay. He decided to mingle and see what the other girls at the party was about. Since he couldn't have the girl of his choice.

Ajay and Ebony was still at it. Their private time was very heated. Ajay had sucked on her breast, her shoulders and even her neck. But he wasn't going to leave passion marks on her. He didn't want to get her in any trouble with her parents. Because they would be on to them and would probably never allow her around him again until she was in high school.

"I like this so much," Ajay said as he continued to kiss her.
He was grinding on her and that felt good to her. She was experiencing feelings she had never had. To be kissed, sucked on and grind on all at the same time was just another experience she had started with Ajay. One she liked and 1 she knew she would look forward too during their private times, from then on.

"I like it too, Anthony," she said, "I always hear my girls talk about it. I wanted to know what it felt like."
Ajay smiled and said, "It felt good to me. You just don't know how many times I laid in my bed and thought about being able to touch you. But I was never gonna go there or anywhere else with you. Without you asking me to first."

"You mean like the *real* thing?" she asked boldly.
"*Damn*! Definitely," he said and chuckled, "After this year we've had. I know we're gonna get there, one day. I can wait until that day comes though and I'll know when you're ready too. I don't want you to rush into it, baby girl. I have girls for that. I don't like none of them either. I don't want to, just like I say all the time to you. I want you and I'm gonna wait for you. I wanna make sure and tell you this part again. I'm not a liar. A lot of guys will tell a lie to their girl. But I won't tell you no lies about other girls. If I was with them and you ask me. I'm gonna tell you the truth. But I want you to know that you are the only girl that I *wanna* be with. And as
244

long as I can be with you. I will not be with no other girl. But as a man. I have needs. The *real* thing kind of needs. And I have to meet those needs. Or it will be hard for me to focus and maintain my cool. I call it the real thing, when I'm talking to you. But the real thing I'm talking about is sex. In my family of men. Sex is something that is *very* necessary. It keeps us from losing our temper and snapping somebody to pieces. My pops and grandpa told me that before I ever started it. I use to fight everyday. Or at least, tell somebody off. Do you remember that?"

"Yes and that's why everybody called you mean," she said.

"It wasn't that I was mean, as much as it was that my hormones was racing," he said and they both laughed. "All the men in my family started young. And when we get married and have a son. He will too. So be ready for that. I'm telling you now that he's gonna be advanced. That's how Jackson men come. Ready for the world."

"You wanna marry me?" she asked as she smiled, "You didn't even ask me to be your girlfriend yet."

They both laughed and he said, "I'm gonna ask you and don't you even have no doubts about that. But I want it to be special. I also wanna do it when it's the right time. Not just because our crew doing it. I told you they're not gonna be as strong as you and me. They're trying to keep up wit each other but not me. I'm following the crew code and my gut feelings too. But I will tell you this. As far as I'm concerned, you *are* my girl. And yes, I wanna marry you one day and have a family. I know I'm gonna ask you before you're thirteen. I just have to make sure my pops is okay wit it and yours too. They didn't do that and they're gonna have to do it that way before the older people in our family take them serious."

"You know a lot."

"Because I was raised too," he said, "You know how my pops and my mama is about me. They not gonna let me slip up. Not when it comes to who I am and what they expect from me. Just since I started being able to spend time with you. The only fights I've had, have been about protecting you. That will not change."

"I know you got that from big Al," she said, "I remember when I was four and you was six. Big Al beat up that man who use to live on the other side of y'all house because he kept trying to flirt with mama Jo."

"That fool was saying stuff to my mama that he had no business saying," Ajay said, "He was talking about her breast and her ass and all that. My pops hemmed him up in that yard, that day. Two weeks later, he moved from the neighborhood and my grandpa bought that property and

245

tore the house down. Those are the men that I come from, baby girl. Now Jan's house is the next one to ours with that empty lot in between. We're not gonna have no neighbors that's not in our crew either. You see that house is gone on the other side of y'all house too, right?"

"Yes but it was a whole family staying in that one when I was little," she said.

"I know but their son was as old as some of our parents and he was always looking at our mothers," Ajay said, "Some men don't understand or respect when a woman is loyal and faithful. When she's taken by her man and she ain't gonna look the other way. He was grown and still living with his mom. He use to come to the card parties too. They was some kin to Neal. The one that Chill killed that day because he jumped on him. After all of that stuff happened. My pops told me that none of his relatives was gonna be safe around us. Sure enough, they moved before Chill finished doing his time in Juvie and big John bought that property. Well papa bought it and big John paid him back. Same way my pops did with my grandpa."

"My daddy bought it?" she asked.

"Yea he did and he said the same thing my pops said," Ajay told her, "He was gonna add on to his house and make it bigger. Or build a new house and rent it to the type of people they want living next door to us."

Ebony had vague memories of Neal Palmer. But she wasn't able to fully recall what had happened that day, to cause Chill to have to be sent away. In another 6 days, it would be the 5th year anniversary of that day. Ebony had blocked it from her memory, for the most part. But Chill, Paul and big Al hadn't and never would. Ajay had everything to do with her failed recollection of that awful day. Because it was at that time, when he came into her life and started to spend all of his free time teaching her to play basketball. She would eventually recall that day again. But it would be a decade later. Her and Ajay would be planning their own wedding. Her memory of it would also assist her in removing any shields about intimacy. And that too, would be due to the comfort she would come to know and feel from Ajay being in her life.

The party was still jumping as Chill came to the living room door. He knocked and quickly identified himself. Ajay went to the door.

"Y'all are gonna eat something right?" Chill asked as he laughed and said, "And you still have to cut your cake. Mama Jo and the ladies about to bring it over here."

"Okay," Ajay said, "Here we come."

He closed the door back and went back to where Ebony was still sitting on the couch. Her dress was still unbuttoned but she had pulled it closed. He liked that she did that before he went to the door. He was already stingy with her. He didn't want anybody to see her compromised except for him.

"We gotta go back in there," he said, "Our mama's about to bring my birthday cake over here and you know I gotta cut it."

"Okay," she said as she fixed her clothes. Then she said, "If I don't have to go home. I wanna come back in here with you."

"I don't have a problem wit that," he said and smiled big, "This has been the best birthday of my whole life. That's because I spent the whole party wit you. Getting to know you and telling you about me."

Ajay's birthday party had been a success on all angles. Those outside hopefuls didn't get within 10 feet of him, the whole night. Ebony on the other hand, was by his side the *entire* night. He and Ebony also got a chance to go back into the private living room for more petting time too.

And they got right back to their talking and everything else they were doing before the food and cake break.

"I'm so glad mama let me stay for the whole party," Ebony said and smiled big.

"You're not happier than me," he replied and they both laughed.

"So you said *we're* not gonna have any neighbors or was you talking about where we live now?" she asked.

"I'm talking about me and you," he said, "Our neighbors are gonna be crew only. I'm playing basketball and I'm gonna make the pro's. I'm just going to the eighth grade and I'm already on the all-state team. I'm gonna make sure nobody lives right next door to me and my wife. We're gonna have our own neighborhood. Watch what I tell you. I've dreamed it and I'm gonna have it. I dreamed about being with you and now it's coming true. I can do anything else after that. Because baby girl, you was the hardest part of all of it."

"I know and I'll never be like that again," she said, "Unless you're messing up. If I find out about it. I'm not gonna like it."

"I knew I had the right girl," he said, "Now we can just chill in here by ourselves. Because I don't even care about seeing nobody else. We can dance in here too. I'm bout to spark up this joint that Chill gave me. You know about weed?"

"Yes I know about it. But I only got to smoke it one time," she said, "I was wit Jb and Bre. They let me and my girls have a hit. After that they let my girls hit it every time we're around them but not me. Jb said I can't

247

have none of it no more. Maybe like, every now and then but not every time. And I don't even know why but my girls can hit it anytime they ask."

"That's cause they don't wanna have to deal with me," Ajay said.

"What do you mean?" she asked, "You smoke it."

"Yea I do. But I don't want you to be high unless you're with me. Or unless you're about to be with me," he said, "Not until I know what it makes you feel like."

"So you told them not to give me none?"

"I told Chill I didn't want you to smoke wit everybody," he said, "Another reason is because I don't want you to smoke it like the other girls do now. I don't want my girl to be a weed head. That's for me."

He laughed and she laughed too. He looked at her. Then he said,

"I told you I want you to be the person that keeps me on solid ground. So I don't want you to crave weed. Because then, all I'll do is smoke more of it. I can handle it and still maintain. But I don't want you to get use to it. I want you to play ball and be a lady. You look so good in this dress and you're smart too. One day you're gonna be the type of lady that wears suits to work. I can't have you getting high before you're thirteen. You'll fry all of those smart brain cells you got."

They both cracked up laughing. Ebony was doubled over laughing on that comment. But then Ajay pulled out the joint that he had.

He said, "I'll let you hit it when I smoke around you. But I only want you to smoke with me. Or when you're with the crew and you're about to be with me. Okay?"

"Okay."

He lit the joint and inhaled it. Ebony watched him. She had to watch how he smoked it and she did. Then he told her he could blow the smoke in her mouth and she could still get a buzz.

"That's called a shotgun," he said, "We just call it a gun. Do you want one?"

"Yes."

He blew her a charge. Then he put the joint out and put it back into his pocket. He was going to save it for later. He watched her and her reaction. He knew instantly when her buzz kicked in because she got all giggly. She was laughing and there was nothing funny being said.

He asked, "Do you wanna see how kissing and stuff feels now?"

"Yea," she said and cracked up laughing.

"You've gotta stop laughing," he said, "You've gotta show me you can handle it. Especially if you want me to let you smoke sometimes."

She made herself calm down and focus. Shortly after that, they were back to their previous activity. It was so much more intense for her after that shotgun. She was very aggressive with her hands. She was holding him and rubbing him a lot. He noticed and commented.

"Do you see how much more relaxed you are and you're doing a lot more now. You notice?"

"Yea."

"That's why I only want you high around me," he said, "I don't want you to be high and some asshole tries to take advantage of you because you're relaxed. You understand now?"

"I do," she said, "I only wanna feel like this when I'm around you, Anthony."

"Very good," he said and they got back to kissing.

The 2 of them would remain in that living room until it was time for Ebony and the girls to go home. Needless to say, Ebony didn't want to leave Ajay. He didn't want her too either but it was almost 11pm and that was all of the girls curfew. He walked her home, just as he'd told the mothers he was going to do when he escorted her over there. His boys walked their girls home too. Jan and Bre was spending the night with Lynn, so Ajay knew Ebony's girls were going to be staying with her. He felt like that was the safest bet for that night. Because if Ebony had stayed with Nina. He would probably have taken things too far, too soon.

Two days after his party, Ajay and Jb had to leave for camps. Ebony was sad to see Ajay leave. But she knew he had to do his thing because he was a superstar and he was going to go to the NBA, one day. Besides, her and the rest of her family would be leaving for 2 weeks in the next 2 days.

By the 15th of July, big John was on vacation and he was taking his family to Houston. That was very hard for Ebony because she was even closer to Ajay than she had been the summer before. She loved her big mama and she loved the talks they would have. But apart of her wanted big mama to come to Cleveland and visit. Rather than her having to go there. She didn't want to be away from Ajay. But he was already gone to camp and he would be doing camps until the day before Rebbie's 11th birthday. Which was the 2nd of August. John, Pearl, Tank, Ebony and Lil man flew to Houston and wouldn't return until the last day of July.

Ebony and big mama had a talk everyday while she was there. She told big mama everything about her new experiences. Well, everything except the weed part. Big mama didn't seem surprised at all about her and Ajay's progress. She seemed to know everything that had happened, up until that point. Maybe not in detail but she knew Ebony had been his date for his 13th birthday. She also knew Ebony got to stay until the regular girls curfew. Something she wouldn't do again until she turned 13, herself. Big mama also told her, she would get to talk to Ajay while she was there.

"I will," she said, "I know he could call when he was in Juvie."

"Well your oldest brother is with him at camps," big mama said, "And his parents are here. Don't you think they're gonna want to talk to him while they're separated?"

"Oh yea," Ebony said and laughed.

"Namesake, you're not even worried about talking to your big brother, are you?" big mama asked, "You just wanna talk to Ajay."

"I know ha?" Ebony said and kept giggling.

Big mama knew right then that her oldest granddaughter was well on her way to falling in love and big mama was all for it. She made sure to cover all of the finer points she wanted Ebony to be prepared for. She also told her that she wanted her to talk with her mother about the new things she was starting to experience.

"I try too, big mama," Ebony said, "But mama still thinks I'm a baby."

"Well you are *her* baby," big mama said, "She's going to be harder at excepting it than anybody else. But you'll have to tell her, okay?"

"Okay, big mama."

Ebony had no idea of how she would approach her mother with a subject which was that mature. But she knew she had too. On her family's honor and her upbringing, she had to be upfront about the decisions she made. That's the way she was raised and she knew there was no way around it.

She did get to talk with Ajay, on every call from Jb. They were having a great time at camp and meeting new players and coaches from all across the country. In the words of Jb, who said,

"I'm doing real good at camp but Ajay's running it. He's hanging wit the top notch players in the nation," Jb told big John, "Everyday out there, Ajay gets picked in the top five and it's a hundred and seventy five boys here."

"Sounds like y'all gonna be ready to claim that state title, this year ha?" big John asked.

"No doubt pops," Jb said, "Ajay is going pro. I'm gonna be his agent because his game is already above average for high school. And he just going to the eighth grade. I'm going to ninth, so I'm balling too."

"You'll be on that high school team with Ajay, this year," big John said, "They already asked me to allow you to move up, so go for it. That's why I convinced your mama to let me send you back to camp. You and Ajay keep each other straight, down there. And I'll see you when you get home."

"Word, pops," Jb said, "In a minute."

"See ya."

Ebony was more than ready to go home when the 31st came. She knew Ajay would be home, the following day and she was beside herself with eagerness. They got home and she went straight to her room to unpack and wait for her girls to show up. She was going to let them have her time, that first day. Because the next day and everyday after that, was going to be Ajay's. Her girls arrived just as she had put all of her clothes away and picked out the outfit she would be wearing when Ajay laid eyes on her, the next day.

"Cousin, I'm so glad you're back!" T-baby screamed as she ran into Ebony's room.

"Just in time for our birthday party," Rebbie said, "We're having it on *my* birthday."

"And we'll all be eleven together," Nina said, "For a few months anyway. Y'all having y'all party together, just like me and Ebony always do. That's how the foursome rolls."

"We're always gonna have two parties for four girls," Ebony said, "Until I get married. Then Anthony is gonna have my party, all by myself." She burst out laughing and her girls laughed too. Nina wasn't going to be out done.

She said, "And Jeremy is gonna have my party with just me too, now!"

"*Whatever*," Ebony said and continued to laugh.

Nothing was going to dampen her spirits *that* day. She had Ajay on the brain. Her girls was staying the night. She had promised her big mama that she would have a heart to heart with her mother. But that was going to have to come later because she had company and she wasn't going to talk in front of all of them yet. Furthermore, she had no clue of how she would tell Pearl nor where to even begin. She knew most likely there would be a few more things to confess, once Ajay was back. They had gotten passed the first pecks, the tongue kissing, the rubbing, grinding and on his birthday. They had graduated to him sucking on the nipples that would start to form breast, in less than a year. She's still young but a lot wiser than the previous year. She was becoming a woman. *No more daddy's little girl*.

251

Chapter 11-She's Becoming A Woman

For this talk, Ajay and his son were riding around Cleveland in Ajay's Jaguar. It was father and son time again. Lil Ajay was super excited. He was ready to talk, listen and learn more about his parents road to the love he sees them display daily.

"What are we gonna do today, pops," Lil Ajay asks.

"It's time for you to start your job at the detail shop," Ajay says as he pulls into Crewland mall and parks next to *Crew Details*.

"My cousin's are all here too," Lil Ajay says as he gets out to greet Brad III, Rich III and Lil Jb. They already have towels in their hands. Ajay grabs towels for him and Lil Ajay and they get started drying cars.

"So this is what you use to do when you was six too?" Lil Ajay asked.

"This was our very first business," Ajay says, "For all the males, from the second generation on down, this was our first job. We all worked for our own company before going into the league or opening the other shops and businesses that you see out here now."

"That basketball court over there," Lil Ajay says, "That's the one my papa Al put up so you would stay at work?"

Ajay laughs and says, "Oh yea he had to, to keep me here. It was a half court then but now it's a full court. My generation fenced it in like that and added the bleachers. Steven and Jamal make sure the staff at Allen Saul keep it cleaned up. But for the most part, the city keeps the grass cut down and all of the major upkeep because we decided to have it opened to the public nowadays."

"It's already two half court games going on, pops!" Lil Ajay says and Ajay can hear the longing in his voice.

"When we help them catch up on these cars," Ajay says, "We can go over there and let you show em some of your skills. You wit that?"

"Yep!"

Ajay laughs. He can remember himself, 23 years ago with that same look of anticipation for getting to the game.

He says, "We've got another car to dry first. Then we can hoop a little bit. I know you got some questions for me, so let it rip."

"I like how you had my mama as your date when you got crewed up," Lil Ajay says, "I wanna do it the same way."

"Any idea who that date is gonna be?" Ajay asks but he's sure he already knows the answer.

"I want it to be Kimmie," Lil Ajay says and smiles big.

"I knew it," Ajay says and chuckles. Then he says, "Well she'll be here this weekend. She's gonna live with Eric and Erica and go to school at Beachwood with you and Lannie."

"*Sweet*," Lil Ajay says with a certain sharpness in his tone.
He's excited to get that news. However, he's more reserved about the next thing his father says.

"Alan is moving here too," Ajay says, "Leilenne will be here and she's bringing her and Lil Arch's one year old daughter Ashley. They're all gonna live with Eric and Erica. But wait until your mom tells all of you."

"I knew Alan was gonna come," Lil Ajay says, "He emailed me last week and said he was gonna go to school with me. But he didn't say Kimmie was coming. I just hoped she was."

"Yes they're all coming," Ajay says, "Leilenne is gonna finish college here and she's gonna work at the complex with Ally and Jamal's girl Holly. They'll get her trained, all next week while Ashley goes to granny's house with Lea and the triplets."

"Man, our crew is gonna be bigger then Bruce *and* Chill's crew," Lil Ajay says and chuckles.

"That was always the plan," Ajay says.

"It was your plan to have our own neighborhood, just like it was our families plan to have our own businesses too, wasn't it?"

"For sho," Ajay says.

"You didn't want nobody trying to talk to my mama, did you pops?" Lil Ajay asked and laughed.

"*Hell* no," Ajay says, "I don't even want nobody looking at her. So there was no way in hell I was gonna have neighbors that I *didn't* know."

"So *that's* why we don't have any neighbors that we *don't* know."

"That's exactly the reason," Ajay says, "I don't want nobody around my home and family, who don't know that I'll take their lives for anything that I view as disrespect."

"So when we was talking the last time. You was at summer camp after your thirteenth birthday," Lil Ajay says, "And you was getting ready to come home. Even when you and my mama was apart. Big mama and nana Jo let y'all talk to each other, didn't they?"

"Yea son, they always had our backs," Ajay says, "Everybody in the family did, for the most part."

"So that was about the time that Kenny's papa got shot up?"

"It was five fathers in that car including your uncle Brad, big Brian, big Archie and big Sam," Ajay says slowly, "Big Jake was trying to
253

take all of them out. He shot that car up and big Paul went to intensive care. And he eventually died, later on that same month. Chill was a beast after that."

"If that was you, I would be too. My crew is gonna get his ass still," Lil Ajay says as he goes into that death stare that his father is known for.

"Most definitely," Ajay says, "After we shoot a game or two. We're going back to the range. I want you absolutely accurate. Because that's one for the ages, right there. My crew got the businesses going and your crew is gonna dead that bitch ass piece of shit."

"I'm looking forward to that, pops," he says, "Papa Al was with you on your first trip to the chamber. Then after all the guys in your crew made thirteen. Your crew took over. So when I get my crew stripes, does that mean you're gonna retire?"

"No," Ajay says, "The men in this crew never really retire, son. We just get bigger and stronger. The active crew will be in the forefront. But if the situation calls for it. Every man in this family will ride with pride and be a force to be reckoned with. We don't retire, seldom die and we always multiply."

"The Jackson man has to be strong and represent *twice* as much as the others because we never have a blood brother," Lil Ajay says, "That makes me more proud to be your son. Because I know I came from men who can stand on they own and get the job done. No matter what it is."

"You sound just like me, son," Ajay says and chuckles, "But you just remember this. Big Jake has never taken a man from your blood line. That's a stat that must never change. He will die before you turn thirteen though. That's my plan. Because I can't relax on his ass, no longer. Not since I learned that he had plans of fuckin with Ebony. I've been putting shit together for him, for a long time. All I'm waiting for now is for you to understand the codes and feel the hunger to rid our family of *any* threats."

"I'm ready, pops," Lil Ajay says, "And to make me even more *amped*. Tell me about how that old fucker killed Kenny's granddad. But I wanna hear the rest about how you and mama got to this point too. Especially now that Kimmie is moving here."

They both laugh and Ajay says, "Alright. The summer of eighty seven continues."

{August 1, 1987}

Ajay was done with his summer camps and returned home on the first day of August, just in time to attend T-baby and Rebbie's birthday party, the next day. He was excited to be home and he wasn't anymore excited than Ebony. She was waiting on their driveways, underneath the basketball goal, when big Al and Paul pulled up and parked. Ajay jumped out of the vehicle before it could even stop rolling. He went straight to Ebony. Ebony smiled as he approached her. He saw a longing in her eyes, for the first time. Ebony got the first hug. Mama Jo got the second one. Big Al and Paul just looked at each other and laughed at the look Jo held on her face, for more 10 seconds. Al could tell she liked what Ajay had done. Al also knew on that day, Jo could tell Ajay was sweet on Ebony. But he also figured she thought it was only puppy love. Al knew it was more than that because Ajay had talked to him, Paul and Jb all the way home from the final camp in Chicago. After Ajay greeted everybody else. He went right back to Ebony.

"How was the trip to Houston?" he asked.

"It was good," she said, "How was the camps?"

"The camps was good," he said, "But like I told you on the phone. I have the best time when I'm at home."

They smiled at each other again. The guys was already talking about what they wanted to do that day but Ajay had other plans.

"I gotta get my bags in and unpack," he said. Then he turned to Ebony and asked, "Will you help me unpack my stuff?"

"Yes," she said and followed him to their car.

Along with Tank and Nina, Ebony helped him get his bags into the house and up to his room. Ajay wanted some alone time with Ebony and Tank was willing to assist him.

"Twin, why don't you help Ajay get this clothes put up," Tank said as he followed Nina into her and Lynn's room.

Ebony stayed in the room with Ajay. She helped him to separate the clothes that needed to go to the laundry and she also helped him put away the rest of them.

"I brought you something back," he said suddenly, "And you're the only one I brought something."

"You did?" she asked.

"Yep," he said as he picked up a stack of folded shirts.

He had brought her 5 t-shirts. 1 from each of the camps he attended. He handed them to her. She smiled as she took them into her arms.

"You brought me some camp shirts?" she asked, "That's so cool."

"Yea, each camp gives us three each, so we can have one for each

255

day of camp," he said, "But I just washed the one I wore the first day and wore it on the third day, so I could bring you some back."

"That's so cool," she said, "Thank you, Anthony."

"You're welcome, baby," he said and smiled. Then he said, "I'm always gonna look out for you. I told you that. Plus I want my girl to have something that match what I wear. You always dress like your girls. So now you can match me when we shoot ball."

"You called me baby and not baby girl," she said and she blushed.

"You are my baby," he said, "It's just a matter of time before I'll be calling you baby. Is that okay?"

"Yes that's okay," she said and she was still smiling.

"I know you're wondering what's taking me so long to kiss you ha?"
She didn't even answer him. She moved up to him and started the kiss *herself*. He put his arms around her and started kissing her hard, the way he knew she liked it. She moaned a lot. She was really into it and he loved it. He knew she missed him and he knew she was ready to be that girl for him.

"I love when we're together," he said, "I feel so comfortable with you, baby girl. I've never felt this laid back with nobody and definitely not with none of those girls I've been with."

"Then you shouldn't be with them," she said.
Then she thought about his hormones and she said, "Well, once that day come when I'm ready to do the real thing. I don't want you to be with those other girls. I just want you to be with me."

"I'm all for that," he said, "I will tell you this. As long as I can be with you. No other girl will be able to take your spot because I know what you're about. You're a good girl and that's why I wanna give my heart to you. I just have to learn how to be in love. I'm gonna need for you to show me that, okay?"

"I've never been in love before," she said.

"You're gonna love me," he said, "And you're gonna love me, the honest way. You've gotta teach me that part. But I'll tell you this today. No matter what I do. You will always be the girl that I look out for. The only one I'm gonna kiss and the only one I will talk to like this. The only time I'm around another girl is for sex. Sex with a condom too. I don't kiss them. I don't suck on them and I barely say anything other than let's do this or I'm outta here."

"That's mean," she said but she was giggling.

"That's me, not liking them," he said, "They wanna be what you

256

are and what I want you to be to me. I've wanted you since before first grade. I just waited for you to start to like me. The other girls will never get that from me. Do you believe me?"

"Yes I do," she said, "You know why?"

"Tell me."

"Because you told me, you wasn't a liar," she said as he kissed her on her neck and sucked on her ears.

She stopped talking right then and there and looked into his eyes. He started kissing her again.

Then he said, "I know our mama's are gonna be looking for us soon. Because we've been up here, a long time. But I'm gonna spend the night with Tank and Jb. After everybody go to sleep, I'm gonna come see you."

"In my bedroom?" she asked in surprise.

"Yes," he said, "Just so we can do what we've been doing. You're not ready for the real thing yet. But I'm gonna start showing you how to move against me, for that day when we do get there."

"I like how that feels," she said.

"What? When we moving against each other?"

"Yes."

"I like it too," he said, "But what I'm gonna be doing is learning what you like *done* to you. Before we even get to that. I wanna know what it takes to *get* you there."

"Anthony, you know everything."

"Not yet I don't but I plan to know everything it is to know about you," he said, "I'm gonna find out everything you like. Because one day, I'm gonna be the man that gives you all of that. I'm gonna be the man that makes you smile."

She was smiling then and kissing him on his face but he wasn't done talking. He said, "I seen you crying when Chill went to Juvie and when Lady got killed. I never wanna see that again. When you cry. I feel so helpless. I don't ever wanna make you cry either."

"I don't want you to make me cry, Anthony," she said, "If I see you with a girl that's gonna make me sad and I'll probably cry too."

"Then I won't do that in front of you," he said, "But until we get to the sex part. I am gonna be hitting other girls, from time to time. I'm never gonna let you see it though."

"I don't even like it when you say it," she said bluntly.

"Well I won't say it," he said, "But I'm not gonna lie. I'm not even gonna start that."

Ajay heard his father come in and call him. He was at the bottom of the stairs.

"Go in Nina's room," he said, "Tank already gonna be coming out. Give me one more kiss for good luck and then I'll see you tonight, in your room."

They kissed once more. Then he opened his door. Tank was already standing there. Ebony went into Nina's room while Ajay answered his dad.

"Sir," Ajay said from the top of the stairs.

"You and Tank come on over to Paul's," Al said, "We're about to have a meeting."

Ajay and Tank knew it was about the beef, just by the tone in Al's voice. They descended the stairs quickly and walked with Al across the street. All of the men and boys were either there already or showing up.

There was more conflict going on with big Jake. By the end of the night, several more of his posse was dead. Ajay had gone along on the trip with the males and added 2 more to his kill count. The only thing that disappointed him about the spree was that big Jake wasn't 1 of the dead. He had never had a problem managing his focus when doing crew deeds. But that ride out was different. During that whole chamber trip, the thought that stayed on his mind was spending that night with Tank and Jb, so he could see and hold Ebony again. That chance would come. But only after a run in with Darlene.

As the men arrived back in Shaker Heights and was preparing to go home, Darlene showed up. It was obvious she had been hanging around their street waiting for a sighting of Ajay. As he got out of the car and was heading toward Pearl's side door with Tank, Darlene pulled up and parked out by the street.

"Ajay, come here baby!" she yelled.

"Ah shit," Ajay said. Then he quickly turned to Tank. He said, "Hey man wait at Chill's house for me. Don't go inside yet. Let me see what this bitch wants. But she gotta move from out here because I'm not about to let baby girl see her."

"Alright cool," Tank said, "You know we roll in two's at least. So I'm going wit you, if you leave."

"Even better," Ajay said, "Come on."

Him and Tank walked out to Darlene's car. She was sitting in it and smiling like the cat that ate the canary.

"What's up baby?" she asked.

"Ain't shit up," he said, "I'm not yo baby. What you want?"

"I came to see you, of course," she said, "What else could I want?"

"Let's ride," he said, "And Tank coming wit me."

Ajay got in the front seat while Tank hopped in the back. Darlene pulled away. Ajay could see the look on his dad's face and he was sure him and some of their fathers wasn't going to lose sight of that car.

Meanwhile Darlene started to make her pitch for taking him to Maple Heights for the night.

"You know I missed you right?" she asked.

"And," was all Ajay said.

"Well I wanted you to come see me," she said.

Ajay knew he wasn't about to go to Maple Heights to spend the night. He was going to stay at mama Pearl's house so he could see his girl. And so he could be there for T-baby and Rebbie's party, the next day. He had to come up with a way to get what he wanted out of Darlene without leaving his Shaker Heights community. He decided to tell Darlene to drive a few blocks away, to a baseball field. It was rarely used for city baseball anymore. Since the city had stopped the regular upkeep. But a lot of the folks in the neighborhood would still hang out there, most likely doing illegal things. He had her to pull in next to the dugouts and park.

"What are we doing here?" she asked.

"I can't be gone that long," is what Ajay came up with. "So whatever you're trying to do. Needs to be done here. I gotta get back soon."

"In the baseball field?!"

"Or you can just take me back now," he said, "Your choice."

"I wanted to taste you but you brought Tank with you," she said.

"You done sucked my dick in front of Tank before," Ajay told her, "What's the problem now? And anyway, what you got for me?"

"What do you mean Ajay?" Darlene asked, "Money wise?"

"Yea," he said.

"Well you was gone, baby," she tried.

"I'm here now and you ain't gave me shit since the day before my birthday," he said.

"But I also bought you three outfits too," she tried.

"So is that a no or what? Cause I can't tell," he said.

"I've got a hundred," she said, "That's all I can do right now because I still gotta pay my rent."

"Cool," he said, "Where is it?"

She reached into her bra and pulled out five $20 bills. She handed them to him. She had it in her breast because she was planning for him to take it out himself. The money was for him before he'd even asked her for it. He took it and stuffed it into the pocket of his jeans. Then he undid his zipper and looked at her.

He said, "Let's make this happen, so I can get back in time and don't get in trouble."

She leaned down over him in the passenger seat and went to work on his dick. Tank was still sitting in the backseat but he had come up with a way he could get in on it too.

"So y'all just gonna leave me back here with no action?" Tank asked, "Ajay come sit in the backseat."

Ajay did just that and brought Darlene back there with him. He removed her clothes. Then put her face back in his lap. He didn't want her pussy. He'd had about all he wanted from Darlene when she handed over the money. But he hiked her ass up and had her to get up on her knees. Tank stood outside of the backdoor and undid his jeans. He strapped on a condom and entered Darlene from the back. She sucked Ajay's dick while Tank fucked her and she enjoyed both. She kept telling Ajay she would like to give him head without a condom, for a change. He wasn't hearing it that night either.

"You know my rule," he said, "No glove. No love. I'm saving my dick for the girl I'm gonna marry."

Darlene went into overdrive with the head job, after that comment. She was determined to be on his mind when he did get old enough to start thinking about matrimony. But she was shit out of luck and would remain that way.

Once the fuck session was over, Ajay was ready to leave, right then and there. But Darlene had a talking bug that early evening.

"When are you gonna come stay with me and let me take care of you *all* night?" she asked.

"I'm not gonna move with you," he said suddenly, "You do know that right?"

"I know you can't now but you *can* spend the night, Ajay," she said, "I know you stay out all night already. So why don't you ever stay with me?"

"I'm not ready for that," he said, "It's time for us to get back home anyway, so let's make it."

Darlene started her car reluctantly. She pulled away slowly but she wasn't done talking.

"I just think you should spend the night with me, one night," she said, "So I can wake you up with some good breakfast and some champion head for my basketball champion. That will help you to relax and have a very good day."

"I'm already gonna have a good day when I wake up," he said, "I know that already too. Just get me home. And look here. You can't be coming by the house anytime you want too either. My mama ain't feeling that shit. I don't want her fussing at me because of you. She said she better not see you, where she can get her hands on you. So be warned."

"Oh baby. Your mama just don't wanna accept the fact that you're a grown man in a teenagers body," Darlene said and laughed.

"I know you're not trying to talk negative about my mama?" he asked, "Ha?"

"I'm just telling it like I-"

"Shut the fuck up," he snapped, "What my mama say is the rule. She's a queen and she's my fuckin mama. Don't you *never* say nothing else that even sounds like you being negative or don't *think* she's right. Do you understand that shit?"

Darlene was quiet. She drove in silence, preferring not say another word but Ajay wanted an answer.

"Do you understand what the fuck I said?!" he asked again with a rise in his voice.

"Yes Ajay! God!" she yelled, "You're not gonna be yelling-"

"You can let me the fuck out, right here," he said, "Stop the damn car."

"I'm sorry," she said gathering herself.

She didn't want him to get out and walk the rest of the way because she knew he wasn't going to talk to her, ever again.

She continued, "I'll take you home. I'm sorry for what I said. I wasn't trying to be negative."

Ajay didn't say anything. He only looked back at Tank who was smiling. Tank knew Ajay was trying to get rid of Darlene because he was into Ebony and he didn't want her coming around their homes. So Tank jumped right in on the conversation, just like crew would.

"Darlene, what do you see for you and Ajay?" Tank asked.

"I want us to be together," she said, "I know he's ten years younger than me. But he's very mature and very gifted."

"You mean like as in *dating*?" Tank asked and chuckled.

"I don't see why not," Darlene said before Ajay jumped in, knowing Tank was painting the picture for her dismissal.

"Because you done fuck all my crew," Ajay said as calmly as big Al

261

would. He continued, "You wanted my pops in the beginning. But that shit was never gonna happen. Then you fucked my big brother Chill, Stoney and Rob."

Tank cut in, "You done fucked every male in our crew except June and Rich. You can't think Ajay is gonna call you his girlfriend. If he did that. I wouldn't even fuck wit him. We wouldn't get along because all his boys done fucked you."

"That was on some hanging out and trying crazy shit, type of action though," Darlene tried.

"That was on some ho shit," Ajay said, "And you call yourself a bad ho, right?"

Darlene was quiet as she pulled in front of the empty lot next to Pearl and John's house. Ajay was persistent. He needed this bitch to stay in her damn lane.

"*Right*?" he asked again.

"I did, yes," Darlene admitted.

"Then why would I call a ho my girlfriend?" Ajay said, "Don't try to change shit now. Because I'm just gone vamp out on you. I hate when fuckers try to change the rules in the middle of the damn game. That shit gets on my damn nerves."

He jumped out of her passenger seat and slammed the door. He summoned Tank to come on too. Tank got out and followed Ajay up the sidewalk which was leading to the front of his house. But Darlene had to say her goodnights and try to make a play for the next evening.

"I'll be by to see you after work tomorrow," she said.

"What the fuck did I tell you?" Ajay said as he stepped back toward her car.

He noticed big Paul's car come back up the street, pull into their yard and park. He knew they had sat outside the baseball field while him and Tank had their rendezvous. He saw the car when Darlene pulled out.

"Okay, well will you call me and let me know when I can see you?" she asked, "Because I do miss you when I don't get to see you."

"Yea," he said, "Now go the fuck home."

He turned and walked with Tank as they headed down the sidewalk and turned onto the double driveways to approach Pearl's side door. Darlene pulled away. As she passed them, she honked her horn. Ajay and Tank heard big Paul and Uncle Greg laughing. They knew what was up with her serenade. Ajay followed Tank on into the house. They spoke to Pearl, who was making her lunch for her graveyard shift job at East General Hospital.

262

It was nearly 9pm and she had to be there for eleven. Paul and Greg were going to drive her to work tonight. Big John always insisted that the males see to her whenever she had to leave home. And even while she was there and he was on the road. Pearl had some last words for Tank before she headed up the stairs to get dressed in her RN uniform.

"Tank I know you're home for the night?" she asked but not really asking but more like telling him.

"Yes ma'am," Tank said, "Ajay wanna spend the night. We gonna go in the basement and listen to some music for awhile."

"Well okay," Pearl said, "But call over to Paul's and tell him that Jb needs to sleep at home tonight too. Baby girl and Lil man are here and I want my oldest child at home. Even though I know your uncle Greg and the guys are gonna be checking the house. Still, I want him to sleep here."

"Yes ma'am," Tank said again as he picked up the phone to call Chill's house.

Pearl went on upstairs to get dressed. Ajay was anxious. He knew his girl was up those stairs in her room. He told Tank he was gonna run home and get a change of clothes and some Pajamas, so he could take a shower at their house. He left while Tank called Jb. But he was back before Tank was done talking to the crew across the street. Ajay talked to Lynn and told her he was staying at Pearl's house and to let their mom know. Because she was in the tub when he'd gone home.

"I was gonna stay over here," Lynn said.

"But Jb gotta come home though," Ajay whispered.

"Well I need to spend the night with Ebony," Lynn said.

"No way," Ajay said, "Not tonight."

"Oh you going in her room ha?" Lynn asked.

"Yep."

"Well I know y'all ain't fucking though," Lynn said.

"No but that's gonna be my girl," Ajay whispered again, "We don't have too. I just wanna do whatever she wanna do."

"My baby brother is in love," Lynn teased.

Ajay didn't respond. He just held the phone. Finally him and Lynn finished their conversation and hung up. Then Ajay and Tank went into the basement and turned on John's stereo and played music.

Upstairs in her room, Ebony had already had her bath. Her mother let her know that Ajay was in the house, so she had to wear her robe if she was to come out of her room.

"Yes ma'am," Ebony said as she closed her door back and smiled.

263

She knew Ajay was spending the night already. She also knew he would be coming into her room as soon as her mother left for work, in another hour. She was excited because this would be the first time she would be in her room alone with Ajay. She had been in his room several times for slow dancing, kissing and petting. She felt anxious. She couldn't wait for her mother to leave. She heard Ajay talking to Tank as they headed up the stairs. Tank was going to the boys room to get their music tapes. Ajay was going into the hallway bathroom to take a shower. She looked out her bedroom door and caught Ajay's eye, just before he closed the bathroom door. He smiled and stood there looking at her momentarily. He had never seen her in her sleeping gown. He thought she looked cute. She was only letting him see her because her mother was shut up in her room getting ready for work. Ebony knew Pearl would fuss if she saw her standing in her doorway in just her gown. But Ebony figured since her and Ajay was going to be husband and wife, one day. Then he needed to see what she looked like in her bed clothes. Little did she know at that time, that when she did start sharing a bed with Ajay. She would be sleeping in the nude.

"Hey baby girl," he said and continued to smile.

"Hi Anthony," she said, smiling and sending chills down his spine. She sounded so sexy and he couldn't wait for their private time. Just as they were about to go into a staring trance, Pearl opened her room door. Ajay closed the bathroom door quickly and turned the shower on. Ebony had ducked back into her room and closed the door.

Pearl came out of her room and stopped at Ebony's door. She knocked and said, "Baby girl, I'm about to leave for work. All of your brothers will be here and Ajay. So you shouldn't be scared because there are plenty of guys around to make sure you're safe, okay?"

Ebony cracked her door and peeked out.

"Okay mama," she said, "I'm just gonna go to bed."

"Okay sweetheart," Pearl said, "I'll see you in the morning."

Ebony said okay and closed her door back. She left it unlocked for Ajay, who was sure to be coming in as soon as he finished his shower.

Pearl left for work before 10:30pm. By 10:45, Ajay was in Ebony's bedroom. She was laying in her bed and when he entered, she sat up.

"Don't get up, baby girl," he whispered, "We never kissed when we was laying down before. Do you wanna try it like that?"

"Okay," she said softly.

He was wearing his pajama pants with a t-shirt to match them and his man sized bedroom slippers. He looked so handsome to her. As he walked from

264

her door to her bed, she watched him. She loved the way he walked. He was so smooth with his steps, each one with a little dip in the middle. He was just cool. Debonair even. *Already*. He made his way to the side of her bed and sat down on the edge.

"How you doing?" he asked with a smile.

"Good," she answered.

"I know that already," he said. Then he asked, "Do you already have a present for T-baby and Rebbie?"

"Yes," she said, "My mama and daddy bought their gifts while we was in Houston. Do you have them one?"

"I'm gonna give them some money," he said, "And let them buy whatever they want."

She could tell he was enjoying a slight buzz too. His eyes were low and slightly red. They looked very sexy too.

"You smoked a joint?" she asked.

"Yea," he said, "I smoked wit Chill and the guys earlier. Is that okay?"

"Yes," she said, "I could tell by your eyes."

"Can I lay down by you?" he asked suddenly.

"Okay."

He took off his slippers and got under the covers with her. He felt her body become very tensed.

"Are you nervous?" he asked.

"A little bit, yes," she said, "Because we never been in my room before."

"You don't have to do this if you don't want too," he said.

That seemed to make her more comfortable. She let out a long sigh and smiled.

She said, "I want you to stay."

He turned to face her and they started kissing. The kissing led to touching and within minutes, he was sucking on her nipples. She tensed up.

"What's wrong?" he asked.

"I wanna turn my lamp off," she said.

He reached over to the lamp and clicked it off. Then the room was pitch dark. He turned back over to her and they resumed their kissing. He sucked on her nipples until they were sore. He sucked a passion mark on each side of her neck. Then he slid on top of her. She was comfortable with him now. She held onto him and he started to grind. She wasn't sure of what to do next and he could tell. He started to coach her and tell her how to move her hips and body next to his. She did as she was told. His breathing was so much heavier than it had been in their previous sessions. She liked the excitement she had and she could tell he was excited too. He started rubbing her face and playing with her hair. She felt beautiful and protected, all at the same time. She felt good too. She knew what that hard object was in his pajamas and just from the grinding. She could tell it was *very* large. He grind harder. He dipped his hips which made the tip of his dick stick straight up against her vagina. He grind even more and she started to moan. She was making sounds she'd never made but it felt great. His dick was touching her clitoris and it was becoming stimulated. He started to lick on her nipples which sent shock waves through her.

"Mmmmm," she moaned.

"You like this, baby girl?"

"Yesssssss," she said as the moan came on the end *automatically*.
She liked the feeling so much. She knew what they were doing, was what men and women did and then some but it felt good to her. She figured she must be becoming a woman because she didn't want it to end. They kept at it for more than 30 minutes until he couldn't take it anymore. He was aroused and he knew he had to stop himself for awhile, just to settle his nerves.

"I'm gonna lay beside you for awhile and hold you," he said, "Is that okay?"

"Yes baby," she said.
He smiled. That was a first too. She had called *him* baby. With that, he knew she enjoyed what they had just done. But she had some questions.

"Is that the things you do when you do the real thing?"

"Oh yea," he said, "And my dick is hard now. That's why I had to stop for awhile. I've never done it like that with no girl. I told you that. I barely touch them and I never kiss em. I just get mine and be out. I don't suck on no titties or none of that. Ooo baby you got me feeling good."
He laid his head back on her pillow and with 1 arm under her shoulders, he stared up into the darkness.
Then he asked, "Can we talk for awhile?"

"Sure."

"I wanna turn on the light, okay?"

"Okay," she said.
He turned the lamp back on, then turned to face her again. He smiled and she smiled back.
He said, "I can already tell that when we do have sex. It's gone be the best I

ever had. I use condoms when I have sex. That's because I didn't grow up with those girls and I'm not about to make no baby with somebody that I don't know."

"Well I know I don't wanna have a baby yet either. But I don't even have my thing yet," she said, speaking about her menstrual cycle.

"I know you don't have your period yet," he said, "But I bet I'll know when you about to start having it."

"How?" she asked and smiled.

"Because your hips will started to form and shape up," he said, "You'll start to look like the big girl you was so worried about being, at one point. But baby girl, I need to know something right now."

"What?"

He looked over on her dresser, her desk and her chest of drawers. There were baby dolls everywhere.

He asked, "Do you still play wit those dolls?"

She giggled and said, "Yes I do."

"The way you're kissing me," he said, "I would never believe you were still playing with dolls. I haven't seen you bring them to my house in a long time."

"Because my girls don't wanna play with them wit me, no more."

"That's because they're trying to act older to impress my boys," he said, "I don't want you to do that. But I can't wait until you stop playing with baby dolls though."

He laughed and she laughed too. She couldn't figure out what it was he had against her baby dolls. She couldn't figure it out. What he was concerned about was her free time. He wanted all of it and he knew she must've been using some it to play with those dolls up in her room, when she could be with him instead. She had more questions.

"Tell me more about the real thing," she said, "How does that go. I mean. I know that you will have to put...."

"....my dick goes in your pussy," he said in 1 breath and his dick jumped up in his pants when he said it.

"Tonya, Renee and Lynn told us that it hurts," she said.

"It does the first time," he said, "It is gonna hurt."

"Why?"

"Because your pussy or vagina," he said, "It has a lining over it. You can't see it but it's there. Like when girls get their period and use those tampons. That don't bother it. It's further up in there. My pops and grandpa told me about all of that kind of stuff. Plus I read about it in sixth

267

grade. You're gonna have that book this fall. What it is, is a lining that covers the entry to another canal like thing, that's inside of females. The only thing that can break through it is a penis. A dick. And my dick is gonna be the one that breaks yours one day. But not until after you're ready and after you get your period. Because that's when you will start to become a woman. I don't wanna do it before that happens, okay?"

"Okay but why is that?"

"Because then I can count the days and I'll know when you can't get pregnant," he said, "I want you to tell me when it starts. I wanna know the day that it come on, every month too. Do you know why?"

"No. Why?"

"Because you're my girl and I don't wanna use condoms with you all the time," he said, "Just the first time because the condom will help me to slide in easier. But just so you know. I think sex is better without them. I just haven't ever had sex without one because I haven't been with nobody that I wanted to feel that good with. I'm saving that for you. But I wanna know the day that your period starts because then, I can count the days until you can become pregnant. It takes fourteen days from the first day of your period. On that fourteenth day, you can get pregnant and for a week after that. And I don't want you to have no kids for me until after I marry you. That's because I have that kind of respect for you and I will not do that to you. I want us to finish high school and college before we have a baby. But if you get pregnant before then. We will *have* to get married before that baby is born. I promised my grandpa I wouldn't break the cycle. I can't break my word to him because that would mess me up. But just know that it is gonna hurt the first time. After that, I'm gonna make you feel damn good every time, from then on."

"I don't want it to hurt though," she said.

"That's apart of it, baby girl," he said, "Every girl hurts the first time. If I could change that, I would."

She looked at him and smiled. She felt so much more knowledgeable after each talk they had. She was glad to know what she had to expect before that time. But she was also embarrassed that he knew more about her body than she did. She smiled and scooted back under him. He set her alarm clock because he was going to sleep in there until 2 hours before Pearl was due to come back home. He was fixed on Ebony. He knew they couldn't wake up to the sun together but he was going to stay in there until pre-dawn. That was something they would do a lot for the next year and a half, before her first time would come. But they both knew it was going to come. He just wanted to make sure she was prepared when it did. They played their kissing game again for another hour before falling asleep.

The next day was T-baby and Rebbie's 11th birthday party. They were having it at T-baby's house after church but it was on Rebbie's actual birthday. Everybody from their schools came, even Brittney Blank. She had brought 2 of her girlfriends with her and also her brother, who's name was Darwin Blank. Darwin was a bad ass kid who stayed in trouble and he went for bad too. That was why Brittney brought him. He was to be a deterrent. A flirt, so to speak. The word around their school last year and all summer long, was that Ajay had a girlfriend named Ebony now. Well Brittney had seen that girl he was with at his party and Chill's graduation party too. So she knew who Ebony was and she planned to interfere. But she had to have someone to get Ebony's attention away from Ajay. As if that could ever happen. Her brother was the someone she'd gotten to come along so he could talk to Ebony, long enough for Brittney to get some time with Ajay. She wanted to fuck Ajay is what she wanted. And she'd bet her girls at the end of last school year, that she would fuck him before the next school year. That was the reason she was coming around for all of the events. But she was running out of time. She was passing to 9th grade while Ajay would be going into 8 and his baby girl had passed to the 6th grade. The school year was a little over a month away from starting.

The party was well underway. The foursome was dancing together and having their usual fun. Their guys had snuck off to the front yard to smoke weed, out of sight of the mothers who was there. It was then that Brittney decided to make her move. She was going to go around there and approach Ajay. But first she had to send Darwin to get to know Ebony. He approached the foursome while they danced and sang together on the make shift dance floor.

"Hey there," he said, "Your name is Ebony Brown, right?"
Ebony looked at him in a strange way because he was acting strange. Plus he was making unusual motions with his body and hands. She didn't answer him and she tried to ignore him but he wouldn't go away.

"She don't wanna talk to you," Nina tried, "You better get your butt away from her before my brother kick yo ass."
Darwin just laughed and kept at it. He wasn't afraid of Ajay. He knew he was a star basketball player and very popular. He knew he'd won a fight at school, a couple of years ago too. Darwin knew he could beat Billy Marshall too, so the thought of fighting Ajay didn't scare him any. He was older than

269

Ajay and had been expelled from school, each of the last 3 years. He was damn near a dropout who didn't care if he ever finished school. He was infatuated with the street and thug life and he just continued to bother Ebony.

"Let me dance wit you, girl," he said as he walked closer to her.

Ebony tried to move away but Darwin just followed her. He kept picking with her and being obnoxious. He would make gestures like he was going to grab her but he hadn't yet. What he was doing was starting to frighten her but she tried to be brave.

Meanwhile, Brittney and her 2 friends had made their way to the front yard. As soon as Ajay saw her coming, he frowned and spoke up.

"Don't bring yo bitch ass over by me," he said, "I done already told you. I'm not about to fuck wit you, so get the fuck on."

But she kept coming. Even Tank, June and Rich tried to discourage her from approaching Ajay but she still came to within 5 feet of him and that's where she stopped.

"How come I can't have none of that, if all these other ho's can fuck you?" she said bluntly.

"Because I don't wanna fuck yo trashy ass," he said, "That's why." He all but started a verbal assault against Brittney while Tank and the other guys laughed. That went on for several minutes until Nina ran up front and told him that there was a boy bothering Ebony. Ajay, Tank, June and Rich took off running to the back yard.

The adults hadn't noticed Darwin pestering Ebony because he was slick enough with it that he didn't draw any attention from them. But Ajay arrived just in time to see him put his hands on Ebony's butt. Ajay didn't even break his stride. He ran straight to Darwin and started punching him with everything he had. That's when the mothers noticed. So did uncle Greg and the fathers, who were off that day and cooking on the grill over in the far corner. Big Al was at work that day. Big Rich was doing yet another bid in jail and big John was on the road. Uncle Greg and June's father Brian Sr saw the fight and started toward it.

Ajay was in undeniable command. He was whipping Darwin mercilessly. No one could see a safe spot to try to intervene. Ajay grabbed a Tiki lamp which was stuck in the ground. He snapped the lamp from the post and started hammering Darwin with it, at a very rapid pace. In between the hammering, he was stomping him about the head and shoulders. Darwin was laying on the concrete slab where Sandy would usually have 1 of her 3 picnic umbrellas. Darwin wasn't moving and Ajay

270

was still hitting him and stomping him. Darwin was very bloody. Uncle Greg, Brian Sr and Brad Sr grabbed Ajay around the shoulders, chest and waist while Uncle Sam and big Arch grabbed his legs. Still Ajay was trying to get free. The 5 fathers got him away from Darwin but that wasn't an easy task. It wasn't easy to keep him away from Darwin, once they had peeled him off of him either. Jo ran over to where they had her son and she started trying to reason with him.

"Ant please," she said in an almost begging voice. "You beat him, son. You've beat him bad and he's not gonna get up. Please stop, son. I don't want you to kill him. I don't want you to murder that boy because they will take you away from me, for the rest of your life. I can't bare to lose my only son."

Jo started crying and that's when Ajay stopped trying to break free. It's like he snapped back into consciousness. He could hear Brittney screaming, "He killed my brother! He killed Darwin! Oh my God! Darwin's not moving! He's not moving!"

Mama Deb had already phoned for a medic to come. But of course, with the ambulance, the police came too.

When the ambulance arrived, the mothers were putting ice on Darwin and trying to wake him up. Ebony had gone to sit next to Ajay. She was scared out of her mind. She didn't know what was about to happen to her man. But she was no longer afraid that Darwin was going to try to feel her up anymore. It was something about him trying to put his hands on her, that scared the shit out of her. She didn't understand why any person would do that. She was crying because she saw mama Jo crying. Nina started crying too but Lynn didn't. She was ready to finish whooping Brittney's ass. She had gotten in a few licks while Ajay was filleting her brother. Nobody even noticed the girl fight because Ajay had all the attention on the melee he'd performed. Ebony was still sitting next to him and she was still crying. He saw her and put his arms around her.

"It's okay, baby girl," he said, "I'm not gonna let nobody hurt you. I told you that. That fool was putting his hands all over you, like he had fuckin permission to even be near you."

Jo had called Al at work and he was on his way to the party scene. The police had filed their report and it wasn't a good 1 for either side. Ajay had an extensive juvenile record and he was going to be arrested. The police had charged Darwin with sexual battery on a minor because he had been emancipated last year. Add in that he'd been expelled from school for the past 3 years. Rightfully, if he had stayed in and passed, he would be going to the 11th grade. He was already 16 years old, the same age as Tonya and Jr. That was the only thing that worked in Ajay's favor. Still Ajay had been charged because of the damage he'd done. The ambulance rushed Darwin to East General hospital. Ajay was taken to Juvenile Detention. Al and Jo went down to the facility where attorney George Wheeler met them.

"What are we looking at?" Al asked Wheeler.

"Another month at the worst," Wheeler said, "And that's only because that kid was older than him and has a worse profile. I'm gonna tell y'all this. I hope that son of a bitch pulls through. Because the only thing that's saving Ajay right now, is that that boy survived."

"I know George," Jo says, "That's what I said to Ant to get him to come back around. He was out of it."

"What happened to make him this angry?" Wheeler asked.

"That boy was molesting Ebony," Jo said, "Pearl and John's little girl. He was tormenting her for no reason."

"And Ajay wasn't gonna allow that ha? Does he like Ebony?" Wheeler asked.

"*Apparently* so," Al said, just to give an answer in front of his wife. He knew Ajay liked Ebony and would protect her, at any cost. Al wasn't upset with what Ajay did. He would've done it himself, had he been there and seen it.

"That's an innocent little girl who has been through enough shit in her life. She didn't need him fuckin wit her. I tell you what. They better get him cured and up out that hospital before John gets here."

"I know that's right," Jo said, "He'll drag his ass up out of that bed, take him outside and finish killing him."

"And he'll have help," Al said.

"I'd be willing to help too," Wheeler added.

About that time, Ajay's youth counselor came out to get them and took them into a room where Ajay was seated and still cuffed. The counselor had the guard to remove the cuffs so he could have time with his family. Then she proceeded to tell them what she was going to ask for and also, what he could possibly get. But Wheeler had already told them those particulars. That's when Jo asked if they could just spend that time with him, talking and seeing what clothes he wanted for the next 2 days. Because he would have to spend at least 1 night. It was Sunday afternoon, so his court would be the next morning and he would have to sit it out and await his appearance before a judge, once again.

Ebony was just sad and distraught. She had gone through this

272

before and she already knew that he would have to stay awhile. She just didn't know how long. Her and her girls were still at T-baby's house but the party ended when Ajay left in cuffs. T-baby and Rebbie didn't even want it to continue. They felt like no event was going to be complete for them without their entire crew.

"This day is just bad," Ebony said and she was still crying, "I don't want him to have to go away again. What am I gonna do?"

"He was protecting you, sis," Nina said, "That's how I know he cares about you. He's not gonna let nobody mess with you. I saw that along time ago. And today my brother went crazy on that boy. He would've killed him, if the fathers wouldn't have been here to stop him."

"It took five grown men to stop Ajay," Rebbie said, "He was mad."

"He beat up Richard for messing with your dog too," T-baby said.

"And when Billy pushed you off the swings," Rebbie added.

"And I know you remember that boy named Carlos who use to say bad stuff about you to people and tell them to say it to you," Nina reminded her. Then she said, "Ajay likes you a lot and everybody is gonna know that. If they mess with you. He's gonna kick their ass."

"I just wish I could talk to him right now," Ebony said, "I don't want him to have to be locked up because of me."

"He's not locked because of you," Nina said.

"That's how I feel," Ebony said and she continued to cry, "I'm sad that he's not able to be at home."

That next morning when Ajay went before the family court judge, the entire crew was there. All 3 generations including poppa and big mama. They had flown in the night before to attend court and to show their support for Ajay. Ebony was there with her family. Big Al had asked Pearl to sit on the front with them and bring all 4 of her children up there with her. She did.

When they brought Ajay in, he had shackles on his feet and his wrist was chained to another shackle which was around his waist. Ebony felt tears well up in her eyes. Ajay looked at her and her only, until he got to his seat at the table where he had to sit with his back to those visiting. The judge opened the proceedings by giving his full name and then reading what he had been charged with. He also informed them that he had 1 statement that would be given by phone from John Brown Sr.

John had called and talked with Al, the night before. As the father of the victim, John was allowed to call in during court since he was unable

273

to be there, in person. When it was time for John to speak, the courtroom speakers were turned on.

"Mister John Brown senior is the father of the female victim whom Darwin Blank has several charges against him, for assaulting," the judge stated, "He would like the courts to allow him to speak via phone today and we have granted him that permission. You may go ahead, mister Brown."

"I'm John Brown senior and I'm Ebony Brown's father," John started, *"I'm a commercial truck driver which takes me away from home for two week intervals. I asked my neighbor mister Al Jackson to look out for my wife and my four children while I'm away. He reared his son to look out for my only daughter as well, along with her brothers. Anthony Jackson is his son and we all call him Ajay. He saw my daughter being assaulted and he only did what came natural. He's doing what he was raised by his father to do. Protect the innocent and those who can't protect themselves. I see no fault in what he did. I do see fault in the young man who for whatever reason, felt he had to assault my baby girl. If Ajay hadn't seen him and took a stance. There is no telling how far he would've gone with it. She's been through enough and I don't want her hurt by anyone. I only hate that I was not there to protect her. That's what bothers me the most. Ajay is a good young man with a promising future. He has already surpassed barriers at his young age, to have our school systems to see fit to have him compete with those a lot older than him. He did a brave thing and something that I will be forever grateful to him for. He protected my baby from being abused. I thank him from the bottom of my heart and ask that the courts please be lenient on him. Ajay, I want you to know that you have my respect, son. I will always be grateful to you for being there and protecting my baby girl. Thank you. And thank you to the courts for allowing me to speak."*

After John was done speaking, the courtroom was quiet for an entire minute. Then the judge ask for others who wanted to speak for or against Ajay. No one asked to speak against him but several others spoke for him. Including his parents, all of the 1st generation, Pearl, Paul, Chill and a coach from each of the school teams he's played for up to that point. Then the floor was rendered back to the judge. The judge admitted that before hearing Ajay's witnesses, he was dead set on sending him to training school until he finished high school. But after hearing all of the testimony for him and none against him. He had changed his mind. He also said he had looked at Ajay's school records. His grades were above average and he attended daily with less than 1 absence per year. The judge then gave his ruling.

"I hereby sentence you to thirty five days in the Cuyahoga County juvenile detention center," he said, "Your release date will be September seventh. Upon your release, you will be on probation for another thirty days. You will be released in time to start school without missing *any* days. Your attendance report his been great and the court does not want to taint it, in any way. However you will have to see your juvenile counselor monthly, for six months following your release. Your parents can set that up with her, prior to your release date. You will not be confined to any certain areas when you're released which will allow you to participate and travel with your basketball team. Young man, what I see in your record tells me that you have the ability to be an upstanding citizen of Cleveland. A real man always defends a lady or a little lady and I applaud you for that. But you must not let it go to the point that the other person is unconscious and/or hospitalized. So I want you to seek counseling to help you maintain your temper and whatever causes you to lose it. I wish you luck. Court is adjourned."

Ajay's sentence was read and understood. He was allowed some time to visit with his family in the back before he had to be taken back to detention and they were going to remove the shackles. The judge stated that only 10 people could go back and visit. Before he was escorted out, Ajay turned and looked at Ebony. He smiled. She managed to smile too. She definitely knew she wanted to be 1 of those 10 who got to visit him. Before she could ask big Al, he turned and said he wanted Tank, Jb, Chill and Ebony to go back with them. Also big mama, poppa, granny and papa. They were gonna try to squeeze 14 because Pam was a baby and being carried by Jo. But then the prosecutor told the judge she would agree to Ajay having a room big enough for all his supporters and family. The judge allowed it. They all moved to a conference room. They were jam packed in there but they made due. Ajay wanted to talk to Ebony, first thing. He moved over to the table where she was and sat in the chair next to her.

"Hey baby girl," he said with a smile, "I don't want you to be sad. I did what I needed to do and I can sit for a month. Just write to me and my pops is gonna make sure you get to see me when they come, alright?"

"Okay but I'm gonna miss you so much, Anthony," she said.
Her eyes filled with tears but she was going to say how she was feeling and she didn't care who was watching them, at that point. Not even her mother. She wanted him to know that she was going to be there for him. She was going to be there when he called and each time he got a visit, she was planning to come then too.

"I know you're gonna miss me," he said, "I would be heartbroken

275

if you didn't. Baby girl, I will always do whatever I have to do to protect you. No matter who it is. Even from yourself."
They laughed together and that made Ajay feel so much better. He visited with all of the family before he had to go back in shackles and be escorted to the van for transport. He hugged Ebony again before they put the shackles on him. Pearl was watching but she didn't object. Within minutes, Ajay was gone and Ebony felt absolutely empty.

{September 7, 1987}

It was Labor day and Ajay's day to come home. Ebony was beside herself. She had talked to him at least once a week and visited him each time his family went. Pearl didn't object but it could've been because big John was home for the first 2 weeks. He went with Ajay's family to visit him and took Ebony, Tank and Jb with him. Ebony had written Ajay letters. He had only answered 2 of them but he was adamant that she kept writing to him. Then he would answer them when she came to visit or when they talked on the phone. Jan and Bre was going to be having their crew induction party in 2 days. They were waiting for Ajay to get home to be apart of it too.
Ebony waited in Jo's living room for Ajay and his parents to arrive home. When the car pulled up, she couldn't stay seated. She ran out the door and met them outside, just like the others. She watched him as he got out. He looked so good and he looked taller too. Everybody was rushing up to him. He gave them half hugs but his eyes never left Ebony. He had a huge smile on his face. She was smiling too but not intentionally. That was just the affect he had on her. She found that she couldn't wait for him to touch her and he got to it quickly.
"Hey baby girl," he said and hugged her tight.
"Hey Anthony," she said, "I'm glad you're home."
"So am I," he said, "Come help me unpack."
She followed him inside. Tank, Nina, T-baby, Rebbie, June and Rich all went in behind them and up the stairs. Chill and the others headed to his house. They knew they would see Ajay later. He had more important things to handle right then and they wanted him to get to it.
Once they got to the top of the stairs, Ajay turned to the others and quickly said, "Y'all go in Nina's room. I just wanna see baby girl, right now. I'll get up with y'all later."
The other 6 went into Nina's room while Ebony followed Ajay into his room and he closed the door. He dropped his bags immediately and grabbed her

276

up in her arms. He started kissing her with fervor and massaging her body. She did the same back to him. It was a great reunion kiss. After the 1st kiss was done, he had something he needed to say to her and it just couldn't wait a minute longer.

"Baby girl sit down in the chair," he said, "I need to talk to you about some things."

She sat down and looked up at him. He sat on his bed in front of her and looked into her eyes.

"You've got the prettiest brown eyes I've ever seen," he said and smiled.

He pulled a picture from his wallet and handed it to her. It was a photo that Arthur had taken of her when she was at Chill's graduation party. Ajay had seen it and gotten it from Arthur, to keep for himself.

"I looked at that picture everyday I was away from you. Even when I was gone to my camps this summer. I had too, baby girl. It was the only way I could make it without going off on somebody. I'm gonna need for you to stay close to me whenever you're outside or away from your house. If I get another charge. They gonna make me stay in detention until I turn eighteen."

"That would be the worst thing that could happen in my life," she said, "The days don't even seem right when you're gone, Anthony."

"Then will you stay close to me where I can know that you're safe and not in any danger?" he asked.

"Yes I will."

"Another thing I wanna know is, will you be my girlfriend?"

"Yes. I already am," she said and smiled.

"I know but I had to asked you the right way," he said, "And I asked big John and my pops if I could go ahead and asked you. Because that would help me to stay calm too and not get into more trouble. The time I spent in detention made me know with no doubts, that I need you in my life. The reason I went was because I beat the fuck outta somebody who was trying to harm my princess. And I'll do that again, in a heartbeat. Chill said all of our parties are gonna be at him and Paul's house from now on. Because big Paul said we had too. So he would know it wasn't no bullshit folks showing up, like that again. Nobody is gonna come over there that don't respect the crew code. Cause they know Chill will take em out the game."

"I love being your girlfriend," she said, "And I promise I'll stay where you can see me whenever I'm outside. I want even come outside if you're not home to watch me. I wouldn't want to anyway."

She smiled and he chuckled. Then he laughed harder. He liked that a lot.

"Good to know," he said, "Now you know I got to get up with my brothers for a little while. But I'm spending the night with Tank. School don't start until Thursday so before the labor day event starts today. We gotta get our bread together. And baby girl, I'm still a man and I've been locked up for over a month. I need some pussy, big time. Do you understand what I'm saying?"

"Yea," she said with a dejected look, "You're gonna see a girl."

"No," he said, "Whoever it is will have to look for me. But they're gonna be looking anyway. It's just about a fuck and nothing more. And remember what I told you when I was in your room?"

"Uh huh," she said, "But I still don't like it."

"I didn't think you would," he said and smiled, "I don't ever expect you to like it. But that's not something that we can do yet. You're not ready to start and if I come in your room tonight, feeling like I feel right now. I'm gonna take things too far. I wanna wait until you become a woman before we do the real thing."

"I know."

"I promise you baby girl," he said, "It won't be no passion involved. All of the passion I have in my heart, my head and my body is for you and only you. I give you my word."

"As long as none of them don't come around our house and think they gonna be in your face," she said, "Then I won't know about it. But if a girl try to disrespect. You're not gonna be the one fighting. I'm gonna beat her ass."

"Don't curse because my woman ain't gonna have no potty mouth," he said and laughed, "I'm gonna be kissing those lips for a long time. For the rest of my life. So keep em clean."

"Nina and my girls curse and you don't say nothing about them," she tried.

"They're not my woman," he said, "You are. Now give me some more of that sweet sugar before I have to break camp."

"I will but don't you stay gone until it's real late," she said, "Cause you just got home today and I'm the one that's gonna be lonely until you get back."

"I'll make it quick, okay?"

"Okay."

"Come here," he said and he started to kiss her.

His hormones were raging and his hands, lips and tongue were telling that

278

story very well. She was aroused too but she knew he had a time table for them, before they would get to the real thing. She decided that tonight it would be time to graduate to the touching stage. She wanted to know what his hands would feel like on her bare skin. Everything in her wanted to show him that she could be all the woman he needed. So he wouldn't have to go out for pussy. But she hadn't gotten her period yet and he wasn't going to go there with her.

After the many kisses were finally done, they came out of his room and went downstairs. Their parents and the other grownups were setting up the tables for their Labor day cookout. Ebony knew she would have to help. Ajay trotted over to Chill's house where the men had gathered to get the meats out to the grills.

Ebony wanted to talk to her big mama. She had to asked a few more questions so she could get a real understanding as to how Ajay really felt about her. She knew he liked her more than any other girl. But he was still going to have sex with another girl and that was bothering her a lot more than she admitted to him. She asked her father if she could call Houston and he said she could. She picked up the phone and called her big mama and poppa's house. Poppa answered on the first ring.

"*Hello,*" he said.

"Hey poppa," she said.

"*Hey there, baby girl,*" he said, "*How are you today?*"

"I'm alright."

"*I figured you'd be in a great mood,*" he said, "*Ajay came home today. I know that's something you looked forward too.*"

"He did and I did, poppa," she said, "But tell me how will I know if he really *really* likes me."

Poppa said, "*The best way you can tell if a young man cares about you, is when he knows he's in trouble with you. If he lets it linger and don't bother to handle it with you right away? Keep moving. But if he doesn't let the sun set on it. Meaning if he comes to straighten it out as soon as possible. Then he's a keeper. But you still have to let him sweat, even if he does come to you right away. That's so he'll remember. If he gets another chance, not to hurt you again.*"

"Well what if he's not in trouble though?"

"*Then you just have to go by how he treats you and Ajay treats you pretty special,*" he said, "*I have to admit that. I'll give him my blessing on that day that he comes to me about dating you. Because I know he's going too.*"

"Okay poppa," she said.

"But he's at a point in his life that you have to wait awhile longer to get too. He knows how the men in this family feel about respecting that time table that we set up for the males and the females. Just be patient and allow him to grow into a man. He's going to get it just right eventually. But for right now, he's still in that young boy stage and he's going to have to grow out of that. He has needs that have to be met and he knows you aren't at the point that any of us would agree that you should be meeting them. Do you understand?"

"Yes sir."

"Then he told you what his plans were for today?"

"Yes sir," she said dryly.

"Then you're already over that hump," Poppa said, *"Because he's being honest with you from the start. That's rare. But you'll learn that later on too. Let him grow up, baby girl. He's gonna be your prince one day. And your's only."*

"Okay poppa," she said, "My daddy wanna speak to you. So I'm gonna take him the phone now. I love you and tell big mama when she come back, that I love her too."

She knew big mama was at their church helping to feed the homeless. She did that every holiday. Whether she was in Houston or Cleveland.

"I'll sure tell her," poppa said, *"Take John the phone and let me see what he's got for me."*

She did just that. Then she went outside to help with the set up. Ajay and the other boys in Chill's crew had already left and all she could do at that point was wait for him and hope that he hurried back to her.

After the festivities and party was done, it was time for Ajay to follow Tank home. Ebony and her girls had to leave early as usual but she knew Ajay would be spending the night at her house. She had told her girls to stay at T-baby's because she wanted to sleep at home alone. She told them she wanted to play with her dolls and they agreed they should stay with T-baby. Their sleeping arrangements would change somewhat by nightfall though. Ajay was on his way and Ebony was planning for him to show her what it felt like to be touched underneath her clothes. She wanted to get just 1 step closer to getting to the point where he wouldn't need a whore for any of his needs. Whether he was a growing boy or not.

By 11:30pm, Pearl was gone to work. John was still at Paul's house enjoying the after party conversation with the rest of the fathers and some of the sons too. Even though 11:30 was an early time for Tank and Ajay to be turning in. They were both ready to come in on that night. Jb was staying at Chill's house. And suddenly, Nina was spending the night with Ebony. By midnight Nina and Ajay had switched places. Nina was in the boys room with Tank. Ajay was in Ebony's bed and she was in rare form. There was something very motivating about knowing Ajay had spent some part of the last hours with an unknown whore. Ebony had to speak on that.

"So where did you go?" she asked.

"Up by the detail shop," he said and kept his answers short.

He could tell by her demeanor that she was uneasy about his confession earlier.

"Who did you get wit?" she asked.

"A whore wit no name," he said defiantly.

He wasn't intentionally trying to be an asshole. But he really didn't know the names of the 2 girls he'd fucked out at the house of 1 of Arthur's girls toys.

"You don't know her name?"

"No."

"How could you be with a girl and not know her name?"

"It's easy," he said, "When I know I'm not gonna look for a girl again. I don't need to know what her name is. Now can we talk about us?"

She could see that he wasn't feeling that conversation. That crease in the middle of his forehead which shows when he's irritated, was very much there. She decided to leave the whore talk alone and get to what was really on her mind.

"I wanna know what it feels like for you touch me under my clothes," she said.

He smiled at her and laid back on her bed. She had shocked him. But she had also gotten his attention in a positive way.

"You mean inside of your panties?" he asked, just to get clarity on her question as he stared at her ceiling.

"Yes I just wanna know what my girls keep talking about."

"What are they saying?" he asked.

"Just how Tank, June and Rich be touching them," she said.

"Alright," he said as they laid together on her bed and he turned to face her.

He started kissing and rubbing on her like they had normally done when they were alone. Within minutes, he was rubbing on her pussy and that felt good. He was sucking on her nipples and her neck too. The better it felt to her. The tighter she held him. Then he inserted his finger into her pussy and

281

she jumped up and slid away from him. The look on her face wasn't a positive one.

"What's wrong?" he whispered.

"I don't like that," she said.

"Okay," he said, "We don't have to try that right now. But that's what they're talking about."

"Then I don't wanna do that," she said.

"Okay we want do it," he said, "I'm sorry if it made you scared."

"I just don't like that," she repeated.

He was okay with that. His goal was to get her to calm down again and get back to what she was comfortable with. Which she eventually did. But she was distant for the rest of that evening.

Ajay noticed a change in her that night which would take another decade to get the answer too. But him inserting his finger into her vagina had brought back to her memory, an action in her young life that had caused her to withdraw from people and not be so trusting.

For the rest of that evening, he just held her, rubbed her, sucked on her nipples and kissed her a lot. She was allowing that and he decided that was far enough for them, at that time.

Chapter 12-The End Of Innocence [The 1ˢᵗ Time]

Immediately Lil Ajay wants to know what the problem was with his mom and why did his pops touching her like that, make her scared and nervous. Ajay tells him the entire story about Neal Palmer. He lets him know that his mother had shot Neal on that day in July 1982 and that his grandpa Al and big Paul had finished killing him.

"So big Chill went to Juvie to keep all of that from coming out, didn't he?" Lil Ajay asks.

"Yes he did," Ajay says.

"That's taken one for my mom and the crew, right pops?"

"Exactly."

"You was going to the eighth grade, still playing for the high school and mama was going to the sixth grade by now, right?"

Ajay is pleased that his son hasn't forgotten any of the things he'd been telling him for the past year.

"Yes you're right son," Ajay says with a smile, "And your mother has always been an over achiever."

Lil Ajay knows his mother had a 4.0 average since 1ˢᵗ grade. He also knows she did a report while in the 6ᵗʰ grade which won her a scholastic achievement award too. That award is framed and hanging in their upstairs library. Which is the one Lil Ajay and his twin sister Lannie use when they do their homework. And he and all of his sisters sit in there when they have reading time with Ebony too. All of their parents plaques, diplomas, degrees and awards are displayed there as motivation for all of their children. So this is the place where Lil Ajay and his dad are having their talk today.

Lil Ajay knows his parents first sexual experience is going to be in today's talk. But Ajay wants to fill him in on all of those things that happened leading up to it, as well.

"I know mama and her girls was still playing ball and cheering," Lil Ajay says, "She tells me all about that. But didn't uncle Tank make the basketball team for seventh grade?"

"Yes and he played for two years until he moved to Houston with your mama, in eighty nine," Ajay says, "After that, he just stuck to running track."

Ajay tells him about Thanksgiving day 1987 when Jo told him she saw a lot of changes in him and she liked what she saw.

"She told me I had calmed down a lot after that last detention stay," he says, "And that was all because of your mama. I wanted to be able to be with her and see her everyday. So I had to stay out here. But what mama was talking about was when a boy at school was bothering Ebony, from Halloween until right before we got out for Thanksgiving that year. Instead of me beating him into a coma, like I did Darwin. I brought Ebony to the principal's office and made her report him. He got suspended for three days. Probably because the staff was trying to save me from missing out on playing ball for them. But that boy left her alone after that. Still Tank and Jb caught up wit him in the streets and beat his ass later."

They cracked up laughing. Then Lil Ajay talks about his mother's 12th birthday which was the first year she didn't get a new baby doll. He talks about when 5 of their fathers was shot up after work, 1 night in 1988 too. That was the shooting big Paul died from, a month later.

"He died right before uncle Tank got crewed up didn't he?" Lil Ajay asks.

"Yes and after his death. Big Chill went on a real rip," Ajay says, "He started planning Eddie Washington's demise *that* year. Because he already knew big Jake had sent him. Chill was trying to smoke out big Jake and kill him because he had caused both of his parent's deaths. That was when Chill let Eddie start selling drugs for him. So he could keep him close enough to take him out. He already knew Eddie was suppose to set me up and Chill wanted to take out that whole posse."

"Lil Kenny was four when his papa died," Lil Ajay says, "He told me all about that and he could remember how mad his daddy was during that time too."

"Renee completely cut off ties with her disgruntle mother, from that point on and stayed by Chill's side," Ajay says, "It was also about that same time when I started experimenting with cocaine. Chill was doing it a little bit before that. But after he lost his dad. He started doing it in front of us guys. I wanted to try it and he let me. That's what let me know later on that Chill was fucked up in the head about losing his mom and dad. Because he would never have been okay with me or any of us doing cocaine in *any* form. But he stopped using by the time your aunt Lynn turned fifteen, that April. Because Renee made him enter a drug abuse clinic or she was gonna leave him. She was graduating from high school that same year."

"She made him get help because Lil Kenny found his stash and he had it all over him, didn't he?" Lil Ajay asks.

"Hell yea," Ajay says, "Seeing his son with coke on his face made Chill get right, right then and there and stay right. I know that feeling now. It would kill me, if you got into some shit like that, son."

284

"Y'all use to supply cocaine and crack to people so they could sell it, ha?" Lil Ajay asks.

"Yes we did," Ajay admits, "And I know for a fact, I got *several* people strung out on coke and crack during the late eighties. I'll tell you about some of them in our later talks. But I was doing coke about once a week. From then until after your mama moved to Houston. I did more of it just to try and keep from missing her. It wasn't working so I'd do more."

"Uncle Tank and auntie Nina started having sex before you and mama did, right?"

"They started on the night of Renee's graduation," Ajay says, "Nina was still twelve and they was at Chill's house. We all use to stay over there after Paul died. But the foursome still couldn't spend the night. I can remember Ebony kept wanting me to touch her private. But if I tried to put my finger in her. She would reject me *every* time. I should've known it was something wrong. But I couldn't figure out what it was until she led me into the background about it. It was six months before our wedding when she remembered what Neal had done to her. When she told me about it. It was like it had just happened that day."

"When I hear about somebody hurting or trying to hurt my mama. I get mad as hell, pops," Lil Ajay says with conviction.

"Then you're just like me, both of your papas, your uncles and your great grandfathers too," Ajay says and laughs, "You didn't steal that, son."

"I liked how you talked to Darlene, that last time," Lil Ajay says, "And Kenny told me about Angel. That bitch ain't no Angel. She's the devil and it's time for her to go to hell. Pops, please let me be apart of it when she dies. Because I know you're not gonna let her live when she gets out, next year."

"I don't plan on none of them bitches living past your tenth birthday, son," Ajay says with conviction, "I've dreamed of so many ways for that bitch to die. I want Darlene gone. I want Alana gone. I want Farah gone. Debra Wittman gone. Nickeia gone. Jarvis wife Gwen gotta go too. Do you know that bitch is still wanting to get with your uncle Tank?"

"He told me that and auntie Nina don't even know about it," Lil Ajay says, "I remember when that Nickeia bitch was in our house. I heard my mama that night, pops. She was pregnant wit Lea. She was in one of the bedrooms on our floor and she was crying so hard. I heard her but she don't know I did. I just stayed by my door so I could hear everything she said in that room. Then when y'all went downstairs to talk. I stood at the
285

top of the stairs. I heard it all. Then I went to check on my twin sister to make sure she was still sleeping and didn't hear it. She was still sleep. So after you and mama went down the elevator to y'all room. I went back in my room and started sharpening my boa knife. I told Lil Jarvis, I don't have no beef with him but he can't date Lannie. *Never*! His family is fucked up and plus, I don't want Nickeia or Gwen to be near my sister. They would be, if she dated him."

"You know before y'all was even born. Jarvis wanted his children and my children to date," Ajay tells him, "But a lot of shit has changed in the eight years since me and Ebony got married. We was on our extended honeymoon, trying to make y'all when he asked me that. Back then, I was actually open to it for *his* sake. But after I saw you and Lannie's faces, the night y'all was born. I knew it was gonna be hard for me to see anybody good enough for my babies. And that takes my mind back to that Angel bitch. If I would never have met her. You wouldn't be my oldest child. So after y'all came. I really felt like she needed to be dead. *That* fuckin day. I will never be at peace until she dies. She killed what would've been me and Ebony's first child. That was my baby, just like you and your five sisters. That bitch robbed me of that joy and it took five years before we were able to make you and Lannie. Ant, I will *never* let that bitch live in peace. She took apart of me, Ebony, you and all of your sisters. I'm getting you that dog and probably a few more dogs too. That bitch will be a meal, one day."

"That's what I'm talking about," Lil Ajay says as he smiles, "I wanna cut her damn head off. That could've been my big sister, like auntie Lynn is to you."

"You're gonna get your stripes, son," Ajay says, "And it will be so many crew members ready to ride on all of the above. But I think your auntie Pam would be willing to help kill Angel. She was so ready to see my baby come. That baby would've been born in ninety four and Pam was gonna be crewed up in ninety five. She had already made plans to be our baby sitter and everything. She cried for the whole two weeks that your mama was in the hospital. That added to my anger. Seeing my baby sister hurt like that, made me boil."

"They all gonna get it," Lil Ajay says, "And pops, before you tell me about you and mama's first time. I need to tell you something about another woman that be around my mama that I don't trust."

"Who?"

"Attorney Wheeler's wife," he says, "She wants you."

"Oh I been knew that but it ain't gonna happen," Ajay says.

"But she said something to me that pissed me off," Lil Ajay says.

"Like what?"

"She said she can't wait until her and my mama start working in the same office, all the time," he says, "She said because she knows she'll get to see *you* more. And she said she can't wait for my mama to get back to her on *when* she can have some of you."

"Oh really?" Ajay says and the anger is visible on his face. He says, "I told Ebony I didn't want her around us. She's been up to that shit since I was at Cincinnati. Ebony was playing with her and told her that she might need a sub for when she's going through her six week healing, after having babies. But Trina Yvette said some shit to me, the other day. She ask me for the dick and said she knows Ebony just had triplets and she knows she'll be out of commission for awhile. And the bitch said just *seeing* me made her pussy wet."

"I hate ho's who don't know how to stay in they lane," Lil Ajay says and he has that same visible frown that his father has.

Then Ajay says, "What she don't know is I recorded her ass on my phone. Not only am I gonna let your mama hear it before our eighth anniversary. Which is in three days. But I'm gonna let Wheeler hear it too."

"That bitch don't know who she's playing wit," Lil Ajay says and laughs, "I just can't wait until we line them all up and do away wit em. That's the day I'm waiting on."

Ajay wants to change the subject. He tells Lil Ajay about June getting crewed up, him turning 14 and when Rich made it into the crew as well. But talking on the ho's has made him antsy. He can tell his son is too. Ajay wants to get back to the point of today's talk because he's feeling like riding on a bitch, right now. He gets back to what makes him smile which is talking about his wife and best friend Ebony. He tells his son about when Ebony turned 13 and her and Nina got crewed up. He couldn't help but mention how Ebony's body had started to change during that time too. He also tells Lil Ajay that he'd told Ebony he could make her breast grow by sucking on them.

"Did she believe you?" Lil Ajay ask and laughs.

"She did at first but by the time she was making thirteen. She knew it was because she was about to get her period," Ajay says and laughs, "But right after her birthday that year. She found out I had put one of her baby dolls in my mama's fireplace."

Lil Ajay cracks up laughing and says, "You was trying to make her grow up with that move, pops."

287

"No not really," Ajay says. Then he chuckles and says, "Well okay. I guess I was by then. But I was so hooked on her by that time, son. Fucking with them ho's I didn't care about, wasn't getting the job done for me no more. And still I had to wait for Ebony to tell me when she was ready."

Ajay tells him about the night in early January 1989 when he killed a guy on his own. Without Chill or anybody else giving him the go ahead. He says it was about an altercation that happened after 1 of his high school games. It was a guy from MLK who had been harassing Bre. Bre was still going to Abe Lincoln where her, Tank, June and Rich was in the 8th grade. Ajay was in 9th grade at MLK, by then. He tells Lil Ajay that Renee, Rob and Stoney had just graduated the May before which was 1988. Tonya and Jr was seniors getting ready to graduate in May of 1989. Jb and Lynn was in 10th grade and the guy that was bothering Bre was a junior at MLK.

"I don't even remember the dude's name, son," Ajay admits as he shakes his head, "I just blacked out and I had to get him done."

"Tell me what went down to cause you to snap out."

Ajay tells him that after 1 of his games before Christmas of 1988, they had all gone out to Gordon park to hang out. It was cold and there was snow on the ground so they wasn't going to stay long. But that guy tried to talk to Bre again, while they were all at the park. When she refused him and was about to walk away. That's when the guy slapped her and knocked her to the ground.

"She was going with Stoney by then and she was playing basketball for eighth grade," Ajay says, "She was a superstar so she got attention from a lot of the high school guys for that and because they knew she was dating older. Because she was with Stoney, who had just graduated."

"So the dude thought with her man outta school. He could just fuck wit her?" Lil Ajay asks with an upset look on his face.

"I don't know," Ajay says, "I guess so, son."

He tells him after the guy slapped Bre, he got away from the park quickly. Before Jan and Lynn helped her up and they got back over by where all of the crew were gathered. They scoured the park looking for him that night but he was gone. Ajay tells him that the crew caught up with him during Christmas week. It was the night of Ebony and Nina's initiation party and of course, Ajay was Ebony's party date. The dude was out by the warehouses in the grove. He tells him that Stoney beat his ass solo. The rest of the crew was just there in case somebody else jumped in. But Stoney had told them he wanted to beat his ass on his own. Because Bre was his girl and that dude had assaulted her so it was on him to check the dude.

288

"Well son, after that bitch ass nigga talked all of that shit about what he would do to Stoney and that he would slap Bre again, if he saw her. He turned bitch," Ajay says, "Auntie Deb and uncle Brad didn't even press charges. They told us to handle him and that's how it was gonna be. Because the dude was talking shit and the streets was bringing the word back. We cornered his ass in the grove and Stoney dusted him off good. He even let Bre slap him until she was tired. Then after he got his ass whooped. *He* pressed charges. Stoney went to county jail for assault on a minor because Stoney was already eighteen and the dude was sixteen. Stoney had to do three months behind that shit and Bre cried everyday. She went to see him on every visit too and so did all of his crew brothers."

"And you got the dude?" Lil Ajay asks.

Ajay tells him yes. He got him, 1 day when he was leaving MLK after after-school basketball practice. He was driving the car that his grandpa Al had left for big Al.

"I was six feet four by then," Ajay says, "Pops was letting me drive home. Him and big John was in the car with me. They wanted to see how I drove with ice on the roads. I was fourteen and gonna make fifteen in six months. I drove good so they had me to go the long way home. I saw the dude walk into an arcade about a mile from MLK. I knew it was against the rules for crew to roll alone but I wasn't caring about that, at the time. I was just thinking about my boy being locked up and the dude swelling up my girl cousin's face. I wanted to dead his ass and I didn't want none of my crew to know it because they was so happy that I had made it through my probation. And then another year with no charges and no trouble."

Ajay tells him he had taken the gun from his mother's van which his grandpa Al had left for him and he'd run through Miss Lou Robinson's backyard. He went through alleys and back streets until he got to a corner and hailed a cab. He went all the way back out to that arcade by his school and waited in hiding until he saw the dude come out. He says he followed him from a distance until he ducked into a path of trees.

"I guess he was going home," Ajay says, "I don't know where he was headed but he didn't make it. I ran up from behind. He heard me when I got within three feet and he turned around. I pulled off my hood, my hoodie and my ski mask. I wanted him to see my face."

Ajay says he asked did he remember slapping his cousin in the face.

"He talked shit cause he knew I was younger than him but he also knew my rep for fighting and all. He was talking shit until I pulled out that three fifty seven and put three rounds in him. He fell back but he was still breathing.

289

I put two more in his head and I stayed there until he stopped breathing, a minute later. I wasn't even thinking about folks hearing the shots. We was way out in the woods. I knew those woods because I had cut out through em one day after school to snort some coke and smoke a cigarette. I knew how to get outta there *five* different ways. I made my way to the street on the opposite side, got another cab and went back to the block where I first got picked up. From there, I walked home. I went and took a shower then went to spend the night at Tank's house."

"That ended that problem for Stoney," Lil Ajay says, "Because he was gonna get him when he got out of county. That's what Kenny and Bruce told me."

"Yes it did," Ajay says, "I didn't want Stoney to go for murder. His dad was already taking one for the crew and he still is, to this day. Stoney is dead and gone now. But he heard about the dude getting killed and he said the police had questioned him about his murder while he was still in county. It was almost a week later when they found him. I was getting ready for the conference tournament. We had after school practice and I remember when the cops had those woods roped off. My teammates and even Jb was saying he wondered what the fuck happened in there. I just acted like I didn't know. The only people who know I killed that dude is that dude, me, my pops and now, you. Pops filed a police report saying the van had been broken into, as soon as I told him. That next night when he went to work he filed that report. The gun was reported stolen before they ever found the body. I hid the gun in an alley on my way home. After the heat died down, two months later. I went and got it and kept it at Arthur's apartment. He had got him a place out by CSU, by then."

"That's gangster, pops," Lil Ajay says and chuckles.

"That's work," Ajay says.

Then he tells his son about the day his mother got her period and started using Pearl and big John's bathroom. Because Tank and Jb didn't want female products in the hall bathroom.

"That was on the third day of February in eighty nine," Ajay says.

"She told Lannie about that day because she's gonna go through that too," Lil Ajay says.

"All of your sisters are, son," Ajay says, "By then, you'll be in the garage apartment. Let them have all these bathrooms on this second floor. Because you ain't gone wanna be in there. And with five sisters? *Man.* Somebody is gonna have one every week."

They laughed. Then Ajay tells him about his aunt Lynn having a fight at the beginning of school with a female from big Jake's family, who was threatening 1 of Lynn's good friends on the track team.

"It was an end of school track meet," Ajay says, "I was gone to my first camp of the summer. The girl was big Jake's grand niece. She was a cousin of Lil Jake, one of them bitch's that killed Stoney and that we laid down out by the U. The female cousin was Addie Johnson. She was bullying one of the girl's on Lynn's track team. Her name is Julie Von Reese. She use to run distance and she was good like Lynn. She was a white girl, so I guess Addie felt like she could punk her out. Lynn beat the breaks off that bitch and they was on the same team. Old man Jake tried to get Lynn suspended but it didn't happen. Lynn was all-state for track and she was getting ready to be a junior in high school. MLK wasn't about to get rid of no star athlete. Plus she was my sister and I was a star basketball player going to the tenth grade. They threw that Addie bitch off the team and expelled her for the next school year. That's when papa Brown stepped in and told them to make them move her to another school because the families were gonna brawl everyday until somebody died. They made big Jake and his family take her to another school and said they would retract the expulsion, if they moved her. So they did. That's power and that's the crew you will be expected to represent, every single day of your life."

"I'm ready pops," Lil Ajay says as he looks his father square in the eyes.

"I know you are," Ajay says.

Then he tells him about the news that eventually led to him and Ebony's *very* first sexual experience. He tells him it was on papa and granny's 36th anniversary, June 30 of 1989. Ajay tells him that was the day Ebony found out about big mama's breast cancer and that she would be moving to Houston to care for her.

"Mama was sad she had to leave, wasn't she?" Lil Ajay asks.

"Ah man, son. She cried that whole day and night. She spent the night with Nina and she slept in my room for most of the night. Just like I would do when I stayed over mama Pearl's house. That shit made me so sad, son. Because it was nothing I could do. I just told her that we was gonna spend every minute that we could together, before she had to move."

"How did you feel about her leaving?" Lil Ajay asks.

"That was the worse day of my life," Ajay says, "Even with me going to Juvie and all of that. Finding out that my baby was gonna be gone for months. It fucked my head up, all over again. I started snorting coke *more* days of the week. I wanted to be numb and not feel it. But it didn't work. I was so in love with your mother by then and we still had never had sex yet."

"But she had her period already," Lil Ajay says, "And you told her you was gonna do it after she got it."

"I did," Ajay says, "It had started back in February, like I told you earlier. It was the third of February, to be exact. I knew from that day on, that she could get pregnant, so I had to know what I was doing if we was to have sex. That's why I tell you about everything too. Guys may think it's not up to them to know how babies are made and how to prevent it from happening. But it's up to the guy as *well* as the girl to take precautions. Don't ever leave it up to the girl to be responsible by herself. Because you'll end up wit a baby before you can map out your life. My father made me aware of what to look for and how to count the days to ovulation. I told your mama about it, back when we first started the touching and all. That's when I made her promise to tell me when her period started and to tell me what day it started, every month afterwards. And she did too. But the morning that we had sex for the first time was 5 months from that first day that she got her period. We was in her room and mama Pearl had worked the swing shift and got off work at eleven that night. I was in Tank's room waiting for her to get home and then go to bed so I could go into Ebony's room. It was after midnight when I got in there and that was the night when she told me she wanted to do the real thing."

"I want you to tell me about that," Lil Ajay says.

"I remember it like it was yesterday," Ajay says and smiles, "Here's how the first day of the rest of our pleasure filled lives happened."

{July 1, 1989}

It wasn't a normal day in Ebony and Ajay's relationship. She had been sad for 24 straight hours and Ajay had been with her, for nearly 20 of them. He didn't know how to keep her from being down about her Houston trip. Only because he was down about it himself. But still he tried to make her smile. Tank and Ebony had stayed at Jo's the night after granny and papa's anniversary party. Ebony cried from the time she learned she had to move to Houston until whatever the hour long after midnight, that she finally fell asleep from exhaustion. She had stayed in Ajay's room until 5am, talking and still crying.

"I can't stand to see you cry," Ajay had said, "I know you're sad cause you have to go stay for so long. But I don't want you to cry no more."

"But I won't be back until my birthday time," she said, *"Christmas* Anthony. That's six months away. Day after tomorrow is the fourth of July and then I'm suppose to leave on the sixth. I won't even be here for your birthday."

"I know but we'll make it work out, some kind of way," he tried, "Just please baby, don't cry."

He kissed her, then held her in his arms while she cried still. They spent that night in his room until before time for mama Jo to get up and start making breakfast.

On the morning of the 2nd before Ebony traded rooms with Tank. Ajay had something to tell her about his plans for the next night. He got the shock of their relationship, once she told him what her plans were for the next night too.

"I know mama Pearl said y'all are gonna pack your clothes today before she have to go to work," he said, "And she said you have stay at home tonight. So I'm gonna spend the night with Tank, so we can still spend the night together."

"My mama's vacation starts tomorrow, once she gets off work," Ebony said, "I gotta watch Lil man while she goes to work at three today. She gets off at eleven. But after she gets home and goes to bed. I want you to come to my room."

"I am," he said, "That's what I was just telling you."

"I want you to come in my room so we can do the real thing," she said while she looked him in his eyes.

Ajay stood there shocked. He couldn't say anything. His insides were happy but his lips wouldn't speak. So Ebony kept talking.

"If I wasn't watching Lil man, I would say we can do it while mama's at work. But I wanna do it before I leave for Houston. You're my boyfriend and I wanna make sure you know that I plan to be with you, for the rest of my life. I want you to know that in every way before I go. Mama's gonna be home for two weeks after her shift today. That means she'll be there, all day for the next three days until I leave. So tonight, when you come to my room. I want you to introduce me to the real thing."

He stared at her, then he smiled and said, "Okay."

That was the longest day of Ajay's life, just waiting for the night time to come. Ebony and Pearl packed her clothes before Pearl had to leave for her 3pm shift. Ebony brought Lil man outside with her. Her and Ajay played basketball against Tank and T-baby while Rebbie and Nina watched Lil man. Ebony was planning to try out for the 8th grade team in Houston and poppa was already getting that arranged. Still she would've rather played with T-baby while Rebbie and Nina cheered on the sidelines.

After they were all done outside, Ebony took her bath and made dinner as Pearl had instructed her to do. It wasn't anything elaborate but she knew how to make Spaghetti noodles and not overcook them. Her mother had already pre-made the sauce and all she had to do was mix that together in a pot and add cheese on the top and then simmer it. She cooked and strained the noodles then cleaned up the dishes afterwards. She let her brothers know they could eat. Ajay had gone home to take a shower and then he joined the 4 of them for dinner.

"My girl can cook," he said as he looked at her and smiled.

"Thank you," she said and smiled back.

They finished dinner quickly. Ebony put 2 plates on the side. One in the microwave for her mother, for when she got in from work. And 1 in the fridge for her father, who would be home early the next afternoon. Her brothers had all gone into the basement to play music. When Ebony was done, she joined them. Ajay wanted to talk to her in private.

"Can we go up to the living room and talk?" he asked.

"Okay."

"Yea go upstairs with Ajay cause me and Jb about to smoke and you ain't getting none," Tank said and Jb cosigned him.

They allowed 8 year old Lil man to stay down there with them. If he wanted to smoke with them, he could but Ebony couldn't. She was use to that part because her brothers had always been strict on her when it came to smoking weed. Especially if she was in charge of the house which she was on that night. Her and Ajay went up to the living room together and sat down on the couch.

"Ebony did you mean what you said in my room today?"

"Yes," she said, "Why? You don't think I'm ready, do you?"

"I do think you are," he said, "But back when I told you that you would have to tell me when you was ready. I never really thought that you would."

He laughed and said, "I was just saying that to try to make sure you didn't feel like I wanted too, real bad. But I've wanted to know what you felt like for years. I told you all those other girls was just substitutes. Your spot in my life is solid. I just had to make sure I didn't put no pressure on you about doing it. That's all it was. I promise you, I'm ready. I *been* ready."

"Just tell me you wanna show me the real thing tonight," she said, "Because you know I'm a virgin, so you'll have to show me all of it."

"Oh don't worry about that, baby girl," he said, "I'll show you everything you need to know. And I'm gonna take my time when we get in your room together. I wanna talk you through it. I told you everything to expect about your first time. Do you remember that?"

"Yes," she said, "It's gonna hurt."

"The first time it will, yes," he said.

"That's the only part that worries me," she said.

Just to be certain, he asked again, "Do you wanna do the real thing tonight?"

"Yes."

"Then we're gonna do it," he said and smiled, "You just made my week, baby girl. I wanna make sure you know that because I know you're a faithful girl. I'm gonna be good to you. After the first time, I want us to do it again before you have to leave. I want you to know it's a lot different the second time. I wanna make it good to you, so *you'll* like it too."

"Okay I'm gonna go to my room and pick out the nightgown I wanna wear for my first time," she said and smiled.

"I'll be in there as soon as mama P goes to bed, okay?"

"Okay."

He put his hands on each of her cheeks and pulled her face to his. He started tongue kissing her. While doing that, he was licking her lips and then putting his tongue back into her mouth again. She liked it. He stopped, looked at her and started to smile. Then he said, "I'm so horny right now. I'm kissing you and trying to imagine how good your pussy is gonna feel."

She blushed and looked away. He pulled her chin up and looked into her eyes and said, "If it's anything about it that you don't like. I want you to tell me to stop, okay?"

She said, "Okay."

Then they kissed again and she got up to head upstairs to her room. He stood at the bottom of the stairs and watched her until she was out of sight. He went back into the basement to smoke with the boys. His anticipation was way up. He really couldn't wait to see Ebony again.

Ebony picked out a new nightshirt. One she had never worn. She pulled the tags off, then went to her mother's room to take another bath. She wanted to be extra fresh for her first night. She used some of her mothers bubble bath oils and scents. She wanted to smell good for Ajay. She turned on the radio in her parents room and let her mother's tape play. It was the *Teena Marie* tape that had the song *Out On A Limb* on it. She was soaking in her bubbles when that tune started to play. She soon heard the door chime. She knew it was just now 11pm so that couldn't have been her mother coming in. She jumped out of the tub and wrapped herself in a towel so she could turn the music down. Then she ran to her parents bedroom door and opened it. She listened to hear who had opened the door. She hoped it wasn't Ajay leaving out. She heard her cousin June talking to Tank. Then they both hurried down the basement stairs. She smiled as she went back to her bath and submerged herself back under the bubbles.

"Anthony's not gonna leave," she said to herself as she smiled, "No way is he gonna leave tonight. He's gonna stay here and wait until he can come to my room. Whoever's looking for him will have to come to my house. Because he's gonna be here with me."

By 11:30 she was finishing up her bath. She got out and dried herself off, then wrapped herself in a fresh towel. She rinsed the tub clean and put on her new nightshirt and her slippers. She turned off the tape and went to her room so she could put on her lotions and her body spray. She was smelling like a lady and she was going to become a woman, within the next hours. She heard the door chime again and this time she could hear her mother come in downstairs and call out to see where they all were. She heard Tank tell her that all of the boys was in basement and that Ajay and June was down there with them. And they wanted to spend the night.

"Twin gone to bed already," Tank told Pearl.
Pearl came on up the stairs and knocked on Ebony's door like she always did before she opened it. That was the reason Ebony hadn't invited Ajay to come up sooner. She knew her mother would check on her before going on to her room.

"Hey baby girl. I'm home," Pearl said.
"Okay mama," she said, "I put your plate in the microwave and I put daddy a plate in the refrigerator."

"Thanks baby but I'm tired tonight. So I'm not gonna eat this late," Pearl said, "I'm going to take my bath and go to bed. We'll be doing prep tomorrow and you and your girls will have to help, like the last time."

"Yes ma'am," Ebony said.
She wanted to talk to her mother again about how she was feeling about Ajay. She'd tried several times to tell her they had been kissing and touching but she couldn't find the courage to do it. She wasn't going to find it that night either. She wanted to get that first time over with and she knew if she told her mother how she was feeling right then. Ajay would most likely not be spending the night. She couldn't risk that, so again she didn't go into it. She decided she would wait and tell her before her Houston trip.

296

Pearl would be on vacation and around the house. She could find a better time to talk to her and let her know about the feelings she'd been having and the things her and Ajay had been doing. Just not that night. She wasn't going to leave Cleveland without knowing what the real thing was that he had been telling her about, for over 2 years.

She heard Ajay come up the stairs and go into bathroom in the hall. She heard him taking another shower and she smiled.
He wants to smell good for me too.

By midnight, Pearl had her mellow moods playing on her radio. Ebony knew her mother was in bed to stay because she would always play music when she went to bed for the night. Whenever John was home, they would play nothing but *Prince, Stephanie Mills, Larry Graham* and *Rick James with Teena Marie.* Later on, Ebony would learn that was their *mood* music. Their good sex music. She hadn't learned to think in terms of sex yet. But that was all going to change after the next few hours.

Ebony laid in her bed with her lamp on and waited. She heard all the boys coming up stairs and felt butterflies in her stomach. Her bedroom door was unlocked for Ajay to come in. He came straight to her door while Jb, Tank and June went into the boys room. They had put Lil man to bed hours ago. Ajay walked into her room quietly and locked the door behind him. He looked at her and smiled. Then he walked over and sat down on the edge of her bed, right next to her. He leaned down and started kissing her immediately. He was rubbing on her vigorously too. She liked how that felt. Then he paused long enough to take off his clothes. He stripped down to his boxers and climbed into bed with her. Then pulled the covers up and over them. He turned to her and smiled. Nervously, she smiled back. He started to kiss and rub on her like he always did as he opened the buttons on her nightshirt. She had on her bra and panties. He smiled because he expected her too. He simply lifted her bra up toward her neck and uncovered her breast. He started sucking on her nipples and she moaned.
"Are you okay?" he whispered.
"Yes."
"Are you still ready to do the real thing?" he whispered.
"Yes."
"I want you to see what I have but I don't expect you to get naked," he whispered, "At least, not on the first night. But the second time we do this. I wanna see your body, okay?"

"Okay," she whispered, "But Anthony, I wanna turn off the light please."

"Sure but I want you to see me first," he whispered, "So you'll know what I have for you. And this is the only dick you will *ever* get. So you need to see it and know what's gonna to be entering your body for the rest of your life. Okay?"

"Okay."

He reached under the covers and removed his boxers, then laid them on the floor on top of his clothes. He pulled back the covers and grabbed his large dick in his hand. She opened her eyes wide. He was *very* large. She looked at his eyes. He was smiling at her because he knew without a doubt, she was nervous about the size of the dick which was going to be entering her.

"I got over ten inches easily," he whispered and started laughing silently, "So we'll just say that I'm gifted in the pants too."

It looked a lot longer than that to her and she said as much.

"What size is it?" she whispered.

"It's really eleven inches," he whispered and laughed, "But I'm not gonna put the whole thing in. I'm just gonna get the tip in because I know it's already gonna be painful. I don't wanna scare you into not wanting to do this again. Because that would ruin my life."

She was already scared after seeing the size of it. But she still wanted to have her first time, so she laid there and waited for him to tell her what to do next. He started kissing her. He was rubbing on her and sucking on her breast again. Then he started rubbing her pussy and she was very turned on by that. It was something about the way he touched her that made her feel safe, secure and loved. He was good with his hands. She figured that was why all the girls wanted him. But what she didn't know at that time was, he didn't give that kind of passion to any other girl. That was for her and her only. He continued kissing, rubbing and sucking on her. He was kissing her ears and that part drove her crazy. They were both moaning and breathing hard. He placed a towel underneath her and continued kissing her. Suddenly he rolled over on top of her. He kept kissing, kept rubbing and sucking on her. He stuck his tongue in her ear and she moaned loud enough to be heard outside of her room.

He smiled and looked at her, then he whispered,

"It's a good thing mama P got her music on and playing loud, baby girl. Or she would've heard you moaning and came beating on the door."

She smiled and looked toward the lamp which was still on. He knew she wanted him to turn it off, so he reached over and clicked it off. Now they were alone in the dark. He was naked. Her nightshirt was unbuttoned to the waist by then and her bra was pulled up. He managed to undo her bra and remove it while they laid there kissing each other. He pulled her nightshirt up to her neck while still rubbing her pussy and kissing her aggressively. He was making his way to the zone. He moved her panties to the side and put the tip of his dick there to keep them pulled over. It was obvious he had done this before because he had skills. She trusted him completely. She could feel his dick on her skin. It was big, warm and it was very hard. She could feel it throbbing as it rested against her. He paused and reach for his pants. He whispered, "I know your period should be coming back on in about three or four days. And it only last for four days, at the most. I'm gonna use a condom tonight because you're in that time when you can get pregnant. That's why I'm using a rubber. But just so you know. I don't wanna use condoms with you. I can't wait until you can get on some birth control pills. Until your period starts again, you can get pregnant. So I'm not gonna take no chances okay?"

"Okay."

She kept her answers to 1 word. She was eager and nervous, all at the same time. She wanted to please him so much. She wanted to be all that he needed when it came to the real thing. The older girls had been telling her what to expect. They had told her that the first time would be painful too. But after she'd seen the size of his penis, she knew it was going to be painful for a long while. Way after the first time and the hundredth time too. He was 11 inches in size and still she prepared herself for him and what was to come next. He was still on top of her. Still kissing, sucking and rubbing on her with the condom already on. She didn't know it but he was nervous as hell too. He didn't want to hurt her nor make her cry. But he knew that both of those things was about to happen. He also knew he had to try to enter her without her expecting it. If she braced for it, she would tighten up even more and make penetration that much more painful and timely too. He decided he would keep kissing her on her neck and chest. Before he entered her, he was going to put his hand over her mouth because surely she was going to scream out. And if she did, there was a good chance her mother would hear her and they would be caught in the act.

"Baby girl I'm gonna keep kissing on you until you relax," he whispered, "I want you to relax because I can't do this if you don't."

"Okay Anthony," she said, "I'm trying too."

"Good," he said and he started sucking on her breast again.

She was moaning and loving that feeling. She was relaxed and holding him close to her. They heard *Voyage to Atlantis* come on in Pearl's room and knew this was the perfect night for their 1st time. He was ready to penetrate. He kept sucking on her breast as he brought his hand up to her face. He covered her mouth and entered her quickly. He could feel her squeals and he felt the tears rolling from her eyes. He kept his hand over her mouth until the head of his penis was inside of her.

"I'm sorry, baby girl. I'm so sorry. I know it hurts but I don't want your mama to hear you," he whispered.

He reached for the lamp switch and turned it on. Her face was soaked with tears, just that quick. He started to cry too.

"I know it hurts, baby girl," he whispered through tears, "But it's the only way to get it in. It's over with. This painful part is over. Please say you know that."

She shook her head yes but her eyes didn't say that to him. She looked like she was scared for her life, so he kept talking.

"Please tell me you know that I never wanna hurt you," he whispered, "I wanna love you. I wanna protect you and make you smile, *all* the time. I'm torn up just because you're crying. That's why I'm crying too, baby girl. But this was the only way to do it for your first time. Do you believe me?"

She was calming down and he was still inside her. He knew there was blood present because he felt it when it trickled down. That's why he had brought a towel from his room. It was a red towel. That way, there would be no blood on her bed sheet and she wouldn't see blood on the towel either. She was looking at him now and she was breathing more settled. He moved his hand and asked, "Are you okay? Please tell me you're okay."

"It hurt so bad," she whispered as those tears continued to flow.

He felt horrible about the look on her face. He couldn't stop his own tears from flowing. Not as long she was still crying. She looked so helpless, so scared and so confused.

"I'm not gonna move around," he whispered, "I'm just gonna lay here, wipe your tears and talk to you. Ask me anything you wanna know."

"Is it blood on me?"

"It was but you're not bleeding now," he whispered, "Just when I first put it in. That happens on the first time too. That's normal. Is it still stinging you?"

"It is but not like it was when you first put it in me," she whispered as she wiped his tears away. She continued, "I know you don't wanna hurt me. And I knew this was how the first time was gonna be. Just promise me that it won't be like this again."

300

"It won't be," he whispered in her ear and then he kissed her. He whispered, "I promise it won't. Every time, after tonight. I'm gonna make you feel *so* good. I've been learning what you like, for 3 years and I can't wait to please you. I want this to be something that you like. Because I know I'm gonna want it everyday that I'm breathing, from now on. So if there's anything you don't like about my touch. Please tell me. I wanna know what it is because I owe you nothing but a lifetime of pleasure. This is gonna be all mine to take care of and to keep with a smile. I'm feeling so honored to be with you. I hope you know that."

"I love the way you touch me, Anthony," she whispered, "I can tell that you care about me. Just seeing you crying, right now. Tells me you hate that it had to hurt me. But I knew it was gonna hurt. There is no other way to give you my virginity without it being painful. I know that. I want you to make love to me and I wanna like it, when we do this."

"It's my job from now on, to make sure you like it, baby," he whispered, "And I'm ready to do my job. I have to make sure you have a smile on your face everyday. Or I'm not a real man."

"It's not hurting as bad now," she whispered back, "But I feel like my private is about to split open."

"It feels like that because your man's gotta big dick," he said in a low voice, then he smiled slightly.

She cracked up laughing.

"Sssssssshhh," he said but he was laughing as well. Just not as loud as she was and that helped to relax her.

He could feel her pussy muscles loosening up and that made him feel a little better too. She was still laughing hard which made him start laughing too. It was a relief for him, just to see her laughing.

"Baby girl, you don't know how good it feels to hear you laugh, sweetheart," he whispered with a bright smile on his face.

She smiled and asked, "Now can we cut the light back off?"

"Do you want me to stop?" he asked, again his voice low.

"No," she said, "You waited for this night too, didn't you?"

"Hell yea," he said and he wasn't smiling.

"Then I want you to finish," she whispered, "Our song's on."

"I hear it," he said, "Our first time was to our favorite Isley song."

His cologne smelled so good to her and it was all over her room by now. She could also smell a different aroma. She knew that was their mixed scent. Their scents blended well together and she loved the new smell. It was her man's scent and it was now on her. A scent she would be so use to, in a few

Years. And the only 1 she would ever know, besides her own. But now she wanted him to feel better about that episode. She didn't want him to look so worried. The way he was, right then. He had a sad look on his face and she wanted to change that. She wanted him to feel comfortable when they did the real thing, from now on.

"Show me what happens after you put it in."

"I wanna leave the light on so I can see you," he whispered, "I wanna know how it's feeling to you. So I don't get outta hand in this good pussy. And baby girl. It *is* good. Lord have *mercy*."

He smiled and so did she.

Then she said, "Okay you can leave the light on. But I'm gonna close my eyes because this is making me kind of shy."

"Okay," he whispered, "But hold me tight."

She did and he started to make love to her. All of the kissing, sucking and rubbing they had done prior to the penetration, was all playing together in a perfect symphony. She was glad there wasn't any new pain. At least, not yet. He started to grind inside of her slowly. His breathing patterns changed often. It was amazing to her how she could feel his heartbeat through his chest and his dick too. He was moaning and breathing faster and kissing her wildly. She could tell he was feeling good. He went to 2nd gear and the pain showed up, deep down in her pussy.

"Ouch!" she said aloud and he paused and looked at her.

"The condom broke. *Shit*," he whispered. Then asked, "Do you wanna stop?"

She shook her head no and he gave her 1 of her pillows and said,

"Bite down on it if it hurts. I want us to finish this too. Because it feels so good to me baby and that's because the rubber broke. I can feel your pussy right next to my dick and it's *so* good baby girl."

She smiled and did as she was told. He went back to grinding. He didn't give her all of him but he gave her enough for him to almost get to his. He felt his climax coming but he didn't want it that night. He wanted her to cum before he did. That was a promise he'd made to himself. He started to work her over, still using only half of his dick. She was still holding him tight but she soon started to dig her nails into his back. He knew it was too much too soon. He stopped and pulled out. It was 2am and he wanted to have time to talk to her before he had to go back to the boys room.

He said, "Let's stop for now. But I wanna do this again before you leave, like I told you earlier. It's my job to make sure you like this and I know what I have to do to make sure you do."

302

"I'm not a virgin anymore," she said and smiled.

He smiled back at her, then laid down next to her. He wrapped her up in his arms and started planting sweet kisses on her face and forehead. At that moment, he was feeling pretty damn good about what their lives was going to be like as a couple. He had found and managed to woo the girl of his late night dreams. He had his wife and she was the perfect girl for his future. They had made it through her first time and she was still looking at him and she was still smiling. He felt damn good.

"No you're not a virgin anymore," he said, "But you will always be a virgin to me."

"And I like that part the best," she said, "The one boy in my crew who everybody thought was mean. Was never mean to me. You always treated me special and that's not just because your daddy and Chill told you too. I know in my heart it's because you care for me and I love you, Anthony."

He pulled her up next to his chest and held her tight. He loved hearing those words come out of her mouth for the first time and he wanted to hear them forever.

"You're gonna teach me what love is all about, baby girl," he said, "Because I've never felt like I feel right now, after having sex. I know I don't want nothing bad to *ever* happen to you. If that's love. Then that's good because it feels good."

"It's love," she said, "Because I've never felt it before either. I like it. I like it a lot."

"Good cause I want you to love me," he said, "Now I know mama P gets up at six o'clock. So I'm gonna set my wrist watch to wake me up at five so I can go back in there wit Tank before she comes outta her room."

"This will be the first morning she want have to wake me up," Ebony said, "When you wake up. I wanna wake up too. You'll know when mama is about to get out of her bed because she'll turn off the radio. Twin told me and Nina did too. That's how she knew to come back in my room."

"Okay cool," he said and chuckled.

"What's so funny," she asked.

"You scratched the hell outta my back," he said, "But I like it. I'll be looking at them scratches later on today and smiling. I ain't never did that before."

They laughed together as he set his watch, then pulled her back close to him. They talked for a few more minutes.

"I got my girl," he said, "Now I know when it's something you really want. You just have to go after it and show how much you want it."

"Uh huh and you did," she said and she yawned.

He continued to talk until he didn't get anymore answers from her. She had fallen asleep in his arms. He smiled, kissed her forehead then turned off the lamp. It only took him a few more minutes to fall asleep himself. He felt so peaceful while he slept, for a change. That was another new thing for him.

His alarm went off at 5am and he woke up to find Ebony still laying in his arms. He turned on the lamp. The light caused her to wake up. The first thing she did was looked at him and smiled.

"Are you sore?" he asked.

"Yes," she said, "I gotta take a bath. Then I have to help my mama get breakfast ready."

He started rubbing and sucking on her. He felt aroused again. He wanted to do it again as he heard *Adore* by *Prince* playing in mama Pearl's room. He was contemplating going for number 2 but suddenly the music stopped.

"I gotta go," he said, "I'll see you at breakfast."

"Okay," she said but she couldn't look at him, all of sudden. She felt shy all over again. He expected that too. He smiled as he got up and put his clothes on quickly. Then he leaned over her and gave her a quick kiss without tongue.

"I don't wanna give you my morning breath," he said.

She laughed as he chuckled and said, "But when I see you after breakfast. I'm gonna get that tongue, okay?"

"Okay," she said.

He got up and started toward her door. She felt sad to see him leaving but she knew he had to go. Before he opened the door, he turned, looked at her and smiled. Then he said, "I'll see ya."

"In a minute," she said back and continued to smile but she still had to look away.

He left her room and closed the door. She laid back on her bed. She felt that towel that he had put under her. She pulled it from under her covers to see the dried blood stain that it still held.

"I'm not a virgin anymore," she said to herself, "I'm a woman."

She laid there until she heard her mother turn on the faucet in the master bathroom. Then she got up, made her bed and changed into another gown. She hid that 1 in her drawer because it had a tiny blood stain on it. Her panties had an even bigger stain. She hid those with the nightshirt in the bottom of her scrap drawer. She would put them in the laundry when her next period started. But at that moment, she needed to talk to her mother.

She wanted her to know that she was a woman. She wanted her mother to know, even before she would tell her girls. She took a deep breath and headed down the hall and into her parents room where she found her mother standing in the bathroom mirror. She was crying and Ebony thought it was about her. She thought her mother knew what she had done. But she would find out that wasn't the case at all.

"What's matter, mama?" she asked.

Pearl turned and saw her standing there. She smiled through her tears and said she was fine. Ebony didn't believe her. But still she knew she wasn't crying about her because she would've said it. So Ebony knew it had to be about big mama. She asked her mother if big mama was doing worse.

"No she's still the same," Pearl said, "I'm just worrying about having to send my baby girl away from home."

That was enough to relax Ebony. She was about to tell her what she had discovered and started to do. But then her brother Tank came bursting into the bathroom and foiled that plan.

Within minutes, their mother had sent him back to wake up his brothers, his cousin June and Ajay. Pearl was about to start breakfast and told Ebony to hurry up and get dressed so she could come down and help her. Ebony said okay but she knew she had to soak in the tub again and try to relieve her pussy of that soreness from her first time. She started her bath and added bubbling oils. She got in and soaked for 30 minutes until she heard her mother yelling from the bottom of the stairs. She hopped out of the tub and got dressed quickly. Then she went downstairs to help set the table. It was another minute or 2 before the boys came down. She tried to look at Ajay but she couldn't. He was all smiles and so was her brother Tank. She knew the boys knew she wasn't a virgin anymore. She had to tell her mother before she found it out from someone else.

{December 28, 2005}

Lil Ajay and Ajay are still in the 2nd floor library talking. Ebony is downstairs in the parlor with Lannie, Lea and the 4 and 3 day old triplet's; Ariel, Arianne and April. Ike had run up to the library and joined the males while Tina stayed down in the parlor with the females.

"It's like Ike knows this is where the males supposed to be, "Lil Ajay says and laughs, "Even our boy dog is up here with us, pops."

"He knows we're out numbered now," Ajay says and laughs too, "He's looking at me like I need to even up the male count in this house."

"I'm gonna be the only Jackson man that's gonna have a brother," Lil Ajay says suddenly, "I already know I am. Just hearing how you and mama came to be like y'all are now. I know y'all are gonna shatter that legacy record. I'm so proud to be your son. I know what I've gotta do and pops. I promise you I'm not gonna let you down."

"I already know you won't," Ajay says, "You're gonna do more than all of the Jackson men before you."

"I am," Lil Ajay says. Then he changes the subject. He wants his father to connect the gaps from that first time until the present. So he sits back in his desk chair and asks, "Okay so now you can tell me about how Anita ended up in your room the day after you finally got your perfect woman."

"Me fucking up," Ajay says and frowns, "See, later on that day after everybody was up and moving around. The mothers started prepping for that next day because it was gonna be fourth of July. Ebony and her girls had all come over to nana Jo's to see Nina. Me, Tank, June and Rich was in my room about to blaze a blunt. They was in Nina's room trying to smoke a joint that Tank gave to Nina. We went in there and got em buzzed. Then I took Ebony back to my room. Son, I was horny as hell and she was all I wanted. I was about to get it in too but mama came back home and called the girls to go back to mama P's house so they could help with prep. They had to clean shrimp that fourth of July and they didn't like that. But son, I didn't get to see Ebony no more until at the Fourth of July cookout."

"And Anita and all the ho's came to that, didn't they?"

"Hell yea," Ajay says, "Well not Darlene. She was down to only calling for me, by then. Or she would try to catch me in public. I was still getting her money but my free time went to Ebony. But that morning before the cookout started. I blew some coke and my dick was extra hard. I wanted to fuck and I knew I wasn't gonna be able to have Ebony because all of the family was out there and they would've noticed if she was gone for that long. That bitch Anita was willing and she wanted to suck my dick. That's something I wasn't about to let your mama do until after I was married to her. I sent Anita to our side door and told her how to find my room. Then I met her up there and she sucked me off like her prostitute ass was suppose too. She wanted some crack. I told you I got her ass hooked on the shit. But then I fucked her cause she was begging for it. I thought she was gone take her crack and leave. She didn't so I fucked her and Ebony walked in my room and caught us."

"Ah man," Lil Ajay says, "I'm gonna have to kill her ass too then."

306

"That crack done already fucked her up," Ajay says, "She got cleaned up a little bit but she ain't never gonna be nothing but an addict."

"My mama girls beat her up too, didn't they?" Lil Ajay asks.

"Hell yea," Ajay says, "And the fathers knew it was about her fucking one of the crew men. Our mama's use to fight a lot too."

"But you and mama made up didn't you?"

"Oh yes," he says, "I was begging her to let me see her that same night but it didn't happen. I had some money from Darlene and I bought your mama a gold necklace. I gave it to Tank to give to her. She had nana Pearl to take her back to that store. She returned the necklace and gave Tank the money back. She told him to give it back to me and tell me to try something else. I went to Chill for some help then."

Lil Ajay cracks up laughing and says, "My mama ain't no punk. But didn't somebody get caught at nana Pearl's house?"

"Your uncle Jb and auntie Lynn got together for his birthday night. They got caught in his bed and that shut all our shit down. We stopped trying to fuck in those two houses forever. We all started going to Chill and Renee's after that. Or Chill would get us a motel room."

"Bruce and Kenny told me about you and mama getting caught in room one eleven," Lil Ajay says and laughs.

"Oh yes indeed," Ajay says with a big smile, "I had already asked Chill for help to make up with Ebony for her catching me with Anita. And he knew I wanted to be with her again before she had to leave for Houston. And with Jb and Lynn getting caught. He knew he needed to get us off the block cause mama and mama P was on the lookout *big* time."

"And they still caught y'all," Lil Ajay says while still laughing.

"Yes *they* did and that changed a lot of shit *that* night," Ajay says, looking guilty as ever. He adds, "That's when the whole crew knew that me and Ebony was getting it in. Every generation knew about it then. Not just ours. But only the mothers were mad. Our fathers knew I was raised to know what came with that territory. Your papa John and Al knew I wasn't gonna wait until she was eighteen and they knew I knew I had to marry her. I was on it. Shit I was on the third story and drawing the room features to this house by then."

They cracked up laughing and Ajay says, "That night in room one eleven was our second time having sex. And it was the first time your mama had an orgasm. I don't be bullshitting wit her. I told her I wanted her to like sex. She was only gonna have sex with me, so it was up to me to make sure that she enjoyed it. I was more than willing to put in the work too."

307

"What happened after that?"

"She got her period the day that we had the family meeting," Ajay says, "So I knew she didn't get pregnant on the first or second time. But we was all put on punishment. See Tank, Chill and Rob had went to county that night after they all road down on some squatters out in the grove. They was squatting at the same warehouses where Stoney whooped that dude ass about slapping Bre. The police was just jacking them up. Junior and the other guys had gone to the chamber with the goods and Chill and them didn't have nothing in his Blazer. I was at the motel with Ebony waiting on our ride that never came because of the police taking them in. But that turned out to be a blessing in disguise for Ebony and me. Because they couldn't leave for Houston on the sixth. Big John had to be here for Tank's court date and his court date was on my fifteenth birthday."

"That's when uncle Tank found out he had to move to Houston wit my mama, right?"

"Yes and I was blowing coke that day too," Ajay says, "I was just depressed because Ebony was gonna leave and I thought Tank was going to detention. But then the judge told him to leave Cleveland. That was a blessing too which we'll get to in a minute. But that night of my birthday, I was high as hell and that's when Chill found out I was still fucking with that powder."

"How did he find out?"

"Because I was bugging out," he says, "I wasn't about to handle the fact that my girl was going away and I was hella mean to her when she went to my room to be with me. Even after she said she'd never go in there again because I had Anita in there. I treated her body the wrong way. After she went back to granny's. I admitted it to Chill because he wanted to know what had Ebony so upset that night that she came back to his house *long* before it was time for them to go back to the point."

"He knew something had happened to her when she was with you?" Lil Ajay asks.

"Yea because everybody knew me and Ebony didn't give up any chance we had to spent every free minute we could get, with each other," Ajay says, "They always had to make sure we didn't get caught somewhere together. But that night, we was the first ones back. They knew I had fucked up because she never did."

"But y'all made up right?"

"Yes we did," Ajay says, "While she was at papa and granny's, she told me she wanted me to come in her window. I went in it too. Thing is, papa and granny knew we was in there and they didn't say nothing about it."

"The great grandparents had y'all backs the whole way, didn't they?"

"Absolutely," Ajay says, "Not about the wrong things. But they knew we had what it took to get to where we are right now. And they knew she was the one person who could save me from destroying my life. And I was the person who wasn't going to allow anyone to ruin hers."

"When she went to Houston," Lil Ajay says, "You still kept up with her, didn't you pops?"

"I called everyday and talked to big mama," he says, "I had to know what Ebony was up too. But I was still immature. I didn't asked to speak to her because I didn't wanna seem weak. That was that powder. She would write me letters and instead of me writing her back. I would call big mama. I would tell her all the things I wanted Ebony to know and give her all the answers to the questions Ebony had put in the letters. Big mama knew I wanted Ebony and loved Ebony since I was the age you are now. She made sure she knew what to say and do when it came to me."

"So when did you know that my mama wanted to be with you for the rest of her life and have me and my sisters?"

"When she was in Houston," Ajay says and chuckles, "She has been telling me since she was in the eighth grade, that we was gonna have a big family and that we was gonna have two Jackson males too."

"That was when that Raymond dude came into the picture too, wasn't it?"

"Hell fuck yea," Ajay says and looks his son square in the eyes, "He was a virus, son. He wanted to ruin my princess. I saw that shit the first time I laid eyes on him. That's why I asked big mama and poppa to make sure she didn't go nowhere alone. Ron and Carolyn got a crew too and they came onboard and started trying to protect her. But Raymond had it in his mind that he was gonna fuck her and he tried too. He was the second man to try to touch her, against her will."

"And she did him in too?"

"At the chamber," Ajay says, "I didn't think she would be able to but Chill said he knew she could."

"Because he knew she had shot Neal Palmer and you didn't know."

"Yes," Ajay says, "He knew that whole story and I didn't learn about it until after Rebbie and June had Orian. I took her to the Fillmore hotel downtown, for some private time. I was thinking she was gonna be depressed because all of her girls had babies and she didn't have one. But she wasn't. She was okay. But once we got into lovers mode, I tried to finger fuck her again and she panicked again. I had to know what was causing that and I wasn't gonna accept that she just didn't like it. Not that night. Raymond was dead and buried but I knew it couldn't have been about when he attacked her. Because she was like that before he ever came into the picture. And I was the only one who knew that besides her. Because she was only intimae with me. She wasn't acting like that when we had sex though, son. She wasn't bothered by me putting my dick in her. But my finger sent her into some kind of frenzy and that shit worried me so bad. That night at the Fillmore, she went back to six years old and I watched her. She told me that bastard tried to finger fuck her when she was six years old. He was my pops age then. What kind of sick fucker would do some shit like that? She told Chill what happened while she was upstairs in his room. Chill went down those stairs and tore into his ass. Chill had just made thirteen and I was eight. It was the same day I got my first piece of pussy, son. She was being abused while I was thinking about myself. I was at miss Lou's house fucking a bitch that I knew then, I didn't even want. The girl I wanted to be here with right now, was being molested. She told Chill and Chill went downstairs to fight Neal. Neal was getting the best of Chill because Neal was a grown ass man. Ebony didn't want him to beat Chill and then hurt her again, so she shot him. But he wasn't all the way dead. He was still breathing. But when pops and big Paul walked in, after the shot. And found out what was going on. They finished him. And son, nobody knows about this but her, Chill, your papa's, the first generation, Neal, me and now you. It stays with us unless your mother decides she wants to talk about it. You got me?"

"Yes sir," Lil Ajay says and he has a look on his face like he's ready to throw something.

"Tell me what you're feeling right now," Ajay says.

"Like I wanna make somebody hurt for all the hurt they did and caused to my mama," he says, "She was the best girl in the world. Why did that grown ass man do that to her?"

"Because he was an evil son of bitch," Ajay says, "Raymond was too and so is Angel. I didn't even like Angel. The only reason I even fucked with her was out of sympathy. She was always begging me to suck my dick. So one night when I was blown. I let her give me head out by Rob and Jan's apartment. Jan came in and busted me and made me take that bitch home and be back in fifteen minutes. That was barely enough time to get her home and get back," Ajay says and smiles, "But I made it back. Jan still let me have it, for even bringing a girl around there. I went on to bed in the spare room. The next morning my pops, mama, Chill and mama P woke me up to tell me that Raymond had attacked Ebony down in Houston."

"Seems like every time you fucked off wit a bitch, knowing you didn't want her…." Lil Ajay starts.

"…. some asshole was fucking with the one girl that I did want," Ajay finishes, "What I got from those two instances was this. It wasn't meant for me to be anywhere except for with Ebony or on the phone with her. Instead of getting my nut off with a ho I knew I didn't wanna be with."

"That was God's way of telling you that you shouldn't have been doing that with them," Lil Ajay surmises and adds, "That made you feel guilty, didn't it pops?"

"Hell yea son," he admits, "I told your mama that too. It was a sign from God that I was suppose to be there to protect her. Because every time I was doing something that went against me and her. Something bad happened to her. I *learned*. I learned that shit quick and got right. Then that nigga big Jake sent a nigga to try to do the same shit Raymond was trying to do. I was on top of that shit from day one. I ended up getting shot behind that too but it was worth it. Ebony was pregnant with our first baby then and I had left Angel by the wayside. She came after Ebony because I stopped fucking with her. She ran your mama's car off a cliff. Ebony survived but my first baby girl died. Still if I had never fucked with Angel. She would never have been in the picture to do that. I was in Cincinnati and I had just left Cleveland that morning. I was still doing blow. But when I got on that call and found out my baby might not live," Ajay says as his voice cracks, "I prayed and asked God to let her live. And if he let her live. I would never do anything that would bring harm to her again. She lived and I kicked that coke habit and them ho's to the curb. It's been about me and Ebony every since and I don't regret one minute of it. My life got better because of her and it keeps getting better. That is a woman who always saw good in me. Even when others thought I was fuckin crazy or mean."

They laugh.

Lil Ajay asks, "Chill and Renee got shot before you did by the same guys who was going after mama and her girls, right?"

"Yep," he says, "Jake's posse. But we did away with the ones who shot them and the rest of em got the fuck out and went out east. We still got a bead on em. They gotta go too, just like big Jake."

"His grandson killed Stoney," Lil Ajay says.

"He sure did. We got Eddie, well before they got Stoney. Then we killed all three of them niggaz that killed him," Ajay says, "Arthur was the lead on that. He got the word to us about them and a lot of other shit too. He's a street reporter like nobody I've ever known."

"Losing Stoney messed y'all up for a minute but it made y'all get all the way right too, didn't it?"

"Exactly," Ajay says, " I see Kenny, Bruce and the guys have been on theirs with you too. That's the crew that yours will follow. Brad the third will be head of your crew and you will have to be a point man. One crew always passes their knowledge on to the next in line. Bruce and Kenny was there for a lot of ours. So I'm loving that they're filling you in."

"They do," Lil Ajay says, "But you always give me more. Pops, you fill in all the blanks."

"That's my job," Ajay says, "And I'm not gonna slack on that job, not one bit. But like I told your mama about Raymond and Angel. I do still have one regret."

"That you didn't do em both?" Lil Ajay asks.

"Fasho," Ajay says and chuckles, "Son, you're just like me. You think like me too. So just know that I expect you to out do me when it comes to your life."

"That's what's up," Lil Ajay says.

Then Ajay talks about the times he wanted to go to Ann Arbor by himself and do Raymond in. But he was in college and it was harder to have an alibi. He also tells him about how he got rid of BJ Johnson, a distant relative of big Jake's and he hasn't told anyone about that but his father.

It was on a weeknight while he was suppose to be in Cincinnati. He had parked his six four at him and Jan's campus condo and pretended to have gone to bed for the night. He knew BJ had a tryout at Ohio State and Ajay was going to make sure he took his last breath in Columbus. He knew where he was staying and he also knew a girl that he was seeing, just off the campus. She was a white girl and BJ was sneaking with her because he didn't want his elder big Jake to know he was race mixing. But Ajay was counting on BJ breaking curfew to go see her and trying to make it back to campus without the trainers knowing he had been out. He tells Lil Ajay that after Jan and Rob went to sleep. He took Rob's car and left a note in Rob's pants pocket saying he was on a creep. He drove to Columbus and stole a car, went and waited outside of BJ jump-off's apartment. When BJ left there creeping back toward the campus. He ran him over several times and left him for dead. Then he ditched the stolen vehicle, made his way back to

312

Rob's car and drove back to his Natty Condo and went back to bed.

"Rob and Jan was still asleep when I got back and went to bed," Ajay says, "You and papa Al are the only people I've told about that one."

"That's one more of big Jake's flock gone and they don't even know the crew did him, do they?" Lil Ajay asks.

"Nope," Ajay says, "It was written off as a hit and run. Ohio State tried to keep it hush-hush so they wouldn't get sued. He was off campus and he didn't have permission to be. His death was buried by the school, just like he was when his family put his ass in the ground."

"And why did you have to get him?" Lil Ajay asks, "I mean that wasn't just about the beef, was it pops?"

"He asked Ebony to the prom during my senior year," Ajay says and laughs, "That was in the spring of ninety two before I graduated. I think he was planning to do her harm, simply because he was from that family. Why else would he ask *my* girl out?"

"I know right?"

"So whether he was planning some shit or not," Ajay says, "He had to go. Simply because he asked my girl out and cause of who he was."

"I'm feeling that," Lil Ajay says and chuckles.

"And we're gonna get them other muafuckahz too," Ajay says, "Tim and that bunch. I wanna get em all. Before we get to big Jake or at the same time. Let Jake see that he's alone. Then cut his fucking limbs off and let his old ass bleed out."

"Ah yea," Lil Ajay says and smiles.

Ajay and his son have to go to the kitchen for lunch. Ebony is calling them. They go in and join Ebony and the girls.

"It smells good in here, ma," Lil Ajay says.

"Well thank you son," Ebony says and smiles. She adds, "You and your daddy was locked up there in that library for so long. We thought y'all went to sleep."

"They were talking mama," Lannie says.

"*Taltin* mama," Lea mimicked her.

"They talk a lot too," Lannie adds, "Just like me and you do. But Ajay thinks he's a man already."

"I am a man," Lil Ajay says, "I'm just not the man of this house but I'm still a man."

"Well to me you're still my baby boy, Ant," Ebony says, "And I don't want you to forget that, okay?"

"I never will ma," Lil Ajay says, "I'm gonna do just like my pops

313

and I'm gonna make you so proud of me. You're gonna see what I mean."

"That's all I want from you," Ebony says, "If you do half as much as you daddy has done, you'll be just fine."

"I'm gonna do more than my pops did, mama," Lil Ajay says, "And I'm gonna take care of you, my sisters and my pops. And my brothers to when I have some. And mama, I know I'm gonna have some because you and my pops are always doing what other people said couldn't be done."

That made Ebony so proud to hear her son express himself. And talk about what he plans for himself and for his family, in the future. She also likes that he can see her and Ajay have overcome and achieved a lot of the things that even some in their crew didn't think was possible. She can't stop smiling as she says, "Ant that's a great thing to hear you say. You are so mature and smart. Just like Anthony was at your age. I am already proud of you. You have straight A's in first grade and so does your twin sister."

She turns to Ajay and says, "I think all of our kids are gonna outdo us. They're already on the right track. I think we're doing great as parents, baby. I'm so proud of my babies!"

"They've got a great mother," Ajay says and chuckles.

"They have a great father too," Ebony says to him and smiles. Then she stresses it saying, "Don't they?"

"Yea I'm alright," Ajay answers and keeps laughing.

Then Ebony has a bit of news that is going to really make Lil Ajay's day and probably Lannie's as well. She's still looking at Ajay as her expression changes.

She says, "Erica and Eric are going to have additions to their household this year."

"For real?" Ajay asks and pretends to be surprised.

He thinks she's talking about Kimmie, Alan and Leilenne moving in with them from Chicago. But she's talking about something else.

"Yes," Ebony says, "Erica is pregnant."

"What?!" Ajay exclaims, "Eric didn't ask me if he could get my Lil sister pregnant! He just ask me if I agreed that he could marry her!"

They all burst out in laughter as Ajay continues to act silly. That gives his 3 oldest kids a treat. They love it when he puts on for them. The triplets are at the table in their high chair reclining seats. Ebony has just finished breastfeeding Ariel. She passes her to Ajay so he can burp her as she picks up Arianne. April will be next, of course. But Ebony is still laughing at her husband. He really didn't know Erica was pregnant. But she can tell he's excited about it. However, the other news she's about to tell them, Ajay

314

already knows. Because he was the person, along with big Al and big John who made it happen.

"They're gonna have four additions that will be moving into that house for two thousand and six," Ebony says before Ajay asks for the floor.

"I need to let them know about that, baby," Ajay says.

Ebony smiles, starts Arianne's feeding and concedes the floor. Ajay looks at Lil Ajay and smiles before he starts to speak.

"Eric junior and Erica have decided to have Alan, Kimmie and Leilenne to come and live with them along with Ashley Josetta."

Lil Ajay smiles big when he hears that news again. Lannie looks at Ebony but she doesn't smile.

Ajay continues, "Lil Arch and Brina are happy about that because Archie the third will be closer to his sister."

"Kimmie and Alan are gonna go to our school too?" Lannie asks.

"Yes unfortunately," Ajay says dryly to his oldest daughter's comment but Ebony checks him immediately as she laughs.

"Kimmie *and* Alan will be at school with you and Ant," she says, "Daddy is just kidding. He's happy about both of them being here and going to school with you two. Aren't you, Anthony?"

Ajay smiles and says, "Uh huh."

Ebony continues to laugh as she hands Arianne to him to be burped and picks up April for her feeding.

"I can't wait until Kimmie gets here," Lil Ajay says, "But Alan can stay in Chicago."

"And Kimmie can too," Lannie fires back at him before Ebony has to step in to settle them down.

"They will both be here and they are both welcome to live in Jackson Heights and go to Beachwood elementary with the both of you," she says, "And your daddy is very happy that they're moving here. He was one of the biggest influences on getting them here."

"Because my pops is the man," Lil Ajay says.

They all laugh and Lannie just smiles. Ebony smiles at Ajay. He has to smile too. He knows their twins are excited that Alan and Kimmie will be moving here and will be closer to them. He's happy about it too. Only he knows Alan has the same excitement that his son does. While his oldest daughter is just as thrilled as Kimmie is about them all being able to see each other everyday. Lil Ajay has another question as they're preparing to clear out their lunch dishes.

"When are they coming?" he asks.

"They'll be here in two days," Ebony says, "On the thirtieth. One day before me and your daddy's eight year anniversary."

"What are y'all gonna do for your anniversary?" Lannie asks.

"I know what we're not gonna do," Ajay says and looks depressed. Ebony just laughs and says, "No baby we're not there yet. Our triplets are three and four days old. We've still got five more weeks to wait for that."

"Yea right," Ajay says and laughs.

"Right!" Lea repeats her daddy and they all laugh.

Then Ajay says, "I'll think of something magical to do for my baby. We got the Pistons that night and we've gotta get them. Since we didn't get the Nets, last night. That was a road win that I really wanted. We all did but they got us by five. No way is Detroit gonna come in here and give us two loses in a row. We're eighteen and ten but we're about to pull this thing together and make the playoffs. Now after the game. We're all gonna come back home and spend some quality family time together and bring in the New Year as a family. I would say the older kids would have to stay the night some where. But your mama want be safe here alone with me."

He laughs and says, "It's really up to you Ebony, as to what you wanna do."

"I say we do the family thing," she says, "We'll all go to the game. This will be the triplet's first game."

"You're amazing woman," Ajay says and smiles, "They will only be a week old. Are you gonna be up for that?"

"I'm a vet, remember?" Ebony says and laughs. Then she says, "You said it yourself. And besides, you have a road game on the fourth of January. We all need to see you while you're home."

"You're just trying to keep everybody here so you'll have some back up," Ajay says and chuckles, "You can't resist me when you're alone."

"True that," she agrees.

Their kids laugh at them. They love when their parents flirt with each other in front of them. Lannie helps Ebony clear the table while 1 year old Lea tries to help too. Ajay and Lil Ajay put the triplets in their baby swings while Lea walks from them to where Ebony and Lannie are, next to the sink. She's giving instructions in her little baby language. Ariel, Arianne and April are already napping and Lea is ready for a nap too. They're done with lunch. Ajay and Lil Ajay leave the females to the kitchen duties and head back upstairs to the 2nd floor library to continue their talk.

As soon as they get back to the library and get seated, Lil Ajay has a request. He asks, "Pops can Kimmie go to the game wit us? And I guess Alan can come too or should he?"

"I think we should invite them both, son," Ajay says, "You and me, we both have to watch him and see if he's gonna be the boy for Lannie. You will be included in those decisions when it comes to your sisters. And you will have to be on top of it, just like I will. Remember when I told you that I want you to know what their actions are online? Well that's period. You're their big brother and I'm their father. They're gonna learn what to look for through us. Just like we learned what kind of lady to look for, through our mothers."

"Yes sir, I got it and I'm so ready for it," he says, "Lannie and me got a *Myspace* page together. Mama said we had to share a page so I already got that covered. That's the only online account mama said we can have. She lets us get on the Disney and Nickelodeon sites and that's it."

"Okay cool," Ajay says, "But we're gonna have Alan and Kimmie over for dinner on Friday when they get here. That way I can start laying down the ground rules, right away."

"And me too," Lil Ajay adds and they both chuckle.

"I just need for you to remember the motto that I give you every time we have these talks," Ajay says, "Can you repeat that for me?"
Lil Ajay looks his father in the eyes and repeats the motto verbatim.
He says, *"The test of being a real crew man is to have the type of control and dominance in your relationship and household, if you're in the same house, that you don't have to give your girl a reason for why she shouldn't do something. Just her man telling her not to do it, is suppose to be enough to insure that she doesn't."*

"That's it. But that word control should not be over used," Ajay says, "You're never to be physical with *any* woman. Whether she's the love of your life or a piece of ass. The control part is mental. As a boy, I took it for granted when I messed around with some other girl and just expected Ebony to take that and still love me regardless. Doing cocaine was a big reason for that. It was that same drug that drove your uncle Richard to be abusive to your aunt Anna. It was that drug that drove Richie Rich to mistreat T-baby and his own son and he eventually took his own life. Even more than that. It drove some of the men in our crew to disrespect their female, in sight of them. I did that once and that was during my senior year in high school. I was mad because Ebony had said she would go to the prom with BJ. I would talk to Angel at school when I knew Ebony was going to be passing through, where we was talking at and see me. That was the most immature and phoniest shit I ever did in my life. It drove me to use more cocaine. I felt like I had to be physically dominant in the form of sex. Twice
317

that happened. In the gym at school. And before that, was on the night of my fifteenth birthday in my room at nana Jo's house."

"That's what made Chill know something was wrong with you?" Lil Ajay asks, "Because that hurt my mama, didn't it? And that's why she left you and went back to Chill house that night?"

"Exactly," Ajay says, "Sometimes it was my way of being physical without using my hands. But it was still a childish thing to do. And even though I was still a child by age. I wasn't mentally. Because I knew it was wrong, each time I did that. Part of that was to keep that control. As a Jackson man, I have a huge dick son and so do you. But there are times when I use it to make a point, which is different. On my birthday, I did it because I didn't know how to express that I loved your mother and I didn't want her to have to go to Houston. In the gym, it was to hide my own mistake of being in that bitches face knowing I never gave a fuck about her. When I knew Ebony was trying to defy me. I used that same thing and she knows the difference. What it did for our relationship was taught us both something. I learned to express how I felt. Whether it was anger or whether I felt disrespected, hurt because someone in our crew was taken from us or whatever. But on the night you and Lannie was made. It was about her disrespecting me and our heritage by crashing our *all* male party. The difference about that night is, she knew that was warranted. And for me, I knew I had to make her think about something else instead of not being able to get pregnant. Because that was keeping us from being able to make a baby. I never took it to the point, at anytime, that it caused Ebony to feel like she had to go and find love somewhere else. That control took some of the guys to the point where they took their female for granted and she strayed or just left him. Because they took that to mean they should be able to do whatever they pleased and their girl was just gonna sit tight. But when those four guys came into the picture, that wasn't the case. Ebony drove them on a movie night and that was only because those were her girls and she didn't want them to be out of her sight with those guys. She was trying to get them not to go. But they're a unit, so she went anyway. We watched them the whole time because we knew big Jake had sent those guys. But the females don't know about that beef. And they are never to know until they have a son who will be affected by it and expected to do what's necessary to stay alive. And see after that movie and pizza night, Ebony admitted all of that to me and then I punished her. She knew it was warranted and she also knew she wasn't gonna go around them again. I got that point across to her without having to leave her scared to death about

318

the Johnson beef. She never went that route again. But T-baby and auntie Nina did go on several dates with two of those guys. But Rebbie, she ended up finding what she needed in Jarvis and that still hasn't come out yet. But Ebony has never been unfaithful to me in *anyway,* other than that movie night. And she stayed in the lobby for all but fifteen minutes of the whole damn movie. She could probably feel that something was wrong because she's always had a sixth sense. And she probably felt my presence too. But that was an understanding that your mother and I found together. And we learned to respect each other with that, for the most part. But mutual respect and understanding was something Tank, June and Rich didn't have that much of, back during that time. Tank got it all the way together and him and Nina are all good now. But that is what eventually caused Rich his relationship with T-baby. June has strayed on Rebbie too and she knows it. So I feel that's the reason she even looked at Jarvis in the first place. But something started with them before Rebbie graduated high school and it's still continues to this day. I'm not sure if there's penetration or not. But they are pushing something. The same day Ebony went to the hospital to have the triplet's. I had to break up a sweet little talk they was having in our parlor. Rebbie looks at Jarvis, the way she use to look at June. I feel it's gonna cost June his marriage eventually. But your uncle Tank got his shit right. And for me, I was never gonna date no other girl and I damn sho wasn't gonna bring her in front of my princess. I fucked around back then. But I was never about disrespecting Ebony or breaking her heart."

"You told me something happened to you when you was in college that helped you understand what had happened to mama in Houston," Lil Ajay says, "I know you said it happened on the same night that Rebbie found her way to Jarvis. So what happened to you, pops?"

"I'll tell you," Ajay says, "But let's go for a ride and check on the complex while we're out. That story is still one that bothers me, son. And I don't even wanna bring it into this house again. It'll mess up the greatness of this place. Let's ride."

Chapter 13-Another Jackson Man Made

Ajay and Lil Ajay arrive at his Allen Saul sports complex. They speak to all of the employees, then head straight into Ajay's office to finish their talk.

"This is where I was the first time I got the story about Katrina Dobbs off my chest," Ajay says.

"That was her name?" Lil Ajay asks.

"Yea."

"So what did she do to you?" Lil Ajay asks.

"Before I get to that, son," Ajay says, "I wanna tell you about a few other things that happened before that. All the things that happened in my life is what brought me to this point. Let me start with *Freaknik*."

"*Freaknik*?" Lil Ajay asks excitedly, "Oh I know I wanna hear about this."

He leans forward, propping both elbows on his knees while he rests his chin on his hands. Ajay cracks up laughing at his son's interest in something with a name like this. But he knows he got it honest.

"It was just what it sounds like," Ajay says, "Ho's was naked and walking the streets, just giving ass away."

"Where this at?"

"It use to be in Atlanta," Ajay says and laughs, "But they don't do it no more."

"Ah man," Lil Ajay says with a disappointed look.

"I went in the summer of ninety three," Ajay says, "Jb and Lynn found out about it when they went down there to attend Georgia Tech. It was off the hook too. Only thing I did wrong down there was fucked with Angel's posse. And son that was the last time I fucked wit her too. A big reason why it was the last time. Was because your mama found out about it and the affect it had on her."

"Uh oh. What happened and how did mama find out?"

"One of my teammates had pictures and Ebony saw one of them. It was a random snapshot that had me on it with Angel in the background. That's how Ebony knew she was down there. They didn't go with us and we didn't know they would be there. It was the same posse it is here in Cleveland. Alana and Darlene included. But it was *Freaknik*, so of course the freaks went. But when Ebony saw that picture, she asked me if I fucked with her while I was down there. I did and I told her the truth. I only fucked her the first night though. Because they found us. We all fucked her and the rest, just like we normally did. Then I just partied for the rest of the week and stayed on the phone with Ebony. Because that was the year I first got a cell phone. After I left for college is when I got it."

"Wait, you didn't have a cell phone until college?" Lil Ajay asks as he burst out laughing.

"Sure didn't," he answers, laughing too as he says, "And look at you. You're six years old and you already got a cell phone. Don't let it get you caught up though, son. I don't think I would've gotten to do half of the shit I did. Especially the bad shit, if I had a cell phone. Because mama and Ebony would've been calling me back to be around them."
They laugh more.

"I'll have to remember that," Lil Ajay says, "But I don't give my number to none of them girls who I don't wanna fuck wit though, pops. And the ones who do get it. Get it because I call them. And they know not to call me, if I don't tell them too. Cause if they do. Then they know I'll never call them no more. And I'll block they number, so they can't call me."

"Very good to hear," Ajay says and smiles.

"So finish telling me about how mama reacted to that picture."

"That shit hurt Ebony's feelings *so* bad," Ajay says with a sad look. "She came to visit me in Natty for the first time, right after we all got back from Atlanta. She was already mad because she wasn't allowed to go. Then after seeing a picture and finding out Angel was there and I had fucked with her. She was thinking that was the reason I didn't want her to go. When the real reason was because I know how the guys act toward any female that show up there. Jb put me up on that part. See if the girl wasn't showing nothing. They would sometimes just rip her clothes off. And son, daddy wouldn't have made it back from Freaknik if that had happened to Ebony. Do you hear me?"

"I hear you and I already know why," Lil Ajay says, "Because you would've killed them or they would've had to kill you."

"Exactly," Ajay says.
Ajay continues, "She saw that picture, then she just went into my room and never came back in the front. I went in there and she was in my bed, crying her eyes out. I can't stand to see her cry. Remember that and don't ever bring no tears to my woman's eyes. Because I'm gonna have a problem with you. That shit tears me up."

"I understand pops and I won't," he says, "So what did you do to stop her from crying?"

"Well we had went shopping before she saw that picture," Ajay
321

says, "And I had gotten her a promise ring. I was getting it so I could give it to her when I brought her back here to Cleveland. But son, after she saw that picture she gave me an ultimatum. I explained myself and that's when I told her that she was the *only* girl that I couldn't be without. She made me promise I wouldn't fuck wit Angel no more and I gave her my word. I cut that shit off from there."

"And that was the end of Angel, ha?"

"It was a wrap from there," Ajay says and smiles proudly, "And me and Ebony was moving on toward what we have now. The real shit with me being faithful to her and looking forward to my future in the NBA. Then Chill and Renee got shot and Destiny was born."

"Kenny told me that's how his little sister came into the world," Lil Ajay says, "On the day their mama and daddy got shot and that's why they named her Destiny."

"That's exactly right," Ajay says, "And I spent the whole time, including my nineteenth birthday, at the hospital."

"And you was running the crew business then too, wasn't you?"

"A lot of it, yes," Ajay says, "The grudge work, Fasho. I was making sure the money stayed straight and kept coming in."

"Y'all didn't have no more of those Eddie Washington type dudes by then, ha?"

"Oh *hell* no," Ajay says, "Big Jake only tried that shit once."

"You popped him out," Lil Ajay says, "You already told me about that. You said you told the crew that he was yours."

"That's right and he was," Ajay says, "He was there to kill me or set me up to be killed. So it was my legacy to do him in."

"That's how I feel about big Jake and *any* other person who did harm to my mama or tried too. It's my legacy to protect my mama and my sisters and my woman too, when I do have her. I'm not taking no shorts on none of the above. You got my word on that."

"Cool," Ajay says before his facial expression changes to 1 of disgust and definite dislike. He's remembering what came next. It was November 1993 and the night he was sexually assaulted.

"Pops you look like you're mad right now," Lil Ajay says as he's learned to pick up on his father moods.

"I am, son," he says, "There's nothing good about having sex with someone that you never wanted. It's a helpless feeling and I can relate to the events your mother went through because of Katrina Dobbs. I sat in this same chair and told your aunt Lynn about it and she got it out in the open.

322

She helped me to tell your mom about it. It wasn't until June of two thousand two when I finally got to where I could tell Ebony. And she was so understanding, that I felt worse for not being able to tell her the day after it happened. She understood how I felt and why I didn't feel like I could tell her, at the time."

"What did Katrina do?" Lil Ajay ask, with a furious look on his face that Ajay recognizes as the 1 before the kill.

"It was two weeks after we moved into the big mansion that mister Parkwood had gotten for the whole crew. Because Tank, June and Rich was there and the foursome was gonna be coming the next year," Ajay says in one breath. He continues, "We had a party to Christian the mansion. All the teams was there and cheerleaders, dance team and students. It was packed and we was getting fucked up. I was doing coke, smoking weed and drinking. That's when Katrina started mixing the drinks. I wanted a refill and she brought it to me. I was buzzing before but after that last drink. I really felt light headed. I just figured I didn't eat enough before I started partying. So I got up and started toward the tables to get some food real quick. I was trying to get something in my stomach because I just thought the alcohol was making me feel like that. But when I got to the table, I felt like I was gonna pass out. Tank noticed me and came over there. I couldn't even walk in the little time that it took for Tank to get to me. That's how I knew June was gone and so was Rich. Because Tank had to get Jarvis and my teammates to help carry me to my room. I remember that part. But son, I don't even remember making it to my bed. I was already passed out before they got me to my room."

He starts to talk slower, "It was much later on when I woke up and I was still dizzy as fuck. I looked at my clock radio and it had five o'clock on it. They took me in there around one in the morning. I was trying to focus on the clock but I could feel somebody sucking my dick. It was still dark in my room so I reached for my bed lamp and turned it on. I could barely see but when my vision came in. I saw that bitch giving me head. Before I knew it, I just pushed her as hard as I could but I didn't have no strength. She just giggled and kept doing it. I was telling her no and she wouldn't get off me. Son it took me five minutes to get myself raised up and propped up on my elbows. During that whole time, she was just going and going and laughing. Finally I found the strength from somewhere and I lifted myself up and flipped myself over, kicking her on the floor at the same time. That bitch just kept laughing. I told her to get the fuck outta my room but she came back at me. I was still weak. It was taking all the strength I had, just to talk.

She knew I was helpless too and she was enjoying that part of it. She came back up to me and grabbed my dick again. And she started back sucking on it. That's when I swung with all my might and hit her across her head."

"Did the bitch stop then?"

"Yea she did and I was getting up and still dizzy," Ajay says, "I was looking for my pistol. That's when she told me that she didn't know why I was bugging out because she had fucked me three or four times. She showed me four condoms in my trash can too. But son, I thought about it after this all came out and I told your mama about this too. There wasn't no sperm in those condoms and I still don't know if she actually put them on me. But I don't think I got a nut. My dick wasn't even hard when she was sucking on it. I mean it wasn't limp but I never am. It wasn't hard like I get when I'm having sex. I don't think she got no cum from me. I think that bitch was just happy to be taking advantage of me."

"Nasty bitch!" Lil Ajay says and he is visibly angry and rocking back and forth in his chair.

Ajay continues, "Once I sat up and I told her again to leave. She was still standing there talking about how big my dick was and it wasn't all the way hard. She told me she fucked me real good. Just a bunch of shit. I tried to stand up and I fell back on the bed. She came back on me. She was holding me down. I didn't have enough strength to overpower her. But when she tried to mount me again, I thought about Ebony and how she had told me she got away from Raymond. Right during that moment, I thought about your mama and how she survived her attack. That shit was weird as hell to me. I also thought about how she would feel about me letting that assault continue. Then somehow I found some strength from somewhere. I got that ho off of me and out of my room. When I got to the living room area, it was nobody sleeping all around in there, like it had been. She knew I was looking for somebody to help me make sure she got outta there.   That bitch was bragging about why nobody was there. She said she had told everybody they had to go to their own dorms and apartments. She said she told them that I said it and that's why they all left. Tank was fucking Gwen, who is Jarvis wife now. So he was on the other end of the mansion in his room, I guess. June and Rich was still gone. Jarvis was gone. I found out he was with Rebbie and that's when their thing started. But for me, I found the strength I needed and I pushed that bitch all the way to the door, out of it and locked it when I got her out. Son I ran back to my bathroom, turned the shower on and jumped in there. I was scrubbing myself and throwing up, all at the same time. Mentally that just fucked me up for *months*."

"Didn't you say she followed you?"

"Around campus and every time she saw me, she made sure I knew she was there," Ajay says, "She would take pictures of me on campus or if she got to come to our games. Then she would send them to my email with messages about how good I taste or how sexy I look when I sleep. She did that shit for years. Even after I was gone from there. Until I changed emails. Her family owned the flower shop right off campus, so she would send me gifts with sexy messages. When I left school and went to Miami. She stole my address when your mama sent me gifts for holidays and stuff like that. But even before she got the address. She would send stuff to the head office and I would just refuse it. That shit went on for years."

"You said it took you a long time before you told mama."

"I told her three and a half years ago," Ajay says, "You and Lannie was born and here, when I told her. It was almost a decade later. But after that shit, things started changing around me too. I couldn't really focus on shit the way I was before that. When my team was getting ready for tournament time, that's when I got Ebony pregnant with the first baby. And son that was because I was in that same bed that I got assaulted in. I knew Ebony could get pregnant that night because I knew how to count her days. But I felt almost desperate and I couldn't stop holding her. Because I was remembering the last sex that happened in that room. That shit Katrina did to me, haunted me for damn near 10 years. But your aunt Lynn knew something was up. She saw that bitch trying to grab me at her welcome back from Afghanistan party and she made me get it out."

"I'm glad she did," Lil Ajay says, "And that Katrina bitch is on my list now. Don't even sweat it pops. I know Kenny already said he plans to do her ass in and I'm gonna be on that hoot ride. I ain't down wit none of my crew being hurt. Not my pops either. You feel me?"

"I know that son," Ajay says, "I'm the same way. I had never felt so helpless in my life. I felt like that bitch took apart of my manhood when she did that. But it was something about the way that I loved Ebony. I gave her my best after that and I wasn't gonna allow her to want for anything. Because she was the woman I wanted in my bed. The *only* woman I wanted in my bed. And that shit Katrina did. Brought me to that realization."

"Mama was pregnant the first time, in ninety four," Lil Ajay says.

"Yes and that bitch Angel still hadn't gotten the clue that I wasn't gonna fuck wit her no more," Ajay starts again, "Before we get to the car accident that Angel caused. Them four niggaz that big Jake sent, started some shit at the U. That was your mama's senior year. It was in April and I

325

got shot in two places. My back and my leg. I went out too. I could hear my baby crying and screaming. But it was getting harder for me to breathe."

"Big Chill said you died off like he did. But you came back before you went to surgery," Lil Ajay says.

Ajay says, "I did. I couldn't put Ebony through that. She was loosing her mind, the same way I would have if it was her on that stretcher."

"You made it and I'm so glad you made it," Lil Ajay says, "There's no way I would be here, if you wouldn't have made it. Is all them niggaz still out farther east?"

"We're getting them too," Ajay says quickly, "No doubt about it. That's the big Jake shit, so they gonna die. And yes, you will be apart of it."

"All I wanted to hear pops," Lil Ajay says and smiles slightly. Then he asks, "Okay tell me how my big sister was taken from me?"

"I was done with Angel and she didn't get it," he says, "Pretty much like she still don't get it now, after doing ten years for killing my child. She started showing up wherever I was and trying to get with me. I told her flat out that I was with Ebony and that's where I was gonna be. I told her I was about to become a father and I was gonna marry Ebony."

"And after that is when she started threatening my mama," Lil Ajay says, "Cause that bitch couldn't *be* my mama. She killed my big sister."

"She would call my apartment phone because it wasn't private," Ajay says, "It was in the phonebook. One night she stayed at the club with no ride. She begged me to get with her and I told her no. She had no ride, so I took her home. That was the second time that I ever hit a woman and didn't feel shit afterwards. She slapped me because I told her for the last time, that it was over."

"She slapped you?!" Lil Ajay ask as his voice rises.

"And I slapped her back," he says, "After that is when she must've started her plan to fuck with Ebony. My pregnant Ebony. She planned that shit and ran my babies off a cliff. I prayed on my own life for them to make it. I promised God that if he didn't let Ebony die. I would not only treat her like she deserved to be treated. But I would stop fuckin with cocaine too. He saved her and I stopped using that shit. *Period*."

"Then you went and got that bitch from Pittsburgh, right?"

"Oh happy day!" Ajay yells as he laughs too. He says, "When that info came in, it was as joyous as it was to find out where Raymond was. Fuck yea, we went and got her ass. The crew plans are brilliant. Together we are great minds and we plan for the day after. Never go into something that could cost you your life or freedom without a plan. Big Paul use to say, *'If you approach it like it's one of many. You'll get to do many. Never enter anything angrily. Give it the thought it needs and always keep your future in mind. Make sure you ask yourself where do you wanna be, the day after? Or who in this world would I be leaving without their heart?'* That was some shit I know for a fact, Chill got from his pops. Chill would never let us go into any hoot ride without a solid plan. No matter how mad we was. And you're my son, so that's a must for your crew too. You understand me?"

"Yes sir."

"We got all the crew in on that damn plan," Ajay says, "We got her and Alana in the process. Got their confessions on tape for the cops and all that. The hardest job my crew had was keeping me from killing her, on the way back to Cleveland. Nobody fucks wit my babies. None of y'all. If I got love for them. Don't fuck with them wrong. Or I'm gonna do your ass in and still enjoy my life."

"That's why you're the man to me," Lil Ajay says, "I've always looked at you as my hero, pops and I wanna be just like you. I promised you before and I'll say it again. I won't let you down and I won't hurt my mama or let her down either. If I ever hurt my mama. That would make me wanna die."

"I had one of those with nana Jo," Ajay says, "I had crack in my pants when she did laundry. Ebony was in Houston alone, then. Mama found it and was getting on me and I felt too guilty to stand there and take the truth. I went to live with Darlene for like two weeks. But I was still at Chill's house everyday or out knocking somebody off. My pops was in touch with me, the whole time and Chill too. They wanted to let me grow as a man and fix my own problems. But it was seeing Ebony, that brought my ass right back to Shaker Heights. She came home for Christmas and I had to have my eyes on her."

"That summer before, is when she had to go back to take care of big mama and uncle Tank was over his court stuff right?" Lil Ajay asks.

"Yes," Ajay says.

"And when she went back by herself. That's when you did your last stay in Juvie for having weed at school in ninety, right?"

"Exactly," Ajay says, "That was the last time. Knowing my baby was coming home and I got arrested, was tough. Then before I got out, she was gone again. Nineteen Ninety was a hard year but she came home for Christmas and brought them stank ass rats from Houston up here. They couldn't get no crew dick like they wanted it and they set your mama up for

327

that bitch Raymond White to attack her. But I think he was planning to do it anyway. Because I found out that was just the type of loser his ass was. Getting rid of him did the world a favor. He wasn't shit."

"We got more favors to do for the world too," Lil Ajay says and they laugh.

Ajay tells him it's time to head back to Jackson Heights and have dinner. Before he has to go practice for their game against the Pistons on December 31, 2005. Which is he and Ebony's, 8th year anniversary.

On the way home, he fills him in on his other life happenings in 1994. He makes sure he knows Ebony met and befriended his Godmothers Yolanda and the deceased April, while she lived in Houston. He also lets him know that's whom his youngest triplet sister was named after. And that April and Ebony had shared a Christmas birthday, same as triplet April.

"My cousin Jerica was the first foursome baby to be born," Lil Ajay adds, "She always brags about that too. And Richie came next."

Ajay laughs and says, "Your mama and her girls always have done things together. That's why they got the name *the foursome*. They was always tight and they still are today."

He tells Lil Ajay about the OJ Simpson not guilty verdict in 1995 which no one thought would happen. For his 1996 review, he tells him about the Columbine shooting, the first 3 foursome girls marriages and his aunt Lynn winning in the Olympics which gives Lil Ajay a thrill.

"She got Olympic gold," Lil Ajay says, "I'm going to the Olympics. I know you didn't go cause you didn't want too but I'm going."

"Do it bigger than me, son," Ajay says, "I'm alright wit that."

"Oh and didn't you say that's when you and cousin Terrell started back being friends?"

"It sure was," Ajay says, "And that's when aunt Jessica and pops got back to being sister and brother. I think she's gonna leave doctor Layton soon too. Terrell told me about it when I was on the road in Chicago, last week."

"From what you told me about him. She *should* leave him."

Then Ajay tells him about the wedding of all weddings. He has a huge smile on his face as he tells his son about the day he gave Ebony his last name.

"That's what it was all for," he says, "We had the house I'd drawn, built and we was ready to get onto being husband and wife and parents. Those was the best days of my life. And son, anything that your mother was apart of, always made my life better. She made everyday of my life worth living. That's why I would do anything to keep her safe and to make her

328

happy. I did it up on the night I proposed to her too. That night had to be magical. She was completely surprised. Son, she's every woman in this world to me. Every woman and she's the best mother too."

"She is the best mama," Lil Ajay agrees, "I always talk about my mama to everybody and you too. People think I'm mean too but I'm not."

"Nah, you're just choosy about who you give your time too," Ajay says and smiles, "You're a Jackson man to be."

They arrive home and join Ebony and the girls as they're just about done making dinner. Ajay gives Ebony a kiss on entrance as he always does. Then Ebony gives Lil Ajay a hug and a kiss too.

"You're enjoying your time with your daddy, aren't you son?" Ebony asks.

"Yes ma'am," Lil Ajay says, "My pops is the man."
Ebony laughs and says, "Okay, well I need for you and the man to go wash up for dinner. Okay? While me and Lannie get the table set."

"Yes Lannie The *girl!*" Lannie yells behind her twin brother and laughs.

They sit down to dinner. Ajay opens conversation with the wedding talk. He knows this is something he wants to share with his girls too.

"I was telling Ant about our wedding day," Ajay says to Ebony and smiles.

"It was perfect," Ebony says with a pleasant smile, "It was the day I had dreamed about, all of my life. Did your daddy tell you he started drawing this house when he was in seventh grade?"

"Yes ma'am, he did," Lil Ajay says as he looks at Ajay and smiles.

"I love my house, daddy," Lannie says.

"My house!" Lea repeats.

"Good baby girls," Ajay says, "Because y'all are gonna be living here until you're in your thirties."
Everybody laughs. Even the triplets seem to be smiling at that comment. Then Ebony tells them she hasn't even had a chance to drive her 2006 Escalade that she'd gotten for Christmas. She poses it as a question for their kids, as she asks, "Do y'all think daddy will let me go to the game and drive my new vehicle?"
Lannie and Aaliyah say yes but Lil Ajay says no. Ajay agrees with his son, of course.

"I'm gonna call my newest three babies, *Tre,*" Ajay says and smiles, "That has more swag than triplets anyway."
They all laugh.

"Anthony I guess you don't want me to go to the game?" Ebony asks.

"Baby, Tre will barely be a week old," he says, "Do you think you'll be up to going? Because I always want you to be at my games. You know that. You're my good luck charm."

"Well that *is* our anniversary," she tells him.

"I'm leaving that up to you baby," he says, "If you feel like going. Then I say you should come."

Then he gets back to the wedding talk as he says, "I remember the day of our wedding when I was thinking about being a father, one day soon. At the time I wasn't sure if it was gonna happen. But nineteen ninety nine was the first of my best years. And I thought I had already seen the best of times. What do you say baby?"

Ebony agrees saying, "Cosign that! Ant and Lannie came into our lives and it changed right there on the spot. Anthony and I knew we'd be together forever for sure, on that day. Because we both knew that neither one of us was gonna go a day without seeing both your faces and hearing your voices. And I also knew I wanted more kids. It was the most complete feeling of my whole life and before that day. I was thinking that having Anthony's love was the top of the pedestal."

Ajay chuckles, looks at his oldest 3 children and says, "It was," then he winks his eye and they all crack up laughing.

Ebony is still laughing when she says, "When I was in the eighth grade and living in Houston with big mama and poppa. I told Anthony I wanted five kids but I had to have two boys. Now we've got a handsome son and five beautiful daughters and our lives would not be perfect without each one of you. But I still do want another son, so we can break that Jackson cycle."

"Y'all got six kids now, mama," Lannie says and laughs.

"Dot six," Lea mimics her big sister and laughs too.

"Lea is the only one who was born by herself and I'm still the only boy," Lil Ajay says, "I'm gonna get things kicked off right first and then I'm gonna have some little brothers. I wanna break that whole legacy thing down too, mama. That's one way to do more than pops. He says I have to do better than him. I'm gonna be the only Jackson man with blood brothers. Full blood brothers, at that."

"Brothers. That's Plural?" Ebony asks him as she smiles before Ajay interrupts.

"You heard the man," Ajay says, "Ant's got that sixth sense thing going on, just like you do Ebony. If he says he'll have more than one

330

brother. Well then that's what its gonna be," he finishes that comment with a huge laugh and they all laugh with him as they dig into their dinner.

On this same Friday, Leilenne, Alan and Kimmie arrive along with little Ashley to stay with Eric Jr and Erica. Ajay and Lil Ajay pick up Alan and Kimmie and they drive back to the Jackson mansion.
Ebony and Lannie have just finished making dinner and are about to set the table when the 4 of them come into the kitchen door.
"Hey misses Ebony!" Kimmie yells with excitement as she runs to Ebony and gives her a hug.
"Hey Kimmie sweetheart," Ebony says as she gives her a kiss. She asks, "How are you?"
Lil Ajay is all smiles as he witnesses this action between his mother and the girl that he has already chosen to be his girl.
"I'm fine," Kimmie says, "I'm so happy that I get to live here and go to school with Ajay and Lannie."
Lil Ajay knows he's going to talk to her real soon. And before too long, he's also going to tell her to call him Anthony and not Ajay.
Ebony smiles at Kimmie and says, "Well Kimmie, Lannie and I would love for you to help us set the table. Will you?"
"Yes ma'am!" Kimmie says excitedly.
While Ebony, Lannie and Kimmie prepare to set the table. Ajay takes Alan and Lil Ajay into the male sanctuary so they can talk until the ladies call them back to eat dinner.
Ajay can see the excitement in both of the young males eyes. He's been there himself and he knows exactly what that feels like. As the adult, he has to make sure and guide them the right way. He also noticed the shyness in his daughter Lannie, when her eyes met Alan's. That brings an uncertainty to him that he isn't familiar with. But he knows he has his father Al who he can go to about how to handle that part and big John also. He likes how his son behaved with Kimmie. Lil Ajay was a perfect little gentleman. That makes Ajay proud. Lil Ajay had opened her car door and helped her into the Benz when they left Eric's house and he did the same thing outside, when they got here. Ajay knows he has only a few minutes to gnaw on the 2 young men's ear about what is to be expected of them. Not only during their dinner today but also in their lives. He gets right to it.
"So we're the men in the house today," he says as Alan and Lil Ajay gives him their full attention. He says, "And we're gonna show that we are gentleman. There are seven beautiful young ladies who will be joining

us for dinner and we're gonna make them all feel like the most important people in the world. That's how you treat ladies. And especially if they're ladies who mean a lot to you. Everyone of those seven females in there, mean the world to me."

"I like Lannie," Alan says suddenly.

For the first time ever, Lil Ajay gives him a positive look and Ajay notices it and says, "Well Ant, this young man seems to have taken a liking to your twin sister. How do you feel about that?"

"I didn't use to like it when he said-"

"Say it to him, son," Ajay interrupts.

Lil Ajay turns to Alan and says, "I didn't use to like it when you use to say you liked Lannie. But I don't feel like that now. I just want you to know that she's my *sister* and if you're gonna like my sister. Then she has to know that too. If she likes you. Then you're gonna have to treat her like a princess. That's my mama's daughter and my mother is a queen. And even if she does like you back. You need to remember that she's in charge of her. Don't ever ask her to do anything. Let her tell you what she wants to do. You good wit that?"

"I'm good wit that," Alan says, "I just like to look at her and I like her smile too. She's the prettiest girl I know. And Ajay, I know you like my sister and I'm good wit that too. I want you and me to be like brothers. Would that be cool?"

Lil Ajay smiles and says, "Yea that's cool. We're gonna be crew anyway. And we have to have each others back. My sisters will only be able to like crew boys because that's what they see from our mama. You just watch how my pop treats my mama and you'll know how to treat my sister. I'll be cool wit you, as long as you don't make her cry. Okay?"

"Okay crew," Alan says and chuckles. Then he says, "That's how I feel about Kimmie too. My daddy told me *and* Eric that we have to take care of Leilenne and Kimmie. So me and you are just alike when it comes to our sisters. We've gotta make sure they know we think they're special too. I'm wit that too. Cool?"

"Cool," Lil Ajay says.

Both young men smile, then look at Ajay so he can have the floor back.

"Wow," Ajay says, "That was *way* easier than I thought it would be. That means the girls are gonna be harder."

They laugh together. Soon Ebony comes to the male sanctuary door and tell them the table is set and they need to come on in for dinner.

"Yes ma'am," Alan says, "It smells good. I can't wait."

Ebony smiles and says, "Thank you Alan. Okay men, us ladies are waiting for you at the table."

Ajay smiles and follows Ebony to their formal dining room as Lil Ajay and Alan follow him.

They all sit down at the table. Alan is sitting across from Lannie with Kimmie next to him. Lil Ajay is across the table from Kimmie, in the chair which is off to Ajay's right side. Of course Ajay is at the head of the table and Ebony is at the other end of the table facing him. Ajay says grace and Ebony begins the passing service with Lannie and Kimmie's assistance.

"I see the ladies got their things in order too," Ajay whispers to Alan and Lil Ajay.

He knows Ebony had a similar talk with the girls. They enjoy a filling dinner. Lil Ajay is very excited and so is Lannie. Ebony and Ajay smile at each other often. They know this is the circle they've had so many talks about, over the last six years. Ebony knows Lannie thinks Alan is cute and she can tell Alan likes Lannie too. Both Ajay and Ebony notice Lannie isn't very responsive to Alan at the table. Ebony finds that strange because Lannie has told her that she likes him. But what Ajay see is that Lannie is very much like Ebony was as a little girl. She doesn't really talk to Alan. While he spends the whole evening trying to get her to have a conversation with him. Ajay and Lil Ajay are watching him. Ajay knows he'll have to have frequent talks with Alan and keep him up on the crew codes. Especially if he thinks he's ever going to be the boyfriend of his oldest daughter. Ajay has dreaded this day since he first saw Lannie's eyes. But he knows life isn't going to wait for his insecurities. He has to give them the guidance that he received at their age. And pay attention to see that they're all following through as they're expected too.

They all attend Ajay's game on New Year's Eve and they win it. After the game, they go by Stoney's for a quick bite while Ajay formally introduces Alan and Kimmie to big Al and big John.

"So Ajay, you have finally turned into me completely ha?" big John ask and releases a roaring laugh.

"Oh big John. I am so sorry man," Ajay says, "I had no idea what I was putting you through."

John laughs more and says, "But at the same time, you now know that I have the highest form of respect for you and trust in you, correct?"

"I do man," Ajay says, "I gotta give you a hug man. Damn the handshake." He laughs as him and John hug each other. Then Ajay says, "I know now why I'm so confident. All I wanted to have was the respect of these two men standing here," he says pointing at big Al and John, "And after this week, I realized that I had to have had it since like age six, at *least*. Because they knew they wanted me to be with Ebony and they knew that I wanted to be with Ebony and they both let me live."

They all crack up laughing as Ajay looks at Lil Ajay and yells, "Son, I *am* the man!"

They have a great time as they finish their late night snacks, then head to Jackson Heights. Lil Ajay is going to spend the night at Eric's house with Alan while Kimmie is coming to stay with Lannie and the girls. Ajay drives all the ladies to his house first, so Lil Ajay and Alan can be the gentlemen they had talked about before dinner, the day before. Plus Ajay insist that his wife gets the royal treatment of being brought home first to feed the triplet's and get comfortable. Alan and Lil Ajay walk Lannie and Kimmie inside the door and tell them goodnight while Ajay and Ebony watch them and smile. Ajay gives Ebony a kiss and says, "I'll be right back. I gotta get little me and Little Tank back around that curve."

Ebony giggles and says, "Exactly."

Ajay, Lil Ajay and Alan head back out to the 2006 Escalade and Ajay drives them back around to Eric and Erica's to spend the night. Then he heads back home for the night.

{*January 20, 2006*}

6 year old, 1st graders Lil Ajay and Lannie are back in school for the winter semester at Beachwood elementary. Alan and Kimmie are there with them. Alan Anthony is in 2nd grade. He's looking forward to his February 12 birthday. He will turn 8 years old. Kimora Lin or Kimmie is in Kindergarten. Today is her 6th birthday.

Today starts out as a typical day for *all* the kids. But it turns bad for 1 of the male students as soon as he decides to take his insulting of Kimmie, *too* far. Only because she has slanted eyes. Dillon Parker is in her class. He has been calling Kimmie *Jap* since their first day of school, 2 weeks ago. No one in the crew knew about these taunts. Not until today while her kindergarten class is in the lunch line. Dillon starts insulting her again. It just so happens Lannie and Lil Ajay's class is lined up right behind Kimmie's class, waiting to enter the lunchroom. It is then that Dillon leaves his place in line and approaches Kimmie. He starts dancing a jig in front of

334

her, while he pulls at his eyes outward to make them appear slanted and pretends to speak another language too.

"*Japanese*! *Japanese*!" Dillon taunts as he continues to dance, giggle and cut up.

Suddenly Kimmie yells, "Leave me alone!"

She starts to cry. She's tired of him teasing her and he has done it since the first day. She *loves* her eyes. They're just like her mother's and the fact is, she *is* half Japanese and half Black. Which she's very proud of. *Blasian* is the name her older sister Leilenne use to reference their heritage. The girls took their features after their mother, who was born in Japan. While their brothers look like their father, for the most part. But Dillon's taunting has caught Lil Ajay's attention. Once he witnesses Dillon. he leaves his class line and heads straight toward him. Lil Ajay goes to Dillon, kicks his legs out from under him which knocks him to the floor and starts pounding on him.

"That's my girl, you *bitch*!" he yells, "Stop fuckin wit her! Do you hear me *fool*?! I'm gonna beat the brakes off yo bitch ass!"

He's doing just that. Lannie ran to Kimmie to console her, as they watch Lil Ajay give Dillon the beating he deserves. The teachers are finally able to pull Lil Ajay off. Lil Ajay bloodies Dillon up good before the fight ends. Teachers are trying to find out what the altercation is about. That's when Alan's class is approaching the cafeteria to form a line behind the last 1st grade class. He sees Lil Ajay being questioned by teachers and his sister being comforted by Lannie. He leaves his line and comes to where they are. And even though his teacher is calling him back, he doesn't stop.

He yells back, "Something is wrong with my little sister and I have to go check on her!"

He goes straight to Kimmie and Lannie. Kimmie has calmed her crying but she's still very upset.

"What happened Kimmie?" Alan asks his little sister.

"Dillon keeps picking at me and talking about my eyes," she says, "Ajay beat him up. Now they're taking him to the office."

Sure enough when the principal gets there, Dillon is taken to the school nurse. Alan watches as they take him away. He's planning on getting in his ass, the first chance he gets. Lil Ajay is escorted to the office and Ebony is called.

Ebony is at home packing her suitcase. Ajay called her at work and asked her to meet him in Utah tonight. The Cavaliers are on the road and have fallen into a losing slump. Since January 10 they've lost 5 games in a row. They have a game against the Warriors tonight. They'll leave San

Francisco heading to Utah, after tonight's game is complete. He wants her to be in Utah when he arrives there. He told her, he needs his woman in the worst way.

Big John and Al drives Ebony to Beachwood to check on Lil Ajay first. On the way, she calls Ajay to alert him about their son.

"Hey baby," he answers, sounding as sexy as ever which makes her pearl tongue tingle.

She know *she's* horny. She doesn't even have to guess about her husband.

"Hey sweetheart," she says in her sexiest voice, "How are you holding up?"

"Not good at all," he says.

"I know you're down about the road trip. But I'll see you tonight," she says, "I'm on my way to pick up Ant."

"What's going on?" Ajay asks.

"He got into a fight with a little boy who was bothering Kimmie," she says, "Daddy and big Al are driving me to pick him up, right now."

"I'm not mad at that," Ajay says.

"I didn't think you would be," she says and smiles. "He's doing what he was raised to do. Look out for those he cares for."

"And to protect his girl too," Ajay says and chuckles.

"He's not being suspended because its his first time getting into trouble, like this," she says, "But he has to come home for the rest of the day."

"That's fine," Ajay says, "I'll call him and get his side of it."

"You sound down," she says.

"I miss my *pussy* Ebony," he says in one breath, "I can't help but think the reason I can't have a complete game is because I haven't had my pre-game since Christmas eve."

"Our Tre is only twenty six days old," she says and giggles.

"It's about that time then ha?" he asks as he smiles.

"I'll see you tonight daddy," she says seductively.

"I can't wait," he says and smiles, "Kiss my babies. Thank big mama and our mama's for keeping the kids so you can fly out to meet me."

"I sure will baby," she says.

He can hear it in her voice. She misses him too and she's in the mood for some hot sex, just like him.

"I'll see you tonight. *All* night," he says and smiles, "I love you."

"I love you too Anthony," she says, "See ya."

"In a minute."

They hang up just as Ebony and their fathers are arriving at Beachwood. Ebony picks up Lil Ajay and Lannie from school. She knows Ajay would never want her to leave Lannie there without her twin brother. They bring them to *Big Mama's House* aftercare. They'll already be there when Kimmie, Alan and the rest of the crew kids get there after school. Big mama, Jo and Pearl will see to Ebony and Ajay's kids until they return from Utah, day after tomorrow. Ebony gives them kisses from both her and Ajay before she heads over to *Granny's House* Pre-Care to kiss Lea and the triplets too. Big Al and John drive her to the airport once she has all 6 children secure. Three of their security team are accompanying her to Utah. She's staying 2 nights. After the Utah game tomorrow night, Ajay and his team will return to Cleveland the following morning for 3 days. Ebony will fly back with the team. They'll play Indiana before leaving again.

Ebony makes it into Utah without any complications. After a long soothing bath, she calls to check on her 6 kids. Lil Ajay is in a good mood. He's just talked to his father and he knows Ajay agrees with what he did today. After hanging up with the kids, Ebony watches Ajay's game on the flat screen. They play Golden State and lose by 20 points. She'll see him in a few hours. She knows she is going to have to make him feel better in a way which only she can. And she's *more* than up for the task.

She calls the front desk and request them to bring room service and a CD player to her suite. She brought along their *Signs O the Times* CD for their musical enjoyment. She's ready and willing to do *everything* in her power as his woman to make sure tonight feels like a 2nd honeymoon. Right down to the musical selection. She sets the CD player up to play *Adore* on repeat. That's the same thing Ajay had done on the 3rd night of their initial honeymoon when he'd finally let her taste him. She lays out the beautiful lingerie set he'd given her 3 weeks ago, as an 8th anniversary gift. He had requested she wear it *only* when she was ready for him to end her celibacy. She's going to be wearing it when he arrives tonight. 26 days is damn near a record for them, after childbirth. She's missing her *14* and that's going to end tonight. In just a matter of hours.

Ajay arrives and comes directly to the team hotel where Ebony is already relaxing with *Prince*. When he opens the door and glides through it, Ebony is standing right next to the roaring fireplace, holding 2 glasses of Champagne. Ajay smiles big when he spots her in the lingerie set he'd bought because he knows their sexual hiatus is going to end tonight.

"Oh baby. You look good!" he yells in a sexy and excited tone.

337

"I am good *now*," she says in a sexy and seductive tone.

He moves in and grabs 1 of the glasses from her. Before even 1 sip, he has to get some of her sweet lips. They kiss with fervor as he grabs her glass. He quickly places both glasses on the mantelpiece and says,

"I don't even need enhancements. I want my pussy. I'm already high baby. Just seeing you in this lingerie and heels *too*? Oh my God."

"I missed you," she says and smiles.

He picks her up cradle style and starts undoing the ribbons and the zipper which holds the tiny little suit next to her firm and voluptuous body.

"Henny and penny missed daddy, ha?" he asks as he sucks on her nipples and carries her to the king-sized bed.

"Henny and penny missed their daddy and Vaginny has too," she says and they both crack up laughing.

He lays her on the bed and finishes ripping away the rest of the lingerie set. He's devouring her breast and making his way to her pussy.

"Baby I *got* to get this sweet pussy, *good* and creamy tonight," he says and he puts his face in the place.

"OOhhhh!"

"Uh huh. I need you to sing for me," he orders as he sticks his tongue into her fresh pussy.

Quickly he raises his head up and captures her clitoris between his lips. He starts to knead it with perfection. He's become quite the professional in the 8 years since he started eating her pussy. He's giving her pearl tongue it's own personal massage.

"Oh daddy!" Ebony yells to this sensation she's missed for almost a month. Her tone turns into a sexy whisper, as she says, "Oh God it feels so good. I missed you Anthony. I missed you baaayybeeeee!"

"Mmmm that shit sounds *so* good," Ajay moans as he eats her pussy perfectly. He whispers, "I missed this sweet shit Ebony."

Ebony starts to feel that uncontrollable arch creeping up into her back. She's trying to make this feeling last as long as possible. But that's going to be a task in itself. She tries to hold out but Ajay is on his job as usual. Her body has missed this actions and it's giving in to what it's missed as well.

"Oooooooooohhhhhhhh bayybeeeeeeeeee!" she yells.

"Sing it baby," Ajay whispers back, "Ebony baby. I missed that damn song. Mmmm huh!"

She's cuming and it's massive. Ajay isn't about to release her pearl tongue until she's done with the gyrating and jerking. And she's nowhere near finished. She's grown from that little girl who was *too* shy to say how she

338

feels when he makes love to her. She's confessing it and confessing it loudly.

"I'm *cumin* baby! Oh! Oh! Oh God I missed you *baaayybeeeee!*"

"Come here sugar," he orders in that sweet sexy voice that always drives her straight on over the edge.

He whispers, "You taste so fuckin sweet Ebony."

She's *out on a limb* like it says in that *Teena Marie* song they started off listening to, together. As Adore is well into it's 2nd play and Prince is singing, *'This condition I've got is crucial. Cru-cial baby. You can say that I'm a terminal case,'* she most definitely is a terminal case. Ajay is singing his way back up to her breast and she's in orgasmic heaven.

"You don't know what you mean to me. Do ya. Do ya. Do ya hear?" He's singing in his baritone voice. She's loving this moment. This night. This *damn good* sexual reunion.

He's still tickling her clitoris with his fingers while his dick is playing tag with her inner thigh. He's hard as a rock and ready to get into his pot of gold. As her orgasm starts to taper off, she reaches down and grabs his dick. *Her dick!*

"I wanna taste my dick tonight," she whispers boldly and in a demanding tone.

"You got three babies nursing from you-"

"-And I pumped enough breast milk to last until we get back *plus* one day after," she cuts him off in a whisper as she's looking him directly in his eyes.

Then seductively she squeals, "I wanna taste you Anthony. *Please!*"

He's *never* seen her like this before but he likes it. He knew that day would come when she would feel free to express her sexual needs and feelings to him. Besides, who else is she going to express them too? He's turned on even more just by the way she's displaying her sexual wants. She even looks like she's about to cry. He know she wants to do him right back and he has no will to tell her she can't. He's horny as hell. So at this point, a disagreement might ruin their whole reunion. He just smiles and she knows he's putty in her hands right now. He's so horny he doesn't even wanna waste time talking about it or trying to talk her out of it.

"Come here," he whispers as he lays on his back and pulls her on top of him while Adore starts a 3rd play.

He has no will to put up a fight. He's ready and willing to accept *whatever* she brings. She straddles him quickly and gives him a very wet kiss. Then she goes from his lips to his neck and chest, on down to his rock hard 14 inches of dick in record time. She's learned to love her chance to take control. Sucking his dick is the only time she can maintain charge, as far as sex goes with them. She figured that out, back when he was hesitate about allowing her to do him in the first place. But that was in their past. Tonight, she's in charge of her future for the moment and her forever too.

She takes him into her mouth and starts to suck on him gently, the way she knows he likes it. His voice is low as he still sings along with Prince. *"I truly adore you. If God one day struck me blind,… your beauty I'd still see. Loves too weak to define,…. just what you mean to me.*
From the first moment I saw ya,……. oooo I knew you were the one…."
She takes his dick to the back of her throat and his body becomes instantly tensed. He hasn't had any parts of sex and wouldn't even let her touch, handle nor play with his dick for the 26 days they weren't able to fuck. Those days are always just as hard for her as they are for him. She wants to make sure he knows her post gestation period is never about her not wanting to have him ravishing her. It's about a vow to God that just like this very moment, they have never been able to fill. They can't seem to do without each other long enough to fulfill it. That 6 week stretch isn't going to happen after their triplets either. She wants to be fucked like she's being punished for something. She's sucking him like she's starving for the taste that only his Mandingo sized dick can give. She missed not touching, tasting and wetting her man's meat. She plans to make up for all of that missed loving tonight.

"I love to suck on this big dick Anthony," she oozes which surprises him too.
But he's in a pleasure zone and all he can do is raise his head up briefly to look at what she's doing *so* well. He's stroking her hair and letting her know he's loving the feeling. She makes eye contact with him and smiles. He's blushing and loving this new side of his wife. He needed to be lifted up from his basketball slump and he knew she was the only somebody who could make that happen. She's humming as she sucks on him. Then she starts to whisper in between sucks.
"I love it….," she whispers and sucks, "Like I love……," she whispers and sucks again, "creeeeamy…," she sucks, "Ice cream," she whispers again as she quickly takes him back to her throat.

"Oh ssss yes! Shhhiiit," he whispers as he grabs 2 fist full's of her silky hair. He moans, "This shit is so good Ebony. Baby. Oh yessss."
She's sucking and licking as she gently grabs his balls and makes them apart of her feast too. His back lifts up off of the bed and her mouth follows his every move. She's got his rhythms down to a science as her lips and

340

tongue provide a musical harmony for his hips to glide too. He could shoot 1 of his famous 3pt jump shots right now and she still wouldn't miss a beat.
"Ebony! Hell fuck yea! Do that shit baby!"
He's no longer whispering. He's pushing his ass up to her mouth and fucking her lips, just as well as he does when he's inside of her.
"You want me to fuck those lips too. Don't you baby?" he asks and he's already doing just that.

"Mmmm hmmm," she hums as she continues to keep his dick moist. His grip on her hair tightens and she knows he's about to cum. He wants that load inside of her pussy. He's at the point where when he's fucking her, there isn't 1 hot point on her body he would miss. She wants him inside of her too. He's pushing her head away from his dick now. He wants his pussy right now. She surrenders the dick to him. He pulls her up and flips her over onto her back, all in 1 motion.

"Bring me my pussy, baby," he oozes and pushes his 14 into her moist tunnel. He's already talking shit, as he says,
"I knew my pussy was still tight. How the fuck am I *ever* gonna loosen this thang up, baby girl? Ha?"

"Oooo OOhhhh!" she yells at the sensation of his penetration.

"Oh hell yea," he whispers, "It's still the same pussy it was in eighty nine," he says and smiles. Then he whispers, "I got six babies out of this sweet muthafucka and these walls still ain't giving in *NONE*."
He starts to kiss her while he works his dick into a good position. He's not done talking yet.
"This pussy don't give for nothing, ha baby? It's undefeated in sixteen and a half years. This sweet muthafucka is a soldier."
He wraps her up tight and starts to fuck her *well*. He's got some catching up to do.

"Mmmm. That's *soooo* good. Oooo," she whispers and moans at the same time.

"Talk to me baby," he oozes, "The look on your beautiful face says I'm fucking you like I should be. Am I baby? Tell me what you want me to do to this sweet pussy."

"Oooo, fuck me baby," she whispers and she knows he's about to do just that.
He raises up and goes to work. He grabs her at the hips for leverage and starts to push into her while he's pulling her hips to him, on every stroke. He wants his payday. That waterfall of sweet nectar he knows he can bring out of her. They don't have anything *but* time tonight. His shoot around

341

before tomorrow night's game, isn't until 11:00am. It's 1:00am now. He figures he can get 2 or maybe 3 more rounds in for this reunion lovemaking session. He raises his body up and pulls her up, just enough to flip her over onto her stomach.

"I miss this position a lot," he says and smiles as he reenters her and lays his weight on her back.

"I gotta keep you in place. Just in case you're planning on trying to run from yo dick."

She smiles to herself. She knew this session wasn't going to be completed without some type of arrogant remark from her *well* endowed man.

He's hitting it hard and she's bracing for the pain because she know he's got a lot to make up for. He's got some proving to do as well. He needs to know he can still make her cum with just the use of his dick.

"Is it deep enough baby?" he asks, shoving his rod into her, over and over.

"Yes baby! Oh God!"

"It's the *man* and you know it!" he says very loudly as he smacks her ass cheeks, a couple of times.

"Give me my pussy woman! Gimme my shit!"

He's in the zone. She knows her orgasm isn't coming right away. He's going to prolong this fucking as long as he possibly can.

"Ouwwwwah!" she screams at the pain that last shove leaves.

"Oh yea," he says with his voice dragging. "I gotta get this dick reacquainted with his pussy *Ebony*. They missed each other. I can feel that. My pussy's wet as *fuck* tonight. I'm bout to make it talk to me."

He pulls her up on her knees and continues to stroke her. Her pussy starts to make farting sounds and he's loving that too.

"Let my pussy talk to daddy. Tell me what you want baby. Tell daddy what you need."

"Oh daddy! I wanna cum!" she yells, "Oh baby! OOhhhh!"

"Ugh. It's *good* Ebony," he says, "Come on. Turn over so I can let you wet me some mo."

He flips her over and goes right back in, so quickly that they keep the same rhythm. He's gently gliding in and out of her now, as he looks down into her eyes.

"I'll never get over this addiction, baby girl," he says, "I don't ever wanna be without this sweet pussy. Do you hear me?"

"Yes baby," she whispers as she feels her pearl tongue throb.

Her sweet ride is on the way and she's *so* ready for it. She knows her man needs her to cum so he can feel whole and accomplished. And to know that

342

he hasn't lost a beat when it comes to giving her the pleasure she's grown to know and love him for.

"I feel yo pearl tongue *jumpin*," he whispers and smiles as he works her over. "Its throbbing. Are you bout to cum for me?"

"Oh yes," she oozes, "I feel it baby."

"Ha? You feel that nut raising up. Don't you baby?"

He starts to suck on her nipples. He's licking them and kissing her lips. Licking on her lips and her neck and then back to her nipples again. She's there. She couldn't hold this one if she was promised *Fort Knox*.

"*OOhhhh* baby! I'm cumin baby! Oooo weeeeee Anthoneeeee! Yes baby yes! Oh God! It's sooooo good baby!"

"Is daddy doing you good baby?" he asks arrogantly, "Wet my sweet pussy baby. Wet it! Wet it Ebony. Yea baby! Ugh!"

He's stroking her again because her prize is here and it's time for him to work toward his.

"Yes it's good baby. OOhhhh!" she screams.

He lays down and holds her tight as he puts his mouth next to her ear and starts to talk to her.

"I need you," he says, "Do you hear what prince is saying? Ha?"

"Yes!"

"*More than your mother. More than your brother. I wanna be… like no other,*" he whispers as he kisses and licks on her ear.

Then he sticks his tongue in her ear. She jerks and grabs hold of him. He's about to hit overdrive. She just needs to hang on to him for the ride. He spreads her legs completely apart for the next run. She's no where near able to handle him but this is *his* show. He has given her hers twice and he hasn't gotten one yet. She can beg and plead but he's not going to take a second off of the fast pace he's on right now. He dips his hips and grunts. He's loving it as he looks at her face which has sweat rolling off of it. Some of its his. He's sweating profusely and grunting. Straining every muscle in his body. He's not trying to save shit for tomorrow night's game and it's apparent, he didn't lose any of his sex muscle in the last 6. She's spent. She's all caught up on the past 26 days and he's still going. His lips are poked out. Every time he pushes into her, he bites down on his bottom lip. He's almost there. She's watching his face through her half closed lids. Her man is definitely, *the man*. Suddenly his face darns an odd look. One that's almost sad as his eyes roll back in his head. He's there! It looks like his nut is toying with him at her expense. But she's going to hang on for the ride, just as she always does.

343

Finally he throws his head back. He's breathing so fast, he almost chokes.

"Geeeeeeeeeeeee. Oooo. Oh yea! Yea! Oh yea yea yea!" he yells.

His nut is here and its taking the scenic route. As Prince is singing, *'You can burn up my clothes , smash up my ride! Well maybe not the ride. But I got to have your face all up in the place. Like to think that I'm a man. I'm a man of exquisite taste. A hundred percent Italian silk imported Egyptian lace. I say nothing baby. I say nothing baby, can compare. Nothing can compare, to your lovely face. Do you know what I'm saying to ya this evening. Just trying, trying to say. Just trying to say. That until, until the end of time. I'll be there for you.'*

He's now able to lay his body down on top of his wife and soothe her. He wipes her tears away and kisses her like his thirst can only be quenched from her lips. She's kissing him back and holding him tight as well.

"I needed that so much," he says breathlessly.

"I needed it too baby," she whispers, breathless too, "I did too."

They hold each other and try to catch up to their breath. He's thirsty and so is she. After he gains a little stretch, he has to have a drink.

"I'm gonna get that champagne and bring it in here," he whispers, "I guess you can have yours too."

She smiles as he peels himself off of her and heads into the living room area of the suite. She looks out of the large window which is next to their bed. Their room is on the 19th floor. She sees that as fitting because in less then 8 months, they will have been a couple for 19 years. Though Ajay counts a few years before that and most of the time he says, all of their lives. She's okay with that too. She's smiling when he returns and hands her, *her* glass.

"It's cold still," she says and she gulps it down.

"I refilled it from the bottle," he says as he lays back down next to her and downs his 2nd glass, "And I brought some Gatorade back too."

She giggles and grabs the Gatorade bottle while he finishes off the Champagne. She knew he wasn't going to let her give him head and have a big share of alcohol too. She's got to keep her system clean so she can nurse his babies in 2 days.

"Well thank you for allowing me to have a glass," she says while she's still giggling. "I didn't think I was gonna get to have *that* one. If you wanna know the truth."

"Oh you earned that one," he says and chuckles. "You went off up in here tonight. My baby has grown all the way up. I knew I got it right, way back in nineteen eighty one. I knew I had to have you as my girl Ebony. You just grew with me, baby girl. Every single step of the way."

344

"I've learned a lot from you baby," she says, "A *whole* lot. I made it a point to learn what you like and don't like. At the same time, I know there's a time for certain things and times when you're just not gonna go for it."

"You paid attention just like I did, ha?" he says and cracks up laughing.

"I did," she says, "I sure did. I love you Anthony."

"You sure did," he says and laughs, "I can sleep all night now."

But she knows he isn't going to sleep, right away. He's going to catch him a second wind and go for round two. But before he gets to that. He has to know what the school officials had to say about his junior.

"Did the principals and teachers seem okay with Ant today?"

"Yes they did," she says, "Of course the ones who were there when we went. Reminded big Al of how familiar they were with *him*."

They laugh and Ajay says, "He whooped his ass for messing wit his girl."

"*Exactly*. Like his daddy," Ebony says and smiles, "He's going to be worse than you was, Anthony. He's already consumed with having to outdo you. Please don't put too much pressure on my baby."

"He's not a baby anymore, Ebony," Ajay says, "You know Jackson men don't stay young for long."

They both laugh again. Ebony thinks about what he'd just said and she has to agree with him. He never seemed like a little boy to her. Ajay was always knowledgeable on things, years ahead of his time. She remembers when she was little and how she use to just stare at him and not say anything when he said something to her. She was that same way with the fathers. But Ajay was patient with her and he found a way to communicate with her and still leave her feeling comfortable to be who she was. That quiet, shy and very particular little girl, about who spent time in her company. That turned out to be a plus for him. He wanted to be in her company and he wanted to be the *only* one she *needed* to be in her company. So he liked that she wasn't open to talking to a lot of people. Neither was he, for that matter. He was a very stand offish little boy. That has carried right on up to today. He's still very particular about who's in his circle and in his space. He was stingy with Ebony, from day one. So he wasn't going to try to get her to open up to others. He only wanted her to open up *to* him and *for* him. She's there. She's there in a major way. She's complete and she completes him as well. The support they had from big mama and granny plus the tutelage he got from his father, grandfather and the males, made him wise enough and confident enough to let down his guard and allow her to find her way to

345

him. While at the same time, the advice and leadership *she* got from big mama, granny, Pearl and even his mother too. Helped her to know how to recognize who was the right boy for her and who would fit into her world and space the best. Ajay is definitely the best fit for her life. He's complete because of her. She's whole because of him. When he refers to her as that female version of him. That is the *highest* form of a compliment he could give. Because everyone who knows Ajay, knows he's not arrogant. He's definitely self assured and more than confident that he can have and hold anything he puts his mind too. He has a wife who is exactly that same way too. Now as parents, their job is to find out how to get their 6 children to this same completeness. It seems that their twins are already at that 1st step. Meeting their futures as very young children. The same way the parents had done it. Their mates are siblings. Just as it is for Ebony and Ajay. They come from a very strong family and background. Same as the twins and their parents, grandparents and so on. Ebony looks at Ajay and smiles. She can tell he's thinking the same thing.

"Let me guess," Ebony says and continues to smile, "You're happy that Ant has chosen Kimmie. Correct?"

"Yes I am."

"But you're not happy that Alan likes Lannie?"

"Does she like him too?" Ajay asks but he already knows the answer.

Ebony smiles but she doesn't offer a response. She just nestles up under him and lays her head next to his, so she can still look into his eyes. He's looking into hers as well. He wants her to answer him. She can tell that much.

"Well?" he asks.

"You never tell me what you and Ant talk about," she says and starts to giggle. "Well not *everything*. But you always want me to tell you about me and Lannie's talks. Why is that?"

"Does she?" he persists.

"Yes. And Anthony *please* don't say she can't like him," she says, "Because she's just like me when it comes to being a little girl. She will not rush into growing up."

"Not until Alan starts burning up her baby dolls," he says and he isn't smiling.

But Ebony cracks up laughing and says, "Alan *does* have your ways, baby. And you said if she started to like a boy who was just like you. You would be open to that."

"Yea but not at six years old, I'm not," he says sternly.

"Alan is gonna be patient with her. Just like you were with me," she says, "He's not trying to press her at all. I asked her."

"And what did she say?"

"She said he told her, he likes to look at her and that's all," she says, "She said he told her all he wants her to do is smile when she sees him and speak to him. Does that sound familiar?"

Ajay laughs and says, "Yes it does. And now I know I have to move his ass back to Chicago."

"Anthony no," she says, "That's just like you were with me."

He smiles and gives Ebony a kiss. Then he stares at her for more than a minute without saying a word.

Finally he says, "I'm not gonna block them. I'm already talking to him too. Eric is too and so is his father. Him and my pops talk on the phone all the time. Pops said he wants Alan to be the man for his Lannie. Poppa Jones said that about me for you. I knew it was gonna be hard for me. *Period*. But I want what's best for her so I'm gonna do what big John did with me."

"And what's that?" Ebony asks.

"He talked to me about what he wanted for you," he says, "He did. He would talk to me damn near every time he came home. Just to see where my head was. And he told me he approved of me being with you as long as I understood what he wanted for you and I was ready and willing to be that. I knew I wanted yo sweet ass. So I had to learn what it took to have you. That's the same thing Alan is gonna have to do."

"And I know he will," she says, "I can see it in Lannie's eyes, baby. She can see her daddy's ways in him. She's best friends with Kimmie already. The two of them, Ashanti and Orian have the makings of another foursome. Just like Jerica, Jada, Destiny and CJ. Lannie's already got a boy who's just like her daddy, that likes her. That's going to save me a lot of time when it comes to wondering who she's going to like and have eyes for."

"Okay baby," he says and chuckles, "I said okay. I'm not gonna stand in the way of it. I'm just gonna make sure he stays on the right track. I needed a lot of straightening to get to this point. Alan has what it takes and I know I'm raising my oldest daughter to know what to look for. I'm exactly that for her. I know that. That's why I make sure she see me loving her mother. She's gonna be okay and so is he. I mean the boy has my father and both of my grandfathers names, for his first name. *My* name for his middle name. God set it right in our laps, just like he did for *our* parents."

She smiles and he smiles back. They realize they are now on the parent side of things. Neither of them have forgotten how much they both put their

347

parents through just to be together. They look at each other and laugh.
"Its about to get real now ha?" he asks as he gives her a kiss.

"It's *been* real baby," she says, "Our twins want love like they see us having. And Anthony I can't blame them. I couldn't imagine what my life would be like or if it would even be worth living if I didn't have the best man growing up right next door to me. Looking out for me and molding me. We just have to guide them and make sure we get big mama in on it too."

"I'll bet she knows already," he says and laughs.

"You're probably right," she says and gives him a kiss.

They wrap up in each others arms and keep kissing until the kissing turns into rubbing, then sucking and eventually their into round 2.

Ajay and the Cavaliers beat Utah by 18 points. The whole team including the coaching staff thanks Ebony for coming. And no one is more vocal than *Lebron James*. He tells her, he was just glad to have some help in the game. They all laugh as they board their flight back to Cleveland.

It's Sunday, January 22nd when Ebony and Ajay arrive home. They attend church with all 6 of their children. This is the triplets 1st church outing so it takes them an extra hour to get away from there after service is done. They head to *Crew's House of Soul Food* for dinner with the rest of the crew families.

At dinner, Alan and Kimmie sit with them as Pearl and Jo give each other the eye then smile. They can see it this time around. They're grandmothers with a more keen eye plus big mama has already told them. They all have a great dinner, then Ajay takes his family home. He wants to sit and talk with his son before he has to hit the road again in 2 nights.

Ajay, Ebony and their 6 kids arrive home and change into some comfortable clothes. They spend a few hours of family time in the 1st floor family room. Lannie has some writings to show her daddy and Lea has pages she colored. She wants him to help her hang them on their refrigerator next to those her twin siblings had done when they attended school at Granny's House. Ajay does both and has some fun time with his triplets too. Then he and Lil Ajay retire to the male sanctuary so they can talk about whatever his son wants to discuss.

"Pops I'm glad y'all won that game last night," Lil Ajay says, "Y'all had lost six in row."

"I know son. But your mama won that game last night," Ajay says and laughs, "I just wore the jersey."

They crack up laughing because Lil Ajay already knows what he means. Then Ajay gets to the problem his son had at school, 2 days ago. He wants to hear his complete side of it.

"So what made you have to fight on Friday?" Ajay asks.

"Dillon was picking on Kimmie," he says, "He's been doing it every since she started going to Beachwood and I didn't even know that part until she got to Crewland. He was picking at her because she's half Japanese. I saw him when me and Lannie class was lining up for lunch. I had to get him."

"I'm not mad at you for protecting your girl," he says, "I expect you too. I'll be there to support you anytime that happens and so will the rest of the family."

"She smiled at me after I beat him up," Lil Ajay says and smiles.

"That made it worth it, did it?" Ajay says and chuckles.

"Ah man yes indeed," Lil Ajay says, "Then when she got to Crewland after school. She told me *thank you*. I told her then, that I'll do that every time and I'm not gonna let nobody disrespect her. *Never*."

"I like that."

"Alan still mad," Lil Ajay says, "His class didn't get there until the fight was over. But he's gonna get him again. He's just waiting until he see him at school."

"I want y'all to make sure and handle it right," Ajay says, "If he don't bother Kimmie anymore. Then don't fight him at school. Let Alan know that he'll see him again somewhere. Just bid his time. But don't get too much on his record at school. Because it won't go away. It'll be there for the next incident. Once those incidences start to build up, then they'll see reasons to send him to juvenile detention and you too. So just be smart about it. You know how I told you I did my dirt. Sometimes you have to be patient and wait for it to come to you, okay?"

"Okay that's a bet," Lil Ajay says, "But when he get to school tomorrow. I bet he don't even look at her wrong, no more. Pops I tried to stomp his face off."

"I want you to breathe right now," Ajay says and smiles, "Pops use to say that to me when we had talks about an incident that I had. He said when I was talking to him. I wasn't even breathing. You're doing the same thing son. You have to allow it to settle in your mind, long enough to think it through. That's the difference between getting away with it or ending up getting caught up with it. You know how a lot of young guys are going to jail for murder because they got pissed off and went out in a blaze?"

349

"Yes sir."

"That's not how the crew do things," Ajay says, "Now you caught him in the act on Friday and you dealt with him accordingly. But you're still heated right now. That's the part that bothers me. I don't want you to do it like that. I want you to learn how to calm it down once the fight is over. I don't even want you to have to be upset to fight. Remember you're fighting for something or someone who means a lot to you, that has been wronged. There's no reason to get upset. Because you're protecting the good. Military people kill and they don't have to be upset to do it. You have to really work on developing those military tactics we talked about."

"Okay pops," Lil Ajay says, "I wanna do this the way you did it."

"Let's take a ride," Ajay says, "I wanna show you the chamber."

They head into the parlor and let Ebony know they're going for a ride and will be back in a few hours.

"Okay baby," she says as she gives Ajay a kiss and she kisses her son on his cheek. Then she asks, "Are you okay, Ant?"

"Yes ma'am," he says, "I'm good."

He smiles to give his mother the look that she needs to see him have. He's thinking about what his father had said about military tactics. He's already trying to apply that and manage his emotions.

Ajay kissed all the girls, he and Lil Ajay head out to his Jaguar, hop in and drive to Shaker Heights. On the way, Ajay is still talking.

"I wanna let you see this place," he says, "Pops and big John are going too and we're gonna stop by and ride with them. I want you to not forget what I'm about to tell you."

"Okay."

"As crew, you are never to go anywhere without backup," Ajay says, "Do you understand me?"

"Yes sir."

"No matter how bad ass you think you are," he says, "Don't do what I did when I went to get the dude who slapped Bre. Or when I went to get BJ because big Jake got lucky a few times. And son, if he was to take you or if anybody does. Everything that your mother and your sisters are use to having is going to change. Because I'm going to kill the muthafucka as soon as I can. I want be able to breathe and think it through. I wouldn't even try too if I lost my son. So please keep your mother and your sisters in mind before you make any move, okay?"

"Yes sir," Lil Ajay says, "I promise I will pops."

350

"Good enough," Ajay says, "And before long, we're gonna start bringing Alan with us. I know he likes Lannie and I already know you and him are gonna be road dogs. I'm cool with all of that. But me and the fathers and uncles have to put him up on crew codes. He's got everything else. You wit me on that?"

"I'm wit you."

"Lannie likes him right?" Ajay asks.

"Yea but not like he likes her," Lil Ajay says, "Lannie's not in that mind frame yet. She just wanna be a little girl and I ain't mad at that."

"Good," Ajay says, "I'm not either."

They arrive at John and Al's double driveway in Shaker Heights. It's snow on the ground but Ajay and his son still jump out and shoot a couple of baskets on that same goal that he'd perfected his game on and taught Ebony to play on too. It's been upgraded a bit but it's still in the same spot and the driveways are ultra smooth now.

Within minutes, John and Al are ready to go. All 4 of them hop in the Cadillac with big John and they head to the chamber. John and Al start talking to Lil Ajay and he listens intensely.

"So grandson you got in that dudes ass about your little sweetheart the other day ha?" big John asks.

"Yes sir."

"That's the girl you want to be in your life, like your mama is with you pop and like your nana's are with us, right? Al asks.

"Yes sir."

"Then you did the right thing," Al says, "Don't get me wrong. If at *anytime* you see a man humbugging a female. You come to her aide. But when they fuckin with your woman. You leave something on his mind."

"Yes," John says, "Like if he fucks with her wrong. He's going to meet his fuckin maker. See a lot of fathers are not raising their sons. I mean they don't even be in their lives. So a lot of these boys you go to school with, don't even know how they're suppose to treat a female. A female that is respectful. If she's a ho, you still don't watch a fool mistreat her. Not with his hands. But you don't have to whoop his ass if he's just talking shit to her. But if he's looking at your woman in a disrespectful way. You get his mind right, right then and there."

"But relax when you do it," Al says, "Don't let your emotions show to the world. Save them for that woman that you want to spend your life with. Let her be the *only* one to see your heart on your sleeve."

"In other words son," Ajay says, "If Kimmie is going to be your girl and it's apparent that you're feeling her. Then she can see your weak side. But only after the two of you have that understanding that's needed."

"Once you know she's ready to bid for you and *only* you," John says, "And all three of us will be here to make sure that you know what the difference is."

"We're gonna guide you son," Ajay says, "Any questions you have, no matter what they are. You can come to us with it. Doesn't matter what it is. If I'm on the road like I'll be after the game Tuesday. And you can't get me. Call one of your grandfather's and they'll get you through it."
John turns on the street which leads to the cul-de-sac where the chamber is located. He pulls up and parks. They get out and head inside.

Once inside, they show Lil Ajay the layout while Ajay shows him where everything had taken place which he's told him about over the 2 years they've been talking.

"Anytime a nigga takes shit too far," John says, "His ass will end up here."

"And we will do whatever we have to, to get him here," Al adds, "But make no mistake about it. Once he's here. He will not leave alive."

"No enemy sees the chamber and lives to talk about it son," Ajay says, "This is the final walk as far as the crew are concerned."

"I was so ready to see this place," Lil Ajay says, "It makes me feel calm, just standing in here. And one day soon, I'm gonna bring big fake Jake here and he's gonna die slow. I already know this."
Ajay, Al and John chuckle which makes Lil Ajay laugh too. He can see in their eyes that what he just said, was exactly what they wanted him to say. He's proud of himself because he has reached the level of trust that he needs from the 3 men, who are going to mold his life. That gives him the last little bit of confidence he needed to move according to his legacy.

"I know Ajay told you that we're gonna mentor Alan too, right?" John asks.

"Yes sir, he did," Lil Ajay says, "And I already know he's gonna like that a lot."

"So are we, Lil Ant," Al says, "We raised our sons and daughters to be together. And we raised them to know what and how we expected them to treat and be treated by their mates."

"And we're gonna do the same with you all too," John says, "You are the same age your father was when I first knew he liked your mother. He was going to first grade and you're in first grade now."

"And we went to work on him and Ebony, right away," Al says.

352

"As well as John junior, Tank, Lynn and Nina too," John adds, "But all of the males in this family have a motto to live up too. We have to have our head of household role *solid*. Our women do not cheat. *Period*. They don't look at another man in a lustful way."

"None of that," Al says, "And it's a motto that you have to know. And you have to live by it and your woman will too. Because it will be up to your leadership to make sure that she does."

"Son you remember the motto we talked about right?" Ajay asks.

"Yes sir."

"And when I ask you for it the last time. You repeated it to me," Ajay says "It was at the time when I told you how I wanted you to live it. As well as make it fit into your life and relationship. So long as the basics are not wavered on. Remember?"

"Yes sir," Lil Ajay says, "I got it and I got it down pat."

"Let me hear it in the way that you plan to live it," Ajay says.

Lil Ajay clears his throat and looks at John, then Al and then to his father Ajay. He stands with his chest out.

He says, "The test of being a real crew man is to have the type of *respectful* control and *necessary* dominance in your relationship and household, that you don't have to give your girl a reason for why she shouldn't do something wrong. Just her man telling her not to do it, will be enough to insure that she doesn't."

His grandfathers and Ajay smile big. They like that he added respectful. They also like that he had taken out the part that said, "If you are in the same house." That let the fathers all know that Lil Ajay plans to have his woman in the same home with him and he plans to be respectful for her and to her.

Afterwards, they pull out the arsenal and let him show them how well he's learned to hit targets. Lil Ajay hits his marks at a 94% rate. Ajay loves that because his first session was 90%.

"You shot better than I did, the first time I was in here," Ajay says with a smile.

"I do think he's living to outdo *you*, son," Al says and smiles too.

"It looks like to me that there has been another Jackson man made," John says and they all chuckle.

THE END!
353

THE TIME WILL REVEAL SHORT STORIES

#1 MORE THAN 4 ADMIRERS-RELOADED
"The Threat to a Legacy."
#2 MR. WRONG AND THE RATS-RELOADED
"Sweet Ray, Sonya, Shuntay & Tina"
#3 THE CREW'S PRIORITY-RELOADED[TBA]
"The Females of the Crew"

ORDER THE FULL SERIES AT:
www.truesrelatepublishing.com
www.blackdollone.com

The Time Will Reveal-Novel series
TIME TO LEARN-RELOADED part 1
TIME TO GROW-RELOADED part 2
TIME TO LOVE-RELOADED part 3
TIME TO KNOW-RELOADED part 4
TIME TO FEEL-RELOADED part 5
The Making of AJAY- Every Man-RELOADED
TIME TO SHOW-RELOADED part 6
AJAY AND EBONY 1- Time To Give part 7[TBA]
AJAY AND EBONY 2- Time To Live part 8[TBA]

All works by Black Coffee at: www.blackdollone.com

Amazon.com Author's page: http://www.amazon.com/-/e/B008S1WOZ2
Join us on facebook: Author Black Coffee & True's Relate publishing, LLC
Group: The Time Will Reveal-RELOADED series Crew Nation #Crew4Life
Twitter: AuthorBlkCoffee
Instagram: AuthorBlkCoffee
Tumblr: Lovely T. Brown
LinkedIn: Lovely T. Brown

WHAT'S NEXT? [A new series, The Organization [NEXT RELEASE]
http://blackcoffee.homestead.com/WHATSNEXTFROMBLACKCOFFEE.
html